Praise for
FOREVER SISTERS

"The stories, memoirs, and essays in this new anthology are vibrant and diverse tributes to the experience of sisterhood. Alice Walker, Olivia Goldsmith, Amy Bloom, Fay Weldon and others illuminate what makes the bond between sisters not just special, but strong, enduring, and complicated." —*Chicago Tribune*

"A powerhouse of eighteen women writers. . . . Vital and celebratory, with no sloppy sentiment, these stories are honest as only sisters can be." —*Kirkus Reviews*

"There are few ooey-gooey tributes here. Instead, the book holds a prism to the word *sister*, reflecting the spectrum of associations it might hold up." —*The Dallas Morning News*

"O'Keefe has keenly arranged prize-winning talent and excellent new voices to illuminate the emotional range inherent in an absorbing subject." —*Publishers Weekly*

MOTHER

"A literary feast." —*USA Today*

"I'd take this book to my mother if she were still alive. . . . She'd love it." —Judith Viorst, *The Washington Post*

"Several generations of acclaimed authors contributed to this collection of short stories and poetry that celebrate women in the role of mother. . . . Each explores a different point in the remarkable journey of motherhood and reminds us of the happiness and troubles we brought our own mothers while they raised us." —*The Bloomsbury Review*

"A wonderful compilation of stories. . . . If you are looking for a perfect gift or book-club book . . . *Mother* is a perfect recommendation." —*Louisville Parent*

ALSO EDITED BY CLAUDIA O'KEEFE

Mother

Forever Sisters

FATHER

Famous Writers Celebrate the
Bond Between Father and Child

Edited by CLAUDIA O'KEEFE

POCKET BOOKS

New York   London   Toronto   Sydney   Singapore

The following non-fiction works appear in this anthology: "Being a Father"; "Comrades"; Messages from My Father: An Excerpt"; Mi Papi"; One Long Celebration"; "Snapshots"; "Mickey Lou, I Was Just Wondering . . ."; "The Wild Russian"; "A Book of Names"; "On Being Daddy's Son and Daughter"; "This Is America, Mom"; "My Real Father"; "Matthew 10, 34–39"; "The Fundamental Things Apply"; "Heavy When It's Empty."

This book also contains works of fiction. Names, characters, places and incidents are products of the authors' imaginations or are used fictitiously. Any resemblance to actual events or locales or persons, living or dead, is entirely coincidental.

An *Original* Publication of POCKET BOOKS

POCKET BOOKS, a division of Simon & Schuster Inc.
1230 Avenue of the Americas, New York, NY 10020

ISBN: 0-671-00791-2

First Pocket Books trade paperback printing May 2000

10 9 8 7 6 5 4 3 2 1

POCKET and colophon are registered trademarks of Simon & Schuster Inc.

Cover design by Joseph Perez
Front cover photo by Darren Modricker

Printed in the U.S.A.

CREDITS

*To the twenty-four and their fathers:
thank you for your steadfast belief,
your inspiration, your stories.*

ACKNOWLEDGMENTS

Special thanks go to Caroline Leavitt and her incredible list of names, Jane Praeger for championing causes, and Mickey Pearlman for her sage advice. My deepest appreciation to John Updike for the wonderful and rare photo of his father. Last, but not least, my heartfelt gratitude to Judith Curr and Wendy Walker. Their thoughtful attentions to this book have made all the difference.

CONTENTS

INTRODUCTION

During the 1950s father always knew best.

At least that was what the producers of television, the ground-breaking new media of the post-war era, wanted us to believe. America was a land swelling with pride in its ideals, its people, and its icons. According to the early sitcom writers, all dads were good dads, loving if somewhat out-of-touch, the dialogue written for them sounding dopey even for that decade. Television fathers back then were antiseptic role models of a time that may not have been simpler, but which we, as a nation, wanted desperately to believe was simple, whole, and socially healthy.

Then came the 1960s, blowing a big fat hole in our image of daddy. For rebellious young baby boomers everywhere, father became a symbol of stodginess, of the tragically clueless, a poster boy for the evils of The Establishment.

Curiously, scripted television still trumpeted its version of dad. Terrified to acknowledge or catch up with the views of the anti-war generation, scriptwriters for film and TV alike continued to portray father as innocent and largely ignorant to the changes happening all around him. When in the late '60s and early '70s modern media finally accepted that fathers no longer controlled the family universe, he was shown bug-eyed in alarm at his daughter's miniskirts or son's irreverent slang and rock 'n' roll ways, perpetually gaping like a dying tuna.

In the mid '70s through early '80s, father as a figure unto himself took the backseat of the family station wagon to the ideology of divorce. Dramas, movies, sitcoms, and yes, books about Splitsville were all pervasive as America's divorce rate skyrocketed. By the time father was rediscovered as a singular theme, it was the '90s, and the media was telling us that he was a deadbeat, abusive, derelict in his responsibilities, absent. With few exceptions, that is all the news, popular literature, and movies had to say about him. What had happened to all those perfect fathers on the tube? What had happened to that mythic figure, who since the formation of the family had been its protector, and who for centuries, through works such as *The Odyssey* and *King Lear*, had such a powerful impact on literature?

Why even concern ourselves with the downfall of a myth? None of the images presented us over the last half century has been a true and complete picture of American fathers, anyway. Not the Hollywood glossovers, nor vilifications by the youth culture, nor the politically correct hyperbole of the '90s. If modern media has been a force to illuminate all that is hidden by society, it has also wielded a tremendous power to distort it.

Why do I keep harping on the role of television and film, when what you are about to read is a book of fiction and memoir? Isn't it true that the 1950s through the 1990s have seen several careful and thoughtful portrayals of fatherhood in literature? Yes, they have. Over the last fifty years, we've been given exemplary writing about fathers by the John Updikes, the Arthur Millers, the Joan Didions of this world.

As we leave the second millennium and enter the third, however, it is the media that has been most influential in shaping our view of the former head of the family. Reality is never a caricature. Life is never a polarization of extremes. Not truly. In everything bad or stupid, there is something good and smart. In every televised hieroglyphic of the man who is critical to the happiness or discontent of son and daughter, there are deeper meanings to be uncovered.

This is what the written word is for and always will be, to delve into, explore, and communicate what we perceive to be the larger truths.

Father, the anthology, is a book for both child and parent, no matter their ages, no matter whether they have close and loving relationships or not. Its twenty-five authors have been brought together to help us on our journey of emotional discovery and fact finding. Within *Father* you will discover straightforward, commanding, and yet openhearted fiction balanced by the warmth, strength, and sometimes provocative search for resolution so often brought to the subject by memoir.

Traditional dads, divorced dads, single dads, older, younger, the fundamentalist, the revolutionary, the alcoholic and lost, or caring and very much involved, you will find many of his faces here. Dad is a person we seek to understand and win approval from, to fantasize about if we've never had one, remember with humor, love, or sometimes even anger once we've lost him. If he abandoned us, we want to know why. If the words have never been spoken, we want to hear him say, *I love you. I'm proud of you.*

He is an individual who hits us at a very private and profound depth. Just as father, the person, can never be distilled to mere code words like loving or deadbeat, one book cannot hope to capture all there is to be said about his character.

We'll be damned, though, if we aren't going to give it a good try.

Claudia O'Keefe
Lexington, Virginia
November 1999

COMRADES

Jane Praeger

SEPTEMBER 1958. A THIN, GRAY LINE OF SMOKE THREADS UP out of the tile ashtray I made for my dad in camp this summer. It's his cigarette, but it looks like it's smoking itself, because my dad is sitting at the kitchen table, lost in *The New York Times*. He's holding a cup of black coffee in one hand and is wearing his flat, brown slippers and yellow terry-cloth bathrobe. My mother hates this bathrobe because it's too short and everyone can see his skinny chicken legs and his you-know-what. But he wears it all the time anyway, even when people come over, which drives my mother crazy and makes me and my older sister, who is really my half sister, giggle.

When I come downstairs, I'm wearing my zebra pj's and the new pink, fluffy slippers I got for my fifth birthday. I'm so quiet, my dad doesn't even hear me come in the room.

"*Dad!*" I say really loudly when I get right in front of him. "*Dad!*" When my dad's reading the newspaper I sometimes have to shout his name two or three times to get his attention. But today I'm not in the shouting mood. So when he doesn't look up,

I slap my hand right into the middle of his newspaper. *"Dad!* My ears hurt. I think I have to go to the doctor."

My dad looks up, and for a moment, he looks really scared, like he just saw a ghost or like I told him we just dropped another bomb on Hiroshima. But then he looks far off to the right (that's where he looks when he's thinking), then back at me, and back to his paper. It's like he already forgot what I said and that he's supposed to say something back. "Dad," I say again, getting my eyes really close to his so they can't get away again, "Dad, my ears really, really hurt. Really!"

He stares at me. "E.! Jane's ears hurt," he calls out to my mother, who is in the living room talking to one of her zillions of friends on the phone. Doesn't he know that when she's on the phone she doesn't hear *anything?* Doesn't he know she *hates* when I get sick? My mother thinks getting sick is just as bad as telling a lie or stealing money out of someone's pocketbook. Whenever I get sick, which is a lot, she punishes me by making me gargle with water that is so hot and so salty it makes me gag and doesn't even make my ears feel better.

I'm staring at the phone cord stretched tight around the kitchen door when I swallow and realize my throat hurts, too. My dad is back with his newspaper and my mother is still on the phone. If my sister was here, she'd probably just spit a big gob of chewed chewing gum onto that newspaper. That would get his attention. But I don't feel like trying anymore. So I just go back to my room without picking my slippers off the floor even once. "Shuffling" my mother calls it. Then I'm back under my covers.

After what feels like forever, my mother sticks her head in. "Do you want breakfast?"

"No," I say. "My ears hurt and my throat hurts. I just want to go to Dr. F. and get the orange pills with the pink 'e' on them." She closes the door. I lay there wondering what would happen if I had appendicitis, like Houdini. My dad says you can die if your appendix bursts. He says that's how Houdini died and he should know because Houdini was his mother's cousin.

The door opens again and this time it's my dad. He stands

there with his hand on the doorknob and says in his lowest, most serious voice, "Your mother is going to take you to Dr. F. in a few minutes so you better get dressed." I feel my whole body flop with relief.

"Are you coming, too?" I say.

"No. I have to go to work."

"Can't you be late?"

"No."

"Why?"

But he's already closed the door. I won, but I don't feel happy, exactly. I'm tired of staring at telephone wires and newspapers and talking to my parents through doors.

For a while, I just lie there pretending I'm Madeline, from my book. Miss Clavel, the school headmistress, is sitting at the foot of my bed, wringing her hands because she is *so* worried about me. She has brought me a tray with a cup of chamomile tea and lots of little sugar cubes. She stays on my bed until she sees I have drunk every last drop. Then she says, "Dr. Cohn is coming over to see you, and I've told the cook, you're to eat only ice cream for a week." Madeline doesn't have any parents. She's an orphan. But sometimes I still think I'd rather be Madeline than me.

October 1960. All the way to school I keep opening and reading the note my dad has given me. It says, "Jane was out of school yesterday because we took her to the march on Washington to protest the Vietnam War." Usually, my mother writes the absence notes because my father's handwriting is so scribbly. But today he wrote it and I can read every word. I'm so proud I got to stay out of school and go on a march. My dad thinks I was the only seven-year-old there.

"Most people don't agree with me," my dad says on the bus to Washington, "but the war in Vietnam is wrong." When my dad talks about the war, he gets very excited. His voice goes up and down and gets much louder than usual. "People should be allowed to choose whatever government they want," he says, "and

America wants to choose for the Vietnamese people. That's why we're going to Washington today. To tell the president that's wrong."

I have a great time on the march. Dad lets me sit on top of his shoulders so I can see Joan Baez and some of the other singers. And he buys me as many bags of potato chips and Cokes as I want. The best is that I get to hold my own sign that says "Vietnam for the Vietnamese. America, Get Out!" I love that sign. Especially the "Get Out!" part.

When I get to my classroom, I get a huge surprise. Everyone is huddled around my teacher's desk, looking at a newspaper. On the cover of the newspaper, right in the middle of the page, there is a picture of the march and me and my dad with our signs. Everyone in my class is so excited. They have a million questions. But before I get to tell anyone anything, Mrs. R., my second-grade teacher, grabs my arm and pulls me out into the hall.

"What'd I do?" I say. Mrs. R. is very old and has a very bumpy face and in the hall light, every bump on her face looks shiny red. I want her to stop squeezing my arm so I stick my note out right in front of her face. She snatches it, reads it, then says in her meanest teacher voice, "You can make up the work you missed yesterday during free time. But please tell your parents that the only excuse for a child being out of school is illness." Then she hands the note back to me, like it was a dirty tissue or something.

I want to yell at her that she's wrong. Kids are always staying out of school to go to Miami and visit their grandparents. But something about her voice and how red her face is makes me too scared to say anything.

Then, at recess, I say to my friend, Karen D., "Let's see how fast we can go on the merry-go-round and then jump off." Karen loves to do this, but today she just looks at me like I have cooties or something.

"My parents say I'm not allowed to play with you anymore because your father is a Communist."

For a second, I wait for her to start laughing, but she doesn't. She's not kidding. Then, Joey D., who is an idiot and a juvenile delinquent, says, "Hey, Comrade Jane, you should go live in Russia with your Commie parents and never come back."

"Oh, shut up," I say. "You should go live in jail." But by lunchtime, everyone else is calling me Comrade Jane, too.

I go home in tears.

"I'm never going on another peace march as long as I live," I sob to my father as soon as he walks in the door.

"At least let him take off his jacket," my mother yells from the kitchen.

But I don't listen to her. I hardly ever do. While he's taking off his jacket, then his tie and his shirt, and before he can even untie his shoes, I tell him everything that's happened. As usual, he doesn't say much. But I can tell he's mad because of the way his jaw moves around in his face.

"Dad, are you a Communist?" I ask.

"No," he says, sighing. "Being against an illegal, immoral war does not make someone a Communist."

I want to believe him, but I'm not so sure. I know he has books about Communism in his underwear drawer, underneath his boxer shorts.

"Then why do you keep those books in your drawer?" I ask.

Now, he's in his yellow bathrobe. He lights up a cigarette, grabs an ashtray from the landing, and leans against the black, steel banister that leads downstairs. He looks serious.

"Jane," he says, "I once had a very bad experience with a man named Joe McCarthy. Mr. McCarthy didn't like that I was defending men accused of being Communists. He thought I must be a Communist, too. So he made sure I lost my job. That's why we moved from Washington to New York."

"Well, is it bad to be a Communist?" I ask.

"No. It's just another way of looking at things. A lot of the Vietnamese people want their country to be Communist, and the United States doesn't like that. So we're bombing them. And we have to tell the president we think he's wrong."

"Well, can't you call Karen D.'s father and Mrs. R. and tell them *they're* wrong," I plead.

"He can't," my mother yells again from the kitchen. I don't know why she always has to answer for him.

"Karen's father is a bigot and Mrs. R. is ignorant!" my dad says. "If Mrs. R. knew any history, she'd know that America can never win a war in Vietnam."

The trouble is, I don't want my teacher to hate me and I want Karen to play with me now, not after America loses the war. I start to cry again.

"You have other friends," my dad says, putting his cigarette out right on the banister. I watch as the ashes flutter down the stairs. "Play with them. It's more important to do what's right than to be liked."

I'm not sure about this either. What if everyone stops playing with me and no one wants to be my gym buddy? What if no one comes to my eight-year-old birthday party?

But my dad doesn't change his mind. Not even when Karen and her mother pretend they don't see us in the A&P, and Mrs. R. gives me an I for "Attitude" on my report card. I means "Needs Improvement," which I don't deserve. Sometimes, I wish I had a father who wasn't so right.

July 1961. My dad is a lawyer and he has two offices: one in the Empire State Building and one in Harlem. I like the Empire State Building office because I love the way my stomach feels when the elevator shoots up to the forty-fourth floor and I love going to the Brooks Coffee Shop on Fifth Avenue to get pastrami sandwiches and chocolate cake for lunch.

But the Harlem office is more fun. My dad goes there every Saturday morning and sometimes I go with him. Lola, his secretary, lets me type on her typewriter and I get to play with all the kids who come in.

The first person who comes in today is a woman with two little boys and a girl who looks about eight. I can tell because I'm eight, too. The girl says her name is Charlotte. I ask her if she knows how to play jacks and she does. So we play on the floor while my dad talks to her mother.

Charlotte and her mother both have very dark skin, but her mother is showing my father the back of her neck, which looks all red and wet, like somebody peeled the skin off. I know I'm not supposed to stare but I can't help it. And while I'm staring, the little red ball bounces across the floor and lands under my father's chair. Neither of us goes to get it.

"You want to know what happened?" Charlotte asks. I nod, yes.

"Well, the landlord was supposed to fix our plumbing and he didn't and the hot water pipe crashed right through the ceiling onto my mama's neck and burned all the skin off."

Just hearing this makes me put my hand on my neck. I wonder if the hot water pipes could fall out of our ceiling.

My dad is asking Charlotte's mother lots of questions, like how many times she told the landlord about the hot water, and on which days. He's using his low, serious voice and scribbling notes on a long, yellow pad, and handing her tissues to wipe her watery eyes. My dad is listening to what she says so carefully, that he doesn't even get up out of his chair. Whenever I get upset or cry, he gets up and starts pacing around. Sometimes he even paces right out of the room.

Charlotte's mother talks to my dad a long time. Her two little brothers, who are wearing white shirts, navy blue jackets, and dark red ties, sit next to their mom on folding chairs, still as stones. I sneak behind my father's chair so I can grab the red ball. Charlotte and I keep playing jacks until she has to leave.

In the car, on the way home, I have so many questions. "Why didn't the landlord fix the pipes?" "What does it mean to sue?" "What happens if she wins? What happens if she loses?" "Could she really lose?" "If she wins, will the landlord go to jail?" "Why not?" "How come there's no bandage on her neck?"

I know my dad doesn't like it when I ask so many questions, but I can't help it. I just keep having them.

Finally he says, "Even if I win her a million dollars in court, she'll be back on welfare next week because she'll have to pay all that money back to the government."

"But that's not fair!" I say. "If she's poor, the government should just let her keep the money." I don't like thinking that Charlotte and her mother are going to be poor forever.

"That's the way the system works," my father says. "The poor stay poor and the rich get richer."

Then, even though he's driving, he turns his head and looks right at me. "Janie," he says, "don't ever, ever be a lawyer. Only poets and artists can save the world."

February 1966. Junior high school is the pits. I hate having to stand on the corner in the freezing cold waiting for the bus. I hate all the seventh grade boys. I hate being thirteen years old and having curly hair and no breasts. And I hate my social studies teacher, Miss B., who is always so mad at her students, you have to wonder why she became a teacher. When she wears her bright red dress with large gold buttons and giant shoulder pads, I want to puke. She's that bad.

All we ever read in class are books by her stupid hero, Ayn Rand. And when I write my term paper on why we should get out of Vietnam, and footnote all my quotes but forget to put quote marks around them, she gives me a big fat F for plagiarism.

My father hardly ever gets mad. But when he sees that big fat F he really hits the roof. He doesn't scream or anything. He just tells me to get in the car, drives me to school, walks right into the principal's office, and makes the principal read my whole term paper, right then and there.

When the principal is finished reading, my father says, "Please ask Miss B. to come in here."

"She's probably with her homeroom class," the principal says. He looks nervous.

"I'm sure she can spare a few minutes," says my father.

I'm surprised at how much shorter Miss B. looks in the office. I never realized it, but she's shorter than me!

Even though the office is teeny-tiny, my father starts pacing, like he's in court.

"Do either of you really believe," he says "that my daughter intended to deceive the reader into thinking that the *indented*, *footnoted*, and *attributed* comments in this paper were written by her?" I love it. He sounds just like Perry Mason.

The principal just stares at the front page of my paper with the F on it. Miss B. goes into her usual bullshit speech.

"Your daughter is in seventh grade, Mr. Praeger. Seventh graders are expected to know that the words of others, used in a paper, must have quotation marks around them. If they don't, it's called plagiarism. And, believe me, it's better that your daughter learn that *before* college."

"Under the law, Miss B.," my father says, still walking, "a person cannot be convicted of a crime unless the state demonstrates that person's intent to commit a crime. You're accusing my daughter of a crime, Miss B. But nowhere, nowhere, have you demonstrated intent."

Miss B. is so mad, that with her shoulder pads, she looks like a rocket ship about to blast off. I can imagine her hurtling through space, a red rectangle with shiny gold buttons. Before marching out of the office, she says to my dad, "You understand, Mr. Praeger, that I will not, under any circumstances, change your daughter's grade."

But she does. Under our "compromise agreement," I have to go back and put quotation marks around all the quotes. For this, she gives me a C−. Some compromise. But I am so happy and proud of my dad, I don't even care.

For weeks after, whenever something bad happens in school, I just think about my dad and Miss B. in that office and start to giggle. Miss B. refuses to look at me or call on me for the rest of the year, but it really doesn't bother me. I'm not scared of her anymore. It's like she and I both know that my dad is standing right there in back of my chair, watching her every move.

October 1970. Our family room is so packed with kids that there's no room to even sit down. My mother would die if she saw the empty pizza boxes and Coke cans on top of the piano, and the donut crumbs all over the couch. But she's upstairs with the grown-ups. Down here, everyone is young, with blue jeans and long hair. It looks like any teenage party. Except that there are cartons of leaflets and a giant map of our town right in the middle of the floor.

Now that I'm seventeen, everything is different. I used to be unpopular because I was smart and my father was political. Now, I'm popular because I'm smart and my father is political. Even my curly hair and skinny body are cool. Everyone is against the war and gathered in our house because my father is running for local office on a progressive anti-war platform. He has, surprisingly, beaten the Democratic incumbent in the primary, a big deal in my conservative township. You can barely walk anywhere in town without seeing his picture plastered in a window.

It's very weird to see him, with his suit and tie and giant smile, staring at me when I go to buy gum at the candy store. Or, on weekend afternoons, to hear his name, bellowed through a loudspeaker, when a blue Volkswagen bug playing Traffic's "John Barleycorn," drives slowly through the streets, urging people to vote in the upcoming election. Then, when I go home, there he is in his yellow bathrobe, slunk in a chair, with his skinny legs sticking out, reading the newspaper.

Our house is election headquarters, so there are meetings here every night. My job is to organize all the high-school students to go door-to-door and give out my father's materials. I have no trouble getting volunteers. Everyone wants to do it. Everyone except my sister, that is. My sister is now twenty-six, teaching art at a Bronx public school, and as angry at my father as ever. "I hate politics," she says when I invite her to a meeting. "And I hope Daddy loses."

My sister has never been able to forgive my dad for leaving her and her mother when my sister was five. And she thinks he loves me better than her, which maybe he does. But every time she's here, she ends up slamming doors and running over to my cousins' house next door. And my dad ends up in his bedroom with the baseball game turned so loud you can hear it in the street. It's like that commercial: Nobody talks, everyone walks.

But tonight, I'm not worrying about my sister, because Ricky

Z., who is quite possibly the coolest guy in my high school, is coming to the meeting at my house.

Ricky Z. has long, straight hair that he wears in a ponytail and is the only person I know who belongs to SDS. He's really smart, too, even though he's kind of a wise ass to teachers and sometimes cuts class to sit out in the schoolyard and smoke dope.

I always look for Ricky Z. in the lunchroom. Sometimes he brings his guitar to lunch and sits on the ledge of the big window in the lunchroom and plays Bob Dylan. When he sings "Boots of Spanish Leather" and "Sad-Eyed Lady of the Lowlands," I love him so much, I can barely eat my lunch. I hardly ever talk to him, though. I'm pretty shy.

Anyway, Ricky comes to the meeting at our house wearing an old T-shirt from a billiard parlor in Macon, Georgia, and blue jeans that have big rips in the knees. I think he looks totally cool. After I've given each person a street assignment for the week, my father comes downstairs. He's looking pretty cool himself, in his blue jeans, a red-and-white-striped T-shirt, and red sneakers. Everyone hushes up the minute they see him. It's like he's a celebrity or something. He says, "Looks like we could use some new music and a new message for the VW propaganda machine. Anyone here want to help to put that together?" Ricky's arm shoots up.

"Yeah, I can do it," he says. "I'll bring over my tape player after school tomorrow and do it with Jane."

"Do it with Jane?" Just hearing him say my name makes my face burn. I'm so flushed, I can't even look at his side of the room.

I know Ricky Z. doesn't have a girlfriend. He doesn't even seem that interested in girls. But he did stop by my locker to ask me about the meeting this morning. And he didn't leave right after I told him it was at eight, did he? I'm already scheming ways to get my mother out of the house tomorrow.

"Jane, is tomorrow okay?" my father asks.

"Oh, yeah, sure," I say.

The next day, miraculously, my mother *is* out of the house. I'm so jittery, I keep running to the bathroom to pee, and while I'm there, check myself out in the mirror. My hair is a mass of frizzy curls as usual. Not much I can do about that. I'm wearing a black, long-sleeved T-shirt, gold earrings, and my most faded jeans, my standard outfit. I've never been pretty. But lately some people have been telling me that I have "presence," so now I'm trying to muster up as much of it as I can.

When the doorbell rings, I almost jump off the kitchen chair. Walking to the front door, I'm so nervous, I'm afraid my heart is going to beat right out of my chest. It's him. Standing right there in front of me. He's wearing the exact same clothes as yesterday, which for some reason, makes me feel a little calmer.

We have a Coke and he shows me some of the music tapes he brought over. Then we go to work. Well, Ricky goes to work. He's got a great voice, like a radio announcer's, and an eight-track tape recorder, because he plays in a band. So after we choose an Airplane tune, he pretty much does everything himself. All I do is listen to the takes and say whether I like them or not. That's fine with me. I'm happy just to sit there and watch his hands fiddle with the levels on the tape recorder.

The recording doesn't take long. When we finish, we sit there on the couch, about two inches apart. Ricky opens two more Cokes and hands one to me. Then, he stubs out his cigarette and leans back on the couch. All I can think about is how much I want him to kiss me. And when he leans forward and puts his hand on my shoulder to get my attention, I think he just might.

But instead, he says, "What's it like to have the coolest dad in the world? You are so lucky to have grown up with such cool parents. You probably don't even know how lucky you are. My parents are idiot Republicans."

I'm speechless. For a moment, I half believe, want to believe, that Ricky is just scared, that it's a case of cold feet. I study his face, his eyes, his mouth. No, he's not scared. He's just in love with my father, not me. How could I be so stupid?

In an instant, my love for him evaporates. I think his torn jeans look ridiculous. His ponytail is a rag. I feel like dumping my Coke over his head.

I also feel like screaming, "You act like you're smart, but you're

so stupid. More stupid than people who voted for Barry Gold-
water."

But I don't say that. I don't say anything. I just shrug, stand up,
and pitch my Coke can into the garbage pail. My mother's right.
I'm growing up to be just like my father.

September 1971. It's my first semester as a freshman at the University of Michigan. My whole family—father, mother, sister—is
driving me out to Ann Arbor. Now that I'm older, my sister and I
have gotten closer. And on this trip, by some miracle, everyone is
actually getting along. The only time I think a fight might break out
is when my sister starts complaining about the assistant principal in
her school. "He's screwing me over," she says. "First, he cut my budget for supplies, then he started making me do lunch duty, and then
when that crazy Charlie C. threw a chair at me in class, that fucker
wouldn't even let me call the kid's parents. He wanted to get Charlie's side of the story. Can you imagine?" That's when my father says,
"You know, P., you're just going to have to start working with your
union if you want anything to change." I see my sister glaring at the
back of his head. But she doesn't say anything. She just crosses her
arms, slams her body into the back seat, and stares out the window.
Nobody talks for a long time. At some point we stop at a HoJo's for
lunch and the tension just kind of blows over. For now, anyway.

When we get to my dorm, we unload all my stuff and take a
look around. My mother and father start acting like self-ap-
pointed tour guides, poking their heads into classrooms, introduc-
ing themselves to teachers and students, loudly noting that
culture does exist outside Manhattan. "Oh, look," my mother exclaims, "Yo-Yo Ma's coming through here next week." I'm mortified, nervously checking around to see which one of my potential
friends they've already alienated.

Now and again they check in with me, the glum tourist, lag-
ging in their wake. The cheerier they get, the more nervous I become. I'm wondering whether everyone in Michigan has blonde
straight hair, and how I'm ever going to find my way around this
gigantic campus, and what it's going to be like to have boys living

on my hall. I just want to go to my room, unpack my things, and start my new life. I'm so anxious to have my family leave, I practically push them into their car.

"Take care, kid," my sister says, planting a kiss on my cheek and hopping into the back seat of the rented car.

"Don't forget to call my cousins in Detroit if you need anything," my mother says. "They're very nice. And they'd probably love it if you paid them a visit."

I go around to the other side of the car to say good-bye to my father. He's having a cigarette and staring at the map he got from AAA. When he sees me, he tries to smile, but he looks like he's about to cry. I give him a long, silent hug, the longest hug I've ever given him, the longest hug he's ever given me. Then, I watch him get into the car and drive off. The minute he leaves, I miss him desperately.

November 1971. Now that I've been in Michigan for six weeks, I'm feeling slightly less miserable. In my weekly phone call, I tell my father about my Marxism class, which is taught by the infamous L., a radical lesbian who wears fatigues and combat boots and has hair that's half an inch long. On the first day of class, L. divides us into Marxist "self-criticism cells" so we can collectively analyze our unhealthy relationship to Capitalism. She tells us that she finally rid herself of the last vestiges of materialism by giving away her stereo system, which she loved. "I've already decided I'm not a Marxist," I tell my dad. "By that definition, neither am I," he laughs. "I like opera too much." It's fun talking to him today, but it also makes me homesick. At the end of our conversation, I say, "I'm thinking about transferring to Columbia next year, to be closer to home," to which my father says, half-jokingly, "I'd stay where you are. Your mother's already turned your room into a walk-in closet."

It's three weeks before I fly home for Thanksgiving and my first weekend away from campus. As part of my psychology class, I'm going on a retreat at a country cabin owned by the university. The cabin is just one big giant room, filled with lots of sleeping bags and backpacks. There are no TVs, no newspapers, and no phones.

A retreat, I soon learn, means that you sit around in a circle with strangers for hours "sharing your feelings." It means some guy I don't know from Adam can tell me that I'm cold and aloof and think I'm better than him just because I'm from New York. I know if my dad was here, and someone was saying this to him, he'd just stand up, excuse himself, and stroll out the front door. I'm tempted to do the same. But instead I try to explain to this guy that I'm just shy and quiet and liked him well enough until he told me I was cold and aloof. This "sharing" goes on all day and well into the evening.

Then, on Sunday morning, while everyone is crying because a girl and a guy who hated each other from the first minute are now hugging, a man shows up at the door of the retreat center looking for me. He's in his mid-fifties, near bald, with round glasses and an edgeless, moon-shaped face. As I get closer, I see a look of pure dread wash over his face. When I reach the door, he says, "I'm your mother's cousin H. from Detroit. She tried to reach you all last night but couldn't get a phone number for you. She called me this morning and asked me to drive out here. I'm very sorry to have to tell you this but your father died last night. Of a heart attack. It was very sudden. Very unexpected. The funeral is tomorrow. I have tickets for us to fly back to New York in three hours. My car is outside."

I feel like a bomb has exploded in my body and all my bones are melting from the heat. With no bones left to support me, my body collapses on the floor. I can hear someone wailing, sobbing, and I know it's me, but it sounds like someone else. I know instinctively that I need another body to help me absorb the impact of the explosion, to keep me from splintering into pieces. But it's like everyone in the room is frozen, the boy who answered the door, my mother's cousin, the circle of people who have been sharing feelings for two days. Everyone is watching me but no one moves toward me. So I just wrap my arms around myself and don't let go.

After that, I barely remember anything. A car. A plane. A cab. On the flight, my mother's cousin and I don't talk at all.

I call my mother from a pay phone at La Guardia Airport. Her voice sounds stuffy from crying, but also bewildered, like a child. She's trying to tell me what happened, but each statement sounds like a question she's still trying to answer. "We had tickets to a concert," she says, "and your father wasn't feeling well. You know those palpitations he always gets? The ones the doctor said were 'nothing'? He was having those. But he just had a complete physical three weeks ago and the doctor said he was fine. So I went to the concert. And he stayed home to watch the baseball game. When I got back from the concert, the baseball game was still on and I thought he was sleeping . . ."

She stops there. She can't say anymore and I don't want her to. I suddenly feel like I'm the mother. "Mom, don't worry. I'll be there soon. I'm almost home."

I come home to a full house. My sister and cousins are slumped on the living-room couch, nursing beers. My mother keeps running to the front door to greet the people who arrive all night. Every time someone new comes in, she bursts into fresh tears. By midnight, most everyone is gone. The few of us that remain sit around the kitchen table drinking coffee and eating coffee cake and talking about my father. Nothing seems real until the next day, at the funeral.

When we arrive at the funeral home the next morning, the place is already packed with people. Despite the gusts of wintry air that blow in every time the door opens, the room feels hot and stifling. People swarm my mother the minute they walk in the door. My sister and I decide to make a getaway to the family room, which we've been assured is "private." So we are stunned when we walk into the family room and see my father lying there in an open coffin.

"He would have fucking hated this," my sister says, incensed. She's right. My father made a big deal about wanting his body to be donated to science, then cremated. He would never have wanted people to see him dead.

I never wanted to see him dead either. But now that he's right in front of me, I can't tear myself away. Under the thick, tan mortician's makeup, his skin looks gray and flaccid. When I put my hand on his and kiss his cheek, his face feels cold to my lips. He doesn't look like my father at all. He looks like a bad imitation.

During the service, I sit between my mother, who is pale but composed, and my sister, who is stone-faced. All around us, people are dabbing their eyes with tissues. Some weep openly. I listen intently as mourner after mourner goes up to the podium to tell stories about the man that has died.

I've heard most of these stories before. There's the one about the time he took my sister and my cousins on a camping trip to Maine "even though he'd never been camping." There are stories about his trips to Mississippi to fight for civil rights and the way he defended alleged Communists in front of the House on Un-American Activities Committee. There are stories about spontaneous acts of kindness, about how when our butcher, J., was running from Mafia loan sharks, my father hid him in our basement for days. Or how my father could never refuse a Bowery bum a dollar, or charge a client who couldn't pay. About how he almost won an election.

Then someone tells the story about how my father helped foot the college bill of a brilliant young black man whose mother was raising five children on her own. The man eventually became dean of an Ivy League college.

I've heard this story many times, but hearing it now, I completely break down. My grief suddenly feels huge and bottomless and unfathomable. I don't know if I'm crying for the father I lost or the father I never had.

One of my aunts, sitting behind me, puts a hand on my shoulder and says, "You've got to be strong now, for your mother."

The elegies continue, all testaments to a man of uncommon generosity, a man who loved and was loved by many. Then, my sister leans over and whispers something to me that almost makes me laugh out loud. She says, "I wonder who's going to get up and say that this venerated man was a selfish, nasty prick, incapable of showing one ounce of affection to his children?"

November 1971. Thanksgiving comes barely three weeks after my father's death and I fly home from Ann Arbor for a short visit.

It's the usual cast of characters, the same oyster-chestnut stuffing and creamed onions, but without my father, it's a strange and somber affair.

The big news of the evening is that my cousin Steven, who is a few years older than me, has baked a nickel bag of hashish into the brownies. Only a few of us are in on the secret and no one is talking. After dinner, everyone downs the brownies with lots of ice cream. By the time the dishes are cleared, my usually boisterous relatives are barely conversant.

I know my cousin's intention was to inject some levity into the proceedings but the opposite has happened. Everyone is so stuffed with food that the hashish turns us into silent, staring zombies. A few people crash out on the couch. One of my aunts throws up in the bathroom. Only my ninety-year-old grandmother seems unaffected. "Ehvreevun is so kuhviet," she says in her heavy Yiddish accent. "Vut kinda pahdy iz dat!"

It's a scene whose weirdness my father definitely would have appreciated. But without him here to enjoy it, no one else does either.

The next morning, my mother and I share an austere breakfast of black coffee and dry toast. While she's pouring us a second cup of coffee, she says lightly, "I found out this week from M. that your father hadn't updated his will in twenty years."

M. was my father's closest friend. Another lawyer.

She puts down the coffee pot.

"M. has been dealing with everything, thank God. You know your father had some very major debts. From that big case that he lost last year. Now his creditors are trying to soak the estate for whatever it's worth. And M. says I have to watch every dime I spend until the suits get settled."

"So what does that mean?" I ask, my hand tightening around my coffee cup. I know she's heading somewhere.

"Well, right now it means there's no money to pay your tuition. But don't worry about it. We'll figure something out."

I feel like I've been socked in the stomach. I try to take a deep breath before talking but the words rush out in an angry blast.

"But Daddy always said there was money for me. Put away. For college. He said no matter what, that money wouldn't be touched. Did it just disappear?"

My mother is wiping off the table with broad, fast sweeps of the sponge. But there's nothing on the table. No crumbs. No spills.

"Well, he did have life insurance. But he canceled it when he lost that case. To pay off some of the debts."

For one panicked minute, I think of calling the dean at the Ivy League school and begging him to take me in. But what if he doesn't remember my father? What if his mother never even told him? What if he doesn't even exist?

"You will get a one-hundred-dollar-a-month Social Security check," my mother says, like it's some great gift.

"That'll help some."

I look at the crusts of toast on my plate and suddenly wonder what I'll be eating a month from now. I have one friend at school whose parents can't give her much help and she eats Rice-a-Roni for dinner every night. I hate Rice-a-Roni. I'm getting queasy just thinking about it.

I go back to school a few days later. And it doesn't take long to figure out the limited purchasing power of $100 a month. I don't even bother enrolling for my second semester. Because I'm an out-of-state student, I don't qualify for much in the way of financial aid. After a few failed attempts at waitressing, I get a job working the midnight shift in a copy shop. While the campus sleeps, I Xerox scholarly library texts for professors. As far as jobs go, it isn't so bad. I find the work kind of meditative and I like hanging out with the oddballs who work there.

A year later, I reapply to school as a self-supporting Michigan resident and am granted a complete financial-aid package. A full-tuition scholarship! Low-interest loans and work-study grants! For a few weeks, I feel like I've hit the lottery. I give notice at the copy shop and they throw me a midnight party. But the euphoria doesn't stick. The money is just something I need because my dad is dead, not a cause for celebration.

*   *   *

December 1978. The apartment is a six-floor walk-up in Little Italy on the edge of what they're starting to call SoHo. It's a minuscule one-bedroom, even by New York standards, but I've bribed the super mightily for the privilege of living there. Taking the advice of my next-door neighbor, I put little white mountains of boric acid in every corner of the apartment, then watch as the cockroaches just scoot around them. The floor is so sloped that dropping a single grape on the kitchen floor immediately sends you under the refrigerator with a broom or into the bathroom at the other end of the apartment. I've actually seen grapes roll that far. Still, it's mine, and I feel lucky to have it.

My whole family is close by. My mother lives on the East Side and works as an account executive at a printing company in TriBeCa. My sister still teaches art in the Bronx and lives in the West Village. We speak often, but almost never about my father.

I'm happy to be back in New York. I don't ever want to live anywhere else. But at twenty-four, I feel like a complete failure. I've already left a graduate program in English because it was too stodgy, and a law school because law really was, as my father said, the opposite of poetry. I guess I just had to find out for myself. I'm dreaming of becoming a documentary filmmaker but working as a secretary.

At night, I sometimes find myself lying in bed, talking to my father, asking for advice. I want to know what I should do with my life, how you're supposed to figure it all out, and what I should do about my mother's crazy new liquor salesman boyfriend. But I don't hear much back.

I've started to sleep in an old T-shirt of his that I've always loved. It has thin dark green and purple stripes and is made of a smooth, soft cotton. It's been laundered so many times it's faded and full of holes. But his smell still permeates it. And I secretly hope that by sleeping in it, I will lure him into my dreams.

I do. But not in the way I've planned. My father appears to me in his best brown suit, the one they dressed him in for the funeral. In the dream, he is vibrantly alive and trying his best to persuade me that he never died. I stand about ten feet away from him, scrutinizing his presence and insisting that he is dead. But he is so warm, so open, so inviting, that my skepticism starts to melt, and I am soon overwhelmed with feelings of love and relief. I run to hug him, weeping with joy. But the moment I fall into his arms, the moment I feel the weight of his body against mine, I wake up and experience the shock of his death all over again. He is, it seems, no more accessible in death than he was in life.

January 1997. When I was growing up, our house, with the exception of my room, was always white-glove clean and organized. Surfaces gleamed. There was a place for everything. But now that I'm in my forties and my mother is in her mid-seventies, I notice that even her well-ordered spaces and lovingly tended possessions are showing signs of age, signs she doesn't always notice.

I'm fixing my children French toast in the kitchen of her new home (my mother remarried over ten years ago), and I'm amazed to see that the Teflon pan has no more Teflon. The morning coffee is bitter, too, probably because of the permanent scum inside of the pot.

"Mom, I need more maple syrup," says my five-year-old daughter, who is already pouring half the bottle onto her plate. But I don't stop her because I'm busy chasing my three-year-old son, who is pulling down spatulas and refrigerator magnets, can openers and pencils, anything he can get his hands on, from my mother's cabinets.

"Leo, those aren't toys!" my mother says to my son when she walks into the kitchen and discovers the disarray. I know she means to be firm, but there's a harshness in her voice, a brittleness that's come with age.

I wipe the spilled syrup off the table, bundle my children in scarves and boots, and send them out with my husband to play in the snow. My mother and I have work to do. We have set aside the morning to go through old cartons in the basement. Many of the cartons were packed up and forgotten years ago.

Each box we open unsettles a new layer of dust and sends me into a fresh sneezing fit. But I love sifting through this stuff. I want to linger over every high-school paper and yellowed paperback.

Not my mother. She is a woman of the present. She is effi-
ciently filling an empty carton with broken and stray pieces of my
children's toys, readying it for the Dumpster.

But as we listen to my kids, who are outside the basement window, screaming with delight as my husband pummels them with
soft snowballs, even she gets nostalgic.

"Your father would have been crazy for these kids, you know.
He loved children," she says.

My father loved kids? I shoot her a look.

"No, really," she says. "Your father absolutely adored you. He
just had trouble showing it."

"That's for sure," I say, continuing to pile up the paperbacks I
want to salvage from the Dumpster.

"Well, he just wasn't good at expressing feelings," my mother
says, folding one of my children's baby blankets, "even to me. I
think it all started with Jeffrey."

"Jeffrey?" I stop flipping pages. "Who's Jeffrey?"

"Oh, I've told you about Jeffrey, haven't I? Your father's son
from his first marriage."

His what? "No. You didn't," I say. I do a quick search of my
memory bank. No Jeffrey.

"What happened?"

"He died. When he was just one."

"He died? How?" I ask. I'm trying to remember my own children at one.

"Well, they put him to bed one night, he had some sort of
upper respiratory infection, and when they came in in the morning, he was dead. It might have been pneumonia. I don't think
they ever figured it out."

I'm reeling. I feel like I want to sit down, but I'm already sitting down.

"He was utterly devastated," my mother says, her voice getting
low and dramatic. "He never got over it, the idea that it was his
fault. That if he had just taken Jeffrey to the doctor, maybe, you
know, who knows?"

"Well what did he say about it?" I ask. "How did he feel? How come no one ever told me about it?" I feel like I've had a black bag over my head for forty years.

"He never wanted to talk about it. Even when I tried to bring it up. But every time you got sick, oh, my God, he went into a total panic. He was convinced you were going to die. He'd become totally despondent. And absolutely nothing I said could reassure him."

My mother suddenly stands up and brushes off her slacks.

"I think I'd better go upstairs and fix some food," she says. "The kids are going to need some lunch."

I watch her climb the black metal spiral staircase, but don't move to follow. I feel glued to this spot on the floor.

I remember as a child, asking my father why the corners of his mouth turned down. "You look like a sad clown," I used to tease. My mother later told me it was because of his Bell's Palsy. But somehow, I knew, the way children often do, that sadness had taken up permanent residence in his face.

Upstairs, I hear my children piling into the house with my husband. City children, they are exuberant to discover that not all snow immediately transforms into wet, gray slush. "Boots on the mat!" my mother yells. "Scarves and gloves on the bench!"

I try to imagine losing one of my own children and I can't. Even to imagine such pain pulls a switch that makes my mind go blank and my body numb.

"What would you do if I died?" my daughter sometimes asks me.

"I would cry every day for the rest of my life and miss you forever," I say, meaning every word.

That my father had endured such a terrible loss and carried it with him silently into the new life he tried to make with us fills me with inexpressible sorrow.

I look around at all the debris on the floor, the books, the papers, the clothes, the toys, the dust. I no longer feel like cleaning it up. I go upstairs and hug my children.

That same evening, back in the city, I call my sister. I can't wait to tell her my news. I expect her to be even more shocked than I was. Jeffrey, after all, was her brother.

"I already knew about Jeffrey," she says flatly. "And I've spent no more than one second of my whole life thinking about him. Who cares why Daddy behaved the way he did? The point is, he did."

I'm incredulous.

"Don't you understand?" I practically shout into the mouthpiece. "That's why he could never get close to us. He never got over Jeffrey."

"Hogwash," my sister says. "That should have made him cherish us all the more."

"But he couldn't," I say.

"Sure he could," she retorts.

And after a pause she says, "Jane, you have to understand. I would have eaten the dirt off the floor if that man threw one crumb of affection my way, just one crumb."

When I hang up the phone, my hands are freezing, but I'm wiping the sweat from under my glasses. Maybe my sister's right. Maybe this is just a convenient excuse for my father's failings.

I know that after my father died, I called all my uncles and aunts and plied them with questions about my father's life. I longed for someone to tell me a story so resonant, so illuminating, so revealing of his character, that I could finally understand the roots of his remoteness, forgive his emotional absence from my life, and move on. It's entirely possible that now that I've heard such a story, I just don't want to let it go.

But by the next morning, I've decided that my sister is wrong. Not wrong, exactly. But missing something. I feel convinced that in withholding his love, and himself, my father thought he was protecting us all from some much greater calamity, the calamity of not being able to control what you love and may lose.

I can also imagine that my father saw nothing in his life that was large enough or strong enough to contain his grief. So he simply lived with it. And lived a little less.

September 1998. My children and I are spending a rainy Saturday morning in the apartment and I'm searching for ways to keep them entertained. I pull some shoeboxes stuffed with old photographs from a living-room cabinet, thinking that the kids will find the shots of their very pregnant mother, and themselves as babies, amusing. They do. But then they want to see what I looked like as a baby, too.

We trudge to another closet where I keep, on a high shelf, my only photo album from my childhood. My parents weren't big picture takers. There's a smattering of professional baby shots, then about one snapshot every other year.

But there's one photograph of my father and me that I've always loved and I show it to them.

"There I am at my cousin Stevie's Bar Mitzvah," I say. "I'm just about your age, Jenne, six."

"I like your dress," my daughter says admiringly, and I laugh.

In the picture, I am wearing a frilly light-pink organdy number with a wide sash and high puffy short sleeves, just the kind of thing my daughter likes. The Bar Mitzvah is being held in my aunt's backyard. My father and I are seated at a table draped with a white cloth against a backdrop of apple trees.

The Bar Mitzvah photographer has caught me making a very important point, my mouth open in a perfect O, my index finger pointing dramatically into the air. My father, wearing a short-sleeved white shirt, is sitting next to me, watching me with unabashed pleasure. Although his face is cocked slightly away from mine, his eyes are fixed firmly in my direction. All the lines of his face, even the creases of his mouth, are pointing upward, toward the bright autumn sky. There is no sadness in his face, no thoughts of a baby who died.

"What are you saying to your dad?" my daughter asks.

"I don't know," I say, wishing I did.

But looking at the photo now, I see something I've never quite seen before. The girl is making an impassioned argument. She knows her father will approve of her sound logic, her emphatic delivery, the moral certainty of her position. And her father is clearly impressed, delighted by the energetic leaps of her youthful mind.

But studying the expression on her face, the way her eyes are fixed on a far spot of sky, I can't help but think that she's working too hard. That she somehow knows that a six-year-old, no matter how precocious, should not have to trade campaign speeches for love. That she might just prefer to be a little girl in a pretty dress at an afternoon party, sitting beside the man she loves.

And him! The more entranced he is by her, the more his eyes bask in her loveliness, the more his head and body pull away from her.

I used to think this was a happy picture. But now, it seems tragically, almost heartbreakingly, sad.

My daughter must notice the change in my expression because she says, suddenly, "He looks happy, Mom."

I look again. And it's true. He is enjoying himself. This party. This daughter. This brilliantly sunny day. And even though it is only proof of a moment, a moment caught by a stranger's camera forty years ago, what I hold in my hands tells me something I have always wanted to know, something I always wanted said, declared, shouted from rooftops: Yes, I love you.

[JANE PRAEGER]

Jane Praeger's riveting memoir showcases the emerging talent of an author who's sole publishing credit is a "My Turn" column in Newsweek.

That column, "When Is a Tree Not a Tree," an essay about the struggle over the presence of a Christmas tree in an interfaith marriage "touched a raw nerve for a lot of people," the writer says. It generated so much mail that Newsweek *devoted a "Mail Call" column entitled "Oy Tannenbaum" to readers' responses the following week. What the essay demonstrated was Praeger's uncanny ability to point out the small events in life that, often dismissed, lead to the most profound personal realizations we will ever make about ourselves.*

Of course, Praeger's facility with prose is not surprising, given that she's written extensively for radio and has utilized her writing skills during a twelve-year career producing documen-

tary films on a variety of topics, including the police response to domestic violence, the story of teenage doo-wap singer Frankie Lymon, and the nation's war on cancer.

"Interestingly," she says, "one of the first documentaries in which I had a major role was a film made for high-school students titled To Be a Father, about the responsibilities of fatherhood!"

Since I had heard through the writers' grapevine that Praeger had a tough time writing "Comrades," and that at several points had almost given up on the essay, I was curious about what the end product had provided her in the way of a new outlook on her relationship with her father. Had it changed it at all?

"Working on this piece did really alter my perceptions of my relationship with my father," Praeger said, "mostly because it forced [me] to think about life from his perspective—something I was not very capable of while he was alive. It helped me to expand my childhood narrative of my father as a man who was 'distant, unexpressive, emotionally withholding' to one which incorporated some of his own longings, his own lifelong struggle with intimacy, his own grief.

"When I first started writing the piece, I wrote it from the perspective of an adult looking back. But the result felt very cold and desolate and intellectual and constrained—too much like him and too much like the person I've struggled hard not to become."

She eventually tossed out that draft and then "discovered that when I started writing as my younger self, the emotions and memories came flooding in. I began to remember feelings and details and sensations that I had long forgotten, or if I hadn't forgotten them, had lodged themselves in my mind in a particular way. I always recalled my father's death, for example, in a series of images that had become frozen and rigid by the passage of time.

"Writing as my younger self actually helped to melt those stale, frozen memories and gave me an opportunity to re-

experience that difficult period of my life. I could see that my re-
lationship with my father was more nuanced, and had more
complex feelings than I had previously allowed.

"My father has been dead for almost thirty years. But
strangely," Praeger observed, "I feel closer to him now than
ever before."

—C.O.

BEING A FATHER

Winston Groom

THIS IS A STORY OF SELFISHNESS AND REDEMPTION, OF ANXIety and love, of resignation and wonderment. It's the story of Carolina Montgomery Groom, age fourteen months, and her papa.

"It will change your life forever!"

This was the cry I'd heard through the years whenever having children was mentioned. It was disturbing, if not frightening. I didn't want my life "changed forever." It was scary enough getting married again. When you get married you have to give up things and at heart I am a selfish person. But life's a trade-off and if I hadn't married the woman I love she would have married somebody else and I would have made the stupidest mistake of my existence.

My first marriage ended childless a few years after it began, a casualty of women's lib and the Age of Aquarius, or so I like to believe. In the late 1960s and early '70s, women were bursting out of their pent-up cocoons and demanding careers, and the economics of life in Washington, D.C., where I was a newspaper reporter, were such that both husband and wife had to work to make ends meet. There was no time for children.

For the next fifteen years I ran amok and studiously avoided marriage at all costs because I was having too much fun. One by one, other friends married and settled down to live what I considered lives of quiet desperation. Not for me. I partied, played rugby, sailed, wrote books, and became something of a gadfly in the New York social scene. Then I met Anne-Clinton who was more than twenty years my junior. I could tell from the outset she was a serious woman, born to be a mother. When it became obvious that there was an earnest and solemn love between us I asked her to get married. She asked me if I wanted children. I truthfully answered yes, but still felt a little uncomfortable about it.

"It will change your life forever!"

The clarion cry rang again in my ears from all my male friends, most of whom at that point had kids of high-school age. They moaned about grades and expenses and having to go to football games and Little League and soccer and so on. But something told me they protested too much—like people complaining about mothers-in-law. But I stayed selfishly complacent. Anne-Clinton and I could travel unhampered by the responsibility of children and of being tied to a place nine months of the year because of school and even of worrying about finding a baby-sitter for the evening.

The years seemed to pass quickly by, yet still we had no child. Most writers are always in a spotlight of sorts, but when they turned *Forrest Gump* into a movie I was suddenly propelled into a kind of celebrity status and was away from home on book or lecture tours sometimes for eight months of the year. There was a lot of time to think during those long stretches on the road and it came to me at some point the greatest gift we humans have is the ability to commit ourselves totally to another human. I was already committed to Anne-Clinton, of course, but even though she's the happiest person I've ever met, I could sense she was feeling tense maternal instincts. All her friends from college had little families by then and she was godmother to several of the children, but it was obvious how much she longed for one of her own. Frequently in our conversations she'd refer to, "when we have our little one," and she was always looking at toys and other children's things and would say, "Oh, wouldn't this be precious for our child." It was heartbreaking, and while I may have a lot of faults, breaking hearts isn't one of them.

It was a spectacular autumn morning at our place in the mountains of North Carolina when she made her announcement. The trees were all shades of red, yellow, and gold and the mountains a riot of color against the backdrop of a sky so clear deep blue it looked like you could drink it.

"I think I'm pregnant," she said.

We were in the bedroom having coffee and reading the papers. The way she said it, I thought for an instant she wasn't happy about it but the tentative note I sensed in her voice wasn't that at all. She was worried that I might not be.

I was stunned for a moment as my heart jumped and then I said, "That's wonderful! Absolutely wonderful!" and we leaped into each others arms and both knew everything was finally going to be okay. When I said it was wonderful I meant every letter of the word.

Actually we weren't completely sure, though. Anne-Clinton's announcement had come as a result of a five-dollar home pregnancy test she'd taken the day before and she wasn't certain that the outcome was correct. Worse, it was Friday and the soonest appointment we could get with a doctor would be Monday so the whole weekend we had to sweat it out along with her mother, Wren, who was staying with us. But you could feel the excitement building by the hour. Anne-Clinton called all her friends with kids and they'd all taken home pregnancy tests. To a person, they told her the tests were accurate and so the weekend passed with an atmosphere of hopeful glee and thankfulness mixed with anxiety until the doctor's pronouncement could be had.

"It's true!" Anne-Clinton's voice came over the car phone as she was driving out of the doctor's parking lot in Asheville, a couple of hours away. There could of course be no drinking toasts for the next nine months but I believe she took a final sip of champagne when she got home. Then the planning began.

Anne-Clinton and Wren are inveterate planners. Everything they do is thought out so well the United States Army would die to have officers of their ability. First, personal obstetricians would have to be secured both in North Carolina and in our main home on the coast in Point Clear, Alabama. Diets, exercise schedules, and other regimens were decided upon. Baby books were poured over and then the buying began. Nurseries were decorated at both homes. I learned to know the difference between Moses baskets, cribs, cradles, and baby beds. Toys began to pile up, mostly stuffed animals and things of outrageous primary colors that gonged, honked, oinked, buzzed, and sang. Friends as far off as New York and California began knitting booties and sewing baby blankets. The newspaper society column ran a story and joy was spread throughout the land.

Meantime, I had to take a back seat to all this hoopla. When the phone rang I knew it wasn't for me but I didn't care at all; in fact, I got in on the act. And soon it started.

"It's going to change your life forever!"

If I heard it once, I heard it a hundred times—well-meaning people giving advice from the height of previous experience.

"No it won't," I told them. At least not the way you mean it, was what I thought.

Now the weeks and months seemed to fly by and on the morning of July 23, 1998, we all packed up early in the morning and drove to the hospital in Fairhope, Alabama for the great event. I had adamantly refused to go to Lamaze classes but Anne-Clinton was determined that I would be with her in the delivery room. I had heard of this practice, though I'm sure it would have horrified women of my mother's generation. Both Wren and I were given sanitary gowns and entered nervously into the delivery room. Anne-Clinton was already there on the birthing table and was the only person who wasn't nervous, except maybe the nurse. I'd never seen her look so beautiful; she'd waited patiently ten years with me without complaint and finally her time had come. Down the hall, twenty or thirty of our friends anxiously occupied the waiting room as well as our room on the obstetric ward and also spilled out into the hall. As the delivery progressed I would sometimes leave the room to give them reports.

We both decided not to know the ultrasound results to find out beforehand if it was going to be a girl or boy. I secretly wished for a girl because, if for no other reason, I didn't want to have to be trying to play touch football at the age of sixty-five or seventy with some big moose of a son. In fact I now knew it was going to be wonderful no matter what it was, but for Anne-Clinton's sake I also wished for a girl. She's a totally feminine personality and all my instincts told me she'd bond with a little girl in a way that would be more than special.

We'd decided that if it was a boy he'd be named after me and after a lot of searching and discussing, a girl would be called Carolina Montgomery, which was the name of both my great-grandmother and my great-great grandmother.

At 2:05 P.M. Carolina Montgomery Groom arrived in the world.

Everybody was laughing and crying. I bit a hole in my lip. Cheering began in the waiting room. I don't remember much except that at some point the nurse handed her to me. I couldn't believe she was so tiny (though that was soon to change—big time). I gave her to Anne-Clinton, whose eyes were glistening and I never recalled a sweeter smile on her face as she cradled her in her arms.

The nurse finally gave her back to me and said we needed to get her to the nursery while the doctor finished up his business. I took her in my arms and with me in the lead we made our way down back corridors until I saw all our friends lined up outside the glass wall of the nursery. There was a door to the hall and I ignorantly started to take Carolina through it to show her to the friends up close, but the horrified nurse restrained me. It had been a long day, but all was truly right with the world. Everybody's heard about the "miracle of birth," but when I finally got to bed that night I lay in awe of what had just happened in our lives. There was suddenly a new, living, breathing little human on the planet among what is now supposed to be six billion other living breathing humans. But this one was ours, by our own creation, and I vowed then and there that she was going to get all the love and care and devotion in my power to give her her chance in the world.

"It's going to change your life forever!" Again the mighty cry swelled up worse than the chorus from the Trojan Women.

At first I was a bit mystified. She was so tiny, Carolina. I didn't know what to do and in fact there wasn't much I could do. We had a nurse and between her and Anne-Clinton and Wren they had things well in hand, so I sort of hung around with the dogs who didn't seem to know what to make of it either. Then one morning Anne-Clinton brought her into bed and we were there, all three of us, and she smiled for the first time I could recall. That was it for me!

Oh, they grow so fast! Everybody says that, but it's too true. Carolina quickly went off the doctor's charts in height. (Both Anne-Clinton and I are tall.) For her first birthday I bought her a rocking horse. Not just any rocking horse but I splurged on an antique English rocking horse that's actually the size of a small pony. When they delivered it, Anne-Clinton was beside herself. "She won't be able to ride that thing until she's three!" she laughed.

I have begun doing all the things I swore always not to do. I carry around baby pictures and show them to people, a thing I detested in others before this. I talk baby talk to Carolina and delight in everything she does. From what people say, she's the best-behaved baby they can remember. She doesn't cry much except when she's hungry, and when she laughs and smiles—which is most of the time—she lights up the universe. She has big blue eyes and strawberry blonde hair and can crawl faster than I can walk. I revel in every new task she learns; she adores picture books and likes to draw and paint and eat crayons. She's so beautiful that someday she's going to accidentally break some boy's heart, but not mine.

I look forward to teaching her to ride and sail and fish and play tennis and to go for long walks in the mountain forests. And if I have to go to Little League or soccer or whatever, I'll do it joyfully. I only hope to live long enough to see how she turns out, but if not that's okay too. I've had enough joy since that day she came into our lives to last a lifetime. When she crawls in bed with us in the morning and says, "Papa," my heart leaps; and then she'll do something nice like stick her finger in your eye. Do you think I would trade it?

"It's going to change your life forever!"

They are right, of course, and so what? You think I'm not looking forward to it!

[WINSTON GROOM]

Forrest Gump—the main character of the 1994 box office hit by the same name—had a father, but he wasn't a longshoreman crushed to death under a load of bananas. He was author Winston Groom, who originally wrote the 1986 novel turned movie starring Tom Hanks.

Gump, the story of an idiot savant, which touched hundreds of millions of moviegoers with its power to describe the powerful simplicity of the human heart, was actually inspired by Groom's own father, a southern lawyer. One afternoon, his father told him the story of a retarded boy he'd grown up with who could do one thing well—play the piano. Groom was so inspired by his dad's story, that he wrote the book in six weeks.

Forrest Gump led to a sequel, Gump & Co., plus a number of tie-ins, most charming among these, the Bubba Gump Shrimp Co. Cookbook: Recipes & Reflections from Forrest Gump, and Forrest Gump: My Favorite Chocolate Recipes—Mama's Fudge, Cookies, Cakes and Candies.

Like Gump, Groom is a tall six foot six. Both grew up in Mobile, Alabama, played football, and served in the Vietnam War. While Gump was an enlisted man, however, Groom was executive officer of the 26th Psyop Detachment on board ship to Vietnam. Like the hero of his famous novel, once in-country, Groom joined the 4th Infantry Division, in Groom's case as a lieutenant.

After the war and writing for the Washington Star until 1976, Groom utilized his experience in the military to author the Pulitzer-nominated Conversations with the Enemy: The Story of PFC Robert Garwood, and to write the 1978 Viet-

nam novel Better Times Than These. Groom's novels also include, Gone the Sun, Only, and Such a Pretty, Pretty Girl. One of his latest successes is an academic military title, Shrouds of Glory: From Atlanta to Nashville—The Last Great Campaign of the Civil War, published in 1998. He is the author of twelve books in all, and divides his time between Point Clear, Alabama and Cashiers, North Carolina.

After reading "Being a Father," I asked Groom to fill me in on his first parenting challenge with Carolina Montgomery.

"Biggest parenting challenge for me so far?" the author writes. "Walking and talking. We waited in awe for these wonderful events. Now she won't sit down and she won't shut up. We call her Conana The Destroyer."

SNAPSHOTS

Claudia O'Keefe

ON THE DAY I WAS BORN, MY FATHER, WHO WAS THE SON OF a then-prominent celebrity, composed a song named for me, "Claudia," and then a week later walked out of my life. He was a genius, my mother told me, who could play anything from Mendelssohn to Gershwin by ear. For years I wondered, what had "Claudia" sounded like? What was the melody? What were the words? Why did my father create such a personal gift for me and then leave?

When I first asked my mother to describe the song, I wasn't surprised to hear her say, "I don't know."

My mother is tone deaf, but even if it weren't for this, I don't think she likes to think much about the day I was born. My father never came to the hospital to visit her or the new baby. After the birth, the nurses asked if they could help her get ready for her proud husband's inevitable visit. Would she like help with her makeup?

"I don't think he's coming," she told them, and so after some mild protest, they left her alone.

In fact, no one came to see us. Not my mother's parents, father's parents, any relatives or friends. Why this was so, I don't know. It does seem strange. It wasn't as if she and my father weren't married, or as if they had been forced to because she was pregnant. They were married first, my mother's pregnancy came later. Neither was distance an excuse for lack of visitors. Every one of our relatives and close friends lived within an hour of the hospital. Three of my grandparents were ten minutes away. It had been my mother's mom who had dropped her off at the hospital entrance when labor pains started, and then drove away.

"What kind of a song was it?" I asked my mother again and again over the years, desperate to find something to celebrate about the day of my birth. "Was it pretty, sweet, haunting, loud, regretful, what?"

"I don't know," she would always say.

"But you heard this song, right?"

"Yes."

"And?"

I'd wait for more from her, but there never was any. Eventually, I gave up asking. My father, whom she went to Las Vegas a year later to divorce, left her with me and no money, no support of any kind. She still resents the no money part, I think, and after a while I knew that this was where I had to leave the discussion about "Claudia."

However, my wonder over a father who could create a song about me, and my longing to hear it, never went away.

Music is something that runs in my branch of the O'Keefe family. My grandfather, who died in 1983, has a star on the Hollywood Walk of Fame. I know, not because I was told about it, but because I happened to walk over it on Hollywood Boulevard one day and did a double take. Walter O'Keefe was a successful Broadway lyricist. He composed the lyrics to "The Daring Young Man on the Flying Trapeze," a song, which though it is from a different time, still lingers in the public consciousness. Most people of my mother's generation remember Walter from the golden days of radio, when he had a game show called *Double or Nothing* and was a summer replacement for some of the biggest stars in show business.

"Think of Bob Barker or Monty Hall," my mother once said. "That's about how popular he was."

Okay, so hosting game shows doesn't rank up there with discovering a vaccine for polio, but as a kid, I felt privileged to be associated with a famous family.

Associated was about it, since I only met my grandfather once, when I was five years old. It was 1963, during a Christmas party at his Palos Verdes estate, a sprawling hyper-relaxed wood-shingled mansion of the 1940s Southern California school. Five thousand square feet if it was an inch, the place was crammed with expensive antiques. When that night my mother used the powder room belonging to Walter's second wife, Terry, she spotted economy-sized bottles of the world's most expensive perfumes on the vanity.

"There was a bottle of Joy that must have set Walter back two thousand dollars," she's told me. "It made me feel crummy, because at the time I was living in a one-room house in Montrose."

Later, the mansion was sold to the owner of Chason's, the legendary Los Angeles eatery, but for years it was the glamorous domain of a man who made everyone he met aware that he was larger than life.

Unlike friends of mine, who can remember events early in their lives quite clearly, and my mother, who claims to remember days in her crib at eighteen months, my recollections before the age of seven are few. They come to me not as flashes, but like the pages of a colorful, if somewhat simplistic, picture book. I remember shapes and the emotions those shapes bring to me, but I never see the whole picture. In my memories, I rarely look at other people. I can't remember my grandfather's face at all from the party. I hear his voice, however, somewhere behind me, huge, like a radio with its volume turned up too high, conveying the sound of dark, supersaturated joy. I have the sense of at least a dozen bodies too tall for me to converse with. I envision white satin, on people, on decorations, on a supernaturally long dining table. I see manzanita branches sprayed with silver paint, a golden reindeer, and a dark study studded with leather.

My grandfather gave me a baby carriage that Christmas, one

of only two gifts I ever received from him. In love with the carriage from the start, I pushed the buggy all over the house for hours. One of its wheels squeaked badly, which must have driven the guests mad, but I countered the annoyance by declaring cutely, "The squeaky wheel gets the oil." Everyone within hearing range laughed or chuckled. After I repeated this a number of times, though, my grandfather pulled me aside and gave me a lesson in comedy.

"Once is funny, Claudia," he said, "but don't milk your jokes. Never milk your jokes."

What I do remember strongly from the evening was that my father wasn't there. Walter and Terry had invited him but he didn't show up. He was off drunk in a piano bar.

Both Walter and Roberta, my grandmother and Walter's first wife, were fabulous alcoholics; Walter in his grandly boozy, entertaining way, and Roberta, whom everyone called Bert, in her good ol' rich gal way. Roberta is someone I really do wish I had had a chance to know. She was already divorced from Walter by the time I came along, but that didn't stop her from visiting her grandchild. A few weeks after I was brought home from the hospital, she dropped in on my mother and me at my maternal grandparents' modest two-bedroom bungalow in La Cañada, bearing the gift of a mink stole, an infant-size mink stole. As my mother tells it, Bert was delighted when, holding me up bare-bottomed, I unexpectedly pooped on her.

"Oh, look," she said, laughing, "scrambled eggs!"

A couple of years later, Bert, who was a big, blonde, bossomy former runner-up in the Miss America contest, was playing "bridge" with some friends in the Hollywood Hills. These bridge games of hers were infamous because very little card playing was ever done. Largely, they were an excuse for her and her pals to get together and spend the afternoon drinking. She was never a mean drunk, but rather a happy, bubbly one.

On that afternoon in the Hollywood Hills, once the friends called it quits, Bert walked out to her car, which was parked at the curb. It was raining. One thing that not even locals seem to comprehend is that each of the major streets winding through the Hills are set at the bottom of individual canyons. The boulevards have names like Laurel Canyon, Coldwater Canyon, and Topanga Canyon. Curbs on these old boulevards can stand a foot tall or higher in places to catch the run-off from powerful storms, which comes rushing down the mountain as flash floods.

Bert, pleasantly wasted that afternoon, toddled on her high heels out to the curb where her car was parked, stepped off into the rain-swollen gutter, and *shwoosh*, was swept into the current racing down from the hills. She drowned under her Mercedes. When the rescue people arrived and fished her out, they discovered that her teacup poodle had drowned with her, shut up in her pocketbook.

How could you not love a woman who expired that way, in such ignoble, but obvious style?

What a shock it was for my mother to learn that her mother-in-law had died by turning on the TV to watch the evening news. Because Walter was still well-known at the time, it made the front page of the *L.A. Times* the next morning, too.

I have no idea what my father thought of his mother's death. He was at every stage absent from my life, so his thoughts and opinions must be, as well. Raised in a household of drunks, he became a drunk himself in his teens. Whereas Walter's alcoholism was halfway tolerated due to his stature in the industry, and Bert's because of her tits and good humor, early on my father suffered from the disease of being a famous man's son. He had the O'Keefe talent for music, which led to an aborted recording career, and then jobs playing in those piano bars he haunted. His genius IQ also enabled him to make several breakthroughs in TV set design, which led to patents for a major manufacturer during the salad days of television. For him, however, it appeared Walter's fame was a personal curse he couldn't lift, and though brighter than his father, with just as much potential, he became a disconnected, angry alcoholic.

His troubles started as early as his drinking. During high school he was sent to a high-brow military academy in New Mexico, and at the age of seventeen ran away to join the marines, serving as an entertainer.

I still have a photo of him in a uniform, standing at a mike singing to the troops. It's a black-and-white photo, with him positioned alone on stage, a simple curtain behind him, like Bing Crosby in *White Christmas*. He's slim and incredibly Irish looking, and I have a hint of what my mother probably saw in him. His nose is my nose; his hands my hands; his black, arched, Irish eyebrows show me where my own came from. The photo is heavily creased now, its corners no longer sharply pointed, but soft.

At the age of six, I joined a swim team and took up the sport competitively. My mother drove me to workouts several times a week, and swim meets on the weekends, which were fun but scary. Once, as we were driving to the Valley, where I was a member of a top swim club, she warned me that my father had called and wanted to see me. He would be coming to watch me.

All during workout, as I chugged up and down the Olympic-length pool in a swimsuit designed to make me resemble a bumble-bee, which it did most successfully, I kept watch on the row of chairs where parents sat and waited. A chair sat empty next to my mother's. I would turn my head up out of the water while swimming freestyle to take a breath and look at the chair, take another stroke, and look again, hoping for a glimpse of the man in the photo I kept in my underwear drawer. After each lap, I paused to look again. In between sprints, I stood on the pool deck behind the starting blocks and stared, afraid to take my eyes off the empty chair.

I never saw anyone sitting in it. My mother says that he came and watched me, but I didn't see him, and he didn't stay to talk to me.

Next year, he called my mother to ask about my favorite color. She told him it was red. At Christmas, I received a warm-up suit in the ugliest red I had ever seen, a sort of dull version of what the inside of my half brother's eyelids looked like when he turned them inside out. I hated the gift and never wore it.

Until I turned eighteen, that was the last I heard of my father. My mother remarried, and my stepfather adopted me, giving me his last name. None of us really liked my stepfather. He drank, too, though not as much as my natural father. He was disgusting when he did drink, smothering my younger half sister and I with big, sloppy-wet kisses. Also, though he knew I hated it, and I pleaded with him not to do it, he would hold me down and tickle me until I started crying. He could be belligerent, was fond of his razor strop and—this only made his leather fetish more danger-ous—was probably the dumbest man of anyone in our nuclear or extended family.

On my eighteenth birthday in 1976, I decided to take back my birth name and began to use O'Keefe again, starting with my col-lege entrance forms. My mother's divorce from my stepfather came through that same year. My half brother no longer lived with us, my half sister barely lived with us, and between my mother and my-self, we looked at my stepfather's departure as our own liberation from a depressing familial wasteland. I began to wonder about my real father. Where was he? What was he doing? Did he ever think about me? Did he want to know where I was and what I was doing?

At the same time, my mother, half sister, and I were com-pletely broke. Though my half sister was his child, my stepfather never paid support. He never paid the alimony the court awarded. He had never paid his taxes while he was married to my mother, so when she attempted to liquidate some assets of hers to help us, the IRS seized them. I was forced to quit college in the beginning of my sophomore year and go to work full-time to help support the family. On top of this, my mother became ill.

It's difficult to be honest, I mean it hurts to be, but I have to admit that part of my longing to locate the lost half of my family was the knowledge that it was a wealthy half. While working the graveyard shift at a large city newspaper for minimum wage, I day-dreamed about being welcomed back into the O'Keefe fold, show-ered with money to make all problems go away and send me back to college, perhaps an ivy league school. My perfectly unoriginal eighteen-year-old brain wrote entire conversations that would take place between Walter and myself once he found me again. "Claudia, where have you been? We've been searching for you for years! Who thought I would have such a bright and talented granddaughter? Do you have a car? Here's a Mercedes convertible.

My God, let's get you some decent clothes. Frank (this spoken to a famous cohort of his), don't you think Claudia and your grandson, the director, would make a terrific match?"

Curious, I think now, that it was Walter I considered contacting, not my father. At the time, I told myself it was because it would be easier to find Walter. Truthfully, though, I was afraid of how my father might react to a reunion. I decided my grandfather would have to love me because all grandparents naturally loved their grandchildren.

One problem, we no longer had any contact, or even knew of anyone who had contact with the O'Keefes. My mother couldn't remember the address of the mansion in Palos Verdes. We were living in Florida then, so on-the-spot sleuthing was out. A friend suggested to me that he might still be a member of ASCAP, and so I wrote to the songwriter and composers organization, a very polite, very gentile sort of request, inquiring if I might have his address. ASCAP's main office in New York wrote back, telling me that they were sensitive to my situation, but couldn't give out members' addresses. They would, however, forward my letter on to Walter, who was still alive.

On the day the letter arrived from Walter, I considered the moment the most exciting of my life. It was typed on pale, celery green stationery, imprinted with his name in Rolling Hills Estates, not far from the old mansion in Palos Verdes, and his words almost lived up to my fantasy expectations. He was impressed with my letter to ASCAP, the old-fashioned good manners I'd employed, combined with a gumption that segued neatly for him into a story about his start in show business. How he had written a bold letter to a big-time Broadway producer that impressed the man so much it landed him his first job. Then he told me that for years, he had been wondering aloud to Terry, "Whatever happened to Claudia?" He didn't add that he had actively been searching for me like I had imagined him doing in my daydreams, but I think I wanted to interpret his words this way, and that's what I did.

Almost like a couple of long-distance lovers, we settled into a romantic, idealized correspondence. I wrote letters by hand on girlish stationery, or a lined, yellow tablet; he typed more on his light green letterhead. Our pen-pal relationship continued through most of 1977 into 1978. I learned about my great-grand-parents in counties Cork and Claire in Ireland, about how he was best buds with the great Sammy Kahn. He told me that he was a recovering alcoholic and would go on for pages about his tour on the AA speaking circuit. I learned that he no longer had a sense of smell and because of that couldn't taste the food that Terry made for him. His years as an alcoholic had bequeathed him numerous medical conditions and resulted in operation after operation, so many in fact, that his doctors were amazed at his survival rate for a man his age. He was seventy-seven when he wrote this to me. I knew because he was born in 1900. One part of me realized that he was just a lonely old man, looking for a way to revive his leonine image, but another part of me still waited and hoped for rescue.

I hinted at it. In retrospect I feel like a slime, but I hinted at my need. Not directly, but in roundabout ways. When Walter asked if I might be planning a visit to the West Coast soon, I let him know that I couldn't afford it. Not wanting to understand that I was just a copy girl then, not yet the correspondent I would become, he set up an interview for me in southern Florida with Susan B. Anthony's daughter. I thanked him, but let him know I didn't know the first thing about how to conduct an interview, and to try to do one with someone that important my first time out was not a good idea. Nor did I keep it a secret that I couldn't afford the gas to drive my beat-up AMC Gremlin down to Deer-field Beach to see the woman. Undaunted, he arranged a press pass for me at JPL when the Jupiter flyby was ready to make the news, and again, I let him know that I didn't have the money for a plane ticket to Los Angeles. I did ask my bosses at *The St. Petersburg Times* if they might sponsor the trip to JPL, but they declined. I wasn't a correspondent, I was a glorified gofer, and they already had a staff writer in place for the event out in Pasadena.

Walter never offered monetary help for these proposed adventures. At the same time, I got the impression that he was disappointed in me for not following through on the journalistic opportunities he offered me. How could I? My mother, half sister, and I were living on around $300 a month, not much, even for the late '70s. I didn't know whether he was broke or just stingy. He told me he was not as rich as he had been, but I didn't believe he was not somewhat well off. People who are poor do not live in Rolling Hills Estates.

It was about this time that I dared to ask Walter about my father. His response was immediate. He sent a recent Polaroid of my father, my uncle Anthony, and himself sitting on a couch at his home. Also sent was my father's address in Alaska, where he was helping to put in the oil pipeline. I took only the slightest glance at the photo. It showed the three O'Keefe men sitting on a white velvet sofa. A pricey-looking oil painting was suspended on the wall behind them. Lush roses sprawled in a vase on a coffee table in front of them. My grandfather appeared as I expected, aged, shrunken, but still full of that hearty personality he was known for. My uncle was to Walter's right, dressed in jeans and a polo shirt. His features were very Irish, but in a way different from the other two. I knew that he had become an architect, and from his appearance, I guessed a successful one.

My father's image, however, alarmed me. He wore brown, navy, and yellow plaid bell-bottom pants with a green, cream, and black striped shirt. Yes, it was possible that even as we verged on the 1980s there were hold-outs still into bell-bottoms, but plaid bell-bottoms?

I put the photo away. I put it away for five years.

My postal conversations with my grandfather petered out. Though I did phone him once to wish him Merry Christmas, during which he bragged at me some more about his AA lectures and told me I should be calling him granfar, in the proper Irish tradition, we just didn't click. I never had the opportunity to see him before he died.

Four years after learning of my father's whereabouts, my family moved to the Northwest. My sister got her own apartment in Seattle and occupied herself with the Seattle Seahawks football team, while my mother and I moved into a house on Mercer Island. My mother was healthy again, thank God, and writing young adult novels. I waitressed, and after having been accepted to an invitation-only writers' workshop, attempted to sell my first novel. We were still poor. Publishing does not pay on any predictable schedule, and we would go for months trying to make it on my tips until another few thousand would come to my mother for work finished half a year before.

We should have been living in an apartment, in a cheesy part of town that we could afford, but my mother said that that would have depressed her so much she might as well commit suicide. Besides, we had a Great Dane. We sat in an empty $700-a-month rental house we couldn't afford, in a stunning neighborhood on the island in the middle of Lake Washington that Bill Gates now calls home. Whatever furniture or belongings we owned, we gradually sold off to make up the difference between my earnings and the rent. When my mother's book money came in, we would catch up on bills and then drop $25 on a Chinese dinner, or lunch at the Tangerine, Mercer Island's small diner.

Friend after writer friend called to ask me to celebrate with them about their first fiction sales. It occurred so often and for such a length of time, with rejection after rejection appearing in my own mailbox, that I began to wonder if I simply didn't have the talent.

Then it happened, one night while watching *Entertainment Tonight*, and wishing I could sell a screenplay, a man called on the phone. I answered hesitantly, worried that it was yet another call from a creditor. I almost pretended I wasn't me, when he announced himself as an editor who wanted to buy my book.

My first book sale significantly changed the way I thought about myself, and just days later, with my confidence at an all-time high, I began to wonder again about my father. My grandfather had died three years before, so I couldn't have asked him for an update on the address. I didn't know this, but it didn't occur to me to ask Walter anyway. I didn't want to wait that long. Finally, at age twenty-seven I was ready to face my father.

Since it was December, I opted to send him a Christmas card

to the Alaska address and hope that it would reach him. I didn't know what to say. *Why'd you run out on us the week I was born, you lousy crud, and by the way, Happy Holidays,* seemed a bit harsh. Leaving it at *Happy Holidays,* I dropped the greeting in the mail.

Two weeks later a special delivery letter arrived from him, and I actually experienced some horror at what I had done. Sure, I was excited, who wouldn't be? Still, I wondered what would really happen if we did as he suggested and spoke immediately to each other on the phone. Would he like me? Would he be proud of me and my few accomplishments? If he met me would he think I was pretty? I had so many flaws.

Be serious, I told myself. You're not the only human in the equation. He'll have flaws, too. I should be ready to overlook them. To this end, I figured I could start with his letter to me. He'd written it on graph paper. His business card, which told me that these days he was a communications contractor working out of Spokane, Washington, was stapled to the top of the letter, as if I was not his daughter, but a salesman's cold call.

I decided to write instead of phone. It was not yet the age of faxes and e-mail.

He called.

I elected not to be home and wrote again, insisting on my desire to take it easy on our way toward this new relationship.

He called again.

I gave up and grabbed the phone, interrupting my outgoing answering machine message. We talked. His voice was deep, just as a father's voice should be, and it occurred to me that it was the first time I had ever heard it. I couldn't tell, was it a good singing voice? Did this voice still remember "Claudia"?

I discovered from him that he had remarried, but that I was still his only child. He no longer lived in Alaska, but on a ranch he'd bought in northern Idaho, near a resort town that was quickly becoming a winter-summer sports wonderland. He had had a heart attack while in Alaska, due to eating too much prime rib, suffered through nine heart bypass operations, and had been so successful in a recent diet that he had lost twenty-seven pounds.

He wanted me to come visit him. We would spend a long weekend getting reacquainted on his ranch. I was hesitant. I needed to think about this, I told him.

My father sent me oversized color prints taken of himself in Alaska and on the ranch. He dated them all on the back, and in addition wrote little descriptions. In the earliest, *Summer 1980,* I saw a middle-aged man sitting in a captain's chair in front of a ship's wheel. He had a graying beard and wore a brown cap and glasses that were almost exactly like the ones my stepfather would wear, big "modish" tinted things I'd always hated. His back was to the camera, and he looked back over his shoulder at the picture taker. I noticed that the hand that gripped the arm of the captain's chair, and forearm above, were chubby. His look was not a friendly one. I wouldn't quite call it angry, but it did not enamor me to him. The notation on the back of the snapshot read exactly in the predictable chicken-scratch handwriting of an engineer type, *At the Helm of The "Glacier Queen" on Prince William Sound.*

Another photo dated *Summer 1980* showed my father lounging at the tiller of his own sailboat in jeans, a white T-shirt, and a moderate gut. His hair was hidden under a captain's cap, his eyes behind dark glasses. The caption read, *Goofing off on board our Sailboat – Contrary to what everyone Thinks, its not all IcebeRGs & Eskimos up here.* He was not smiling in the photo.

In none of the seven snapshots he sent me was he smiling. To be fair, I don't think I can count the seventh one. It was a photo of a German shepherd sticking its head up through the forehatch on a smallish sailboat. It was a gorgeous dog, labeled on the back of the picture not with a name, but the words MY FEARLESS DOG + SAILBOAT.

His other two photos from 1980 were at his Prudehoe Bay job site. The first depicted a man in work shirt, jeans, green hard hat, and the same moderate gut, standing arms akimbo beside a bank of unrecognizable electrical equipment. His eyes stared straight into the camera, his mouth tight-lipped. In the second, he was outdoors in a snowfield, standing astride a snowmobile, that same fixated stare on his face.

His last two snapshots were better and presented me with some hope. *Winter 1985* he stands dramatically in front of another snowmobile at the bottom of a hill and more Alaska scenery. He is in red shirtsleeves, with a gun in a holster on his right hip. He looks off camera, his stance and facial expressions undeniably rakish. The caption tells me that this startling hero is standing there five months after the heart attack.

My final look at my father is in a photo taken just a week before. Seated backward on his favorite mount, the snowmobile, a great microwave tower rises out of his head in the background. His head is tilted this time, with a touch of personality, his expression not so hostile or intimidating.

"He looks sort of like Pernell Roberts in this photo, don't you think?" I asked a co-worker at the Mexican restaurant where I was waitressing. "I don't mean the young, *Ponderosa*, Pernell, but the older, *Trapper John, M.D.*, Pernell."

My co-worker grunted noncommittally.

I decided I had no choice but to go see Dad. I scraped together the plane fare from Seattle to Spokane.

At 30,000 feet I was nervous. On touchdown I needed heavy tranquilizers. He'd done a lot, my dad, or so he'd told me over the course of our phone conversation earlier. Like his father, he was a recovering alcoholic. He had been sober for more than ten years. Up in Alaska, he'd had his highly successful career as a communications engineer. When mobsters weren't chasing him because he'd denounced one of their pioneer town gambling saloons as crooked, he'd be jumping out of helicopters in a blizzard to install satellite dishes atop mountains where it was so cold the average wrench would snap in your hand at first use. From time to time the "black bag" people would send him on discreet jobs as an independent contractor to third-world countries, where he would set up intelligence equipment for "certain government agencies." He was so bright, I remembered my mother once saying, that during idle moments he would scrawl complicated chemical equations on cocktail napkins just for fun.

Then there was the money factor. Evidently he had plenty of

the stuff. His new consulting business had supposedly brought in one million in contracts during the six months since he had started it, while the novel I was completing would only net me $5,400 advance money for two years work. When I had boarded the Alaska Airlines jet for the short hop to Eastern Washington, I couldn't help but think about my mother, who would remain at home in a freezing house because we couldn't afford heating oil, the only furnishings being a redwood bench brought in from outdoors and a kitty litter box.

My father's version of himself was completely different than the picture I'd built up of him in my mind, drunken looser ex-patriot of La-La Land. He was successful. Would he detect how strapped I was and think I was after his money? Would he become tired of me after the first flush of our meeting?

I wondered, would he remember the song he wrote for me on my birthday and still be able to play it?

"Dad?" I said, as I saw him waiting for me at the mouth of the deplaning tunnel. He was wearing one of those weird hunting caps with the ear flaps, a bright orange camouflage print jacket, and the dirtiest pair of jeans I'd seen since the '60s. Hanging from his belt were all these survival tools. I was so startled, I can't remember if we hugged.

"Dad," I said, "how wonderful to meet you at last."

He never changed his outfit the entire time I was there.

It was Valentine's week 1986, and the runway at touchdown had been white with ice. He led me outside to his car, a crummy looking Ford Escort with a bumper sticker that read SAVE THE WHALES, HARPOON A FAT CHICK. I studied his stomach. He may have lost twenty-seven pounds, but he still had a ways to go and was actually heavier than in his early photos.

Those who live in glass houses, I thought.

More importantly, though the roads all the way from eastern Washington to his ranch in northern Idaho were covered with snow, the Escort wasn't wearing snow tires or chains. I tried not to think about this fact, keep my mind on what he was saying, as we drove.

". . . wonderful wife of fifteen years who you are *really* going to love because she's only five years older than you," I heard one part of the sentence as he whipped around a turn as if in a chase scene from a Bond movie set in the Alps. I dug my fingers into the armrest on the passenger's door. He filled me in on all the fun we'd be having soon. Snowmobiles figured largely in the scenario. "I sure hope you have some better clothes than that in your bag," he said. "Or else you're going to freeze."

Locals called Kathy, his wife, "The Wilderness Lady." As far as I could see, she had earned the title. Dressed in greasy coveralls, she stomped through the snow to greet us. Dad told me she had bagged both caribou and moose, and I was impressed enough with her build to imagine that she could easily toss a two-wire bale of hay over three cows lined side by side.

Kathy had two topics of conversation that weekend, snowmobiles and snowmobiles. My father was more diversified. His hot topics were snowmobiles and the various frozen lakes he was under the impression I was eager to explore.

I was given a quick tour of the ranch, which included a small, old farmhouse filled with a jumble of stuff that left no clear impression on my mind and a barn deserted except for an expensive speedboat. His property stretched up the side of a mountain, which had been mostly denuded of timber. By cutting down the trees on his property, he told me, he'd made a hefty profit selling them to a lumber mill.

As we walked the property, we genuinely bonded. About artificial sweeteners. I don't recall how the subject was brought up, but I happened to say that I preferred sugared Coke over Diet Coke because I didn't trust Nutrasweet not to give me cancer.

"Hey!" he said brightly, his first sign of true animation since my arrival. "Me, too! I don't trust those chemicals at all."

We spoke a little more, drifting onto the topic of the space shuttle. My father doubted humans would ever experience meaningful, useful travel into space. His reasoning? The shuttle and everything in it was too big, too heavily weighed down with the bulky machines and mechanisms necessary for running it that there would never be room for more than a few passengers and a scant amount of real cargo.

I stopped, quietly stunned. This was my father, the genius, talking? What had happened to his fabled IQ?

"Dad," I said, "they'll make the machines smaller. That's the way technology goes. Things get smaller, more compact, and lighter weight. Think about the first engines that were ever invented. What about cars? Haven't they improved over the years, sleeker, better, packed with more bang for the buck?"

"Oh," he said. "You're right."

And we walked on.

Our first evening together, I was subjected to viewing countless slides of beheaded deer, strings of fish, the U-Haul they rented to transport their worldly goods from Alaska to Idaho.

Hungrily, when he brought out his slides, I noticed his professional quality 35mm outfit. I mentioned to him that I had been a news photographer in the past and missed taking photographs. To my credit, I didn't tell him that I'd been forced to pawn my beloved Canon AE-1 and lenses the year before. I don't think it would have made a difference. Whenever I told him things about myself, there would come a pause and he would get a look on his face like the ones in the photographs he'd sent me, that stare that was not quite a glare. Then the moment would pass and his conversation would resume.

One intriguing slide show was about "Beefy." Kathy narrated this one. They had about a hundred slides of a calf they'd once owned. You know, pics of the day he was born, bottle feeding Beefy, Beefy growing up as a member of the family, Beefy playing with fifty-five-gallon drums in his paddock.

Then Beefy as beef, dead beef.

A few differences of opinion rose between the couple and myself when it came to personal hygiene and grooming. Neither my father nor Kathy could understand why I wanted to shower every day, since they kept regaling me about their life in the Arctic, where they had spent eight years "shitting in a five-gallon bucket of water," because their cabin in the woods didn't have any plumbing. They had bathed once a week at the local Laundromat. My blow-dryer was a concept totally beyond them, and I had to wait for them to go to the barn to gaze wistfully at their speedboat so I could sneak on the light makeup I wore, using a television screen as a mirror. Except for when I asked if I could use the bathroom to, well, go to the bathroom, I had the impression that it was off limits to me. God, why? Had they gone for so many years without, that they were now reluctant to share with anyone else?

On Valentine's Day there was a blizzard, but my father was determined to keep our dinner reservations at upper Idaho's only expensive restaurant. He looked charming as ever in his post–nuclear war ensemble. Kathy wore rubber mud boots and a surplus parka. During dinner, while my father munched away on a huge slab of ultra-rare prime rib, I glanced around at the other people in the dining room. To a one, all were couples dressed romantically for the occasion, some of the women showing off jewelry their dining partners had given them, one or two with orchid corsages.

I felt supremely ugly. I had not been able to score any makeup time in front of the television screen before going out and I had yet to have a shower. I had not brought anything dressy, and to top off my misery, Kathy had insisted on loaning me her spare pair of rubber mud boots.

At dinner, conversation between my father and myself concerned the direction and distance a radioactive plume would drift were the military base in Spokane to be hit with a nuclear bomb. They were downwind here in Idaho, approximately sixty miles from the base, but my father told me he wasn't worried.

"By the time the effects of exposure could show up as cancer," he said, "I'll be dead of old age." No mention was made of Kathy, who would probably outlive him by at least a couple of decades, but then she kept quiet during this whole discussion anyway.

On the way home, the Escort racing once again chainless through the driving snow, she was more in her element. "I know!" she said. "Let's take sleeping bags and see if we can survive outside tonight." She was completely, utterly serious.

"That doesn't sound fun to me," I said.

Though I'm now confident Kathy's suggestion was meant to show me up in the eyes of my father, pointing out what a wimp I was, I suspect she would have happily tromped out to a snowbank and settled down for the night. My father was silent on the subject and we drove on through the storm.

Once back at the ranch, he proudly showed off the piano he had there, an old upright. He volunteered to play it for me.

Now was my chance to ask.

Gershwin, Kathy said as he began. I listened.

Would he remember "Claudia"?

I don't know. I was afraid to ask. The piano was so far out of tune I couldn't recognize "An American in Paris."

A little while later, while I struggled to assimilate the loss of a dream, my father pulled out the convertible sofa for me in the living room. "You know," he said, cautioning me, "if you have to go to the bathroom tonight, be careful what you touch. I've got guns hidden all over the house, just in case."

I nodded. "Oh. Right." Then as if he'd said something perfectly natural, "Yes. Of course."

I spent a miserable night on the hide-a-bed, afraid to get up to go to the bathroom.

Next morning, when my father asked me to pose on the sofa with his two favorite firearms, I knew it was time to go.

"I'd love to, Dad," I said, "but I think I really should get to the airport."

THANKS FOR VISITING COEUR D'ALENE, the sign read as we drove out of town. Coeur d'Alene? I thought. Isn't that the headquarters for the Aryan Nation?

"I couldn't believe it when you walked off that plane," my mother told me the other night when we were reminiscing about my return from Idaho.

"Your hair," my mother said. "I'd never seen your hair like that before. I remember thinking, *This is my daughter? Oh, my poor child!* I've never seen you look so horrible in your life. You looked like you'd been on one of those treks to the outer wilderness."

She expressed profound relief that she was no longer married to my father. "Their love life must have been a thrill," she said. "Two Sasquatches mating."

Not terribly charitable, I admit, but in a figurative sense, she is the other woman now.

"Oh, my God," she said. "That could have been me shitting into that five-gallon bucket of water!"

I know I missed out on a lot growing up without a positive male role model in my life. I know that at forty-one, I'm single rather than married because I was afraid to get close to men. I was afraid of sex. Men were strange physical creatures to me.

I never got to finish college because I had to help support my family. My father wasn't there. For years I took the most menial jobs available because I didn't believe I was qualified for anything better. I didn't have the confidence I do now and have earned on my own without his help.

What were my feelings for him? I don't know. It was as if I had none, and yet did. It was as if he was a blank in my life that had been deeply burned into me, a harsh brand smoldering with no discernible pattern. Why didn't I try to initiate a conversation which delved beneath that mutilated surface? Why didn't I ask him why he had deserted me? I guess it just didn't seem appropriate at the time. Our weekend together was supposed to be a familial meet-and-greet. We were supposed to be getting to know each other before we moved into the heavy emotional stuff, except that no-getting-to-know occurred, and I had no desire to go back for more of the same. I thought he was a selfish, self-absorbed jerk. I considered him to be an incomplete personality, fractured before it could be finished. It was a pathetic situation. For both of us.

Even all these years later, my sadness remains. I know, however, that what I am mourning is not the absence of a father, but the loss of heritage. So much is spoken about it these days. Other Irish-Americans celebrate theirs, African-Americans, Jews, Hispanics, Italians, everyone, it seems, celebrates their heritage, but the only heritage I wish I could be celebrating right now is the very personal traditions of a father and daughter who knew each other well.

It would be a tidy ending to the story to say that I've never seen my father since, but that wouldn't be true. He called me a couple of weeks after my visit, and I could tell he was drunk. He talked to me as if I was someone other than his daughter. It was not a deep conversation, nor an entirely coherent one, and after he sent a couple of unmistakable sexual innuendos in my direction, I told him I had to go and hung up. A few days later, he phoned again and got my mother instead of me. She informed him that my birthday was coming up. He said he would be flying over to Seattle on business around that time and thought it would be a good idea if he took me to dinner. He asked my mother what I would like as a birthday present. A camera, she said, telling him what I hadn't been able to, about my having to hock all of my photo equipment, $900 worth, including a wide-angle lens I'd saved for more than a year to buy. I know how much she misses it, she said. She'd really like to have a camera again.

When we met for lunch, not dinner, in a restaurant at SeaTac airport, he presented me with my birthday present. Excited, having a notion that this was going to happen and what the gift would be, I opened the box. Inside was a small automatic camera, the type that tourists pick up to take on vacation. I couldn't help it; I compared it to his own equipment I'd envied on slide night at his ranch.

"Thank you," I told him, but couldn't make myself be effusive. The camera was next to useless, perfectly fine for snapping pics of a baby shower, but not for professional photography.

Why did my feelings for my father have to end up being about money? Was I that superficial? Or was it, as my mother suggested, that he had not thought enough of me to buy me a real camera, and that was what hurt. It left me feeling shallow when I didn't want to feel shallow.

As if to underscore this, the last two conversations I had with him revolved around money. Both times I called him. Once, it was because I was about to lose my Honda Civic to the bank. He sent me enough to make one payment, a pointless gesture, since I lost the car two months later with only three payments left on the loan. The final time I spoke with him I had been laid off after the restaurant where I worked closed. I was having trouble finding another position.

"Hi, Dad," I said, when I phoned. I managed to interrupt him and some friends watching *The Equalizer* in his living room.

"Would you happen to know of any jobs over in your area?" I asked him following a few seconds of small talk. "I know that there's a big resort over in Coeur d'Alene."

I heard him turn away from the phone and ask the people in the living room, none of whom I knew, "Does anyone here know of any jobs in town? My daughter needs a job."

Assorted murmurs came to me through the phone line, and I imagined his friends shaking their heads, looking uncomfortable.

"Nope," my father said. "Guess not."

[CLAUDIA O'KEEFE]

Family themes are the core of O'Keefe's career as an anthologist, beginning with Mother: Famous Writers Celebrate Motherhood with a Treasury of Short Stories, Essays, and Poems, *published in 1996, and* Forever Sisters, *which has an equally long subtitle, and which first appeared in hardback in 1999.*

Her anthologies have received critical acclaim from The Washington Post, USA Today, Chicago Tribune, Publishers Weekly, *and* Kirkus Reviews, *among others, but her favorite quote is from* The Tampa Tribune. *Said reviewer Keith Blouin of* Forever Sisters, *"O'Keefe's selection of stories shows great sensitivity toward her subject, as well as a heap of humor that makes the volume hard to put down."*

A writer first, anthologist second, among her credits are the novel Black Snow Days, *chosen by the late editor Terry Carr to be in the prestigious debut line of Ace Science Fiction Specials; short stories in several anthologies; and hundreds of arti-*

cles, most notably as a former correspondent for The St. Petersburg Times in Florida.

Though she has done the usual writer gambit of waitressing tables, her other careers have included graphic designer, keno girl, and civilian shepherdess for the Air Force. With her mother, she co-owns Swan & Grace, an antique linens business, and resides on a restored farm in the Appalachians.

MESSAGES FROM MY FATHER

AN EXCERPT

Calvin Trillin

HE WAS TRULY FUNNY. HE HAD A LARGE COLLECTION OF marching-band albums, and, when Sukey and I were children, there were times when one of them would set him to marching himself. This happened rarely and spontaneously; my father did not march on command. We would wait in one room while he circled the ground floor of our house. Every time he entered the room we were in, he would be marching in a different way—one time listing precariously off to one side, the next time rolling along in a Groucho Marx stoop, the time after that marching in a sort of hip-hop—pretending to take no notice of the fact that Sukey and I were both on the floor, helpless with laughter. In conversation with children who were not his own, he had some set routines. When he met someone who was studying a foreign language, he always asked for a translation of the same sentence: "The left-handed lizard climbed up the eucalyptus tree and ate a persimmon." I have continued to use that sentence from time to time—I have some set routines myself, some of them his—and I have to say that the responses do not build confidence in the level of language instruction in this country. He also had a special word

60

that he challenged any schoolchild to spell. It was, phonetically, "yifnif." I can present it only phonetically, because I never learned how to spell it.

Many years later, after I had mentioned "yifnif" in print, I was informed that Milt Gross, a humorist who captured the Yiddish accents of his characters phonetically, sometimes wrote about a woman named Mrs. Yifnif. It wouldn't surprise me to learn that my father, who loved dialect humor, had read Milt Gross's work. I can picture him chuckling over the beginning of a letter Mrs. Yifnif sent to her son's school principal in Gross's *Nize Baby*, published in 1925: "Mine Joonior hinforums me wot yesterday hefternoon in de school one from de pyoopills trew on heem a speetz-ball. So mine Joonior, wot he ain't, denks Gott, a cowitt, trew heem beck a speetz-ball wot de odder goot-for-notting docked so it flew gredually de speetz-ball de titcher in de faze." If Mrs. Yifnif did put the word in my father's mind, though, that association and that spelling had faded away. In my father's version, "yifnif" had no meaning. It existed only to be spelled.

Or to defy efforts at spelling. I once wrote a story based on the attempts to spell "yifnif" made by a carful of Boy Scouts on those occasions when my father drove us to a meeting. He always offered an array of prizes for the correct spelling, and in the story I mentioned as many as I could remember: a new Schwinn bicycle, a trip to California, a lifetime pass to Kansas City Blues baseball games, free piano lessons for a year, a new pair of shoes. I can't imagine that any of us would have been interested in free piano lessons for a year, but we made attempt after attempt to spell "yifnif" anyway:

"Occasionally some kid in the car would make an issue out of yifnif's origins. 'But you made it up!' he'd tell my father, in an accusing tone.

" 'Of course I made it up,' my father would reply. 'That's why I know how to spell it.'

" 'But it could be spelled in a million ways.'

" 'All of them are wrong except my way,' my father would say. 'It's my word.' "

There was, I knew, no chance that my father could have simply called any spelling we came up with wrong and thus avoided handing out the prizes; as I said in the story, "His views on honesty made the Boy Scout position on that subject seem wishy-washy." I never had any doubt in my mind that there was one correct way to spell "yifnif" and that my father knew what it was and that anyone coming up with it would get every single prize that had been offered.

I was convinced that he had in mind some enormously complicated spelling of what sounded like an extremely simple word. In the story, we wily Boy Scouts brought in a ringer—my cousin Keith, from Salina, Kansas, who had reached the finals of the Kansas state spelling bee. I really do have a cousin Keith who got to the finals of the Kansas state spelling bee—his mother was my aunt Hannah; his father, my uncle Jerry Cushman, was at that time the city librarian of Salina—but Keith never came with us to Boy Scout meetings and he doesn't know how to spell "yifnif." I've asked him. The fictional Keith's try was Y-y-g-h-k-n-i-p-h. At some point, I had become certain that "yifnif" began with a double "y"—"y" used as both a consonant and a vowel. I can't imagine what made me so sure of that. My father didn't give hints. As you were picking your way through the first syllable, he never said anything like, "You're doing fine so far." You tried to spell "yifnif," and when you were through he said, "Wrong." On the way to Scout meetings, when other boys in the car were waiting their turn to take a flier at winning a new pair of shoes, he'd say, "Wrong. Next."

He was a collector of curses, particularly old Yiddish curses of the may-you-have-an-itch-where-it's-impossible-to-scratch variety. Once, while he was visiting Alice and me in New York, he came back to our apartment with an addition to his collection which he had unexpectedly bagged on the Lower East Side. He had been in Katz's Delicatessen, where sandwich-makers stand above the crowd behind a long counter, piling on pastrami and maintaining a strict form of queue discipline ("And who are you—a movie star maybe?"). My father put in his order with the sort of little joke he might have used with a waiter in Kansas City. "Give me a corned beef sandwich," he said. "Make it lean, and I'll recommend you to the boss." The sandwich-maker looked down at him and said, "The boss! May the boss's nose fall off!"

Washington Avenue in South Miami Beach was where my father expected to find curses. Sometimes known as Yenta Alley, it had grocery stores that had become the central battleground in South Florida for daily wars of nerves between the proprietors and retired Jews whose resources consisted of small fixed incomes and extensive experience in negotiating with the butcher. Yenta Alley in South Miami Beach is to collectors of curses what the Serengeti is to connoisseurs of lions. My father liked listening to the arguments even when they didn't contain curses. It was in a grocery store on Washington Avenue that he collected his favorite curse: an elderly woman shouted at a butcher, "May you have an injury that is not covered by workmen's compensation."

After loitering in the grocery stores on Washington Avenue for a while eavesdropping on arguments, my father sometimes went to the beach with his old 16-millimeter movie camera and took a reel or two that consisted entirely of fat women approaching the ocean. When it came to a willingness to traffic in humor that would now be seen as demeaning to women, he was not ahead of his time. If the subject of what to look for in a wife came up, for instance, he always raised the question of teeth. Occasionally, one of the young salesmen who came into Trillin's restaurant for lunch would announce that he was engaged to be married. "Abe," the salesman would say, as I imagine the scene, "I have met the girl of my dreams, my true love, the woman who was meant for me. I have asked her to be my wife, and—thank God, because I cannot live without her—she has agreed. We are engaged to be married."

"Did you check her teeth?" my father would reply, before he even offered his congratulations. One of his antic theories was that flaws of personality or looks or background could be corrected or adjusted to but bad teeth represented a lifelong financial drain that could undermine the strongest union.

My father liked names. When he told stories to small children, there was often a character whose name sounded like Stoolie-allahmalochas. His version of Joe Blow was someone named Schlayma Puch, whose last name rhymed, more or less, with "shnook." He handed out names to real people, and some of them stuck. His name for my mother's first bridge-and-gossip set was the Clique Adorables. Eventually, my mother called them that, too. One of his friends was a small, cigar-smoking man we called Little Stuff Silverstein. He referred to many animals he ran across—occasionally including a fish he'd caught—as Fred. He got fancy, though, with the name of the only pedigreed dog we ever owned—a lazy, rather dim English bulldog. Although we referred to the dog as Buck, the name on his papers had been Sir Lancelot. My father, not considering that quite grand enough, extended it to Sir Lancelot O'Pujilus.

I believe that for my father the perfect anecdote would have featured a man with a funny name who finds himself in an embarrassing situation. The stories he told about old days in the grocery store leaned heavily on the humor that comes from someone backing into something that isn't what he thinks it is—the most ribald word I ever heard my father use was "goosey"—or of being frightened by something that turned out to be harmless. He enjoyed teasing people. When I was a little boy, he teased me about a temporary but intense devotion I had to Gene Autry, the singing cowboy—a devotion I would make some lame attempt to justify if I could remember anything about my hero except for the sponsor of his radio show, Doublemint chewing gum, and the name of his theme song, "Back in the Saddle Again."

He liked Jewish humor. We had some record albums by Jewish comedians that my parents and their friends found enormously entertaining and I found enormously frustrating. A long buildup that was at least partly in English always ended in a punch line—an uproarious punch line, judging from the response in my living room, and, I always suspected, an off-color punch line—that was inevitably delivered in Yiddish and thus lost on me completely. Like a lot of people from Eastern European Jewish backgrounds, he found Litvaks—Jews from Lithuania—such a rich source of humor that the word alone made him smile. My mother's family had come from Vilna—or near Vilna, really; their village was called something like Munchnik—and my father sometimes seemed to imply that their peculiarities had something to do with their Litvak origins. I was never quite sure what was so funny about Litvaks—I'm not sure now, even though I, too, tend to smile when I hear the word—but I accepted the fact that Litvaks were figures of fun as one of the elements that separated my mother's family from the band of stubborn Kiev suburbanites I identified with.

A lot of my father's own humor was strongly Midwestern. The joke I heard him tell more than any other was about a man who, travelling along a country road, sees a boy lying in the shade of a tree with a piece of grass in his mouth and his hat pulled down over his head. "Boy, if you can show me a lazier act than that, I'll give you a dime," the man says, and the boy replies, "Put it in my pocket." Once, when I was trying to describe Midwestern play-dumb humor, I used the real example of my father's visit to Tiffany's when he was in New York visiting Alice and me. He and my mother and Alice and I were standing at the counter, looking at something like silver pins, when he said to the salesman, "What's the name of this store again?"

"Why, Tiffany's, sir," the salesman said.

My father said that he had never heard of it, and asked if it had just opened. "I'm from Kansas City," he added, by way of explanation.

"Oh, no, sir," the salesman said. "It's been here for a number of years. It's quite a well-known store."

"Does it have anything to do with Cartier's?" my father asked. "I've heard of Cartier's."

"No, sir," the salesman said. "Nothing at all to do with Cartier's."

"Tiffany's," my father said, rolling the word around as if testing how it might work out as a name for a jewelry store. "Tiffany's. Well, that's a new one on me."

[CALVIN TRILLIN]

He's been called "perhaps the finest reporter in America," and "a classic American humorist," but Calvin Trillin is also a devoted father.

"Your children are either the center of your life or they're not, and the rest is commentary," he has written.

Trillin, who has contributed articles to the New Yorker for over two decades, beginning with his roving reporter "U.S. Journal," pieces, also writes a weekly column for Time magazine. USA Today pronounced his humor column in the Nation, "simply the funniest regular column in journalism." His nineteen books include three on America's cuisine, recently published in one volume titled The Tummy Trilogy, which inspired Craig Claiborne of The New York Times to dub him "the Walt Whitman of American eats."

After the debut of his latest book, Family Man—a quasi-memoir regaling readers with the adventures of family life for Trillin, his wife, and two daughters—the author told interviewer Mark Bazer, "I am the comic figure . . . I think the sort of traditional American father's role of being present to be manipulated by the rest of the family is definitely the role I play."

—C.O.

THE GOLDEN DARTERS

Elizabeth Winthrop

I WAS TWELVE YEARS OLD WHEN MY FATHER STARTED TYING flies. It was an odd habit for a man who had just undergone a serious operation on his upper back, but, as he remarked to my mother one night, at least it gave him a world over which he had some control.

The family grew used to seeing him hunched down close to his tying vise, hackle pliers in one hand, thread bobbin in the other. We began to bandy about strange phrases—foxy quills, bodkins, peacock hurl. Father's corner of the living room was off limits to the maid with the voracious and destructive vacuum cleaner. Who knew what precious bit of calf's tail or rabbit fur would be sucked away never to be seen again.

Because of my father's illness, we had gone up to our summer cottage on the lake in New Hampshire a month early. None of my gang of friends ever came till the end of July, so in the beginning of that summer I hung around home watching my father as he fussed with the flies. I was the only child he allowed to stand near him while he worked. "Your brothers bounce," he muttered one day as he clamped the vise onto the curve of a model-perfect hook. "You can stay and watch if you don't bounce."

So I took great care not to bounce or lean or even breathe too noisily on him while he performed his delicate maneuvers, holding back hackle with one hand as he pulled off the final flourish of a whip finish with the other. I had never been so close to my father for so long before, and while he studied his tiny creations, I studied him. I stared at the large pores of his skin, the sleek black hair brushed straight back from the soft dip of his temples, the jaw muscles tight-ening and slackening. Something in my father seemed always to be ticking. He did not take well to sickness and enforced confinement.

When he leaned over his work, his shirt collar slipped down to reveal the recent scar, a jagged trail of disrupted tissue. The tender pink skin gradually paled and then toughened during those weeks when he took his prescribed afternoon nap, lying on his stomach on our little patch of front lawn. Our house was one of the closest to the lake and it seemed to embarrass my mother to have him stretch himself out on the grass for all the swimmers and boaters to see.

"At least sleep on the porch," she would say. "That's why we set the hammock up there."

"Why shouldn't a man sleep on his own front lawn if he so chooses?" he would reply. "I have to mow the bloody thing. I might as well put it to some use."

And my mother would shrug and give up.

At the table when he was absorbed, he lost all sense of any-thing but the magnified insect under the light. Often when he pushed his chair back and announced the completion of his latest project to the family, there would be a bit of down or a tuft of dub-bing stuck to the edge of his lip. I did not tell him about it but stared, fascinated, wondering how long it would take to blow away. Sometimes it never did and I imagine he discovered the fluff in the bathroom mirror when he went upstairs to bed. Or maybe my mother plucked it off with one of those proprietary ges-tures of hers that irritated my brothers so much.

In the beginning, Father wasn't very good at the fly-tying. He was a large, thick-boned man with sweeping gestures, a robust laugh, and a sudden terrifying temper. If he had not loved fishing so much, I doubt he would have persevered with the fussy business of the flies. After all, the job required tools normally associated with woman's work. Thread and bobbins, soft slippery feathers, a magnifying glass, and an instruction manual that read like a cookbook. It said things like, "Cut off a bunch of yellowtail. Hold the tip end with the left hand and stroke out the short hairs."

But Father must have had a goal in mind. You tie flies because one day, in the not-too-distant future, you will attach them to a tippet, wade into a stream, and lure a rainbow trout out of his quiet pool.

There was something endearing, almost childish, about his stubborn nightly ritual at the corner table. His head bent under the standing lamp, his fingers trembling slightly, he would whisper encouragement to himself, talk his way through some particularly delicate operation. Once or twice I caught my mother gazing silently across my brothers' heads at him. When our eyes met, she would turn away and busy herself in the kitchen.

Finally, one night, after weeks of allowing me to watch, he told me to take his seat. "Why, Father?"

"Because it's time for you to try one."

"That's all right. I like to watch."

"Nonsense, Emily. You'll do just fine."

He had stood up. The chair was waiting. Across the room, my mother put down her knitting. Even the boys, embroiled in a noisy game of double solitaire, stopped their wrangling for a moment. They were all waiting to see what I would do. It was my fear of failing him that made me hesitate. I knew that my father put his trust in results, not in the learning process.

"Sit down, Emily."

I obeyed, my heart pounding. I was a cautious, secretive child, and I could not bear to have people watch me doing things. My piano lesson was the hardest hour in the week. The teacher would sit with a resigned look on her face while my fingers groped across the keys, muddling through a sonata that I had played perfectly just an hour before. The difference was that then nobody had been watching.

"—so we'll start you off with a big hook." He had been talking for some time. How much had I missed already?

"Ready?" he asked.

I nodded.

"All right then, clamp this hook into the vise. You'll be making the golden darter, a streamer. A big flashy fly, the kind that imitates a small fish as it moves underwater."

Across the room, my brothers had returned to their game, but their voices were subdued. I imagined they wanted to hear what was happening to me. My mother had left the room.

"Tilt the magnifying glass so you have a good view of the hook. Right. Now tie on with the bobbin thread."

It took me three tries to line the thread up properly on the hook, each silken line nesting next to its neighbor. "We're going to do it right, Emily, no matter how long it takes."

"It's hard," I said quietly.

Slowly I grew used to the tiny tools, to the oddly enlarged view of my fingers through the magnifying glass. They looked as if they didn't belong to me anymore. The feeling in their tips was too small for their large, clumsy movements. Despite my father's repeated warnings, I nicked the floss once against the barbed hook. Luckily it did not give way.

"It's Emily's bedtime," my mother called from the kitchen.

"Hush, she's tying in the throat. Don't bother us now."

I could feel his breath on my neck. The mallard barbules were stubborn, curling into the hook in the wrong direction. Behind me, I sensed my father's fingers twisting in imitation of my own.

"You've almost got it," he whispered, his lips barely moving. "That's right. Keep the thread slack until you're all the way around."

I must have tightened it too quickly. I lost control of the feathers in my left hand, the clumsier one. First the gold mylar came unwound and then the yellow floss.

"Damn it all, now look what you've done," he roared, and for a second I wondered whether he was talking to me. He sounded as if he were talking to a grown-up. He sounded the way he had just the night before when an antique teacup had slipped through my mother's soapy fingers and shattered against the hard surface of the sink. I sat back slowly, resting my aching spine against the chair for the first time since we'd begun.

"Leave it for now, Gerald," my mother said tentatively from the kitchen. Out of the corner of my eye, I could see her sponging the kitchen counter with small, defiant sweeps of her hand. "She can try again tomorrow."

"What happened?" called a brother. They both started across the room toward us but stopped at a look from my father.

"We'll start again," he said, his voice once more under control. "Best way to learn. Get back on the horse."

With a flick of his hand, he loosened the vise, removed my hook, and threw it into the wastepaper basket.

"From the beginning?" I whispered.

"Of course," he replied. "There's no way to rescue a mess like that."

My mess had taken almost an hour to create.

"Gerald," my mother said again. "Don't you think—"

"How can we possibly work with all these interruptions?" he thundered. I flinched as if he had hit me. "Go on upstairs, all of you. Emily and I will be up when we're done. Go on, for God's sake. Stop staring at us."

At a signal from my mother, the boys backed slowly away and crept up to their room. She followed them. I felt all alone, as trapped under my father's piercing gaze as the hook in the grip of its vise.

We started again. This time my fingers were trembling so much that I ruined three badger hackle feathers, stripping off the useless webbing at the tip. My father did not lose his temper again. His voice dropped to an even, controlled monotone that scared me more than his shouting. After an hour of painstaking labor, we reached the same point with the stubborn mallard feathers curling into the hook. Once, twice, I repinched them under the throat, but each time they slipped away from me. Without a word, my father stood up and leaned over me. With his cheek pressed against my hair, he reached both hands around and took my fingers in his. I longed to surrender the tools to him and slide away off the chair, but we were so close to the end. He captured the curling stem with the thread and trapped it in place with three quick wraps.

"Take your hands away carefully," he said. "I'll do the whip finish. We don't want to risk losing it now."

I did as I was told, sat motionless with his arms around me, my head tilted slightly to the side so he could have the clear view through the magnifying glass. He cemented the head, wiped the excess glue from the eye with a waste feather, and hung my golden darter on the tackle box handle to dry. When at last he pulled away, I breathlessly slid my body back against the chair. I was still conscious of the havoc my clumsy hands or an unexpected sneeze could wreak on the table, which was cluttered with feathers and bits of fur.

"Now, that's the fly you tied, Emily. Isn't it beautiful?"

I nodded. "Yes, Father."

"Tomorrow, we'll do another one. An olive grouse. Smaller hook but much less complicated body. Look, I'll show you in the book."

As I waited to be released from the chair, I didn't think he meant it. He was just trying to apologize for having lost his temper, I told myself, just trying to pretend that our time together had been wonderful. But the next morning when I came down, late for breakfast, he was waiting for me with the materials for the olive grouse already assembled. He was ready to start in again, to take charge of my clumsy fingers with his voice and talk them through the steps.

That first time was the worst, but I never felt comfortable at the fly-tying table with Father's breath tickling the hair on my neck. I completed the olive grouse, another golden darter to match the first, two muddler minnows, and some others. I don't remember all the names anymore.

Once I hid upstairs, pretending to be immersed in my summer reading books, but he came looking for me.

"Emily," he called. "Come on down. Today we'll start the lead-winged coachman. I've got everything set up for you."

I lay very still and did not answer.

"Gerald," I heard my mother say. "Leave the child alone. You're driving her crazy with those flies."

"Nonsense," he said, and started up the dark, wooden stairs, one heavy step at a time.

I put my book down and rolled slowly off the bed so that by the time he reached the door of my room, I was on my feet, ready to be led back downstairs to the table.

Although we never spoke about it, my mother became oddly insistent that I join her on trips to the library or the general store.

"Are you going out again, Emily?" my father would call after me. "I was hoping we'd get some work done on this minnow."

"I'll be back soon, Father," I'd say. "I promise."

"Be sure you do," he said.

And for a while I did.

Then at the end of July, my old crowd of friends from across the lake began to gather and I slipped away to join them early in the morning before my father got up.

The girls were a gang. When we were all younger, we held bicycle relay races on the ring road and played down at the lakeside together under the watchful eyes of our mothers. Every July, we threw ourselves joyfully back into each other's lives. That summer we talked about boys and smoked illicit cigarettes in Randy Kidd's basement and held leg-shaving parties in her bedroom behind a safely locked door. Randy was the ringleader. She was the one who suggested we pierce our ears.

"My parents would die," I said. "They told me I'm not allowed to pierce my ears until I'm seventeen."

"Your hair's so long, they won't even notice," Randy said. "My sister will do it for us. She pierces all her friends' ears at college."

In the end, only one girl pulled out. The rest of us sat in a row with the obligatory ice cubes held to our ears, waiting for the painful stab of the sterilized needle.

Randy was right. At first my parents didn't notice. Even when my ears became infected, I didn't tell them. All alone in my room, I went through the painful procedure of twisting the gold studs and swabbing the recent wounds with alcohol. Then on the night of the club dance, when I had changed my clothes three times and played with my hair in front of the mirror for hours, I came across the small plastic box with dividers in my top bureau drawer. My father had given it to me so that I could keep my flies in separate compartments, untangled from one another. I poked my finger in and slid one of the golden darters up along its plastic wall. When I held it up, the mylar thread sparkled in the light like a jewel. I took out the other darter, hammered down the barbs of the two hooks, and slipped them into the raw holes in my earlobes.

Someone's mother drove us all to the dance, and Randy and I pushed through the side door into the ladies' room. I put my hair up in a ponytail so the feathered flies could twist and dangle above my shoulders. I liked the way they made me look—free and different and dangerous, even. And they made Randy notice.

"I've never seen earrings like that," Randy said. "Where did you get them?"

"I made them with my father. They're flies. You know, for fishing."

"They're great. Can you make me some?"

I hesitated. "I have some others at home I can give you," I said at last. "They're in a box in my bureau."

"Can you give them to me tomorrow?" she asked.

"Sure," I said with a smile. Randy had never noticed anything I'd worn before. I went out to the dance floor, swinging my ponytail in time to the music.

My mother noticed the earrings as soon as I got home.

"What has gotten into you, Emily? You know you were forbidden to pierce your ears until you were in college. This is appalling."

I didn't answer. My father was sitting in his chair behind the fly-tying table. His back was better by that time, but he still spent most of his waking hours in that chair. It was as if he didn't like to be too far away from his flies, as if something might blow away if he weren't keeping watch.

I saw him look up when my mother started in with me. His hands drifted ever so slowly down to the surface of the table as I came across the room toward him. I leaned over so that he could see my earrings better in the light.

"Everybody loved them, Father. Randy says she wants a pair, too. I'm going to give her the muddler minnows."

"I can't believe you did this, Emily," my mother said in a loud, nervous voice. "It makes you look so cheap."

"They don't make me look cheap, do they, Father?" I swung my head so he could see how they bounced, and my hip accidentally brushed the table. A bit of rabbit fur floated up from its pile and hung in the air for a moment before it settled down on top of the foxy quills.

"For God's sake, Gerald, speak to her," my mother said from her corner.

He stared at me for a long moment as if he didn't know who I was anymore, as if I were a trusted associate who had committed some treacherous and unspeakable act. "That is not the purpose for which the flies were intended," he said.

"Oh, I know that," I said quickly. "But they look good this way, don't they?"

He stood up and considered me in silence for a long time across the top of the table lamp.

"No, they don't," he finally said. "They're hanging upside down."

Then he turned off the light and I couldn't see his face anymore.

[ELIZABETH WINTHROP]

Elizabeth Winthrop, daughter of the late Stewart Alsop, the political journalist, is an important author in her own right. Among her forty books for children, The Castle in the Attic, *has sold more than a million copies. Twenty-three states nominated it for their top book awards. In Vermont it won the Dorothy Canfield Fisher Award and in California, the Young Readers Award.*

Winthrop's writing isn't limited to the younger members of the family, however, as "The Golden Darters" demonstrates. Recently she published her second adult novel, Island Justice, which in a starred review, Publishers Weekly dubbed "an absorbing novel," with "chillingly realistic scenes." People magazine had praise for it, too, naming it as their beach book of the week. Recently Island Justice was published in trade paperback by Quill.

About the genesis for "The Golden Darters," Winthrop says, "I wrote 'The Golden Darters' one summer when I had promised myself I would take a break from writing and did not even take my computer with me on vacation. But stories seem to happen to writers when we least expect them, and most especially when we shut the door on them.

"Friends asked me for dinner and afterward, the husband suggested I try tying a fly with him. It was a grown woman who accepted the invitation, but a twelve-year-old girl who lowered herself into the chair, a girl who had always hated performing in front of any audience, no matter how small. The grown woman was angry at herself for accepting the invitation to the fly-tying table while the young girl was trying to concentrate on the patiently delivered, yet imperative, instructions. When I got up from that table with an aching back and a golden darter in my pocket, the story was already starting in my head."

Editor Robert Stone chose the piece for inclusion in the 1992 edition of The Best American Short Stories. More accolades are no doubt in store for this Washington, D.C. native and graduate of Sarah Lawrence College. Children will also be delighted to hear that three additional books by the author from publisher Henry Holt are on the way. Her most recent children's book, Promises, about a girl adjusting to her mother's illness, was published this spring.

—C.O.

DADDY'S GIRL

A STORY

Jonathan Kellerman

SHE WOKE TO FIND HERSELF BEING MURDERED.

She was twelve, three weeks past her birthday, felt the cold-leather pressure around her neck, saw the barest outline looming over her, and thought, "This is a nightmare," then: "No, it's not!"

The night-light had been switched off and her bedroom was void-dark.

She tried to move but her arms were pinned under the covers. She always slept swaddled for security and now the duvet was her trap. Despite that, she continued to buck, squirm, twist away from the claws around her neck.

They clamped tighter, her throat hurt so bad, no matter how hard she tried to suck in air she couldn't, as if he'd shut her off completely.

Now, a different kind of darkness, cold, wet, strangely sweet, took hold of her, creeping upward from her feet but even as she felt herself dying she fought, so angry, thinking this isn't fair, what did I do to *deserve* this?

And then it stopped and bright lights popped in her head and

77

she thought she'd passed to the other side but she was sitting up, being held, being held . . .

Cradled. Aqua Velva. *Daddy.* Sweaty wool, stale breath, Aqua Velva, had to be Daddy.

She heard him say, "It's okay, baby, it's okay."

The lights had been turned on but her head was pressed against the bone and gristle of his shoulder and she never actually saw what he looked like the instant he saved her.

Later she found out the bogeyman had been a known hot-prowl burglar and rapist named Bush Bromet, recently paroled after a two-year B & E sentence handed down by one of those "soft-brained idiot judges" Daddy despised. Targeting their house had been a break in routine for the scumbag; Bromet's usual turf was miles south, in a bad part of town. But like Daddy said, even roaches got tired of the same garbage.

Thinking how close she'd come froze her spine.

Daddy had gone for a late-night walk, returning just in time to see the jimmied back door, pulling out his service revolver. But he couldn't shoot Bromet, the guy was all over her, so he pulled the scum off, breaking Bromet's neck with a reflexive one-two twist. Bromet died before he hit the ground.

The irony—a burglary detective's kid nearly savaged in her own bed—would have made a great story, but Daddy knew people on the paper—reporters for whom he'd been a dependable, anonymous source—and none of it got into print.

So that was the end of it.

Except, things were different now. Daddy had always been her hero. A solid, stocky man with hard, pale eyes and oversized hands and a full head of unruly ginger hair, he'd raised her alone after Mom died. The years chasing bad guys had seamed his face and he looked older than forty-nine. And those eyes . . . Not much for conversation, he liked to listen to talk radio, garden, fall asleep on the couch. He rarely told a joke but when he did, he knew how to deliver a punch line. He made sure to do his drinking after she went to bed. She never saw him with a woman but sometimes he came home later than usual, looking grim, and when she learned about sex from girls at school, how guys needed it all the time, would do anything to get it, she wondered if he was out taking care of himself, maybe the grimness was guilt. She sensed guilt was a part of his makeup, though she couldn't say why. He wasn't religious, never had a kind word for God.

He had perfect posture except when he sneaked a look at Mom's picture on the mantel and his shoulders bowed, or when he talked about some scumbag who'd gotten away, cold cases years old, and they bunched up tight around his neck.

Sometimes you just couldn't win, he said. She was never sure how he felt about that.

Now it was different. He was a *real* hero—how many kids get their lives saved by their dads?

For the first few days after, she thanked him and hugged him a lot, told him he was the greatest. She thought she was making a pretty good show of being strong until he asked her if she wanted to go see someone to talk about what happened. She laughed it off and said, "What? Some shrink?"

"If you need it."

"No way! Shrinks are crazier than anyone, right? Anyway, I don't remember a thing—just some noise and then you were there. It was no big deal."

He stared at her but didn't argue, never mentioned it again.

When the nightmares did come, she kept them to herself. When she hugged him, he allowed it but she thought she felt resistance and eased off.

He'd never been a demonstrative man. The closest thing to affection that she remembered was when she was much younger: tiptoeing into her room late at night when he thought she was sleeping, placing a cool, dry kiss on her forehead, then standing there for what seemed like a long time, sighing and trudging heavily to his room next door. When that ended, exactly, she couldn't recall. Some time before she'd turned ten.

They had no family; he'd been raised in an orphanage and Mom's cousins were "lowlife grifters" living down south—people he made clear she should have nothing to do with and she saw no reason to protest.

He did her laundry and cooked for her till she was eleven, working cases all week, then spending weekends in the kitchen preparing stews and soups, salads—tuna, canned salmon, and crab, chicken, anything you could bind with mayonnaise and celery—pickling cucumbers and tomatoes from the little garden he kept out back, constructing pies from yeasty ready-made crusts and gluey canned fillings. He made chocolate pudding, Jell-O, peas and ham, bowls of Minute rice. Putting away weeks' worth, freezing everything, so that she'd always have something to eat if he got called out.

In sixth grade, she took home ec and learned how to cook and from then on she was in charge of the kitchen and they ate Italian and Mexican, roast chicken, Swedish meatballs, Spanish casserole, once in a while a shoulder roast. Sometimes, standing at the gas range, wearing an apron that said "Come and get it!" she felt like a miniature wife and it thrilled and upset her. He had beautiful table manners, courtesy the orphanage, always spread his napkin precisely over one knee, never began till she was ready, wiped his lips frequently, cut his food surgically. They never said grace. He came no closer to faith than the secular rituals of December.

Two weeks after he saved her life, he quit the police department, explaining to her that he'd seen enough filth for one lifetime, had put away some pension, was ready for something new.

It crushed her, she'd always seen him as a detective and his choice of a new job—salesman at a sporting goods store—depressed her. So . . . regular.

He claimed he liked it, but she knew the pay was low because sometimes he worked double shifts, and he brought her fewer gifts, cheaper ones, and stopped buying himself new clothes. She did her best to feed him, searching out new recipes, figuring protein would help and looking for budget cuts of beef, but he lost weight and his trousers bagged. White hairs appeared at his temples. He took to wearing murky-colored cardigan sweaters over short-sleeved white wash-and-wear shirts and cheap sneakers when his cop-oxfords finally wore out. Years later, she realized he must have been a dreadful salesman—that tight mouth, those cold eyes, no penchant for small talk.

He got even quieter. Alcohol remained a clandestine pleasure and when his eyes grew pink around the rims, she began checking the bottom drawer in his nightstand where he kept the pint bottle under the blue velvet bag, gauging the descent of the tea-colored liquid and realizing how much more he was putting away.

Despite being thinner, he got soft around the middle. She found herself having to remember the night he saved her in order to see him as a hero. Mealtimes were now silent. He took to watching reruns of TV shows he'd never seen in the first place and had more patience for mediocrity. They had nothing in common but blood and love and when adolescence slapped her across the face, that ceased to be enough.

She never rebelled the way some of her girlfriends did—no tattooes, no weird piercing or heavy dope, just a few joints now and then and never booze because she saw that as *his* thing, sharing it would be a violation of his privacy.

When she was fifteen, his hair went completely white and acquired a slight curl.

She found excuses for missing dinner and he frowned but never argued. When boys discovered her and she chafed at ever being home, it was all she could do to watch him eat without screaming, "It's so fucking quiet in here!"

Her anger inflated by the week and she wondered how much longer she could stand it. Then he'd do something unexpected—compliment her cooking, tell her she was a regular chef. Tell her she was smart. And she'd find her tongue frozen, her airways asthma-tight—like that night!—and all the resentment would be sucked out of her and she'd barely be able to mutter a "Thanks, Dad," before they each looked away.

One of the boys she hung out with told her, "My dad told me he knew your dad when they were kids. He said your dad never screwed around with the guys, he was always real straight."

She came home especially late that night and he looked upset but he didn't say a thing.

She *was* smart, but a reluctant student, and at eighteen, she began junior college, declaring no major, hating the place, barely able to concentrate, feeling totally out of it.

After two semesters, she quit and got a summer job flipping burgers. One afternoon after work she drove over to the police academy and filled out a form, waiting a week before telling him, not sure how he'd react, figuring at least part of him might think it was okay.

His hands began to tremor and he shook his head back and forth, saying, "No, no, you don't want to do that."

"Why not?"

"Because it's not right for you."

"Why not?"

When he didn't answer, she said, "It think it's *absolutely* right and I'm *doing* it."

"Believe me, you don't want to." She could smell scotch on his breath. He sounded smug. It got to her.

"I want to be like you," she said. It came out as mockery.

"Don't be an idiot!"

"You're weird!" She jumped up from the table. He made a grab for her wrist. She broke away viciously, fighting the urge to swing at him, racing out of the house to the street. He followed her, both fists waving in the air, mouth open for the scream that never came. The two of them airing their dirty laundry in front of the entire neighborhood like one of those nutcase domestic calls he used to talk about.

Maybe he realized that because he stopped on the porch and just stood there, legs planted wide, hands still balled, his hair all over the place. She was out by the curb by then, not wanting to look at him but unable to stop herself. The stare he shot her was hard to classify but she thought she still saw the smugness, plus rage, fear, not a little contempt—the self-righteousness of a reformed drunk.

Far as she was concerned, he was a *real* drunk, now, putting away a pint a day, hiding the bottles in his bedroom closet in a shiny black lawn bag that he snuck to the trash every Thursday night.

And his clothes never smelled clean! He washed them with cheap soap; who was he to tell her a goddamn thing?

She left him standing there, took a long walk, ended up at a girlfriend's apartment, a cheap little student dive. Some people came over, they all did some partying, she slept over, didn't return home till the next afternoon.

When she arrived, the house was hot and close. He was out in back gardening, tying up vines. The tomatoes were already dead but he kept working with them like some maniac. That night she heard him through the wall that separated their bedrooms, sobbing.

I can't take this, she told herself, and a few days later she talked to that same girlfriend and they agreed it made sense to share expenses.

She loved the academy, every bit of it. Physical training, marksmanship, even the textbook stuff held her interest the way school never had. Through the whole course, he never phoned but she did, starting the second week. Home visits became every other Sunday. She cooked in her two-step kitchen and brought the food over wrapped in foil. He'd lost more weight, his hair was coarser and there was less of it. He couldn't be that old; she was only twenty.

Their conversation was sparse, almost surreal. He'd ask her how she was doing she'd say fine, they'd chew and clear the dishes and that was it. If she asked him how he was, he'd shrug.

A dozen Sundays passed like that as graduation approached. She was at the top of her class, thinking about becoming a detective, eventually. What would he think of *that?*

Two weeks before the end of the course, she found herself rotating through Central Records, a moldy, yellow barn of a building next to the coroner's office, right on the waterfront, you could smell the crab nets. The place was crammed with bolted iron shelves, the aisles so narrow you had to pass through sideways. The shelves held tens of thousands of case folders and a few cartons of computer disks. At the front of the room were makeshift tables loaded with antiquarian personal computers. The walls were sweating concrete. Every dark corner revealed wriggling tribes of silverfish.

The class assignment was: familiarize yourself with the new data-processing methods. Like most of the cadets, she had little interest in high-tech but she learned fast—the academy had taught her she really *was* smart.

She finished early, felt restless, started wandering among the shelves. A century and a half's worth of crime, alphabetized by perpetrator.

The B section jumped out at her like a mugger. *Bromet, Bush* was right there, on an outer shelf, so it had to be some kind of kharma, right?

She gazed around the barn. Her classmates were typing away. No instructor in sight.

She pulled out the folder, amazed that she felt nothing, not the slightest rise of heartbeat—no, that wasn't true, here it was, her pulse *was* racing, she was vibrating at every pressure point and all of a sudden her hands were icy and wet, barely able to hold onto the manila.

Slipping out of sight, she found a dimly lit spot, opened, and read.

She waited till the next Sunday visit. He was sitting at the kitchen table in his undershirt, empty glass at his fingertips, amber stain at the bottom, not even bothering to hide it anymore.

Usually she sat across from him but this time she pushed her chair next to his. His fingernails were filthy. Garden dirt, she hoped.

"Dad," she said. "I know."

She'd phrased it obliquely to snag his attention, but he just rotated his head slowly and looked at her, barely focusing. Their faces were inches apart. He'd used mouthwash and put on the Aqua Velva. Something new. Or maybe he did it every Sunday and she'd never noticed; she no longer trusted her own perceptions.

"I read the file, Dad."

Still, no response.

"I read Bromet's file, Dad."

He closed his eyes. She could see tiny, twitchy movements along his jawline.

"It's no big deal," she said.

He smiled horribly, eyes still shut. "No big deal."

"He was a scumbag, Dad. With all the ones you busted, one was bound to try to get back at you—"

"Get back at me?" Suddenly his eyes were open, flashing, his voice strong, deep, the way she remembered it. "You think he was the first? Let 'em try, any of them. Let 'em take their best shot with me, the stupid fu—But my family? No way you go after my—"

"I'm sure it was you he was after," she said, not sure of it at all. A rapist?

"Damn right he was," he nearly shouted. "Right in court he made threats. Told me when he get out—so what happens? *This* idiot isn't there." Punching his chest.

"How could you know? They all make threats, Dad—"

"Exactly. So you keep your damn wits about you," he said. "Wear the eyes in back of the head, that's the point of the goddamn *job*. That's what I tried to tell you. Fifty-nine minutes of boredom, one minute of panic. You can't turn off, ever. You become a machine—that what you want? Be a machine instead of a human being? I thought I had it down. Hell *no*, I didn't."

It was the longest speech he'd ever made. His hands were flapping, out of control. Foam flecked the tiny triangles where his upper lip curled away from its mate.

She said, "You took a walk, Daddy. You couldn't be expected to be a twenty-four-hour prisoner—"

"Yeah, I could." He wheeled on her. "You're not *hearing* me: that's the goddamn *job*, you're a prisoner—*worse* than a prisoner. The scum gets *paroled*."

He punched himself harder. "He warned me, so what do I do? Leave my little gir—"

"You took a *walk*, Dad."

"Yeah, a walk," he said. "A little walk." Digging the nails of one hand into the knuckles of the other and suddenly she knew he'd gone out that night to see one of his women, maybe a whore for money.

"I thought I knew," he said, "but I didn't know crap."

"You saved my *life*, Daddy."

He shook his head. The nails had drawn blood, tiny globules, red and shiny as a fire ant's body segments, pimpling up from the grimy skin. She tried to wipe them with her palm but he jerked away.

"I'm alive because of you," she said.

"Your mother gave you life." He swabbed his hand with his napkin, showed her the back of his head.

"You kept me going," she said, wanting to pound sense into him. "You were always my hero, Daddy. For God's sake, you're *still* my hero."

"Yeah, a hero," he said furiously, and now she was sure he'd do something sudden and violent and irrevocable.

Instead, he began to cry, tearing at his hair, growling at the humiliation but unable to stop. Finally, he accepted defeat, giving himself over to the shameful display, letting the tears flow, sobbing harder than he had that night, through the walls.

Oh, Lord, I want to be anywhere but here, she told herself. She waited a while, tried to embrace him. He didn't reciprocate but he didn't shove her away. Had he shoved her, she wasn't sure what would have happened, but he didn't, he sat there and wept and let her arms remain clenched around his neck.

She could feel the musculature of his shoulders. He'd shrunk but there was plenty of substance left. She wanted him to hug her back, one big happy catharsis, move on, happy ending, but that was movie crap, she'd settle for no earthquake.

They sat that way for what seemed a long time until he unfolded her arms, got up, went to his bedroom, stayed there even longer, came back in a fresh shirt, saying, "Okay, what's for dinner, chef?"

She put the franks-and-beans casserole in his fridge and half-dragged him to a Mexican restaurant she frequented with her friends. No one she knew was there tonight and they got a corner booth and she chased away the mariachi band with a five-dollar bill that raised his eyebrows.

"Academy pays, nowadays?"

"Yeah, I'm rich, Daddy." In her purse was fake I.D. for a margarita but she didn't dare use it, wanted to cry into her cola.

He had on a suit she vaguely remembered, a gray twill antique, way too big for him, shiny around the lapels, but not bad at all, dressing up helped his appearance. When she ordered him a scotch he made no excuses and sipped it slowly.

He wore the same suit at her graduation, sitting in the front section reserved for families. Not smiling with pride like some of the other parents but managing to tolerate the ceremony, back straight, oversized hands folded in his lap, freshly shaved, a brand-new haircut.

Later, at the buffet, a few people his age came up to him, all respectful. Some of them called him "Detective." The first time he heard that, his eyes slitted and he started to say something but checked himself. She felt his hand brush against hers, grabbed his pinkie, dropped it because she wasn't sure.

Somehow, they made it through the day. He hung back when her friends congratulated her, waited patiently as they snapped her picture. When she pulled up in front of his house, he said, "You want to come in, I made a pie? No great shakes just one of those—"

She silenced him with a finger across his lips. "Strawberry?"

He nodded.

"My favorite." Finishing the rest of the sentence in her head: *Dammit, no one else knows that.*

[JONATHAN KELLERMAN]

Even were he not the author of fifteen consecutive best-sellers and a series of novels featuring psychologist sleuth Dr. Alex Delaware, it would be difficult to find someone more qualified to write about the complexities of the relationship between father and child than Jonathan Kellerman.

Trained as a child clinical psychologist, Kellerman was founding director of the psychosocial program at Children's Hospital of Los Angeles, and is currently clinical professor of pediatrics and psychology at USC School of Medicine. He is the author of three volumes on psychology, including Savage Spawn: Reflections on Violent Children, inspired by the schoolyard shootings that took place in Jonesboro, Arkansas, and Springfield, Oregon, in 1998. He has written numerous essays and scientific articles, as well as two books for children. Among his best-sellers are Bad Love, Billy Straight, Blood Test, and the first of the Delaware books, When the Bough Breaks, made into the movie starring Ted Danson.

Because fatherly expectations are the springboard for "Daddy's Girl," I asked Kellerman what expectations he, himself, has had as a parent.

"Before I became a parent, I worked for several years as a child clinical psychologist," Kellerman told me. "Much of my time was spent with gravely ill children and I learned that life's full of surprises, not all of them pleasant. Perhaps because of that, I didn't enter fatherhood with any conscious expectations of my four children. Of course, I wanted them to end up as moral, responsible human beings and I did my best to train them as such. But I also relished their individuality and was loathe to impose upon them my interests or goals.

"So far, so good: they're all fascinating, gifted people whose company I'd enjoy even if they weren't my progeny. Of course, having a terrific mother helps. In fact, it's probably ninety or more percent of the recipe."

Kellerman's latest novel is Monster, and celebrates the return of his trademark character after a brief hiatus.

—C.O.

TWILIGHT OF THE DAWN

Dean Koontz

"SOMETIMES YOU CAN BE THE BIGGEST JACKASS WHO EVER lived," MY wife said the night that I took Santa Claus away from my son.

We were in bed, but she was clearly not in the mood for either sleep or romance.

Her voice was sharp, scornful. "What a terrible thing to do to a little boy."

"He's seven years old—"

"He's a little boy," Ellen said harshly, though we rarely spoke to each other in anger. For the most part ours was a happy, peaceful marriage.

We lay in silence. The drapes were drawn back from the French doors that opened onto the second-floor balcony, so the bedroom was limned by ash-pale moonlight. Even in that dim glow, even though Ellen was cloaked in blankets, her anger was apparent in the tense, angular position in which she pretended to seek sleep.

Finally she said, "Pete, you used a sledgehammer to shatter a little boy's fragile fantasy, a *harmless* fantasy, all because of your obsession with—"

"It wasn't harmless," I said patiently. "And I don't have an ob-session."

"Yes, you do," she insisted.

"I simply believe in rational—"

"Oh, shut up."

"Won't you even talk to me about it?"

"No. It's pointless."

I sighed. "I love you, Ellen."

She was silent a long while.

Wind soughed in the eaves, an ancient voice.

In the boughs of one of the backyard cherry trees, an owl hooted.

At last Ellen said, "I love you too, but sometimes I want to kick your ass."

I was angry with her because I felt that she was not being fair, that she was allowing her least admirable emotions to overrule her reason. Now, many years later, I would give anything to hear her say that she wanted to kick my ass, and I'd bend over with a smile.

From the cradle, my son, Benny, was taught that God did not exist under any name or in any form, and that religion was the refuge of weak-minded people who did not have the courage to face the universe on its own terms. I would not permit Benny to be baptized, for in my view that ceremony was a primitive initia-tion rite by which the child would be inducted into a cult of ig-norance and irrationality.

Ellen—my wife, Benny's mother—had been raised as a Methodist and still was stained (as I saw it) by lingering traces of faith. She called herself an agnostic, unable to go further and join me in the camp of the atheists. I loved her so much that I was able to tolerate her equivocation on the subject. Nevertheless, I had nothing but scorn for others who could not face the fact that the universe was godless and that human existence was nothing more than a biological accident.

I despised all who bent their knees to humble themselves be-fore an imaginary lord of creation: all the Methodists and Luther-ans and Catholics and Baptists and Mormons and Jews and others. They claimed many labels but in essence shared the same sick delusion.

My greatest loathing was reserved, however, for those who had once been clean of the disease of religion, rational men and women, like me, who had slipped off the path of reason and fallen into the chasm of superstition. They were surrendering their most precious possessions—their independent spirit, self-reliance, intellectual integrity—in return for half-baked, dreamy promises of an afterlife with togas and harp music. I was more disgusted by the rejection of their previously treasured secular enlightenment than I would have been to hear some old friend confess that he had suddenly developed an all-consuming obsession for canine sex and had divorced his wife in favor of a German shepherd bitch.

Hal Sheen, my partner with whom I had founded Fallon and Sheen Design, had been proud of his atheism too. In college we were best friends, and together we were a formidable team of debaters whenever the subject of religion arose; inevitably, anyone harboring a belief in a supreme being, anyone daring to disagree with our view of the universe as a place of uncaring forces, any of *that* ilk was sorry to have met us, for we stripped away his pretensions to adulthood and revealed him for the idiot child that he was. Indeed, we often didn't even wait for the subject of religion to arise but skillfully baited fellow students who, to our certain knowledge, were believers.

Later, with degrees in architecture, neither of us wished to work with anyone but each other, so we formed a company. We dreamed of creating brawny yet elegant, functional yet beautiful buildings that would delight and astonish, that would win the admiration of not only our fellow professionals but the world. And with brains, talent, and dogged determination, we began to attain some of our goals while we were still very young men. Fallon and Sheen Design, a wunderkind company, was the focus of a revolution in design that excited university students as well as longtime professionals.

The most important aspect of our tremendous success was that our atheism lay at the core of it, for we consciously set out to create a new architecture that owed nothing to religious inspiration. Most laymen are not aware that virtually all the structures around them, including those resulting from modern schools of design, incorporate architectural details originally developed to subtly reinforce the rule of God and the place of religion in life. For instance, vaulted ceilings, first used in churches and cathedrals, were originally intended to draw the gaze upward and to induce, by indirection, contemplation of Heaven and its rewards. Underpitch vaults, barrel vaults, grain vaults, fan vaults, quadripartite and sexpartite and tierceron vaults are more than mere arches; they were conceived as agents of religion, quiet advertisements for Him and for His higher authority. From the start, Hal and I were determined that no vaulted ceilings, no spires, no arched windows or doors, no slightest design element born of religion would be incorporated into a Fallon and Sheen building. In reaction we strove to direct the eye earthward and, by a thousand devices, to remind those who passed through our structures that they were born of the earth, not children of any God but merely more intellectually advanced cousins of apes.

Hal's reconversion to the Roman Catholicism of his childhood was, therefore, a shock to me. At thirty-seven, when he was at the top of his profession, when by his singular success he had proven the supremacy of unoppressed, rational man over imagined divinities, he returned with apparent joy to the confessional, humbled himself at the communion rail, dampened his forehead and breast with so-called holy water, and thereby rejected the intellectual foundation on which his entire adult life, to that point, had been based.

The horror of it chilled my heart, my marrow.

For taking Hal Sheen from me, I despised religion more than ever. I redoubled my efforts to eliminate any wisp of religious thought or superstition from my son's life, and I was fiercely determined that Benny would never be stolen from me by incense-burning, bell-ringing, hymn-singing, self-deluded, mush-brained fools. When he proved to be a voracious reader from an early age, I carefully chose books for him, directing him away from works that even indirectly portrayed religion as an acceptable part of life, firmly steering him to strictly secular material that would not encourage unhealthy fantasies. When I saw that he was fascinated by vampires, ghosts, and the entire panoply of traditional monsters that seem to intrigue all children, I strenuously discouraged that interest, mocked it, and taught him the virtue and pleasure of rising above such childish things. Oh, I did not deny him the enjoyment of a good scare, because there's nothing essentially religious in that. Benny was permitted to savor the fear induced by books about killer robots, movies about the Frankenstein monster, and other threats that were the work of man. It was only monsters of satanic and spiritual origins that I censored from his books and films, because belief in things satanic is merely another facet of religion, the flip side of God worship.

I allowed him Santa Claus until he was seven, though I had a lot of misgivings about that indulgence. The Santa Claus legend includes a Christian element, of course. Good *Saint* Nick and all that. But Ellen was insistent that Benny would not be denied that fantasy. I reluctantly agreed that it was probably harmless, but only as long as we scrupulously observed the holiday as a purely secular event having nothing to do with the birth of Jesus. To us, Christmas was a celebration of the family and a healthy indulgence in materialism.

In the backyard of our big house in Bucks County, Pennsylvania, grew a pair of enormous, long-lived cherry trees, under the branches of which Benny and I often sat in milder seasons, playing checkers or card games. Beneath those boughs, which already had lost most of their leaves to the tugging hands of autumn, on an unusually warm day in early October of his seventh year, as we were playing Uncle Wiggly, Benny asked if I thought Santa was going to bring him lots of stuff that year. I said it was too early to be thinking about Santa, and he said that *all* the kids were thinking about Santa and were starting to compose want lists already. Then he said, "Daddy, how's Santa *know* we've been good or bad? He can't watch all us kids all the time, can he? Do our guardian angels talk to him and tattle on us, or what?"

"Guardian angels?" I said, startled and displeased. "What do you know about guardian angels?"

"Well, they're supposed to watch over us, help us when we're in trouble, right? So I thought maybe they also talk to Santa Claus."

Only months after Benny was born, I had joined with like-minded parents in our community to establish a private school guided by the principles of secular humanism, where even the slightest religious thought would be kept out of the curriculum. In fact, our intention was to ensure that, as our children matured, they would be taught history, literature, sociology, and ethics from an anticlerical viewpoint. Benny had attended our preschool and, by that October of which I write, was in second grade of the elementary division, where his classmates came from families guided by the same rational principles as our own. I was surprised to hear that in such an environment he was still subjected to religious propagandizing.

"Who told you about guardian angels?"

"Some kids."

"They believe in these angels?"

"Sure. I guess."

"Do they believe in the tooth fairy?"

"Sheesh, no."

"Then why do they believe in guardian angels?"

"They saw it on TV."

"They did, huh?"

"It was a show you won't let me watch."

"And just because they saw it on TV, they think it's true?"

Benny shrugged and moved his game piece five spaces along the Uncle Wiggly board.

I believed then that popular culture—especially television—was the bane of all men and women of reason and goodwill, not least of all because it promoted a wide variety of religious superstitions and, by its saturation of every aspect of our lives, was inescapable and powerfully influential. Books and movies like *The Exorcist* and television programs about guardian angels could frustrate even the most diligent parent's attempts to raise his child in an atmosphere of untainted rationality.

The unseasonably warm October breeze was not strong enough to disturb the game cards, but it gently ruffled Benny's fine brown hair. Wind mussed, sitting on a pillow on his redwood chair in order to be at table level, he looked so small and vulnerable. Loving him, wanting the best possible life for him, I grew angrier by the second; my anger was directed not at Benny but at those who, intellectually and emotionally stunted by their twisted philosophy, would attempt to propagandize an innocent child.

"Benny," I said, "listen, there are no guardian angels. They don't exist. It's all an ugly lie told by people who want to make you believe that you aren't responsible for your own successes in life. They want you to believe that the bad things in life are the result of your sins and *are* your fault, but that all the good things come from the grace of God. It's a way to control you. That's what all religion is—a tool to control and oppress you."

He blinked at me. "Grace who?"

It was my turn to blink. "What?"

"Who's Grace? You mean Mrs. Grace Keever at the toy shop? What tool will she use to press me?" He giggled. "Will I be all mashed flat and on a hanger when she's done pressing me? Daddy, you sure are silly."

He was only a seven-year-old boy, after all, and I was solemnly discussing the oppressive nature of religious belief as if we were two intellectuals drinking espresso in a coffeehouse. Blushing at the realization of my own capacity for foolishness, I pushed aside the Uncle Wiggly board and struggled harder to make him understand why believing in such nonsense as guardian angels was not merely innocent fun but was a step toward intellectual and emotional enslavement of a particularly pernicious sort. When he seemed alternately bored, confused, embarrassed, and utterly baffled—but never for a moment enlightened—I grew frustrated, and at last (I am now ashamed to admit this) I made my point by taking Santa Claus away from him.

Suddenly it seemed clear to me that by allowing him to indulge in the Santa myth, I'd laid the groundwork for the very irrationality that I was determined to prevent him from adopting. How could I have been so misguided as to believe that Christmas could be celebrated entirely in a secular spirit, without risk of giving credence to the religious tradition that was, after all, the genesis of the holiday. Now I saw that erecting a Christmas tree in our home and exchanging gifts, by association with such other Christmas paraphernalia as manger scenes on church lawns and trumpet-tooting plastic angels in department-store decorations, had generated in Benny an assumption that the spiritual aspect of the celebration had as much validity as the materialistic aspect, which made him fertile ground for tales of guardian angels and all the other rot about sin and salvation.

Under the boughs of the cherry trees, in an October breeze that was blowing us slowly toward another Christmas, I told Benny the truth about Santa Claus, explained that the gifts came from his mother and me. He protested that he had evidence of Santa's reality: the cookies and milk that he always left out for the jolly fat man and that were unfailingly consumed. I convinced him that Santa's sweet tooth was in fact my own and that the milk—which I don't like—was always poured down the drain. Methodically, relentlessly—but with what I thought was kindness and love—I stripped from him all of the so-called magic of Christmas and left him in no doubt that the Santa stuff had been a well-meant but mistaken deception.

He listened with no further protest, and when I was finished he claimed to be sleepy and in need of a nap. He rubbed his eyes and yawned elaborately. He had no more interest in Uncle Wiggly and went straight into the house and up to his room.

The last thing that I said to him beneath the cherry trees was that strong, well-balanced people have no need for imaginary friends like Santa and guardian angels. "All we can count on is ourselves, our friends, and our families, Benny. If we want something in life, we can't get it by asking Santa Claus and certainly not by praying for it. We get it only by earning it—or by benefiting from the generosity of friends or relatives. There's no reason ever to *wish* for or pray for anything."

Three years later, when Benny was in the hospital and dying of bone cancer, I understood for the first time why other people felt a need to believe in God and seek comfort in prayer. Our lives are touched by some tragedies so enormous and so difficult to bear that the temptation to seek mystical answers to the cruelty of the world is powerful indeed.

Even if we can accept that our own deaths are final and that no souls survive the decomposition of our flesh, we often can't endure the idea that our *children*, when stricken in youth, are also doomed to pass from this world into no other. Children are special, so how can it be that they too will be wiped out as completely as if they had never existed? I've seen atheists, though despising religion and incapable of praying for themselves, nevertheless invoke the name of God on behalf of their seriously ill children— only to realize, sometimes with embarrassment but often with deep regret, that their philosophy denies them the foolishness of petitioning for divine intercession.

When Benny was afflicted with bone cancer, I was not shaken from my convictions; not once during the ordeal did I put principles aside and blubber at God. I was stalwart, steadfast, stoical, determined to bear the burden by myself, though there were times when the weight bowed my head and when the very bones of my shoulders felt as if they would splinter and collapse under a mountain of grief.

That day in October of Benny's seventh year, as I sat beneath the cherry trees and watched him return to the house to nap, I did not know how severely my principles and self-reliance would be tested in days to come. I was proud of having freed my son of his Christmas-related fantasies about Santa Claus, and I was pompously certain that the time would come when Benny, grown to adulthood, would eventually thank me for the rigorously rational upbringing that he had received.

When Hal Sheen told me that he had returned to the fold of the Catholic Church, I thought he was setting me up for a joke. We were having an after-work cocktail at a hotel bar near our offices, and I was under the impression that the purpose of our meeting was to celebrate some grand commission that Hal had won for us. "I've got news for you," he had said cryptically that morning. "Let's meet at the Regency for a drink at six o'clock." But instead of telling me that we had been chosen to design a building that would add another chapter to the legend of Fallon and Sheen, he told me that after more than a year of quiet debate with himself, he had shed his atheism as if it were a moldy cocoon and had flown forth into the realm of faith once more. I laughed, waiting for the punch line, and he smiled, and in his smile there was something—perhaps pity for me—that instantly convinced me that he was serious.

I argued quietly, then not so quietly. I scorned his claim to have rediscovered God, and I tried to shame him for his surrender of intellectual dignity.

"I've decided a man can be both an intellectual and a practicing Christian, Jew, or Buddhist," Hal said with annoying self-possession.

"Impossible!" I struck our table with one fist to emphasize my rejection of that muddle-headed contention. Our cocktail glasses rattled, and an unused ashtray nearly fell to the floor, which caused other patrons to look our way.

"Look at Malcolm Muggeridge," Hal said. "Or C. S. Lewis. Isaac Singer. Christians and a Jew—and indisputably intellectuals."

"Listen to you!" I said, appalled. "On how many occasions have other people raised those names—and other names—when you and I were arguing the intellectual supremacy of atheism, and you joined me in proving what fools the Muggeridges, Lewises, and Singers of this world really are."

He shrugged. "I was wrong."

"Just like that?"

"No, not just like that. Give me some credit, Pete. I've spent a year reading, thinking. I've actively resisted the urge to return to the faith, and yet I've been won over."

"By whom? What propagandizing priest or—"

"No person won me over. It's been entirely an interior debate, Pete. No one but me has known I've been wavering on this tightrope."

"Then what started you wavering?"

"Well, for a couple of years now, my life has been empty. . . ."

"Empty? You're young and healthy. You're married to a smart and beautiful woman. You're at the top of your profession, admired by one and all for the freshness and vigor of your architectural vision, and you're wealthy! You call that an empty life?"

He nodded. "Empty. But I couldn't figure out why. Just like you, I added up all that I've got, and it seemed like I should be the most fulfilled man on the face of the earth. But I felt hollow, and each new project we approached had less interest for me. Gradually I realized that all I'd built and that all I might build in the days to come was not going to satisfy me because the achievements were not lasting. Oh, sure, one of our buildings might stand for two hundred years, but a couple of centuries are but a grain of sand falling in the hourglass of time. Structures of stone and steel and glass are not enduring monuments. They're not, as we once thought, testimonies to the singular genius of mankind. Rather the opposite: They're reminders that even our mightiest structures are fragile, that our greatest achievements can be quickly erased by earthquakes, wars, tidal waves, or simply by the slow gnawing of a thousand years of sun and wind and rain. So what's the point?"

"The point," I reminded him angrily, "is that by erecting those structures, by creating better and more beautiful buildings, we are improving the lives of our fellow men and encouraging others to reach toward higher goals of their own—and then together all of us are making a better future for the whole human species."

"Yes, but to what end?" he pressed. "If there's no afterlife, if each individual's existence ends entirely in the grave, then the *collective* fate of the species is precisely that of the individual: death, emptiness, blackness, nothingness. Nothing can come from nothing. You can't claim a noble, higher purpose for the species as a whole when you allow no higher purpose for the individual spirit." He raised one hand to halt my response. "I know, I know. You've arguments against that statement. I've supported you in them through countless debates on the subject. But I can't support you any more, Pete. I think there *is* some purpose to life besides just living. And if I didn't think so, then I would leave the business and spend the rest of my life having fun, enjoying the precious finite number of days left to me. However, now that I be-lieve there is something called a soul and that it survives the body, I can go on working at Fallon and Sheen because it's my destiny to do so, which means the achievements can be meaningful. I hope you'll be able to accept this. I'm not going to proselytize. This is the first and last time you'll hear me mention my religion, because I'll respect your right *not* to believe. I'm sure we can go on as before."

But we could not.

I felt that religion was a hateful degenerative sickness of the mind, and I was thereafter uncomfortable in Hal's presence. I still pretended that we were close, that nothing had changed between us, but I felt that he was not the same man as he had been.

Besides, Hal's new faith inevitably began to infect his fine ar-chitectural vision. Vaulted ceilings and arched windows began to appear in his designs, and everywhere his new buildings encouraged the eye and mind to look up and regard the heavens. This change of direction was welcomed by certain clients and even praised by critics in prestigious journals, but I could not abide it because I knew he was regressing from the man-centered architecture that had been our claim to originality. Fourteen months after his embrace of the Roman Catholic Church, I sold out my share of the company to him and set up my own organization, free of his influence.

"Hal," I told him the last time that I saw him, "even when you claimed to be an atheist, you evidently never understood that the nothingness at the end of life isn't to be feared or raged against. Either accept it regretfully as a fact of life . . . or welcome it."

Personally, I welcomed it, because not having to concern my-self about my fate in the afterlife was liberating. Being a nonbe-liever, I could concentrate entirely on winning the rewards of *this* world, the one and only world.

The night of the day that I took Santa Claus away from Benny, the night that Ellen told me that she wanted to kick me in the ass, as we lay in our moonlit bedroom on opposite sides of the large four-poster bed, she also said, "Pete, you've told me all about your childhood, and of course I've met your folks, so I have a pretty good idea what it must have been like to be raised in that crackpot atmosphere. I can understand why you'd react against their religious fanaticism by embracing atheism. But sometimes . . . you get carried away. You aren't happy merely to *be* an atheist; you're so damn eager to impose your philosophy on everyone else, no matter the cost, that sometimes you behave very much like your own parents . . . except instead of selling God, you're selling godlessness."

I raised myself on the bed and looked at her blanket-shrouded form. I couldn't see her face; she was turned away from me. "That's just plain nasty, Ellen."

"It's true."

"I'm nothing like my parents. Nothing like them. I don't *beat* atheism into Benny the way they tried to beat God into me."

"What you did to him today was as bad as beating him."

"Ellen, all kids learn the truth about Santa Claus eventually, some of them even sooner than Benny did."

She turned toward me, and suddenly I could see her face just well enough to discern the anger in it but, unfortunately, not well enough to glimpse the love that I knew was also there.

"Sure," she said, "they all learn the truth about Santa Claus, but they don't have the fantasy ripped away from them by their own fathers, damn it!"

"I didn't *rip* it away. I reasoned him out of it."

"He's not a college boy on a debating team," she said. "You can't reason with a seven-year-old. They're all emotion at that age, all heart. Pete, he came into the house today after you were done with him, and he went up to his room, and an hour later when I went up there, he was still crying."

"Okay, okay," I said.

"Crying."

"Okay, I feel like a shit."

"Good. You should."

"And I'll admit that I could have handled it better, been more tactful about it."

She turned away from me again and said nothing.

"But I didn't do anything wrong," I said. "I mean, it was a real mistake to think we could celebrate Christmas in a strictly secular way. Innocent fantasies can lead to some that aren't so innocent."

"Oh, shut up," she said again. "Shut up and go to sleep before I forget I love you."

The trucker who killed Ellen was trying to make more money to buy a boat. He was a fisherman whose passion was trolling; to afford the boat, he had to take on more work. He was using amphetamines to stay awake. The truck was a Peterbilt, the biggest model they make. Ellen was driving her blue BMW. They hit head-on, and though she apparently tried to take evasive action, she never had a chance.

Benny was devastated. I put all work aside and stayed home with him the entire month of July. He needed a lot of hugging, reassuring, and some gentle guidance toward acceptance of the tragedy. I was in bad shape, too, for Ellen had been more than my wife and lover: She had been my toughest critic, my greatest champion, my best friend, and my only confidant. At night, alone in the bedroom we had shared, I put my face against the pillow upon which she had slept, breathed in the faintly lingering scent of her, and wept; I couldn't bear to wash the pillowcase for weeks. But in front of Benny, I managed for the most part to maintain control of myself and to provide him with the example of strength that he so terribly needed.

I allowed no funeral. Ellen was cremated, and her ashes were dispersed at sea.

A month later, on the first Sunday in August, when we had begun to move grudgingly and sadly toward acceptance, forty or fifty friends and relatives came to the house, and we held a quiet memorial service for Ellen, a purely secular service with not the slightest thread of religious content. We gathered on the patio near the pool, and half a dozen friends stepped forward to tell amusing stories about Ellen and to explain what an impact she'd had on their lives.

I kept Benny at my side throughout that service, for I wanted him to see that his mother had been loved by others, too, and that her existence had made a difference in more lives than his and mine. He was only eight years old, but he seemed to take from the service the very comfort that I had hoped it would give him. Hearing his mother praised, he was unable to hold back his tears, but now there was something more than grief in his face and eyes; now he was also proud of her, amused by some of the practical jokes that she had played on friends and that they now recounted, and intrigued to hear about aspects of her that had theretofore been unknown to him. In time these new emotions were certain to dilute his grief and help him adjust to his loss.

The day following the memorial service, I rose late. When I went looking for Benny, I found him beneath one of the cherry trees in the backyard. He sat with his knees drawn up against his chest and his arms around his legs, staring at the far side of the broad valley on one slope of which we lived, but he seemed to be looking at something still more distant.

I sat beside him. "How're you doin'?"

"Okay," he said.

For a while neither of us spoke. Overhead the leaves of the tree rustled softly. The dazzling white-pink blossoms of spring were long gone, of course, and the branches were bedecked with fruit not yet quite ripe. The day was hot, but the tree threw plentiful, cool shade.

At last he said, "Daddy?"

"Hmmmm?"

"If it's all right with you . . ."

"What?"

"I know what you say . . ."

"What I say about what?"

"About there being no Heaven or angels or anything like that."

"It's not just what I say, Benny. It's true."

"Well . . . just the same, if it's all right with you, I'm going to picture Mommy in Heaven, wings and everything."

He was still in a fragile emotional condition even a month after her death and would need many more months if not years to regain his full equilibrium, so I didn't rush to respond with one of my usual arguments about the foolishness of religious faith. I was silent for a moment, then said, "Well, let me think about that for a couple of minutes, okay?"

We sat side by side, staring across the valley, and I knew that neither of us was seeing the landscape before us. I was seeing Ellen as she had been on the Fourth of July the previous summer: wearing white shorts and a yellow blouse, tossing a Frisbee with me and Benny, radiant, laughing, laughing. I don't know what poor Benny was seeing, though I suspect his mind was brimming with gaudy images of Heaven complete with haloed angels and golden steps spiraling up to a golden throne.

"She can't just end," he said after a while. "She was too nice to just end. She's got to be . . . somewhere."

"But that's just it, Benny. She *is* somewhere. Your mother goes on in you. You've got her genes, for one thing. You don't know what genes are, but you've got them: her hair, her eyes. . . . And because she was a good person who taught you the right values, you'll grow up to be a good person as well, and you'll have kids of your own someday, and your mother will go on in them and in *their* children. Your mother still lives in our memories, too, and in the memories of her friends. Because she was kind to so many people, those people were shaped to some small degree by her kindness. They'll now and then remember her, and because of her they might be kinder to people, and that kindness goes on and on."

He listened solemnly, although I suspected that the concepts of immortality through bloodline and impersonal immortality through one's moral relationships with other people were beyond his grasp. I tried to think of a way to restate it so a child could understand.

But he said, "Nope. Not good enough. It's nice that lots of people are gonna remember her. But it's not good enough. *She* has to be somewhere. Not just her memory. *She* has to go on. So if it's all right with you, I'm gonna figure she's in Heaven."

"No, it's not all right, Benny." I put my arm around him. "The healthy thing to do, son, is to face up to unpleasant truths—"

He shook his head. "She's all right, Daddy. She didn't just end. She's somewhere now. I know she is. And she's happy."

"Benny—"

He stood, peered up into the trees, and said, "We'll have cherries to eat soon."

"Benny, let's not change the subject. We—"

"Can we drive into town for lunch at Mrs. Foster's restaurant—burgers and fries and Cokes and then a cherry sundae?"

"Benny—"

"Can we, can we?"

"All right. But—"

"I get to drive!" he shouted and ran off toward the garage, giggling at his joke.

During the next year, Benny's stubborn refusal to let his mother go was at first frustrating, then annoying, and finally intensely aggravating. He talked to her nearly every night as he lay in bed, waiting for sleep to come, and he seemed confident that she could hear him. Often, after I tucked him in and kissed him good night and left the room, he slipped out from under the covers, knelt beside the bed, and prayed that his mother was happy and safe where she had gone.

Twice I accidentally heard him. On other occasions I stood quietly in the hall after leaving his room, and when he thought I had gone downstairs, he humbled himself before God, although he could know nothing more of God than what he had illicitly learned from television shows or other pop culture that I had been unable to monitor.

I was determined to wait him out, certain that his childish faith would expire naturally when he realized that God would never answer him. As the days passed without a miraculous sign assuring him that his mother's soul had survived death, Benny would begin to understand that all he had been taught about religion was true, and he eventually would return quietly to the realm of reason where I had made—and was patiently saving—a place for him. I did not want to tell him that I knew of his praying, did not want to force the issue, because I knew that in reaction to a too heavy-handed exercise of parental authority, he might cling even longer to his irrational dream of life everlasting.

But after four months, when his nightly conversations with his dead mother and with God did not cease, I could no longer tolerate even whispered prayers in my house, for though I seldom heard them, I *knew* they were being said, and knowing was somehow as maddening as hearing every word of them. I confronted him. I reasoned with him at great length on many occasions. I argued, pleaded. I tried the classic carrot-and-stick approach: I punished him for the expression of any religious sentiment; and I rewarded him for the slightest antireligious statement, even if he made it unthinkingly or if it was only my *interpretation* of what he'd said that made his statement antireligious. He received few rewards and much punishment.

I did not spank him or in any way physically abuse him. That much, at least, is to my credit. I did not attempt to beat God out of him the way my parents had tried to beat Him *into* me.

I took Benny to Dr. Gerton, a psychiatrist, when everything else had failed. "He's having difficulty accepting his mother's death," I told Gerton. "He's just not . . . coping. I'm worried about him."

After three sessions with Benny over a period of two weeks, Dr. Gerton called to say he no longer needed to see Benny. "He's going to be all right, Mr. Fallon. You've no need to worry about him."

"But you're wrong," I insisted. "He needs analysis. He's still not . . . coping."

"Mr. Fallon, you've said that before, but I've never been able to get a clear explanation of what behavior strikes you as evidence of his inability to cope. What's he *doing* that worries you so?"

"He's praying," I said. "He prays to God to keep his mother safe and happy. And he talks to his mother as if he's sure she hears him, talks to her *every* night."

"Oh, Mr. Fallon, if that's all that's been bothering you, I can assure you there's no need to worry. Talking to his mother, praying for her, all that's perfectly ordinary and—"

"Every night!" I repeated.

"Ten times a day would be all right. Really, there's nothing unhealthy about it. Talking to God about his mother and talking to his mother in Heaven . . . it's just a psychological mechanism by which he can slowly adjust to the fact that she's no longer actually here on earth with him. It's perfectly ordinary."

I'm afraid I shouted: "It's not perfectly ordinary in *this* house, Dr. Gerton. We're atheists!"

He was silent, then sighed. "Mr. Fallon, you've got to remember that your son is more than your son—he's a person in his own right. A *little* person but a person nonetheless. You can't think of him as property or as an unformed mind to be molded—"

"I have the utmost respect for the individual, Dr. Gerton. Much more respect than do the hymn singers who value their fellow men less than they do their imaginary master in the sky."

His silence lasted longer than before. Finally he said, "All right. Then surely you realize there's no guarantee the son will be the same person in every respect as the father. He'll have ideas and desires of his own. And ideas about religion might be one area in which the disagreement between the two of you will widen over the years rather than narrow. This might not be *only* a psychological mechanism that he's using to adapt to his mother's death. It might also turn out to be the start of lifelong faith. At least you have to be prepared for the possibility."

"I won't have it," I said firmly.

His third silence was the longest of all. Then: "Mr. Fallon, I have no need to see Benny again. There's nothing I can do for him because there's nothing he really needs from me. But perhaps you should consider some counseling for yourself."

I hung up on him.

For the next six months Benny infuriated and frustrated me by clinging to his fantasy of Heaven. Perhaps he no longer spoke to his mother every evening, and perhaps sometimes he even forgot to say his prayers, but his stubborn faith could not be shaken. When I spoke of atheism, when I made a scornful joke about God, whenever I tried to reason with him, he would only say, "No,

Daddy, you're wrong," or, "No, Daddy, that's not the way it is," and he would either walk away from me or try to change the subject. Or he would do something even more infuriating: He would say, "No, Daddy, you're wrong," and then he would throw his small arms around me, hug me very tight, and tell me that he loved me, and at these moments there was a too-apparent sadness about him that included an element of pity, as if he was afraid for me and felt that I needed guidance and reassurance. Nothing made me angrier than that. He was nine years old, not an ancient guru!

As punishment for his willful disregard of my wishes, I took away his television privileges for days—and sometimes weeks—at a time. I forbade him to have dessert after dinner, and once I refused to allow him to play with his friends for an entire month. Nothing worked.

Religion, the disease that had turned my parents into stern and solemn strangers, the disease that had made my childhood a nightmare, the very sickness that had stolen my best friend, Hal Sheen, from me when I least expected to lose him, *religion* had now wormed its way into my house again. It had contaminated my son, the only important person left in my life. No, it wasn't any particular religion that had a grip on Benny. He didn't have any formal theological education, so his concepts of God and Heaven were thoroughly nondenominational, vaguely Christian, yes, but only vaguely. It was religion without structure, without dogma or doctrine, religion based entirely on childish sentiment; therefore, some might say that it was not really religion at all, and that I should not have worried about it. But I knew that Dr. Gerton's observation was true: This childish faith might be the seed from which a true religious conviction would grow in later years. The virus of religion was loose in my house, rampant, and I was dismayed, distraught, and perhaps even somewhat deranged by my failure to find a cure for it.

To me, this was the essence of horror. It wasn't the acute horror of a bomb blast or plane crash, mercifully brief, but a chronic horror that went on day after day, week after week.

I was sure that the worst of all possible troubles had befallen me and that I was in the darkest time of my life.

Then Benny got bone cancer.

Nearly two years after his mother died, on a blustery day late in February, we were in the park by the river, flying a kite. When Benny ran with the control stick, paying out string, he fell down. Not just once. Not twice. Repeatedly. When I asked what was wrong, he said that he had a sore muscle in his right leg: "Must've twisted it when the guys and I were climbing trees yesterday."

He favored the leg for a few days, and when I suggested that he ought to see a doctor, he said that he was feeling better.

A week later he was in the hospital, undergoing tests, and in another two days, the diagnosis was confirmed: bone cancer. It was too wide-spread for surgery. His physicians instituted an immediate program of radium treatments and chemotherapy.

Benny lost his hair, lost weight. He grew so pale that each morning I was afraid to look at him because I had the crazy idea that if he got any paler he would begin to turn transparent and, when he was finally as clear as glass, would shatter in front of my eyes.

After five weeks he took a sudden turn for the better and was, though not in remission, at least well enough to come home. The radiation and chemotherapy continued on an outpatient basis. I think now that he improved not due to the radiation or cytotoxic agents or drugs but simply because he wanted to see the cherry trees in bloom one last time. His temporary turn for the better was an act of sheer will, a triumph of mind over body.

Except for one day when a sprinkle of rain fell, he sat in a chair under the blossom-laden boughs, enjoying the spring greening of the valley and delighting in the antics of the squirrels that came out of the nearby woods to frolic on our lawn. He sat not in one of the redwood lawn chairs but in a big, comfortably padded easy chair that I brought out from the house, his legs propped on a hassock, because he was thin and fragile; a harder chair would have bruised him horribly.

We played card games and Chinese checkers, but usually he was too tired to concentrate on a game for long, so mostly we just sat there, relaxing. We talked of days past, of the many good times he'd had in his ten short years, and of his mother. But we sat in silence a lot too. Ours was never an awkward silence; sometimes melancholy, yes, but never awkward.

Neither of us spoke of God or guardian angels or Heaven. I knew that he hadn't lost his belief that his mother had survived the death of her body in some form and that she had gone on to a better place. But he said nothing more of that and didn't discuss his hopes for his own place in the afterlife. I believe he avoided the subject out of respect for me and because he wanted no friction between us during those last days.

I will always be grateful to him for not putting me to the test. I am afraid that I'd have tried to force him to embrace rationalism even in his last days, thereby making a bigger jackass of myself than usual.

After only nine days at home, he suffered a relapse and returned to the hospital. I booked him into a semiprivate room with two beds; he took one, and I took the other.

Cancer cells had migrated to his liver, and a tumor was found there. After surgery, he improved for a few days, was almost buoyant, but then sank again.

Cancer was found in his lymphatic system, in his spleen, tumors everywhere.

His condition improved, declined, improved, and declined again. Each improvement, however, was less encouraging than the one before it, while each decline was steeper.

I was rich, intelligent, and talented. I was famous in my field. But I could do nothing to save my son. I had never felt so small, so powerless.

At least I could be strong for Benny. In his presence, I tried to be cheerful. I did not let him see me cry, but I wept quietly at night, curled in the fetal position, reduced to the helplessness of a child, while he lay in troubled, drug-induced slumber on the other side of the room. During the day, when he was away for therapy or tests or surgery, I sat at the window, staring out, seeing nothing.

As if some alchemical spell had been cast, the world became gray, entirely gray. I was aware of no color in anything; I might have been living in an old black-and-white movie. Shadows became more stark and sharp edged. The air itself seemed gray, as though contaminated by a toxic mist so fine that it could not be seen, only sensed. Voices were fuzzy, the aural equivalent of gray. The few times that I switched on the TV or the radio, the music seemed to have no melody that I could discern. My interior world was as gray as the physical world around me, and the unseen but acutely sensed mist that fouled the outer world had penetrated to my core.

Even in the depths of that despair, I did not step off the path of reason, did not turn to God for help or condemn God for tor-turing an innocent child. I didn't consider seeking the counsel of clergymen or the help of faith healers.

I endured.

If I had slipped and sought solace in superstition, no one could have blamed me. In little more than two years, I'd had a falling out with my only close friend, had lost my wife in a traffic acci-dent, and had seen my son succumb to cancer. Occasionally you hear about people with runs of bad luck like that, or you read about them in the papers, and strangely enough they usually talk about how they were brought to God by their suffering and how they found peace in faith. Reading about them always makes you sad and stirs your compassion, and you can even forgive them their witless religious sentimentality. Of course, you always quickly put them out of your mind because you know that a sim-ilar chain of tragedies could befall you, and such a realization does not bear contemplation. Now I not only had to contemplate it but *live* it, and in the living I did not bend my principles.

I faced the void and accepted it.

After putting up a surprisingly long, valiant, painful struggle against the virulent cancer that was eating him alive, Benny fi-nally died on a night in August. They had rushed him into the in-tensive-care unit two days before, and I had been permitted to sit with him only fifteen minutes every second hour. On that last night, however, they allowed me to come in from the ICU lounge and stay beside his bed for several hours, because they knew that he didn't have long.

An intravenous drip pierced his left arm. An aspirator was inserted in his nose. He was hooked up to an EKG machine that traced his heart activity in green light on a bedside monitor, and each beat was marked by a soft beep. The lines and the beeps frequently became erratic for as much as three or four minutes at a time.

I held his hand. I smoothed the sweat-damp hair from his brow. I pulled the covers up to his neck when he was seized by chills and lowered them when the chills gave way to fevers.

Benny slipped in and out of consciousness. Even when awake he was not always alert or coherent.

"Daddy?"

"Yes, Benny?"

"Is that you?"

"It's me."

"Where am I?"

"In bed. Safe. I'm here, Benny."

"Is supper ready?"

"Not yet."

"I'd like burgers and fries."

"That's what we're having."

"Where're my shoes?"

"You don't need shoes tonight, Benny."

"Thought we were going for a walk."

"Not tonight."

"Oh."

Then he sighed and slipped away again.

Rain was falling outside. Drops pattered against the ICU window and streamed down the panes. The storm contributed to the gray mood that had claimed the world.

Once, near midnight, Benny woke and was lucid. He knew exactly where he was, who I was, and what was happening. He turned his head toward me and smiled. He tried to rise up on one arm, but he was too weak even to lift his head.

I got out of my chair, stood at the side of his bed, held his hand, and said, "All these wires . . . I think they're going to replace a few of your parts with robot stuff."

"I'll be okay," he said in a faint, tremulous voice that was strangely, movingly confident.

"You want a chip of ice to suck on?"

"No. What I want . . ."

"What? Anything you want, Benny."

"I'm scared, Daddy."

My throat grew tight, and I was afraid that I was going to lose the composure that I had strived so hard to hold on to during the long weeks of his illness. I swallowed and said, "Don't be scared, Benny. I'm with you. Don't—"

"No," he said, interrupting me. "I'm not scared . . . for me. I'm afraid . . . for you."

I thought that he was delirious again, and I didn't know what to say.

But he was not delirious, and with his next few words he made himself painfully clear: "I want us all . . . to be together again . . . like we were before Mommy died . . . together again someday. But I'm afraid that you . . . won't . . . find us."

The rest is agonizing to recall. I was indeed so obsessed with holding fast to my atheism that I could not bring myself to tell my son a harmless lie that would make his last minutes easier. If only I had promised to believe, had told him that I would seek him in the next world, he would have gone to his rest more happily. Ellen was right when she called it an obsession. I merely held Benny's hand tighter, blinked back tears, and smiled at him.

He said, "If you don't believe you can find us . . . then maybe you *won't* find us."

"It's all right, Benny," I said soothingly. I kissed him on the forehead, on his left cheek, and for a moment I put my face against his and held him as best I could, trying to compensate with affection for the promise of faith that I refused to give.

"Daddy . . . if only . . . you'd look for us?"

"You'll be okay, Benny."

". . . just please *look* for us . . ."

"I love you, Benny. I love you with all my heart."

". . . if you look for us . . . you'll find us . . ."

"I love you, I love you, Benny."

". . . don't look . . . won't find . . ."

"Benny, Benny . . ."

The gray ICU light fell on the gray sheets and on the gray face of my son.

The gray rain streamed down the gray window.

He died while I held him.

Abruptly color came back into the world. Far too much color, too intense, overwhelming. The light brown of Benny's staring, sightless eyes was the purest, most penetrating, most beautiful brown that I had ever seen. The ICU walls were a pale blue that made me feel as if they were made not of plaster but of water, and as if I were about to drown in a turbulent sea. The sour-apple green of the EKG monitor blazed bright, searing my eyes. The watery blue walls flowed toward me. I heard running footsteps as nurses and interns responded to the lack of telemetry data from their small patient, but before they arrived I was swept away by a blue tide, carried into deep blue currents.

I shut down my company. I withdrew from negotiations for new commissions. I arranged for those commissions already undertaken to be transferred as quickly as possible to other design firms of which I approved and with which my clients felt comfortable. I pink-slipped my employees, though with generous severance pay, and helped them to find new jobs where possible.

I put my wealth into treasury certificates and conservative savings instruments—investments requiring little or no monitoring. The temptation to sell the house was great, but after considerable thought I merely closed it and hired a part-time caretaker to look after it in my absence.

Years later than Hal Sheen, I had reached his conclusion that no monuments of man were worth the effort required to erect them. Even the greatest edifices of stone and steel were pathetic vanities, of no consequence in the long run. When viewed in the context of the vast, cold universe in which trillions of stars blazed down on tens of trillions of planets, even the pyramids were as fragile as origami sculptures. In the dark light of death and entropy, even heroic effort and acts of genius appeared foolish.

Yet relationships with family and friends were no more enduring than humanity's fragile monuments of stone. I had once told Benny that we lived on in memory, in the genetic trace, in the kindness that our own kindnesses encouraged in others. But those things now seemed as insubstantial as shapes of smoke in a brisk wind.

Unlike Hal Sheen, however, I did not seek comfort in religion. No blows were hard enough to crack my obsession.

I had thought that religious mania was the worst horror of all, but now I had found one that was worse: the horror of an atheist who, unable to believe in God, is suddenly also unable to believe in the value of human struggle and courage, and is therefore unable to find meaning in anything whatsoever, neither in beauty nor in pleasure, nor in the smallest act of kindness.

I spent that autumn in Bermuda. I bought a Cheoy Lee sixty-six-foot sport yacht, a sleek and powerful boat, and learned how to handle it. Alone, I ran the Caribbean, sampling island after island. Sometimes I dawdled along at quarter throttle for days at a time, in sync with the lazy rhythms of Caribbean life. Then suddenly I would be overcome with the frantic need to move, to stop wasting time, and I would press forward, engines screaming, slamming across the waves with reckless abandon, as if it mattered whether I got anywhere by any particular time.

When I tired of the Caribbean, I went to Brazil, but Rio held interest for only a few days. I became a rich drifter, moving from one first-class hotel to another in one far-flung city after another: Hong Kong, Singapore, Istanbul, Paris, Athens, Cairo, New York, Las Vegas, Acapulco, Tokyo, San Francisco. I was looking for something that would give meaning to life, though the search was conducted with the certain knowledge that I would not find what I sought.

For a few days I thought I could devote my life to gambling. In the random fall of cards, in the spin of roulette wheels, I glimpsed the strange, wild shape of fate. By committing myself to swimming in that deep river of randomness, I thought I might be in harmony with the pointlessness and disorder of the universe and, therefore, at peace. In less than a week I won and lost fortunes, and at last I walked away from the gaming tables a hundred thousand dollars out of pocket. That was only a tiny fraction of the millions on which I could draw, but in those few days I learned that even immersion in the chaos of random chance provided no escape from an awareness of the finite nature of life and of all things human.

In the spring I went home to die. I'm not sure if I meant to kill myself. Or, having lost the will to live, perhaps I believed that I could just lie down in a familiar place and succumb to death without needing to lift my hand against myself. But, although I did not know how death would be attained, I was certain that death was my goal.

The house in Bucks County was filled with painful memories of Ellen and Benny, and when I went into the kitchen and looked out the window at the cherry trees in the backyard, my heart ached as if pinched in a vise. The trees were ablaze with thousands of pink and white blossoms.

Benny had loved the cherry trees when they were at their radiant best, and the sight of their blossoms sharpened my memories of Benny so well that I felt I had been stabbed. For a while I leaned against the kitchen counter, unable to breathe, then gasped painfully for breath, then wept.

In time I went out and stood beneath the trees, looking up at the beautifully decorated branches. Benny had been dead almost nine months, but the trees he had loved were still thriving, and in some way that I could not quite grasp, their continued existence meant that at least a part of Benny was still alive. I struggled to understand this crazy idea—

—and suddenly the cherry blossoms fell. Not just a few. Not just hundreds. Within one minute every blossom on both trees dropped to the ground. I turned around, startled and confused, and the whirling white flowers were as thick as snowflakes in a blizzard. I had never seen anything like it. Cherry blossoms just don't fall by the thousands, simultaneously, on a windless day.

When the phenomenon ended, I plucked blossoms off my shoulders and out of my hair. I examined them closely. They were not withered or seared or marked by any sign of disease.

I looked up at the branches.

Not one blossom remained on either tree.

My heart was hammering.

Around my feet, drifts of cherry blossoms began to stir in a mild breeze that sprang up from the west.

"No," I said, so frightened that I could not even admit to myself what I was saying no *to*.

I turned from the trees and ran to the house. As I went, the last of the cherry blossoms blew off my hair and clothes.

In the library, however, as I took a bottle of Jack Daniel's from the bar cabinet, I realized that I was still clutching blossoms in my hand. I threw them down on the floor and scrubbed my palm on my pants as though I had been handling something foul.

I went to the bedroom with the Jack Daniel's and drank myself unconscious, refusing to face up to the reason why I needed to drink at all. I told myself that it had nothing to do with the cherry trees, that I was drinking only because I needed to escape the misery of the past few years.

Mine was a diamond-hard obsession.

I slept for eleven hours and woke with a hangover. I took two aspirin, stood in the shower under scalding water for fifteen minutes, under a cold spray for one minute, toweled vigorously, took two more aspirin, and went into the kitchen to make coffee.

Through the window above the sink, I saw the cherry trees ablaze with pink and white blossoms.

Hallucination, I thought with relief. Yesterday's blizzard of blossoms was just hallucination.

I ran outside for a closer look at the trees. I saw that only a few pink-white petals were scattered on the lush grass beneath the boughs, no more than would have blown off in the mild spring breeze.

Relieved but also curiously disappointed, I returned to the kitchen. The coffee had brewed. As I poured a cupful, I remembered the blossoms that I had cast aside in the library.

I drank two cups of fine Colombian before I had the nerve to go to the library. The blossoms were there: a wad of crushed petals that had yellowed and acquired brown edges overnight. I picked them up, closed my hand around them.

All right, I told myself shakily, you don't have to believe in Christ or in God the Father or in some bodiless Holy Spirit.

Religion is a disease.

No, no, you don't have to believe in any of the silly rituals, in dogma and doctrine. In fact you don't have to believe in *God* to believe in an afterlife.

Irrational, unreasonable.

No, wait, think about it: Isn't it possible that life after death is perfectly natural, not a divine gift but a simple fact of nature? The caterpillar lives one life, then transforms itself to live again as a butterfly. So, damn it, isn't it conceivable that our bodies are the caterpillar stage and that our spirits take flight into another existence when our bodies are no longer of use to us? The human metamorphosis may just be a transformation of a higher order than that of the caterpillar.

Slowly, with dread and yet hope, I walked through the house, out the back door, up the sloped yard to the cherry trees. I stood beneath the flowery boughs and opened my hand to reveal the blossoms that I had saved from yesterday.

"Benny?" I said wonderingly.

The blossomfall began again. From both trees, the pink and white petals dropped in profusion, spinning lazily to the grass, catching in my hair and on my clothes.

I turned, breathless, gasping. "Benny? Benny?"

In a minute the ground was covered with a white mantle, and again not one small bloom remained on the trees.

I laughed. It was a nervous laugh that might degenerate into a mad cackle. I was not in control of myself.

Not quite sure why I was speaking aloud, I said, "I'm scared. Oh, shit, am I scared."

The blossoms began to drift up from the ground. Not just a few of them. All of them. They rose back toward the branches that had shed them only moments ago. It was a blizzard in reverse. The soft petals brushed against my face.

I was laughing again, laughing uncontrollably, but my fear was fading rapidly, and this was good laughter.

Within another minute, the trees were cloaked in pink and white as before, and all was still.

I sensed that Benny was not within the tree. This phenomenon did not conform to pagan belief any more than it did to traditional Christianity. But he was *somewhere*. He was not gone forever. He was out there somewhere, and when my time came to go where he and Ellen had gone, I only needed to believe that they could be found, and then I would surely find them.

The sound of an obsession cracking could probably be heard all the way to China.

A scrap of writing by H. G. Wells came into my mind. I had long admired Wells's work, but nothing he had written had ever seemed so true as that which I recalled while standing under the cherry trees: "The past is but the beginning of a beginning, and all that is and has been is but the twilight of the dawn."

He had been writing about history, of course, and about the long future that awaited humanity, but those words seemed to apply as well to death and to the mysterious rebirth that followed it. A man might live a hundred years, yet his long life will be but the twilight of the dawn.

"Benny," I said. "Oh, Benny."

But no more blossoms fell, and through the years that followed I received no more signs. Nor did I need them.

From that day forward, I knew that death was not the end and that I would be rejoined with Ellen and Benny on the other side.

And what of God? Does He exist? I don't know. Although I

have believed in an afterlife of some kind for ten years now, I have not become a churchgoer. But if, upon my death, I cross into that other plane and find Him waiting for me, I will not be entirely surprised, and I will return to His arms as gratefully and happily as I will return to Ellen's and to Benny's.

[DEAN KOONTZ]

Dean Koontz is one of those bootstrapper success stories which aren't as common as moviemakers would like us to believe, but which everyone loves to hear about. Born in the Allegheny Mountains of Pennsylvania, he was raised until age eight in a tar-paper and clapboard house where his alcoholic father took out his anger on Koontz's mother. His first job after graduating from college was as a tutor in the Appalachian Poverty Program. He got the job only after the kids he was supposed to be tutoring had put his predecessor in the hospital.

A year and a half later, Koontz met Gerda, who would become his wife of thirty-four years, but who at that time presented him with a challenge he vowed to meet.

"I'll support you for five years," she said, "and if you can't make it as a writer in that time, you'll never make it."

Five years later, Gerda was handling the business side of Koontz's writing career. Today, with two hundred million of his books in print worldwide, he now owns a neo-Victorian and a 1936 Art Deco beach house in Southern California, is building a palatial mansion nearby, and cruises around Newport Beach in a Mercedes S600 sedan.

Seven of Koontz's novels have shot to number one on The New York Times *hardcover bestseller list, among them* Lightning, Cold Fire, Intensity, *and the recent* Sole Survivor. *Intensity was made into a Fox Network miniseries, which aired in August of 1997, and* Sole Survivor *is currently in development as a miniseries as well. Koontz, himself, wrote the screen-*

play and executive produced the movie Phantoms, starring Peter O'Toole and Joanna Going. It was adapted from his novel of the same title.

I asked Koontz if he might share with readers his goals in writing "Twilight of the Dawn."

"I had intended to write about faith and hope," Koontz responded, "in a story from which I had stripped all sentimentality while preserving genuine sentiment. I had hoped this would give the narrative a harder emotional impact. I also wanted to explore the curious fact that a passionate atheist can be as dogmatic, narrow-minded, and self-righteous as the worst religious fanatic, and that in fact atheism is a belief system that, often, is expressed as if it's a religion—a narcissistic religion in which there is no god but self."

Added Koontz, "This story has drawn hundreds of letters over the years, more than ninety-five percent positive. Weirdly, the mail from committed atheists has in every instance degenerated into vicious, name-calling rants; I say 'weirdly' 'cause one would think that in trying to convince me that the father in [the novella] is an utterly atypical atheist, they would not adopt the ugliest aspects of his character!"

—C.O.

MI PAPI

Ana Veciana-Suarez

FOR A GOOD PART OF MY CHILDHOOD, I REMAINED CON-
vinced that all fathers, while working, smelled of chalk and
mildew—a scent that was as strong as it was strangely sweet when
it permeated a room, entered the nostrils, and finally home-
steaded there. It is perhaps one of my most enduring memories of
Papi, this smell, and it is also probably the most untrustworthy
one. Memory deceives, distills, defines. I cling to it, however, because it is something to hold on to, something tangible and at
least partly true.

When I was a child, Papi and his friends met regularly in a
rented storefront in Allapattah, a Miami neighborhood where
the whites were fleeing the incoming Cubans and the native
blacks, a neighborhood in transition, like the exiled revolutionaries who came. The shop was not far from Jackson High School
and a stone's throw from an ice cream shop, which we visited
often because back then a single scoop did not break a piggy
bank. It was in this storefront where I learned to read Spanish,
where I memorized the first verses of Cuban poet José Martí, and
where the geography and history of my Caribbean homeland was

taught by the wives of the men who wanted to liberate the island through war.

This is also where my father kept his guns.

Now he says he didn't. But fact plays no part in my story. Truth, my memory of it, is more important. If he and the anti-Communist commando group he helped found did not keep guns, they kept something just as powerful: passion and righteousness.

I cannot remember much else about the storefront, or what was in it. Except, of course, the chalk because the mothers needed it to teach us, and because the men used it, too, to plot whatever it was they plotted on the blackboard. Perhaps there was a map of Cuba taped to the wall, and alongside it a color rendition of its flag and a pencil sketch of Martí the Liberator, complete with bushy moustache and wide forehead. There may have been photographs of the oceanfront Malecón and the Cuban Capitol, of a peasant's thatched roof *bohio*, of El Morro castle and numerous other scenes of a country my six-year-old mind was quickly and inevitably forgetting.

But maybe not. Perhaps the walls were left blank, a surrender to peeling paint and rusty nails. I'm not sure. Sometimes I wonder why I even want to know.

I loved going there. I loved the way the mothers wrote lessons on a large portable blackboard, with efficient, elegant handwriting and yellow chalk that dusted our clothes. I loved the way we started class, with the U.S. Pledge of Allegiance and the Cuban National Anthem. I loved the soft, melodious sound of children's voices reading their Spanish: *Mamá bebe agua. José bebe leche. ¿Qué bebe el bebé?* I loved straining to listen to my father's muffled voice in the other room, using his own chalk and blackboard, and to feel the important bustling of busy men who sometimes argued so loud we could not hear our teachers above their din. I loved, too, the pastries at mid-morning because the guava was always warm and the crust flaky. It did not matter summer rains gave this storefront a perpetual smell of mildew that stuck to our clothes. Nor was it important that most other children I knew spent Saturday mornings watching cartoons.

It didn't matter because my Papi was there.

One year, with the help of the women and the encouragement

of the men, we children staged a show of Cuban folkloric dance
and song. For my number, I wore skin-colored tights, T-strap black
shoes, and a dress my mother sewed, a white, frilly country gown
with red satin ribbons at the cinched waist and scooped neckline.
Mami painted my lips the color of cherry and circled my eyes in
blue. With a black pencil she darkened my eyebrows and rubbed
a beauty mark near my mouth. Standing beside my dance partner,
the white-shirted, straw-hatted, red-kerchiefed older brother, I
was immortalized in this flouncy outfit by a family photographer,
probably my father. I keep this photograph in an old scrapbook,
proof that I danced the *zapateo* on a well-lighted stage. But I have
no other confirmation except a deceiving memory to recall the
initial vertigo of stage fright and that awful moment after the
dance when, panicked by applause, I froze in the lights and refused to shimmy behind the curtains until my father called.

Never happened, he tells me. I danced without misstep or fault.

Over the years we participated in many events other than indoor activities. Namely, we marched. A lot. On these parades, the
men led us through Miami streets and over bridges, past gaping
motorists and pedestrians, all of us walking proudly, walking stri-
dently, waving the Cuban flag and singing, a veritable conga line
of politics and purpose. *Al combate corred bayameses que la patria os
contempla orgullosa* . . . I try to sing the anthem now, a melody
that echoes in my head, but I stumble over the words. How long
ago this must have been!

So, yes, we marched and we walked and we skipped, the
women and children behind the men, until we arrived at Bayfront
Park or the Cuban Refugee Center or some other important place
of commerce that has long since been razed and redeveloped.
Once there, one of the men, often my father, would roar words of
justice, and his voice would rock the ground and move the
women to tears and we the children of revolutionaries, thirsty,
sweaty, and eager to play among our own, stood restless at attention by our mothers' sides for fear of getting smacked. It was always hot on those marches, and my thighs chafed and the men
got dark rings of sweat under their arms and the women's dresses

stuck to their backs. Police escorted us everywhere, usually on motorcycles, which, as you can imagine, thrilled the children in a way few things could. Sometimes the cops led us on large brown horses, too, and because we behaved, our mothers allowed us to pet their manes.

The speeches, I don't remember what they were about, but they always finished with the hopeful shouts of *"Viva Cuba Libre!"*—shouts I recognize now as plaintive cries of dreams broken and promises disavowed. They ended, too, these marches, with everyone rushing the speaker to reach for that voice of confidence and authority. Entranced, bewildered, and jealous in a way I could not explain, I watched these people, their tangle of arms, their all-too-visible hopes, and knew they possessed my father in a way I never could. I was simply a little girl, powerless and shy, and all I could offer was to adore him from afar.

My father doesn't deliver speeches anymore. The last time he spoke in public was in an auditorium where I was reading from my first novel. I recognized him in the audience and introduced him. Graciously he declared, "She used to be my daughter. Now I am her father."

We did not take many vacations when I was a child, but the few we did were memorable and exciting. One in particular, across the heart of South America, comes to mind. This is how I remember it, true or false:

The road ended abruptly and without explanation at the banks of a clear, cold river. Papi stopped the four-door blue sedan, a vehicle he had borrowed for our vacation, opened his door, and trudged to shore. I watched from the back seat, feeling that too-familiar wave of anxiety ebbing in. We were travelling from Bolivia, through Peru, and into Chile. If roads in this part of the world are bad now, they were dismal then, pockmarked with craters if they were paved, and dirt and rock if one was lucky, or, during the rainy season, mud and puddles. Now we had run out of luck, and there was not even a recognizable path across.

Papi ordered us out of the car and sent us looking for shallows. My older brother, fifteen at the time, found it near a foot-bridge the Indians had built. We drove to the spot. In the distance, across the potato farms of the altiplano, I noticed how the Quechuas stopped their tilling to watch the white city folk cross their bridge. We carried bundles of clothes and heavy boxes. Then my father sped the car across the gurgling waters and met us on the other side. The wind was harsh, like a scorned lover's slap, and the landscape brown and desolate except for scrub plants.

That was just the beginning of fun.

Later, in Peru, on a winding mountain road that descended into a village of some renown (it appeared, at least, on a map), the car wheezed, sputtered, coughed, then began to smoke. Nearing town it gave out completely, and we climbed out to push. Because it was Sunday, my father had to pay an exorbitant price—months' worth of wages in those parts—to find us lodging, food, and auto parts.

Undaunted, we continued south on the spine of the Andes. Two days later we crossed into Chile. Guards stopped us at the border and would not let us pass. My mother and the three children were given the run of a room. Somebody brought us sandwiches, soft drinks. We played, we must have. And, I'm sure, we fought. My father was gone for hours, sequestered in a room, I was told, getting our documents in order. It was nightfall before we saw him again. I don't remember the expression on his face, though I imagine now that it must have been ashen and preoccupied. I do remember thinking, with my primitive child's logic, that my family had the most adventurous holidays of any family I knew.

Our vacation in Santiago, a cosmopolitan city with some of the best food I have ever eaten, coincided with Fidel Castro's 1971 visit to the then Communist-controlled Chile. Under the seats of the blue sedan my father drove—the car that forded a river, that motored some of the steepest roads imaginable, that konked out in the middle of nowhere, that actually belonged to the United States government—somewhere in the bowels of that car a rifle and ammunition were stored. We sat on these valuables, my older brother, my younger sister, and I, singing "One hundred bottles of beer on the wall."

In September 1979, I was twenty-two years old and a year and a half out of college when my father was shot in the head. He was driving home from work, his regular route, when the driver of a brown Buick station wagon pulled alongside him and fired four shots. Blood spurted on Papi's clothes, over the dashboard and steering wheel. Shaking and disoriented, he drove home, stumbled into the house where the youngest of my siblings were playing, and collapsed in the living room. Blood, blood everywhere.

I was working as a reporter at that time and had just returned from an assignment when one of the other city desk writers, covering my father's shooting, pulled me aside and told me about it. My knees buckled.

Papi underwent surgery and was eventually sent home from the hospital two days after the shooting. Miraculously, only one small-caliber bullet had lodged just above his ear. The others dented the car or ricocheted off. Despite several leads, police never found the gunman, and the assassination attempt was attributed to "political circumstances." The FBI had warned him about the possibility of an attempt on his life several months before.

Following the shooting, an editor asked me to write about my experience with political violence. My father's shooting had come on the heels of another assassination, this one in Puerto Rico. I did write a piece—and won a national journalism contest, my first. Now, two decades later, I cannot remember a single line in that article, but that dry-mouth sensation when my colleague delivered the news remains vivid, a reminder of that oh-god-what-now feeling that was as much part of my childhood as squabbles with my sister and cold lemonade in the summer.

An accountant by trade and a revolutionary by vocation, Papi was an unlikely leader of any sort. He was the son of Catalonions who migrated to Cuba, poor peasant stock with a knack for hard work and a spirit of sacrifice that has served me, two generations removed, in good stead. Though an only child, he grew up in a large, raucous house in Havana, with aunts and uncles and cousins and grandparents, a place everyone of that generation called La Finca, The Farm, a name he would later give another home in exile. He was brilliant and bookish as a child, a baseball fanatic of the most virulent kind, and spoiled by a mother who personally cut his filet steak well into his adolescence. (She, of course, ate whatever the butcher was giving away.) He grew tall and lanky, traits I inherited from him, a serious man with deep-set eyes, an aquiline nose, and a large mole over his lip that he hid as soon as he could grow a moustache.

He is still brilliant, still a baseball fanatic, but no longer lanky. He has filled out with age, and sometimes he stoops. My children, his grandchildren, tease him about his choice of clothes. At home, he prefers colorful plaid shirts, Bermuda shorts, and black over-the-calf socks. His legs are as white as a Canadian tourist's, and he always manages to appear a bit disheveled, despite my mother's valiant attempts. He forgets to zip his fly, his shirttail scoots out, and his hair sometimes sticks up every which way. He has a sweet tooth of the worst sort. He has been known to gorge on three and four desserts.

He tends to sentimentality. I can recall, on the fingers of one hand, the times I've seen my mother cry. I've lost count with my father. His eyes water in joy, in sadness, in resignation. This is not a man of the old school, a patriarch removed by choice, mythological by his very absence.

And yet . . . and yet. The father of the child I was is a phantom, a mirage, a hologram. He was more presence than reality. I must often ask myself how much I truly remember about those years, and how much is imagination eager to fill in the blanks. I love to look at the photographs of that time in my childhood, probably in hopes of recapturing what I could not possibly remember—what I may never have had and so might have made up.

In a worn, green scrapbook, there is a telltale photo of the young refugee family, a black and white taken in January '63 in front of the rock fireplace in the ramshackle house we lived in when we first arrived from Cuba. My mother looks painfully young, her face unlined, her lips full and smiling. My father wears baggy pants and his hair, raven black and full, is cropped close. I can't tell if he's smiling. The three oldest children are in the foreground in donated clothes, pretty clothes, mind you. I am, as expected, at my father's side; he is caressing my cheek. Behind us, on the mantel, are the Cuban and American flags.

Another snapshot, June '63: In the front yard of the same house in our Easter finery. My brother wears a plaid jacket, my sister and I have matching purses and hats. Of course I pose next to my father, his arm around my shoulder.

June 1980, color photograph: My father, in a gray tux, walks me down the church aisle to the muted strains of a wedding march. I have filled out, but I'm still a child. His hair is graying on the side. The photographer captures our smiles but not our words or actions. My father's arm shakes, tears roll down his cheek. "Will you calm down?" I whisper hoarsely.

Papi was not a roll-up-his-sleeves kind of father. He did not change diapers, give baths, or sing lullabies at bedtime. He neither helped us learn our timetables nor taught us to play ball. He never roughhoused with me, and if he did so with my brothers, I cannot remember, though my youngest sister, sixteen years my junior and the youngest of five, insists our father told her elaborate, comical stories about a cow at bedtime. I was out of the house by then, in college first, then married.

My father rarely disciplined us, and that I am sure was part of his charm for us as children. My mother wielded a mean belt, and she was quick to pinch. Later, much later in life, when the father of my own children left the dispensing of privileges and punishments to me, I was bitterly resentful. Disneyland Dad, I called my husband, for he was the one associated with fun, and I with routine and wrath. Our good cop–bad cop routine, however, helped to shed a different light of understanding on my mother, my father.

I was a child known as much for my rages as for my quiet stubbornness. *Fosforito*, they called me during adolescence. Little match. I was fifteen the only time my father hit me. We had had an argument at the table. He wanted me to do something; I refused. I ran into my bedroom and locked the door. He pounded on it. As he picked the lock, I climbed onto the windowsill. From the second story, it was not a bad jump to the garden. We had tried it before, my middle sister and I, but somehow this time . . . this time . . . The hesitation cost me. He grabbed me by the hair and pulled me down. He slapped me. When we calmed down, he lectured then apologized for hitting me. I turned my face away. I wouldn't talk to him—for days. It was my opportunity to make him pay for every trespass I could imagine. I wonder now who punished whom.

I'm sure he was reluctant to spend the little time he had with us in forcing us to do things we did not want to. On the rare occasions he was home, when he was not at the chalky, mildewy Allapattah storefront or at the various jobs he held during those first years of exile (always abroad), it was Christmas, New Year's, and the end of school all rolled into one. As the oldest daughter and the most verbal of his children, I was allowed to tag along with him wherever he went, to stores, to offices, to government agencies, wherever I could. I learned to blend in, to not speak loud, certainly not unless I was spoken to, and to observe. I translated when journalists interviewed him about Cuban exile politics and when investigators from the House Select Committee on Assassinations initially contacted him to find out what he knew about John F. Kennedy's murder. (He eventually told the committee that in 1963, through a CIA contact, he had met Lee Harvey Oswald in Dallas three months before Kennedy was killed there.)

As I matured, I began to witness my father's growing frustration with *la lucha*, the struggle for a free Cuba, and his bewilderment over a misguided perception others had about those who fought against Castro as right-wing thugs. He learned, as I did, that the printed word, the filmed image, and the broadcast voice can be as far from reality as a cartoon show. Because of him, I became a woman with sharply defined political ideas, liberal values that are also deeply held. Because of him, I refuse to discuss them aloud, however. In fact, I'm allergic to public discussion of politics of any kind. I learned very early on that arguing politics is as useless as describing color to the blind. We believe what we want to believe, regardless of the facts. Why waste time in talk?

But my father influenced more than political thought. What he is, what he would have hoped to be, has defined me as much as my own dreams. It is a verity of life that *all* fathers cast a long and wide shadow over their children's lives, even if we never meet them, even when they're gone long before we are born or possess memory. I owe my work habits to Papi. I have yet to meet anyone who works harder and longer and with as much passion. He always carries a file of some sort with him, or a stack of important-looking papers. Not in a briefcase, no, but bound together with a rubber band or ensconced in a plastic bag: notes, budgets, receipts, letters, many of which bear his telltale loopy writing that seems more flourish than practical. He refuses to retire, and I wonder if he enjoys running a business so much he cannot imagine staying at home—or if he is afraid of what comes in old age, the whispering quiet, the questioning time, the inevitable knowing of what might have been but wasn't.

As the first man I loved, he has, in one way or another, been a template for all the relationships that followed him. He taught me that virility and nurturing are not mutually exclusive and that the complicated matters of love can bring joy as well as pain, disillusion along with hope. And so I have had good luck in the affairs of the heart. I have loved and been loved passionately, freely, without doubts. I've always expected to be pampered, to be doted on, to be admired—but also to be respected and encouraged. For a Latino man, my father was—and still is—incredibly ambitious for his three daughters. He has pushed us to strive, to be at the top of our class, to be the best at our careers. We are all well-educated professionals, all women with minds of our own. Though my mother was very much of her generation and her culture—in other words, she knew her place—I was never raised to be somebody's wife. I was expected to be somebody in my own right. For that I am eternally grateful.

Still, I tend to be inexplicably anxious about what he will

think. So much of my life has been spent in an effort to not dis-
appoint him. Not because of fear that I would not make the cut
in his eyes. I could, and did, measure up. But because I needed to
be better than he expected, better than my siblings, the out-
standing among the extraordinary, the one he would notice in
whatever way I could manage to get noticed. It wasn't, and isn't,
enough to succeed in the public arena. A triumph doesn't count
unless he witnesses it, unless I tell him about it.

Papi became gravely ill in 1993, when I was pregnant with my
last child. After emergency open heart surgery, he is said to have
blinked awake in the recovery room and asked the nurse for his
wallet. Barely conscious, barely able to move, he wanted to show
her a letter to the editor that had recently appeared in the *Miami
Herald* about my writing. My younger brother, who discovered
this scene when he walked into the room, repeated the story so
many times that its retelling was enough to cheer my father, to
keep him motivated for months. Thus, it entered the annals of
family lore, a story that, with embellishments and a little editing,
underscored the slow evolution of our relationship—a relationship I once described to my second husband as: "I'm the son he's
always wanted."

For me, that hospital stay was more than yet another family
tale, however. It marked the beginning of something and the
end of another—a changing of the guard, the leveling of the
field, if you will. Not long ago, driving out of a parking lot, my
father blacked out at the wheel and smashed into another car.
When I saw him shaken but unharmed at home, I recognized
that vulnerability I had first seen at the hospital years earlier,
after bypass surgery. There was something more, too, a soften-
ing of the features, an acceptance that suffuses us when we
come to terms with our own faults and frailties. Inevitable,
some might say, that I am parenting him more and he fathering
me less.

The more successful I become, the more I learn about the
world and the farther I venture, the less it seems I need him. But
I wonder about that. The ties that bind aging parent to adult child

are like elastic, to be stretched and tested before returning to form. I've been known to snap that elastic a few times.

When my first husband died suddenly of a heart attack at thirty-seven, leaving me with five children ages sixteen to one, it was the kind of devastating loss that gave my father a renewed purpose in life. He is, if anything, a man for impossible missions, and I, once again, needed to be rescued. It was an awkward time for us, however. Pain takes many forms, some which cannot be explained, and there were times I lashed out when I really wanted to be held tight.

"*Mi palomita herida*," he called me. My injured dove.

He held me tight, oh, yes, he did, but sometimes with a suffocating grip. I thought he was making up for lost time, for a childhood that neither he nor I can ever get back. Now I know different. Now I know that it was heartbreakingly difficult for him to watch me struggle alone through grief, for that is the only way to deal with sorrow. He could not abide his own helplessness. So we argued about my decision to continue living alone with the children. We argued about money, career moves, new interests, even eventually about dating. Suddenly, I was seventeen all over again.

Yet, the death of my children's papi helped me view my own father with compassion and forgiveness. My children, left fatherless too soon, idolize their daddy, much the same way I adored mine as a little girl: from afar. But mine does not remain frozen in time, a perpetual thirty-seven-year-old, and I must be ever thankful for that. He has taken human form as I age, become a man like other men, with annoying habits and inexplicable idiosyncrasies, virtues, too, all real, all tangible and true. He no longer smells of chalk or mildew. Maybe he never did. His scent is of deodorant and musky aftershave, sometimes of the seasoning in my mother's black beans.

The other night, he phoned to complain we had not spoken in two days. I chided him for whining, explained about deadlines, children's practices, church commitments, household duties: excuses he did not accept.

"*Pio, pio, pio,*" he joked before hanging up. "*La palomita vuela.*" The little dove flies.

I swear I detected a note of pride.

[ANA VECIANA-SUAREZ]

After reading Ana Veciana-Suarez's moving account of her father, and the gifts his full, relationship-rich life has given her, I found myself wondering about the effects her husband's death at an early age has had on her own children. So I asked her if she had noticed anything that was different about their outlook on the world compared to herself as a child, which she could attribute to them no longer having a father in their lives.

I was prepared for a "no comment" answer, the subject being too sensitive, but Veciana-Suarez was generous in her response.

"I don't mind answering at all," she told me. "As a matter of fact, I've long thought about precisely this. I've noticed that each of my children has reacted in a different way. Two of them—the middle boys—seem very resentful of the fact that their father died. They don't say it in so many words, but in other ways. Like: 'Everything happens to us!' 'It's not like this in other families.' My oldest, the only girl, feels a little like that, too. On the other hand, two of my other boys don't dwell as much on that. Their attitude has changed in the sense that they try to squeeze as much fun and pleasure from the moment as they can because, as my seventeen-year-old once told me, 'You can just drop dead at any time.'

"All of them suffer in various degrees from what I call 'father hunger,' " Veciana-Suarez says. "The youngest, who is six now, was a baby when his father died and has no memories. Ironically, he's the spitting image of his father, and he's always asking questions about him. 'Did my father like to do this?' 'What did he say when he . . . ?' Things like that."

Veciana-Suarez's latest book, Birthday Parties in Heaven: Thoughts on Life, Love, Grief and Other Matters of the Heart, *will be published in the fall of 2000, and with it, continues this very theme. She is also author of a novel,* The Chin Kiss King, *which* The New York Times *called, "piquant and aromatic, written with a spirited sense of inner worlds and human foibles . . . an impressive debut."*

Her day job as a columnist for The Miami Herald *garners her national and local journalism awards on a routine basis, including one in 1996 for Excellence in Feature Writing from the American Association of Sunday and Feature Editors, a Penney-Missouri Award in 1995, and the 1998 State Sunshine Award for Commentary from the Society of Professional Journalists. She and her husband, David Freundlich, live in Miami with her five children.*

—C.O.

THE LAST VACATION

Caroline Leavitt

HE WOULDN'T COME OUT OF THE WATER. SADIE SAT ON THE beach blanket, slathered in a greasy skin of lotion, as breaded with sand as a cutlet, hot and itchy and tired. The sun was in her eyes but still, she watched her father's head bobbing out in the ocean. He was so far apart from the other swimmers, he seemed alone.

The beach was cooling down. People were gathering their things: blankets, beach rafts, and the squirming hands of their kids. They were heading out to the drive-ins, the restaurants, the shade of their own cottages. They walked past Sadie and her mother, shifting the sands, laughing, and talking. Sadie brushed herself off.

Her mother, Louise, shielded her eyes with the flat of her hand and frowned. "He always does this," Louise said wearily. "Once again, we're going to be the last ones on this beach." She stood up, tugging down the high-cut legs of her red two-piece, her stomach brown and flat, her long pale hair unfurling like a flag to her waist. Louise was forty-three years old and men on the beach still looked at her, women still turned their heads, appraising, more than they did at Sadie, who was built like a swizzle straw, whose suit was plain and one-piece and deep blue, with padding at the bust, whose hair wasn't the thick gold gloss of her mother's, but a dirtier blonde fizz to her chin.

Louise scanned the horizon and waved. "Yoo-hoo, Bill," she said weakly. She glumly sat down. She rested her chin on her knees.

"There. Here he comes," Sadie pointed. Her father began swimming back to the shore, stepping onto the sand, water sluicing from his plaid boxers, his black hair slicked back. He was freckled and tanned both. He was thin and sharp featured. He shook the water from him, sprinkling them with droplets, the way a dog might. "Cut it out!" Sadie said, and he laughed and kept shaking. The water droplets made her feel hotter than ever. She got out of his way. He shook at her again deliberately and then picked up the blanket.

"We'd better get going if we're going to make our reservations," Louise said. "I still have to shower off this salt."

"It's too late to go out," he said. "Let's just eat at home."

"It's not a vacation if I have to cook."

"Well, Louise, it's not a vacation if I have to pay for something we can do ourselves."

Bill gathered up the beach things. "Let's go," he said.

Sadie knew this scenario. Hot weather. Hot tempers. Nobody and nothing ever really cooling down.

Every July since she could remember, it went this way. Her family rented a cottage on Cape Cod for two weeks. You always knew what you were getting. Yarmouth or Hyannis Port. A too-small box of a cottage with no air-conditioning, the windows flung open for the nonexistent "nice fresh breeze" Louise assured everyone was about to come in any moment. Pine needle lawns and no front porch. Crowded beaches buzzing with horseflies and kids and the tinny scratch of radios, the high point of the day being when the ice cream trunk came, and all of this because they couldn't afford the more deserted, gentile richness of Truro.

For two weeks, they all had a routine. Beach in the morning, lunch at home, more beach, maybe a little shopping and then, the one thing that gave Bill real pleasure, a drive-in movie at night, where they all sat silently together. They were all exhausted by the heat, by the things they did each day as if they had to do them.

The first thing they did was hit the Cape library and stock up on books, as thick as fists. Bill grabbed nonfiction, Sadie and Louise dreamily devoured novels. Sadie liked to read on the beach, getting lost in what she was reading. She wasn't stuck on a hot beach with her parents. She was in love in Paris. She was walking on the moon. She was anywhere and everywhere else. "Let me see," Louise said, tapping Sadie. Paris vanished. A toddler screamed. Louise peered over Sadie's shoulder and then looked back at her own book. Sadie coughed and Bill looked up at her, distracted.

"Is your book good?" Sadie asked him. He shrugged and turned a page, looked down.

This was the year Sadie was sixteen, the summer she had her first boyfriend. His name was Danny. He had gone to Sadie's school, but they didn't share classes, and he almost always had a pretty blonde girlfriend on his arm who looked right through Sadie, the same way he did. He was smart and funny and going to MIT on full scholarship in the fall, and there was no reason for him to be interested in Sadie. He never spoke to Sadie, not until the first day of summer, when he came into the Sweet Dreams bakery where she was working, her hair a nimbus of curls, her pink uniform dusted with sugar, and he suddenly seemed to see her. He blinked, shaking his head, as if he were trying to clear something.

"I know you," he said. He put his hands in his pockets. He looked down at the cupcakes. "Sadie." It startled her, hearing him say her name. It worked its way deep into her bones. "You're always reading," he said. She drew back, stung, but then she saw that he was smiling at her, that he kept smiling even after he bought a dozen chocolate chip cookies. "Reading's good for you," he said and bit into a cookie. He stopped at the door, considering, and then opened it, and left.

Every day after that, he came in for cookies. He took his time. He talked about MIT, about the stars, and sometimes, too, about his mother, a divorcée who went out every night to the Holiday Inn to husband hunt. "People think I'm a golden boy, but it's not that at all," he told Sadie. "We don't have money. I had to work hard to get into school, even harder to get a scholarship, and every day, over my head, like this drumbeat, I keep hearing 'you can't fuck this up, you can't fuck this up.'" He leaned on the counter. "You're a good listener. You understand me."

She couldn't tell him that he was making her so nervous she couldn't speak. Not with words, anyway. Instead, she tucked extra chocolate cookies into his bag, a pair of mint clouds and a macaroon, her own whole sweet language. The air sugared around them, sweeter and sweeter the more he came in for cookies, and then one day, he came and put his hands, broad and flat and beautiful on the glass case, making prints she'd have to wipe off. "I didn't come for brownies," he said. "I came for you."

She blinked at him, shocked. "I'm not blonde enough," she blurted, and then flushed, humiliated.

He laughed. "Who wants you to be?"

She shrugged. "Well, your other girlfriends . . ."

"I like you because you're different. I'd like to get to know you."

She swallowed. "I'd like to get to know you, too."

"So let's do something."

She stood still.

"Say a movie. Say something to eat afterward. Say this Friday." He waited. "Say yes."

"Yes," she said.

"You're too young to date," Bill told her that evening.

"She is not," Louise said. She was giddy. She acted as if it were happening to her and not Sadie. "I can take you shopping, buy you a dress."

"No one wears dresses."

"Well, they should."

Bill frowned. "She's too young," he repeated.

Louise met his gaze. "I was her age when I fell in love."

Sadie moved away from both of them. She knew her mother didn't mean with her father.

Sadie's parents were a couple but Sadie didn't know why or how. They slept in twin beds with a red maple nightstand smack in the middle, the same way as those 1950s sitcoms everyone was always making fun of. They didn't hold hands or do more than peck kisses at each other and late at night, the only murmur of voices Sadie ever heard was coming from the radio, from one of the talk shows her mother loved to listen to.

Sadie knew how her parents had met. Louise told her it was at an adult camp, a month after Louise had been jilted by the man she really loved. Sadie had seen his picture, a gleaming blond with a mischievous smile, who had run off and married someone else, and if Sadie wondered why Louise kept the photo, she didn't ask. According to Louise, Bill had fallen in love with her at first sight. He hadn't cared that her eyes were red from crying, that the name she sometimes murmured wasn't his. "I was twenty-six and already an old maid," Louise told Sadie, and so, two months later, she and Bill were married, and a year later, Sadie arrived.

Early on, Sadie knew her father wasn't like other fathers. She couldn't remember him reading her a story, taking her to the park or the zoo or anything other than a movie, and that didn't count because he was silent then, and they always saw movies he wanted to see and he didn't like to talk about them afterward, either. He didn't laugh with her or hug her much or ask her what she had done that day. He didn't have a passion for golf or badminton the way some of the other fathers did, men who took their girls with them and taught them a little something. Instead, Sadie's father's passion was for the vegetable garden that took up half their backyard, and when she even got close to it, he shouted at her, so loudly, she burst into tears.

He spent hours ordering seeds from catalogs, whole weekends mulching and planting and spraying, whistling to himself. It was Louise who filled Sadie's days, who took her shopping and out to eat, who sat for hours talking to her. Louise who made dresses for Sadie's dolls and brushed Sadie's hair.

Bill was gone before Sadie even woke in the morning. When he came home, he sat in the leather chair in the living room and read the paper, or a book, and after dinner, he went to his den and worked. When she thought of it now, she could remember two nice things he had done for her. When she was ten, he had confronted the librarian who had refused to let Sadie into the adult section. "This is my daughter and she has my permission to be anywhere she wants. And when she can read these books, she can take out whatever book she wants," he said. He guided Sadie toward the adult books. "Don't you dare try to stop her." And once, when Sadie was coloring a picture, he walked behind her and put his hand on her hair, stroking it, and when she turned around, starting, he was already in the other room. Two nice things. It didn't seem like very much.

One night, when she was five, she woke to hear her parents arguing. "Who's her nursery school teacher?" Louise shouted. "What's her favorite thing to do? You don't know, do you? You don't have a clue?" Sadie pressed her ear against the wall. Her father's voice was low, insistent, muffled.

"Wrong," Louise shouted. "Everything about you is wrong."

Hearing them argue made her afraid. Suddenly, she saw ghosts in the closet, a big black dog growling just under the bed. She got up and switched on her light and then she padded into her parents' room, her flowered flannel nightgown frilling about her knees.

The room was dark. Her parents had stopped arguing. She crawled into Louise's bed. Even at night, her mother smelled of gardenia and powder. Sadie snuggled against Louise, who sighed, and then Sadie slept.

It became a habit. She'd go to bed and wake up and crawl in bed with Louise, who never seemed to mind, who never told her she was too big a girl for such nonsense.

And then one day, Bill asked if Sadie would sleep with him, too. "You used to sleep in my arms when you were a baby," he said.

Sadie blinked at him. Her heart hammered in her chest.

"Don't you think I can keep away the bogeyman as well as your mother?" He sat in the kitchen chair. He looked defeated and sad, and Sadie suddenly felt so responsible she couldn't bear it. "Yes," she said.

"Ah, that's my girl," he said. He ruffled her hair, leaving the kitchen, and as soon as he did, the enormity of what she had done struck her like a blow.

*   *   *

The night Sadie was to sleep in her father's bed, he came home at six, the way he usually did, but he was smiling. "Hi Sadie," he said. The three of them ate dinner as if nothing were wrong. Lamb chops and baby peas and bright yellow corn from the can, Green Giant, the kind Sadie liked. Chocolate pudding peaked with Cool Whip for dessert. Sadie dallied that night, brushing each tooth, washing her face two times, getting in and out of three different pairs of pajamas. Sadie padded into her parents' room. They were both in bed, reading, both in pajamas, both smiling. "Here's our girl," her father said. Sadie climbed across her mother and into his bed. Sadie curled toward the wall and he curled against her, and where her mother was soft and warm, her father was angular and unyielding. Sadie felt the press of him against her.

"Nighty night," her mother said, switching off the light. Sadie's eyes flew open. Her father flung one arm about her, trapping her. Sadie pretended to be asleep. She made her breathing long and even. She snored, and then her father hoisted himself up. She felt his breath on her face, and then he lowered himself down again. He stroked her hair and then he slept.

Sadie didn't sleep. She didn't like her father's breath on the back of her neck. Sadie didn't like his body so close to hers. She shifted, but she wouldn't turn toward him. She didn't want to see him facing her. Sadie kept her eyes open, and on her mother, in the bed next to them. She tried to will Louise to open her eyes, to see her discomfort and rescue her. Come on, she begged. Come on. Louise stretched and pulled the blanket over her. Sadie kept her eyes wide open.

In the morning, Sadie was exhausted. She couldn't remember sleeping, but she must have, because the bed was now gloriously empty. She could look across and see Louise sleeping, her hair tumbled across the pillow. She looked up and there was her father, walking across the room naked. There was his penis! Long and dark, like poop, bumping against his leg. She recoiled and her father suddenly saw her, and he covered himself with his hands. He frowned. "Aren't you ashamed of yourself, Sadie?" he demanded. Sadie shut her eyes so tightly, she saw pinpoints of light.

Bill walked to the closet, jerking down his robe, belting it tight, and then strode from the room. She stayed in bed until she heard his car.

No one talked about that night again, but Sadie stopped crawling into Louise's bed. That night and every night after. Instead, she learned to sleep with her covers hooded over her face against the ghosts she heard whispering, calling her name. Her father never asked her to share his bed again, and Sadie never offered. "You're growing up," Louise said, approvingly.

Sadie didn't realize you could have a different sort of father until she was ten and became friends with a girl down the street named Judy Harper. Judy was skinny and pin-dotted with freckles. She had long red hair and laughed with her mouth wide open. She was an only child and her father was warm and funny, with the same red hair as Judy's, the same bountiful laugh. He always gave Sadie a hug. He seemed genuinely happy to see her, genuinely interested in what she had to say. He'd sit opposite her and lean forward. "Tell me what's going on in Sadie's world." Mr. Harper piled Judy and Sadie into the car and took them to the park and the diner. He joined in when they sang hit tunes in the car. He gave Sadie and Judy bites of his sundaes, fries from his plate. "Now, what do you say we go shopping?" he said. Judy clapped her hands.

They went to the mall, to the TeenScene shop. All the new sweaters were in, rows of golds and greens and blues. Sadie flipped the price tag over on one of the sweaters. $80. Louise would never pay that. She got all their clothes in Filene's Basement. "This, and this, and this," Judy said, piling sweaters into her father's arms. Sadie leaned along the racks, feeling her heart split with yearning, and then Mr. Harper came over and studied Sadie. "You know, I think blue is your color," he said, and then he whisked one off the rack and held it up against her. "I was right," he said. "I'm going to have to buy it for you as a present."

"Oh, yeah, get the blue!" Judy called, grabbing down a two-tone stripe. Sadie threw her arms around Mr. Harper. "You're the best father in the world!" she said, and he laughed, and she meant it, but not the way he thought.

She wore the sweater home. She modeled it for Louise and Bill, her face shining. "You have to take it back," Bill said. "You want sweaters, we'll buy them for you."

"Mom."

"You're bringing it back," Louise said. "It's too expensive to keep."

"Fine," Sadie said, bunching up the offending sweater. She never brought it back. Instead she had brought it to school, she had kept it in her locker and changed into it until it got so dirty and stained, she couldn't wear it anymore.

After that, it wasn't as much fun being at Judy's house. She began to hate Judy for having a father who asked about your day, who talked to you and took you places and gave you hugs just because he felt like it. She began to hate Mr. Harper, too, for being so kind, so open. "Honey, is something bothering you?" he asked the last time she was there. He sat down opposite her. He tried to get her to look at him. "Well, I'm always here to talk. You know that, don't you?" His voice was kind, but she couldn't listen. She couldn't hear. All his kindness did was remind her how much she was missing. It hammered home what it was she didn't have. It was better not to see him, better not to be reminded of what you did and didn't have.

She stopped going over to Judy's. "But why not?" Judy asked. "I never get to see you anymore." Her voice was soft, plaintive.

"I can't," Sadie said. "I have to go to the dentist."

Then, while Judy was bowling with her father, or eating out with her father, or watching a movie with her father, Sadie sat in the backyard leafing through magazines, thinking about her parents being killed in an accident. Killed suddenly, before they knew what hit them. The cops would come to the door, or maybe a kindly social worker. They'd tell her and then before they could take her to an orphanage, because there was no other place for her, no living relatives, Mr. Harper would come to her rescue. "I've always thought of her as mine," he'd say.

Sometimes she imagined her parents divorcing, instead, arguing over who would take Sadie. The judge, a kindly man with long white hair and blue eyes, would call Sadie into his study. "So

Sadie, who would you like to live with?" No matter how many times she played the game, she always said Louise.

It wasn't until Sadie began dating Danny that Bill suddenly seemed to take new interest in her. The week of her first date, he began to ask her questions. "What does this boy do? How did you meet him?"

"He went to my high school. He's going to MIT next year. I met him at the bakery."

"Who are his parents?"

"I'm not marrying him!"

"Things happen."

"Bill, for God's sakes," said Louise. "It's a date."

The night of Sadie's date she wore new blue jeans and a tight black blouse. "Don't you think your guy would love to see you in a dress?" Louise coaxed. Bill frowned. "You be home by eleven," he said. Danny was supposed to come inside, to meet her parents, but as soon as Sadie heard his car, she was so keyed up she bolted outside to meet him. She jumped in his car. He was in a black T-shirt and jeans. He smiled at her.

"Go, go, go," she ordered.

He buckled her in beside him in the car, tightening the seat belt, tugging her close.

They didn't do much that night. They walked by the Charles River and when she stubbed her toe, she pretended nothing had happened. Her whole foot throbbed, and she was grateful when he suggested they sit on the banks.

They didn't talk much, but it didn't matter. She was already so in love with him he could have suggested they bay at the moon and she would have, so when he took her back to his house, to his mother's basement, she followed along. He lowered her onto a black leather couch so that when she looked up she saw a Venus paint-by-number deer on the wall. He undid her blouse a button at a time, and he shook his head in admiration. "I have never seen anything like you in my life."

He kissed her stomach, her knees, knobby as teacups, her feet, her flossy hair. Sadie had never had a real boyfriend before. "I'm not ready," she whispered, and he nodded at her. He lay back down and cradled her in his arms. "That's okay," he told her. "I can wait."

She could tell he was asleep by the way he was breathing. His arm was thrown across her, his eyes rolled in dreams, and then she looked up and saw the time. One in the morning. She bolted up. His arm fell from her. "What?" He blinked at her. She grabbed her purse. "I'm half an hour late," she said, panicked. She didn't want to admit she was really two hours late, didn't want him to think she was terminally uncool.

"How can you be so beautiful?" he said, but he got up, he pulled on his clothes and helped her with hers, and then right before they got to the door, he pulled her to him and kissed her again.

She was nervous all the way home, but he played the radio. He tapped his hand on the dashboard. "I'll come in with you," he said.

"No, yes-no," she said, flustered.

Inside, the house was cool and dark. "They're out looking for me," she said, humiliated. Danny smiled. He tilted her face up to him. "Then we have time," he said and started kissing her again. She shut her eyes and then she heard something and her eyes flew open and there was her father, in his gray robe, striding out, his face set and furious. His robe opened up. You could see his underwear, and Sadie flushed, shamed. "Where were you?" he said. "Your mother is out looking for you."

"Sir," Danny held out his hand. Bill looked at it for a moment and then back at Sadie. "It's very late," he said. "You were supposed to come inside and meet us before you took our daughter out." He looked at Sadie. "And you were supposed to be home on time."

"Sir, it's my fault," Danny said.

"You had better go now."

Danny nodded. He opened the door and stepped out, and then Bill shut and locked the door behind him. "How could you do this?" Sadie asked.

He looked at her as if she were a stranger. "How could you?" he said.

She was grounded for two weeks. She had to apologize to Louise, apologize to her father, but she didn't care, because every day during her lunch hour at Sweet Dreams, she met Danny and they drove someplace. They went to the next town and had coffee, they went into Boston and walked around and went on the swan boats, and they sat in his car and kissed.

When she wasn't grounded anymore, he made sure to show up on time, to talk to Bill and Louise, and show them the itinerary for the dates he had planned. "Dinner in the Square, then a movie at the Brattle," he said.

They never went. Instead, they went to Danny's house, because his mother was never home. They sprawled on her bed and watched TV or cooked dinner, and then ten minutes before Sadie's curfew, he drove her home. It was a whole secret world no one knew about but them.

The first time they made love was in his den. She felt small electric shocks. She tugged back, panicked. "I'm still not ready," she whispered. He stopped, so suddenly she felt stunned, and all she could think of was how much she wanted his hands touching her again, telling her secrets she didn't even know about her own self.

She didn't know what to do.

"You're everything to me," he said. And then he kissed her neck, her face, her fingers, and then she forgot to stay his hands, to protest. Instead, she shut her eyes. "I'm not ready," she whispered, but she arched her back and moved toward him, as if he were her fate. She memorized every part of him she could touch and see.

Afterward, she was silent. "Did I hurt you?" he asked. She looked up, rolling to her side, her face away from him, and he leaned over to her, brushing her hair from her face. "Sadie?" he said, and then she looked at him. She lifted up one hand and put it against his face. "Mine," she said.

* * *

It was that summer, just a month after she had started dating Danny, that Bill decided to go on vacation three weeks instead of two. "Three!" Sadie said. She couldn't imagine being away from Danny for three days, let alone three weeks. "I'm sixteen. Why can't I just stay home?" she said. "I could watch the house, get the mail, water the garden."

Bill shook his head. "This is a family vacation."

"That's right." Louise nodded.

Sadie argued and fought and finally Louise said, "Well if you really hate it, you can leave after a week, I suppose. You could take a train back." And Sadie threw her arms about her mother. Already, she was seeing it. The whole house and no one but her and Danny in it. This was it, she told herself. This was the last vacation.

The ride up to the Cape seemed longer than before, crawling with traffic. The drone of the radio bothered her. Bill was now completely silent, and Louise was talking far too much, making Sadie respond when all she wanted to do was sleep and dream about the way Danny kissed her. Sadie felt cramped in the backseat with the suitcases, the wicker picnic basket of sandwiches everyone was too hot to even nibble at. Her legs were too long. Her arms too ungainly. She sat in the car and thought about Danny. She stared out the window, while Karen Carpenter crooned that she had always just begun.

Sadie had taken her time packing for the beach, but once they got there she found that she had forgotten essential things. Her favorite sunglasses with the fake jewel tips. Sundresses. The library hadn't had any books she felt like reading so she was forced to take a trilogy about a young French wife living in Paris with her husband Pierre. Sadie kept the suitcase on her bed like an open mouth, telling everyone just how she felt about being there. She kept Danny's photo tucked in the bleary mirror over her dresser and every night she kissed it. She whispered endearments to him, as if he could hear her. I love you. I want you. I need you desperately. Desperately. She liked that word. It fit her. "Desperately," she said out loud.

Her parents got ready to go to the beach and she sprawled on her twin bed reading. Louise came in and frowned. Her hair was pinned up with a flower clip. She was in a bright yellow bikini and flip-flops and she smelled of lemony perfume. "You're not in your suit?"

"I'm not going. I hate the beach," Sadie said.

"Since when?"

"Since now."

Bill walked by, an armful of the ice-cream-colored shorts he liked to wear folded across his arm. "Come to the beach."

"I don't feel good." She put her hand on her head.

It was four days into the family vacation and her parents were fighting again over what to do about dinner. Louise wanted to go to Thompson's Clam Bar. Bill wanted to have corn on the cob at home. Bill sat silently in the kitchen, drumming his hands on the table and finally Louise jerked open a cabinet and slammed two plates down on the table, so forcefully one of them broke in two. "Fine," she said. "Here's your plate." They fought all that evening and that night when Sadie woke up to get a drink of water, she found her mother sleeping alone on the couch, her back to her, the sheets thrown off. Sadie crouched and picked up the sheet. She put it over her mother. She didn't stir.

Her parents fought when they went to Trader Vics, a tacky three-story souvenir shop Sadie had loved when she was in grade school. Her father refused to come inside but sat out in the broiling heat, waiting for them, his eyes hidden behind dark glasses. They fought at dinner—a cheap Italian restaurant with checked oilcloths on the tables—because her father still thought it was too expensive. "Look at these prices."

"This is a vacation!" Louise hissed.

"Can't you please just stop?" Sadie said.

"Watch your tone," Bill said.

"Eat your fries," Louise angrily ordered.

"What did I do?" Sadie demanded.

"Your fries—" Louise said. Sadie bolted up to find a phone, to call Danny, and found one in the back, and when she picked it up, there was no dial tone.

She came back to the table to find Bill handing the waiter the money, Louise shaking her head at the dessert menu, getting her sweater.

On the ride home, no one spoke. Bill turned on a droning ball game, and in minutes, Louise and Sadie began to sleep. Sadie dreamed. Danny was in front of her, telling her something, his words getting lost in the ball game. "Look," he said. He pointed to the highway, which had forked in two and was suddenly alive, curling up like a serpent about to strike.

And then she heard a shout, and a scream, and her eyes fluttered open and she saw that Louise was screaming, too, and that Bill was careening the car down the grassy embankment of the highway, frantically trying to steer, his feet banging on the breaks. The car rolled and bumped. Sadie's head snapped back. Louise braced her hands along the dashboard and then Bill jerked the wheel to the side and the car stopped. For a moment, no one moved, and then Louise scrambled out of the car, panting. She jerked open Sadie's door and then Bill's. She waited for him to climb out, and then she struck him so hard in the chest, he fell back a step.

"You fell asleep!" Louise screamed. "You fell asleep on the highway!"

Stricken, he stepped back. He ignored her. He crouched and studied the car. "We're alive," he finally said, but he kept looking at the car, touching it. He reached for Louise and then for Sadie, holding her so close she could feel his heartbeat. But Sadie didn't feel alive.

Sadie wanted to be anywhere but where she was and then Louise whirled around and glared at her. "Look at that face on you. You don't care if we died, do you?" she demanded. And for a moment, standing there in the shimmer of the heat and the road, the cars moving past like a river, Sadie didn't know.

They got back in the car. "I'm driving," Louise announced, and then Bill sat beside her, not saying a word, not commenting on the way she drove five miles below the speed limit, the careful way she took her turns.

As soon as they were back at the cottage, Sadie went outside and called Danny from the phone at the convenience store. "Come before I kill myself," Sadie urged.

He was driving to see her the next day. She kept repeating it to herself, imagine, he was driving all that way to come and see her! He couldn't stay, but he'd be there just when her parents went to the beach, which was perfect timing. He'd leave a half hour before they usually got back. She wouldn't tell them a thing.

The next day, before Danny was due to arrive, Sadie rushed her parents out of the house. Louise looked at her doubtfully. "Maybe I'll meet you at the beach later," Sadie faltered. Louise beamed.

They were gone only half an hour when Danny showed up, and then Sadie didn't quite recognize him. She couldn't tell if anything was different or not. She had never seen anyone so beautiful. She wanted to touch him, to swallow him whole inside of her. It was as if he had a sheen about him, like a kind of suntan oil, glossy and inviting, and if anyone had told her you couldn't fall in love more than once with the same person, Sadie would have told them they were nuts, because that was exactly what was happening to her.

Danny leaned forward and kissed her. His mouth tasted like salt, but not ocean salt. More as if he had been eating french fries. They went inside and sat on the couch and he smoked a cigarette and then he leaned forward and touched her, and then they were tumbling. They rolled on the ground, the windows wide open, they made love, and every time she dared to look at him, he had his eyes wide open. He was watching her.

"Well," Danny said. He stood up. Beautiful and naked, so easy in his own skin, Sadie couldn't help but admire him.

She listened to the water in the shower. One of them had to stand as lookout otherwise she would have just gone in there with him. Sadie tapped her fingers on the glass. She bent and picked up Danny's denim shirt and held it to her face. It felt as if a whirlpool had formed within her, spinning deeper inside. She put the shirt down, dazed. She picked up his pants and his wallet flew out. She knew she shouldn't. What kind of a girl was she? Didn't she trust him? She opened the wallet. A stick of gum. A driver's license with his blurry face. And a piece of paper. Evelyn, it said, 555-4577. Sadie felt sick. She went over to the phone and called. A girl answered. "Hello?" she said, and Sadie hung up. When Danny came out, his hair slick like a seal, his face sunburnt, Sadie was crying.

"Did I miss something?" Danny said, puzzled.

"Who's Evelyn?"

"She's no one." He looked around. "Why would you even say that name?"

"You had her name on a piece of paper. It . . . fell out of your wallet when I was picking your things up."

He sighed. "Sadie, I want you to come home."

He cupped her chin in his hands. He kissed her. "I'll call you tonight," he said and then Sadie made a decision. "I'm coming home," she said.

She was sprawled on the couch reading when her parents came back in. "You missed a wonderful day," Louise said.

"I'm going home," Sadie blurted. She stood up. "I'm going to take the train. I hate the beach. I hate the sun. No one else my age has to take vacations with their family." She looked at Louise. "You said if I stayed the week, I could go home. We agreed."

"You're staying here," Bill said.

Sadie shook her head. She looked at Louise. "You said if I had a bad time—"

"Sadie," Louise said, wearily, "can't you just stay?"

"You are staying. I'm your father and I say you're staying."

Sadie turned around, grabbed her purse, and headed for the door. "My father!" she cried angrily. "I'm going."

And then Louise was suddenly crying, suddenly grabbing for Sadie's arm. "Don't leave me here with him," her mother whispered and Sadie walked out the door.

* * *

Sadie wasn't sure where she was going. She had ten dollars in her pocket, and she jabbed her thumb out to hitch, but the only person who picked her up was a woman who scolded her for hitching and a guy who wanted to know if Sadie knew what fellatio meant. He smiled at her, clean, scrubbed, friendly. "It means I call the cops," Sadie told him, and he peeled to a stop. He leaned across her, making her stiffen, but all he did was pull up the button and jerk open the door. "Get out," he said, still smiling.

There was no place to go but the beach. She'd think what to do. Maybe she'd hitch. Maybe she'd get to the Greyhound Station and have enough to get somewhere. The beach was cold and dark and deserted. Kind of spooky, she thought. And then she heard a car slowing behind her. Great. The fellatio guy coming back to show her what he meant. Some other pervert. Some maniac. Well, she was in no mood to take anything from anybody. Sadie jammed up her third finger. She kept walking along the road and then she heard someone speak. "Sadie." Her name pulled like a hook deep in her throat. "Sadie." Sadie turned and there was her father in the car, and he was crying, his face crumpling. It was the first time she had ever seen him weep. It pinned her in place. "Please," he said. "Please get in, Sadie. Oh God, please."

He started to put his head on the wheel and then looked back at her. His face was streaked with tears. Sadie got into the car. He turned the motor off. He swiped one hand across his eyes. "I thought you had gone." His voice sounded different to her. "I didn't know what to do." His shoulders shook. His eyes were so swollen they were pin dots. He touched her and Sadie jolted back. "You're all I have."

"You have Mom."

He shook his head. "I never had your mom." He swiped at his eyes. "Your mother has no use for me. She never did. You think I don't know that?"

Sadie looked at him, shocked. Her side of the door was unlocked. She could jump out again. All she had to do was put her hand on the door and turn it. All she had to do was move one leg after the other.

"You said I don't know anything about you," her father said.

"But do you know anything about me? Did you know I wanted to be a doctor? That my father said fine, pay for it yourself. Did you know that? I tried to. I went to work, I saved, but I couldn't make enough to do more than go to community college and be a salesman. Did you know I suffered, too?" He looked at her. "Don't you love me? I know I'm not your mother's dream. I'm not the doctor I wanted to be. If you say I'm not your father, then what am I?"

He pulled her against him. She felt herself stiffen.

"Your mother said if I couldn't find you she would divorce me. She said I couldn't expect her to be in the cottage if you weren't with me." He kissed Sadie's face, her chin, the tips of her fingers.

"She wouldn't leave."

"She got the suitcase out." He held Sadie's hand in his right hand, and with his left, he snapped on the radio. A peppy tune chirped on. "You like this song?" he said hopefully. His grip tightened.

She had never heard it before. It sounded like an advertising jingle to her. "Sure. Sure I like it."

"See? Now I know something about you. I know you like this song. And you know something about me. That I like it, too. Now we know something about each other. It's something to build on, isn't it?"

He was staring at her, pinning her in place. Sadie nodded.

"Do you want to talk more? Is there anything else you'd like to know?"

"No." All the questions she had ever had about him folded back like a row of dominoes.

"Well, then, let's head back." He smiled at her. He stroked her face.

The drive home, he had one hand on the steering wheel, the other clasping her hand, tightly, as if he'd never let go. She sat as closely to him as she did with Danny. He parked in front of the cottage and ran around to her side to open the door, and as soon as she stepped out, he put his arm about her shoulders. His grip was tight. He was standing so close she could hear him breathe. He guided her back into the cottage, matching his steps to hers.

Inside, Louise's suitcase was open in the middle of the room. It was almost packed, blouses and swimsuits crammed in, shoes, and when Louise strode in, Bill pulled Sadie closer to him. "Everything is just fine now," he said boisterously. Sadie couldn't have moved even if she had wanted to. Sadie saw the look on Louise's face, an expression that struck her like a slap. Trapped. Louise was trapped. Sadie had given her a way out by leaving. And Sadie had betrayed her by coming back.

That evening, they went to dinner at The Clam Bar, the place Louise had been trying to convince Bill to go to all week. Bill ordered wine and they all clinked glasses and no one talked about anything. When Bill got up to go to the bathroom, she leaned toward her mother. "Are you mad I came back?" she said.

Louise looked at her.

"I didn't know what else to do," Sadie said.

"Why would I be mad? I was worried sick about you." Louise looked away, down at her plate, at the leftover lobster.

Sadie pushed her plate away from her. The lobster looked suddenly glutinous. "You could still leave." She made her voice low, as if she were telling a secret she didn't dare have anyone else know.

Louise laughed. "You think it's so easy?" she said, and then there was Bill, sitting down, and Louise seemed focused on something else now: her lobster, the napkin, the waiter.

"Who wants dessert?" Bill said. He looped one arm about the back of Sadie's chair, one arm about the back of Louise's. "Let's all get some."

They drove back to the cottage, the radio on, Bill and Louise talking about the beach, the weather, the things they might do the next day. Sadie pretended to doze. As soon as they got to the cottage, she yawned loudly. "I have to go to sleep," she said. She kissed Louise. She kissed Bill and then she sat in her room, listening, trying to hear what they were talking about, and then after a while, the cottage was silent.

She couldn't sleep. She quietly got up and went outside, walking to the pay phone by the beach. She squinted at her watch. It was two in the morning, but she had to call Danny.

"Yes?" A woman's voice, soft with sleep.

Danny's mother, Sadie thought, and it struck her suddenly that in all the time she and Danny had been going together, she had never met her.

"I'm sorry to call so late. I wouldn't if it wasn't an emergency. It's—it's Sadie."

"Sadie?"

"Sadie London. His girlfriend."

Danny's mother was quiet for a minute. "What's the matter, Sadie?"

"Please." Sadie couldn't help it. She started to cry. She sluiced at her tears with her fingers.

Danny's mother sighed. "Don't make this a habit," she said, and then there was the clunk of the phone and silence and then Danny got on, his voice slow and heavy. "Hello?" he said and Sadie burst into fresh tears. Please, she wanted to say. She wanted to tell him about her parents, to tell him how lonely she was, but instead her mouth just opened, it had a life all its own. It said what it wanted.

"Who was Evelyn?"

"Sadie, do we have to do this now? Can't this wait?"

"Look, I love you." Her own words shocked her. "If you can't handle it, tell me now. We can just forget everything."

He was silent. She could hear his breath moving through the wires. What have I done? she thought.

"Say it!" she screamed. "Just be honest!"

There was silence again. She heard something clicking through the wires. She'd hang up the phone, she'd walk right into the sea and hope for sharks. Or maybe she'd just hitch to New York.

"Okay," he said.

"What, okay," she said wearily.

"I love you." His voice was quiet. "Okay, I love you."

"What?"

"I love you."

"And you'll stop seeing Evelyn?"

"Evelyn who?" he said.

Sadie hung up the phone. Her heart was racing. She couldn't catch her breath. She turned and kept walking, to the beach. No one was there. The sand felt gritty. The water looked black. She thought of the movie *Jaws*, the first time she had seen it. There was a whole media blitz about it in Boston. Some theaters said right in their ads that they were going to hire ambulances to wait outside for customers who might faint, the same way they had for the opening of *The Exorcist*. She had gone to the movie alone. Before the movie even started, someone had run out screaming and the woman next to her had laughed and said, "That's a good sign." Sadie had watched *Jaws* with her feet up on her seat. She hadn't gone to the beach all the rest of that summer. She had been so terrified Louise had called up a marine biologist friend of hers and put him on the phone with Sadie. "Sharks don't act like that. That's the movies," he assured her.

"Oh." Sadie pretended to believe him.

She walked to the water, let it lap at her toes. A shark would be a huge white flash under all that water. You could disappear in ways no one could even imagine. She kept walking. She sat down, close to the waves. She thought about all the ways a family could configure, how you could spend your whole life just wanting to get out from under.

And then, she remembered this one time. She was six, her buttery curls flying about her head, untamed, playing this game with Louise. They ran around and around the house, racing out the front door and in through the back door, zooming through the messy kitchen, the dining room where the breakfast dishes still sat, the living room with Louise's fashion magazines sprawled across the floor. Nothing cleaned up. "Run!" Louise called, her voice a challenge. Sadie ran, tumbling and bolting up, scampering, the two of them laughing harder and harder. Stamping their feet, making a mess. "Run!" Sadie screamed. And then Louise zoomed out the door, and Sadie banged into the front door, smashing it into a million pieces. Everything went still. Glass sparkled across the front steps, through the front lawn. Sadie kept her head down. She clapped her hands over her ears, waiting.

And then Louise laughed, a bright bell. "Don't touch anything," she said, and then she crouched down. She cleaned up the glass herself. She called a glass man to come and fix the door and by the time Bill came home, he hadn't even noticed that anything was different, not even that the glass looked cleaner. Sadie waited, but Louise didn't say a word. Instead, when Bill was plunking down in the big brown chair by the window, leaning over to untie the shoes he hated, Louise winked broadly at Sadie. It was funny, but every time after that, every time Sadie passed the glass door, she remembered the chasing game. She remembered Louise's wink. The bright chiming bell in her laugh.

Sadie stood up. In a few hours, this beach would be mobbed again. Families. Lovers. Kids. Louise and Bill. And Sadie. She shucked off her shirt, her shorts, everything but her panties and bra, and then she ran into the water. She swam. Sharks or no sharks. Danny was coming again. They'd make love. He'd say sweet things, and maybe, if she was lucky, she'd believe them.

In the end, Sadie was right. It was the last vacation. The week before Danny was to leave for MIT, a girl named Betsy called her up and told her she was Danny's new main squeeze and had been for months. Why couldn't Sadie leave him alone? Why couldn't Sadie see how desperately Danny wanted to be free?

"Why couldn't you just tell me?" Sadie asked Danny, and he shrugged, embarrassed, and that was that. He went off to MIT and she went off to high school. She left early and came home late, and at night, she always said she had studying. Weekends, she had papers. Nothing changed in her family. The only change was that every time she looked at her parents, she knew what was keeping them in place, and it was too big a responsibility.

When Sadie went to college, she went to Stanford, as far away as she could get, and she found reasons not to come home. Summer school. An internship. New boyfriends, none of which ever worked out. She came home every Christmas, every May, just for a week, and every time she did, Louise had a million things planned, and Bill said hello and then went into his garden. Sadie sat in the kitchen, watching Louise peeling the skin from a chicken before she cooked it. "Fat," Louise said, tossing out the skin. "Your father's blood pressure has hit the roof. We eat like Spartans these days. The days of Cape Cod lobster dinners are over."

Sadie told Louise about a woman her mother's age who was taking classes, going for a new degree. She told Louise how a friend of hers had seen Louise's photo and exclaimed about her beauty. "Isn't that nice," Louise said.

"You could do that," Sadie said and Louise rolled her eyes. "Don't start with me, please," Louise said.

"Are things better? Are you happy?"

Louise laughed again. "Oh, to be young again," she said, "and believe in everything being possible."

Sadie spent all her time at home crazy to get away, but as soon as it came time to leave, she felt herself coming undone. It hurt her the way Louise looked so tired. It hurt her the way her father, even on his special diet, seemed to be putting on weight. She hadn't even left and already she missed them, but maybe it wasn't them she missed, maybe it was just the idea of them, the idea of family. She got back to her dorm room and flopped on the bed, depressed. She thought about her father, thought about the divorce/car wreck game she used to play, and then panic set in. What if there really was a car wreck? What if something really happened? She bolted up from her bed. She didn't have a boyfriend. She didn't have a best friend at school. She couldn't make the right connections, not the ones that stuck. She was alone in the world. She thought of her father saying, "If I don't have you, what do I have?"

She got up and grabbed a sheet of paper. She drew little hedgehogs on it, a summer garden sprouting from the margins. Hi Daddy, she wrote. I just wanted to tell you I love you and miss you! And then before she could change her mind, she mailed it.

A week later, she called home and Bill answered. "Did you get my letter?" she asked.

"Oh yes," he said. "Very nice." There was a silence. "Oh, here's your mother," he said. "She wants to speak to you."

That night, she got out her watercolor paper, two dollars a page, and painted a Garden of Eden. She put in Adam and Eve and the serpent, too. She gave him blue eyes and a bright red tongue. She wrote a one-page letter to her father. *We should have dinner together when I get home, just the two of us. We could talk.* She mailed it to Bill. She put on a return address so it wouldn't get lost. "Did you get my card?" she asked when she called, and he always said yes, as if it were the most usual thing in the world.

She began sending him more and more cards, each one more elaborate than the next. She bought special watercolors from France, she bought sable brushes and a rapidograph and hand-made paper with blue threads running through it. She felt guilty and made some for Louise, who gushed and carried on and called the moment the cards arrived. Finally, Sadie asked Louise, "Does Daddy look at my cards?"

"Of course he does, honey," Louise said.

"Does he say anything?"

"Oh. You know your father," Louise said. "What does he say about anything?"

Sadie was a senior in college when the call came. Stroke. In the garden, releasing a mail-order praying mantis Bill had special ordered, just as Louise was calling him in for the special nonfat healthy meal she had prepared for them, the no-fat dessert. Sadie flew home for the funeral.

She stayed two weeks. Her father hadn't had many friends, but the house was crowded with people Louise knew, all of them rubbing Louise's back, fitting cups of tea into her hand. "It wasn't a love affair," Sadie heard someone say to Louise, and Louise snapped up. "I liked him," she said furiously. "He was my husband."

Sadie drifted through the house. People were polite. They asked her how school was, if she had any boyfriends, and she was polite back. They told her stories about her father that she had never heard before, and then they waited, but the only story she could think about was that last Cape Cod vacation, and she didn't want to tell that. She felt as if she should be weeping, as if she should be telling stories, but instead, the only thing she felt was numb.

It wasn't until everyone left, until the house had emptied out, that she felt panicked. Louise looked around. "Let's just try to sleep. People will be here again tomorrow," Louise said.

They slept in Louise and Bill's bedroom. Sadie hesitated and then crawled into her mother's bed, the same way she used to when she was a little girl. Louise smelled of powder and sweat and starch. "I'm so tired," Louise said. "I'm so tired of everything." She shut her eyes. She looked to Sadie as if she were a hundred years old.

All that night, Sadie lay awake while her mother slept, watching her, and then, toward morning, Louise bolted up, crying, terrified, her hands washing over her face. "I'm here!" Sadie cried. "I'm here!" Louise blinked, and flung herself into Sadie's arms. "I want him back," she wept. "I want him back."

Sadie soothed her mother's back. She clutched her mother's hand. She said whatever she could think of. "I'll come back more often. I'll call every night."

"I want him back!" Louise wept. Sadie spooned as close as she could, rocking Louise, until morning, until it was time to get up all over again.

Sadie stayed for another week, until she had to go back for finals. The house was always crowded with people, the phone never stopped ringing, and Louise began thanking God for what she had. "Thank God I have my work," she told Sadie. "Thank God I have the neighbors. Thank God I made so many friends."

Sadie waited. Thank God I have you, she heard, but her mother didn't say it.

"Go. I'll be fine," Louise said. "Really. Thank God I'm not the kind of mother who lives through her kids."

On Sadie's last day, all the company began to be too much for Sadie. She was tired of dressing up, tired of having to avert the plates of food handed to her. Her mother was sitting on the couch, deep in conversation with a neighbor. Someone touched Sadie's arm. She turned. "You're so thin," a woman Sadie didn't know said to her, and Sadie half-smiled, thinking it was a compliment. "You look like a skeleton," the woman said.

Sadie excused herself. She went into her parents' room and shut the door tight.

Sadie sat on the bed, staring around the room. Her mother had made arrangements for Goodwill to take Bill's things away. "I don't want to have to touch anything. I don't want to be reminded," Louise said. Sadie slowly got up and opened her father's closet. There was his heavy jacket. There were his gray ties. She opened his drawers. Tucked under his socks, she found a high-fat candy bar, a half-eaten bag of potato chips, a package of Chips Ahoy cookies. She pulled them out and threw them into a wastebasket. She opened the second drawer. Socks, balls of color, lined up like little soldiers. She ran one hand over them and as they parted, she spied something. An envelope.

She pushed the socks aside and pulled it out. She opened the clasp and there, inside, were all the letters she had sent him, all the decorated envelopes. She sat down on the bed. The edges of her letters were dog-eared, as if he had read them more than once. Sadie fanned through the letters and began to cry.

"Sadie?" Someone rapped on the door. "Sadie, are you in there?" She didn't recognize the voice. Sadie swiped a hand over her eyes. She rubbed at her drippy nose. And then she pulled out her suitcase from under the bed and opened it, and gently lay the letters in it, under her blue sweater, carefully, so they wouldn't crush. "Sadie?" the voice called again. Sadie shut the case and pushed it under the bed. She stood up.

"I'm here," she said, "I'm right here," and then she opened the door.

[CAROLINE LEAVITT]

According to Caroline Leavitt, this novelette started with a single image, that of "a teenage girl alone on a dark beach at night, her father weeping in a car on the street." Almost immediately, the image took on a life of its own, and the novelette was well on its way to completion. No other writer I have known can match the speed at which Leavitt turns out narratives with such complexity, poignancy, and staying power as "The Last Vacation."

"I was really interested in the proverbial ties that not only can bind a family together," says Leavitt of the story, "but also can act as a garrote. And I also wanted to explore how abuse doesn't have to be as violent or dramatic or physically obvious as it is often portrayed, but that it sometimes can be subtle, delicate, and even more difficult when there is also genuine love involved."

Her novels include Family, Jealousies, Into Thin Air, Lifelines, *and the more recent* Living Other Lives, *which received a starred review from* Publishers Weekly. *Her short prose, for which she is a National Magazine Award Nominee, has appeared in* Parenting, Redbook, McCalls, New Woman *and* Salon.

Praise for her writing has come from such auspicious sources as The New York Times Sunday Book Review, *which cited "her ability to create believable characters who can behave badly without forfeiting the reader's sympathy."*

After meeting her for lunch at Zen Palate in Manhattan one March afternoon, I can see how this is not only possible but would be expected of her writing. Leavitt, the person, is so unaffected and kind, that even the worst of her characters can't help but have redeeming qualities.

Her newly completed novel will be published by Saint Martin's Press.

—C.O.

ONE LONG CELEBRATION

Martha Coventry

CLOSE TO DINNERTIME, AN OLD FRIEND AND I WALK OUR dogs on the path around a city lake. Near the place where I turn off to my house and she continues on to hers, the smell of something cooking on an outdoor grill comes to us in the autumn wind. I raise my nose and sniff. "Hm . . . Tuna," I say. My friend looks at me, amused. "That's your father in you, isn't it?"

He was a Minnesota boy, my father. Born in Duluth with Lake Superior dazzling before him and behind, woods that stretched all the way to Canada. On the canoe trips he took as a young man in the boundary lakes and tannin-dark rivers of that country, he was always the cook—minutes-fresh trout filets fried fast and hot in a cast-iron pan, scattered with bits of almost-burnt bacon, pineapple upside-down cake, the fruit caramelized around the edges when he lifted the pan off the fire and flipped the cake over onto the lid. He grew up with the solid cooking of the Swedes, Finns, and Cornish people who came to work the mines and log the white pine, and he developed a desire for the more elusive and remarkable flavors of the world. As a young wartime surgeon in 1945, he wrote home to my mother from the Philippines that he had seen some men cutting down a palmetto. He drove back to camp, got a machete, and returned quickly to harvest the hidden heart of palm. He steamed it, chilled it, and served it to his friends with a homemade vinaigrette.

When I was born seven years later, a shining and unbreakable filament of love attached itself between my father and me. On early summer evenings, playing in the house as a little girl, I would hear car wheels on the gravel driveway through the windows wide open to the still-cool Minnesota air. My father coming home from work. I would run to be the first to greet him—his hand reaching for the knob on one side as I reached for the knob on the other side of the thick plate glass of the back door. He'd stoop to hug me, or I would wrap my arms around his legs and he would thump me on the back while he leaned over to kiss my mother on the mouth.

Trailing him through the kitchen and up to his dressing room, I chatted away like he'd been gone for a month. When he changed out of his suit and tie and into an old shirt and khakis, he'd say, "Let's go see what's in the garden for dinner," and back we'd go to the kitchen. My father would grab the chipped enamel colander and a knife and I'd take his hand. In the garden, he'd cut off the short, thick stalks of new asparagus where they grew out of their bed of straw. Then we'd pick some lettuce for the salad my mother would make. On the way back to the house with the vegetables, we'd discuss whether to steam the asparagus just right and eat the spears with our fingers, or cut them up and poach them in milk like my father's stepmother used to do. I liked asparagus in milk, then, with butter melting yellow against the green and white, the fresh-cracked pepper floating spicy and dark. As my father mixed a drink for my mother and him and got to work on the rest of the dinner, my mother soaked the lettuce in cold water. Then she would drain it, gather it in a dish towel, and send me outside to swing the bundle round and round. I'd see how fast I could go, bare feet planted in the dewy grass, watching the drops of water spinning off like fat diamonds into the sky.

On the weekends, my father went to the hospital in the mornings and Saturdays were taken up with errands and friends. But

Sunday afternoons were sweet fragrant hours in anticipation of the dinner to come as my father and I worked side by side. We lived in the country and there were always chores to do—fallen trees to cut and potatoes to dig, bonfires to tend and fences to repair. And each task had its companion smell of fresh sawdust or black dirt, wood smoke or the metallic sharpness of barbed wire. Sometimes, we'd head south to the Root River where an old patient of my father's lived. He'd show us where to hunt for morels under oaks or dying elms and the best streams for watercress growing piquant and clean in the chilly springtime waters.

In the quickly darkening days of winter, my father and I would spend most of the afternoons cooking—a beef daube, perhaps, or some more complicated dish that we seemed to have all the time in the world to make. We'd add this and that and then taste, add more things, then taste again. "What does it need!" my father would ask, eyebrows raised, as I'd gingerly slurp some hot broth or long-reduced sauce from the wooden spoon he held out to me. We'd admire the little stars of anise before tossing them into a simmering pork loin, or grind cardamom and coriander in the wooden mortar and pestle releasing their faraway flavors into our familiar kitchen. My father would strip basil leaves from the stalks he'd cut from the garden the summer before and rub them in his big hands. "Here. Smell this basil," and he'd stretch out his dusty hands for me to bury my face in. There would be good music on the radio and the sound of logs snapping in the fireplace in the living room. My mother would be somewhere around the house knitting or reading, wandering into the kitchen every once in awhile to smile at us. Even as a child, I knew there was something precious about those times with my father, as we moved easily with each other from cutting board to sink to stove and oven.

My father drank California wines when he was stationed there at the start of the war, and in the 1950s, he began to study wine in earnest. When I got old enough, eleven or twelve, to taste a little wine, I became his avid apprentice. "So, what smells do you get?" he'd ask after we'd whirl the wine around to coat our glasses, I always careful not to slosh any over the rim. "Blackberries, maybe?" I'd offer. "Do you get a little damp earth, too?" he'd wonder. My father always asked, never told me what to find in the tangle of flavors in my mouth and nose. We honed our palates together, learning to pick up nuances of taste. He drank more wine more often than I did, obviously, and his knowledge quickly surpassed my own, but he was proud of my fledgling skill and I loved it that he was proud of me. With a friend, he founded a chapter of the International Wine and Food Society in our little prairie town and I'd crouch on the floor of my bedroom with big white sheets of poster board and make maps of the wine regions of France or Italy or Germany for the dinners and wine tasting we'd have at our house.

My father and I were held together by much more than food and wine—we talked about art and books, rode horses and skied together, and explored the woods. But food and wine just made us both absurdly happy. We could spend hours clarifying butter, cutting translucent thin slices of potatoes, drying each one, arranging them in layers with spoonfuls of butter to make a perfect pommes Anna—a crispy tender masterpiece of a potato cake. When it stuck to our American pan and looked not quite like its picture, we didn't much care. And wine was an intricate, joyous adventure—we'd pour over the wine catalogs and place an order, then the wooden crates would arrive with the name of the wine and picture of the vineyard burned into the smooth pine. We'd unpack the cool, shiny bottles, brushing off the strands of excelsior clinging to them, and decode their pristine labels, plain and ornate. Then the first tastings. My mother was the blissful recipient of our enthusiasms. Good wine and food came to her as marvelous gifts, appearing to her delight in her glass and on her plate.

While in her sixties, my mother began to show signs of Alzheimer's and ten years later she was dead. After her death, I returned home even more often to see my father. As I drove up to the house, he would come out to meet me and we would hug each other long and hard. He was still robust and stoic, but cancer was making its way into his body. I'd walk into the kitchen of my childhood and something lovely and special would welcome me—gravlax made with dill from the garden, an apple tart with crème fraîche, a wine waiting to be uncorked and shared. Dumping my stuff in my old room, I would see the flowers next to my bed. Always a few newly cut blooms in a small vase.

My father and I called each other on the phone almost every night before dinner. We talked about what books we were reading and about my daughters. He would tell me how he was feeling and I'd ask, "What are you making for dinner, Dad?" It was invariably something good like poached halibut and sautéed peppers, garlic mashed potatoes, and a salad. Even alone and ill, he never gave up on food.

When it came time for him to die, my father had a hospital bed set up in what we called the music room—a butternut-paneled, cork-floored room with a small hearth in the corner where, when my sisters and I were children, my father cooked legs of lamb on a spit, basting them with oil and vinegar, garlic and rosemary. This is where we often ate dinner together, on an old English pub table, candles glowing soft against the worn wood. He placed his bed so he could look both into the room and out the big picture windows to the lawn and pasture beyond.

My father was fairly keen until the last few days, when the pain got worse and the morphine dose increased. Then his eyes became unblinking and his great handsome head fixed toward the ceiling. I sat by his side and stroked his hand. I felt I needed to help him die. After quietly talking to him on this last afternoon, I thought I would read out loud a little. I looked at the bookshelves behind him, and saw M. F. K. Fisher's *As They Were*. It seemed fitting to read of food and cooking, to visit one last time the place that brought us so much joy. But perhaps I read more for myself, the one left behind, than I did for my father. By that time, his soul was already somewhere else.

On Labor Day, five years after his death, I gathered around the table with my closest friends at the cabin my parents built. My mother had died before any of them knew her well, but they all had known my father and loved him. We were eating chickens cooked crackly-skinned and smoky from the Chinese oven my father built and drinking a few of the last wines from his cellar.

When it came time for a Château Lalande-Borie, which I guessed might be the best of the evening, I poured some in a glass to take to my daughters. I went into the other room where they were playing board games with their friends, and they turned from Risk and Monopoly to focus their adolescent pleasure on the taste and smell and color of their grandfather's wine.

I miss my father most in the late afternoons. The September sun is pale today as it slants into the cabin through the birch trees and spruce outside the windows. Everyone has gone back to the city and I am alone here. If my father were with me, we'd be talking about food. How to cook a piece of lake trout or whether we have time to make floating island for dessert. My father would open a bottle of wine as we talked in the kitchen and pour us each a glass. We would stand for a moment and touch our glasses together and I would feel, as I did every time we made that gesture, an inward bowing to each other, an unspoken gratitude that we got to go through this life together.

Walking up through the woods from the lake after the last swim of the season, I heard a faint chirping in the ground near a fallen split-top balsam. I squatted quietly next to the stump, hoping I could follow the sound back to the insect that was making it. I wasn't quiet enough and it stopped, but as I waited, the little sunlit patch of forest floor before me suddenly looked as beautiful as any place on earth. And I wondered if when my father taught me how to love wine and food, he taught me how to love the world. It is the small things that matter—the raisiny gold of a Sauternes, a hint of tangerine in a fish velouté, one freshly plucked rose petal curling on a dish of chilled rice pudding. And here in the woods, the underside of a wood orchid leaf brightened by the setting sun, or the delicate softness under my fingers of the tiny green tendrils reaching up from a thick billow of moss. Every ingredient, every thing, is perfect in its own right. Each eggplant, torn basil leaf, chive flower. Each duck wing and squid sac. Each raspberry and muddy potato. And everything is waiting to meet another swirling wonderful thing of the world to create an astonishment, a comfort, a memory.

[MARTHA COVENTRY]

Two accomplishments that give this fourth generation Minnesotan a sense of personal pride and happiness are learning French and starting a school.

"I fell in love with French and France when I was probably about nine or ten and I began looking at those lovely wine labels on my father's wine," she says. "They were so beautiful and instilled in me not only a curiosity about the language, but about the place. Where were these vineyards? What was their climate? What was the entire region like where the grapes grew? What food did they eat there?"

Coventry started taking French lessons. "I was a lousy student," she admits, "but my love of French kept me going. I went away to school in Massachusetts in the tenth grade, but my prep-school career was cut short by the fact that I was getting failing grades in French—I could not keep up academically and was not asked to return. But I had some kind of devotion to French that wouldn't let go."

In fact, she worked so hard at it that she earned both a B.A. and master's degree in the discipline. As a result, she ended up teaching it, as well as translating a book, *Rose Blanche*, from the French, which went on to win the Batchelder Award for children's literature.

What about the second accomplishment?

"The school I founded with three other friends is a Waldorf school," she says. "It grew out of kitchen-table conversations and a kind of naive *why don't we start a school! impulse.* Never once did we think we couldn't pull it off. We just plugged away at it.

"My daughter was gravely ill at the time and somehow the planning and dreaming for this place for her and her sister, as well as other children, helped me. My daughter survived and is thriving and she will graduate this year from a Waldorf high school. The school that started in the living room of a little house in my neighborhood now has 200 students and is about to move into a beautiful new building of its own."

Upon tasting the rich literary textures Coventry freely gives to readers in her essay for this book, I needed to ask her about her father's effect on her own children. Had the legacy of love for food that he had passed down to her been willed to her children, as well?

"You know," she tells me, "I think about that all the time!

"My daughters spent a lot of time with my father—they were nine and thirteen when he died—and he had a huge influence on how they see the world. He left many things in my children's hearts—a capacity for kindness and a sense of service among them. But love of food is right up there, providing them and me with so much pleasure every day.

"With my children, there was never any neurotic, picky stuff around food, no intense dislikes, no 'I'm not eating anything green!' kind of thing, and I attribute that to my father, to a large extent. We spent a lot of time with my parents at my childhood home or our cabin, cooking and eating the most wonderful food. And it was always presented as if it were both special and totally ordinary. As if this delicious stuff was part of the world like trees and bird songs and snow. Sometimes, now, they will cook for me—mostly pastas with a simple sauce and salads with homemade dressing—but mostly I cook for them, and it is a terrifically gratifying experience."

Coventry sums up: "Food is a very joyful thing in our house, thanks to my father. And my children are consciously and gratefully aware that this is a gift that he has given to them."

Coventry works for Utne Reader and is currently writing a memoir.

—C.O.

MY REAL FATHER

Jane Bernstein

My real father is gone, I tell myself when I enter the nursing home to visit the man with my father's name. Downstairs is the easy part—highly polished cherry furniture and reproductions of Impressionist paintings of girls in bonnets with streaming ribbons and bouquets of flowers. The elevator is straight ahead. It takes only a moment—never enough time—to go from that pleasant lobby to the dementia unit, where I will find the person who is not my father, but bears the name and some outward resemblance to the man I call "Daddy."

I find him right away. The man who is not my father sits for most of the day in a plastic-covered wing chair. A year before, I could touch his loose, mottled skin—not my father's skin—and gently wake him. I could get him to walk with me. I could convince myself that my hand in his did some good. But now it is hard to rouse him, and even if I can get him to open his eyes, he looks at me blankly and shuts them again, sleep as compelling to him as a ball game once was. So I leave my father, the dementia unit, the benign, motel-like lobby, and go on with my life. But that day or the next, I will see a man in a cap and windbreaker, and imagining for an instant that it's my father I will hurry close. When I glimpse his face, I find it's not him, of course, nor someone who looks like him now, but a much younger version of my father, a daddy from decades back.

My father was a travelling salesman and most weeknights was out of town, and so when I remember him, what I remember is his absence. These are not sad memories: when Daddy was on the road, we told stories about him and created a daddy for ourselves, a perfect daddy, who was *"shane v'ya madel,"* in my grandmother's words. Handsome like a girl, loved by everyone, a great athlete. When my father was travelling, my sister and I liked to page through my mother's old-fashioned photo album, with its black pages, the captions beautifully written in white ink below the small, sepia photos. My father is in motion in most of the shots—rowing a boat, carrying a sled, holding a bat. In that last photo, small, soft, bleached-out, he wears a uniform and a beanie-type cap. I studied that photo and when I was young showed it as proof that my father played for a minor league team. I told this story so many times that I became proud of my father for doing this thing that I had imagined.

My real father was not boastful. Except for his triumphs as a high-school sprinter, he never bragged or postured or pretended to be anything but what he was—a Jewish guy from Brooklyn. He never spoke of his childhood poverty, though his parents, Russian immigrants, crammed their six children into a tenement and tried to feed them on his father's salary as a presser in the garment industry. They weren't the kind of Jewish immigrants with a reverence for books and education, like my mother's parents, whose hopes were pinned on the next generation. Surely my father's success was more than his parents might have dreamed possible. But he never spoke of his past struggles or thought of himself as successful, though of all the brothers, he was the one who bought a house, and a new car every second year, the one who made "good money."

Until the day he lost his language, he described himself as a travelling salesman. His line was kitchen gadgets. Pennsylvania and New York was his territory. When I was young, there were as many "travelling salesman," jokes as jokes about farmers' daughters. You said, "travelling salesman," and people thought of shabby hotels, bar flies, beat-up cars, sample cases, desperation. They thought Willy Loman. I learned that I could call my father a "manufacturer's representative" and say he sold housewares to customers like Macy's and Bloomingdale's. But it was not the way he described himself.

When I was young, he left home every Monday morning and returned home Friday night. Picture this as a jumpy home movie. Two little girls in pajamas, balanced on the top of the sofa, jumping, kicking, pinching each other, angling for Indian burns. Suddenly the dog stands: his ears go erect. A car door slams. The girls are up in a flash, jiggling in the doorway, pushing each other, waving, yelling, calling "Daddy, Daddy."

Then after that it is blank, for I remember what it felt like to love my father, and I remember being proud of him for things he did and things I imagined him doing. And that's about it.

My father woke early on Saturday mornings. He took the dog out for a walk, smoked his first cigarette, drove to the bakery for rye bread or jelly donuts. And then, after breakfast, he strolled down our street. There were eleven split-level houses on our block, all of them built in 1954. Everyone moved in that year; everyone stayed. My father played with whichever boys were outside or picked crabgrass with the screwdriver or awl he kept in his back pocket for this purpose. In summer, he meandered in old shorts, shirtless, feet bare. If he mowed the lawn, he put on old shoes for safety and tied a rag around his brow to soak up the sweat. He was a warm, brown, well-muscled man who liked the sun. I remember how he would go outside, take a deep lungful of air, and say, "Ahhhhh!" as if feeling the sun was enough for him to experience the sheer pleasure of being alive.

My father liked to grow things, so our yard in New Jersey was verdant. We had strawberries all along the perimeter of the back yard, grape vines, peach trees, a vegetable patch. In the first few years, before we ran out of space, he would occasionally dig up a sapling from the woods or parks in Pennsylvania and replant it in our yard. We got our locust tree that way, and a mimosa that he had transplanted when it was no more than six inches high. The tree grew well, spreading its graceful branches and pink, fringed flowers.

I knew my father loved people, though it never occurred to me that what he loved was people in general, their warmth and conversation. And I knew he had a special feeling for my older sister, Laura. My sister and I had comfortably acknowledged that she was Daddy's favorite and Mommy liked me best, dividing our parents as if they were a deck of cards. All this was fine, until I was around eight and began to hanker for something more tangible than the stories we created about him. I did not know what I wanted or how to get it, though if I could have put it into words it would have been a simple thing: Look at me. Everything I did rephrased this same request.

I sang all the verses to "On Top of Spaghetti All Covered with Cheese," told elephant jokes, ate dog biscuits. Shy of any obvious talent like singing or dancing, I learned to wiggle my ears while my eyes were crossed and to bend my fingers at odd angles. I may have lacked dimples and blonde ringlets, but I could laugh convulsively and stand on my head.

My mother was not fooled. I was just looking for attention, she said. Trying to be cute. Such an actress.

And my father? What was his opinion of my clever tricks? Where was he, while Mom and Laura begrudgingly watched me straddle my desk chair and pluck out an approximation of "Mary Had a Little Lamb" on the instrument I had created by weaving rubber bands at different tensions through the rungs of the chair.

Weeding the Perlmutters' lawn. Bringing tomatoes to the Schwartzes. Playing ball with Fred Fatell.

I tried to be my father's son. I had worked up a story about how disappointed he was that I was a girl and tried to make myself into a boy. Because this was the 1950s, when the roles for boys and girls were so rigidly defined, to me, being a boy meant playing sports. I hid from him all the things I thought made me a girl and begged him to teach me how to throw, catch, and bat.

I begged in an annoying, exaggerated, trying to be cute, please-oh-please-pretty-please-with-sprinkles-on-top kind of way. One night after dinner, he oiled up his baseball mitt, and after a long discourse on the importance of keeping the leather supple, walked me to the playground across the street. But the gnats were swarming and so we went right home. On another morning, some time later, he agreed to teach me to play tennis. We found a can of balls and two rackets in their screw-corner frames in the recreation room closet. Then we drove the half mile or so to the tennis court at Glen Rock High School, a ride that seemed interminable because of my father's conviction that all of the courts would be taken.

They weren't. I walked through the gate onto an empty court, stood at what I now know is the service line, and waited. My father handed me a ball. "Here," he said. "Hit a few against the backboard." Then he disappeared.

I did not feel neglected by my father after these failed attempts at being a boy. Nor did it occur to me, even once, that perhaps my father wasn't interested in teaching me to bat or play tennis, that perhaps he did not have a clue how to teach a kid anything. My father was godlike to me, utter perfection. The nicest father on the block. When someone asked Dickie Paganello, our eight-year-old neighbor, to name his best friend, he said, "Dave." My father. When my friends came over, he made them borscht or offered them chocolates he brought home from Reading, Pennsylvania.

I saw my failures as proof that I was a klutz, a girl. I was not unloved, like my friend Faye. Her father, a handsome, strapping, one-legged Veteran of World War II, was so cold, so mean that he bought Faye a chair for her thirteenth birthday. (A chair! we whispered in horror.) Faye and I hatched a plan to get our fathers to take us fishing. It was a fix-up date really. Our dads had a lot in common, we decided. They had curly hair, were Brooklyn born and bred. Both were "in sales."

We were successful. Our fathers agreed to take us deep-sea fishing on a party boat down on the Jersey shore, not far from where we lived. During the drive to the marina, the men talked the whole time. Faye and I sat in the back, squeezing each other's hands in excitement. They were still talking when we arrived. My friend and I lugged the coolers and towels onto the dock, then seeing our fathers strolling together with the fishing gear, we whispered: Look, they like each other.

We boarded the boat, and they said: Here, let the captain show you how to bait the hook. And then left us to dream about sinking our hooks and reeling our daddies back in.

Didn't you ever get angry? Didn't you resent your father?

Yes! I did get angry with my father, and I stayed that way. It was 1967, and I was eighteen and a freshman in college. My sister had been dead for a year by then, and my father was hardly my only target. I was angry with my school for its ties to the military-industrial complex, with the U.S. government for its imperialistic policies, with my old friends for being apolitical, with my mother for being "such a liberal." I was angry that when I came home from school, my mother always woke me at 8 A.M., made me stumble downstairs for breakfast, where I would always find a glass of orange juice at my place. I was angry that she could not remember that I hated juice.

I went to school in New York, only twenty miles from home, but I wrote letters instead of phoning. I was angry that I addressed these letters "Dear Mom and Dad," and that only Mom answered, though at her urging, I suspected, Dad sometimes added a postscript sending love and kisses.

At home, the anger I felt was channeled into fierce battles about politics. My father was not part of these fights—he seemed not to have any opinions about world events. He did not play Scrabble with us or sit with us in the living room until the timer switched off all the lights. Instead, he would be off somewhere, working at his desk, or watching a game on TV, magically appearing only if I tiptoed into the kitchen for a late-night snack, and then to offer me some bizarre concoction, like ice cream and prunes.

Sometimes during the visit my mother would say, "Your father is delighted to see you." Or: "Your father says you look well."

It was as if he lived in a different country and spoke another tongue, and my mother was his sole interpreter. Occasionally there were messages from his land. "Your father hates patent-leather shoes," my mother might say. Or, "Your father is very proud."

"Why doesn't he tell me?" I asked, as if once he had and now he didn't.

One weekend I came home to tell my parents that I had moved in with my boyfriend. This was in 1970, before cohabitation had made the cover of *Time*, and I was thought by my friends to be uncommonly bold. No one could imagine telling their parents they were having sex. Now I see this as yet another attempt at getting my father to talk to me, though at the time I believed I was doing this for moral reasons. To have them pay for an apartment I no longer used was wrong, I thought. Sleeping with my boyfriend was not. Still, I could barely breathe, I was so nervous about speaking the words.

I remember the weekend well. I arrived late on Friday. The next morning, my mother woke me from a deep sleep at 8 A.M. I appeared at breakfast, bleary-eyed, dressed in the old bleach-stained robe I had left in my closet and moved the glass of juice off my place mat. Why don't you drink your juice? My mother asked. I hate juice, I said between my teeth. Later that day, my mother and I argued loudly but amiably about politics. My father visited people and watched football. Late at night, he offered to make me a chicken and cranberry relish sandwich.

I took the train back to New York. As soon as I was in my apartment, I sat down at the phone and made myself call home. I had trouble fitting my shaking fingers into the dial.

"Ma," I said. "I'm living with Allan."

My mother said, "I thought so."

The next day she phoned. "Your father wants to talk to you," she said. "He's very upset."

When I went home a couple of weeks later, I placed myself in the same room as my dad—timid, nervous, yet anxious to have his eyes meet mine, to hear him say something directly to me. I stood by his desk. I followed him downstairs to the recreation room. I sat on the front steps while he mulched the shrub beds.

On my next visit I waited, and on the one after that. "And I'm still waiting!" I heard myself say at a dinner party, ten years later, laughing hard, enjoying the story.

Twenty years later, thirty. I was still waiting for my father to talk to me, still waiting like a chick with my beak open, cheeping, flapping my wings. And so my grudge toward my father deepened. I did not quarrel with him, but something hardened inside me. The stories that come out of this hard place continued, for wasn't it true that when I became a runner and wanted so much to share my enthusiasm with him, he could only speak of his high-school triumphs? And wasn't it true that when my husband said, "We're talking about *her* race, not yours," my father proclaimed my performance, "piss poor." And wasn't it true that even after I published my first novel, my father could not seem to recall that I had accomplished something, did not remember that I worked?

At the time, I was living in a suburban town in New Jersey. My father had a customer there, whose housewares store was around the corner from my house. "He wants to visit you when he calls on Jack," my mother said.

I was sitting in my parents' kitchen, eating the orange my father had cut in quarters for me.

"I work during the day," I said.

"You have a job?" he asked. "What do you do?"

"I'm a writer," I said. "I'm working on a new book."

We had this conversation several times, and each time, my father seemed momentarily surprised to hear I had a job. And then he simply forgot it. When he came to town, he stopped at my house. I am ashamed to remember the time I did not answer the doorbell when it rang. When I think about it now it makes me weep, for I also remember the times I did answer the door, and there he was, handsome in a tweed sports jacket, arms full of gifts for me—a turnip, a Vidalia onion, beefsteak tomatoes wrapped in newspaper. There would be a gadget or two, returns that were slightly banged up, or gadgets that were oddly repaired by him, like the vegetable steamer with a screw for its third leg. Often there was an item he had found in the street—a man's hat or a sweater—for my father was always picking up things "in the gutter" and pressing upon me strangers' clothing that was "perfectly good."

Later, I moved to Pittsburgh and had a title—"professor"—and a business card. Though I still worked in my house, when my parents visited, I had to dress up and leave, if I expected my father to recall that I worked. I remember him sidling up to me as I was on my way out, saying, "When do you knock off?"

And I said, "Five," as if that was the time I would punch out. Then I drove to a coffee shop, sat at a small table in the back, and did the work that was meaningless, utterly forgettable in his mind.

My parents' neighborhood changed first. By 1992, most of the original neighbors were gone, their houses bought by young Russian émigrés who paid top dollar for the split-level houses that were so much the image of U.S. postwar prosperity. My father, at eighty-one, was at last retired. He settled into a routine of swimming three times a week at the Jewish Community Center. But there were no more kids on the block, and hardly anyone to visit.

That summer—my parents' last in New Jersey—I began to notice my father's lapses in memory, the small things that suddenly confused him. But I tucked this knowledge neatly out of reach. It was easy to do, for my father was still broad-shouldered and handsome, so fit he competed in the Senior Olympics. I competed in the triathlon that same summer and finished second in my age group. While I had no need to talk about it, I boasted to everyone about my father's gold medals in discus and in the 50-meter freestyle, neglecting to mention that in several events, he was the only competitor in the over-80 division. I was so childlike in my pride at having a dad who was stronger and faster than anyone. I never really imagined that time would catch up.

With my father, it wasn't a broken hip that set off his decline. It was his teeth. Shortly after my parents moved to Pittsburgh, his implants began to loosen. He had lost so much bone in his lower jaw that the posts had to be surgically removed. It took months for his gums to heal. During that time, his appearance changed radically, transforming my father from a handsome gentleman to a geezer with a sunken mouth. His face was often nicked and poorly shaven. It was hard to understand his speech. My father did not want to swim or have lunch at the new Jewish Community Center. My mother said it was because he didn't know anyone. But I knew there was something else. It was too difficult for him to make conversation. Even after he got dentures, he could not shmooz, could not win people over, could no longer make strangers into friends.

What followed next was worst, for over these next months, my father was often frustrated and confused. "The marbles are rattling in my head," he told me once. He was still going to movies and concerts, still driving, but his lapses were odd and alarming.

"Wasn't there another one?" he whispered to me one day.

"Yes," I said. "Laura."

Another time, he asked, "Wasn't there a Martha?" using the name I had stopped using over thirty years before.

I saw what was happening to my father. Alzheimer's, I had begun to think. Now that I could no longer expect recognition, the knot of anger dissolved. I noticed then how he brightened when I visited, saying, "I'm tickled to death to see you!" and laughing his velvety laugh.

My house was two and a half hilly miles from my parents. When my father began to wander—to run away, really—he often ended up at my door. The wandering made my mother frantic, for my father would sneak out early in the morning or he would leave after a quarrel.

I took my father in after these long journeys, oddly pleased to be alone with him. I would make him a cup of tea and give him cookies, then watch him turn the cookie in his hand and take a bite. Noticing the pleasure he took in its taste, I saw my father for what he had always been, a man who liked to eat, to talk to strangers, to walk, a man whose joys were elemental—sunshine, green grass, food, people's voices. He was not a thinker, driven and analytical. Nor was he a dad from a 1950s TV sitcom, who would put his arm around my shoulder and say, "Son, you want to hold the bat like this." The kind of attention I had demanded had never been in his repertoire—ever. He had always been scattered, distractible, inarticulate. His gifts were his good cheer and love of life, his simple innocence, his affection for everyone, his blind trust in a world even after it had not treated him well.

There is one other sweet memory of this dreadful time, two years after my father's decline had begun. I had just moved to a different house, with a back room that had windows on three sides, and above them, stained glass. One day, shortly before my mother could no longer care for him, she brought him to my new house. His language was almost gone by then. I walked him into the back room, helped him into a chair. My father sat straight and turned in every direction. He took a deep breath. "This is," he said, and paused, the word stuck, elusive. He gestured then to the stained-glass windows. "Beautiful," he said. "Beautiful," he said again.

My father's first home away from my mother was in the personal-care unit of a nursing home, on a floor where the residents were still ambulatory, still partially functional. His language by then was mostly "Word Salad," words in no obvious order, random, meaningless. Still, when my mother visited, she would always ask, "Who am I?" and he would say, "Ruthie." Sometimes, he would ask to come home or he would push against the locked door and try to leave. When my mother wasn't there, he walked in the corridor, holding hands with another resident. She called my father "Howie," her husband's name. My father called her "Ruthie." When I saw them, I thought: This is my father—warm, affectionate.

I listened so hard to him in those days, sure that I would be able to understand him when he spoke, for there was still an inflection, a tone, a spark of life inside. Though I never could catch any meaning, in time, he would always respond to my presence. Once in a while, a favorite expression would emerge. "I'm tickled to death!" he'd say when I approached. Or: "That's neither here nor there."

Once, we were doing our slow walk down the halls, when our path was blocked by the housekeeper, a huge woman in leggings and a T-shirt, who was leaning over to plug in the vacuum. My father shuffled closer. At the sight of her massive buttocks, his arm went out, thumb and forefinger poised to goose. The woman stood. My father's fingers retracted. We continued our way down the hall.

Yes, I thought, laughing. This, too, was my father. But not the belligerence so common to people with Alzheimer's, for my real father did not strike anyone but was the nicest man I've ever known.

By the summer of 1999, my real father is completely gone. He no longer opens his eyes when I sit next to him. His skin still has a familiar smell and texture, but my touch is completely irrelevant to him. I cannot pretend that it matters in the slightest that I am beside him. If he's sleeping, I cannot nudge him awake. If he is eating, the only thing he does with any gusto, nothing else enters his consciousness—not the aide who calls to him in a booming voice, not the fight across the table, where one resident has stolen the cake off another's plate—only the pulverized pieces of food before him.

Late one afternoon, when I am overwhelmed by the fact that my father is gone, and there is no sign of him in the man with my father's name, I go home to take a run. I strip down as far as is legally permissible—sports bra, shorts—check the leaves of the dozens of plants I have, and then I go outside. I inhale very deeply. The light is low, and the air is dry and fragrant. And when I set out, I feel my father's presence within me and thank him silently for his innocence and kindness, for the strong legs I inherited from him, for this joy I feel.

[JANE BERNSTEIN]

Including this essay on her father, Jane Bernstein says she's "written about nearly everyone in my family, including my childhood dog, Buster; my children's dog, Lexington; and Madison, a stray dog."

"*Sometimes,*" *says the author,* "*I think, Enough already, back to fiction!*"

Bernstein did start off as a fiction writer, but is finding herself doing more and more essays and memoir. Her fourth book, Bereft: A Sister's Story, *was released this spring. She also teaches creative writing at Carnegie Mellon University, where* "*I don't tell my students to 'write what they know.'* "

Of "My Real Father," *she says,* "*In its earliest draft, this piece was about taking up tennis in my late forties. The parts about my father seemed full of old grudges, since my father would never teach me tennis or any other sport. Other parts of this draft were about my sheer enjoyment of this sport—of lots of sports. As I was struggling through this essay, I found myself redefining what my father passed on to me.*

"*My father didn't share any wisdom or moral code with me,*" *Bernstein maintains,* "*but in an unconscious and genuine way, passed on a way of finding pleasure in the world.*"

—C.O.

A BOOK OF NAMES

Sylvia Watanabe

RECENTLY I HAVE CAUGHT MYSELF, MORE OFTEN THAN I'D like, beginning sentences with the word *remember*. During one of our weekly phone conversations I told this to my father, who laughed. "I do that myself," he said; my father will turn eighty in October.

When I visit him in Honolulu we go for walks, just as we have always done. In the last several years these walks have become a ritual of naming what is there and no longer there—the koa grove, long since cut down, where we once found a blackburn butterfly; the ponds, where we looked for skimmers, now filled in and paved over. My father says, "If you live in a place long enough it begins to forget you."

Fifteen years ago I left the island for graduate school and did not know I was leaving for good. I went to say good-bye to my grandmother, who lived with my mother's older sister.

"Don't go, there will be strangers there, you'll forget who you are," Grandmother said. This woman who, at the age of nineteen, divorced her husband in Japan, entered a paper marriage with a man she didn't know, sailed alone across the Pacific Ocean to a place she'd never seen, then spent the whole rest of her life remembering.

"But look at you, Obaasan," I reminded her. "You've never forgotten."

Grandmother waved out the door. "Go then, go," she said, turning back to the television.

A year later she fell and broke her hip, and my aunt placed her in a facility for elderly care. At first Grandmother called home every day. "You have forgotten me here," she said.

Then she forgot where she was.

Forgetting comes to us inside our skins. I think of my uncle who forgot and forgot. As names came undone and slipped away, he forgot that a broom was not a tree, that the sky was not a sail. Desperate, my aunt thought to cure him with a health regimen. She put him on a special diet and fed him fish oil capsules, said to be rich in memory substances. She took him for constitutionals on the beach, so he could take in the salt air. Sometimes he hummed, my aunt said, a kind of singsong; she could not make out the words. They sounded like either sea or she, forgets or forgives.

The sea, the sea where forgetting is.

My father finds refuge in the microcosm. By training and habit his gaze seeks out what is small. He says it gives you a different sense of time, the same sense you might get from looking at something vast.

When I was a child and he was late coming home from work, my mother never worried; she knew to send me only as far as the front yard, where I would find him lost between the front door and the garage, investigating the underside of a leaf or the creatures emerging from the cracks in the walk.

I remember her asking him once, dinner cold again, what he hoped to see, and he said, "Something I've never seen before."

The bookshelves in his study were filled with books naming all the things he'd seen and hadn't seen. In these books—he called them keys—were the names of rare and common insects, their habits and habitats and significance to human beings. On Saturday mornings, if there was nothing my mother needed us for, we packed the car with insect collecting equipment and a box lunch of rice and salty Japanese pickles, then headed off to see something new.

On green days, smelling of fern, it rained on the mountain. Fern wings overhead, our gazes down, we hunted for damsels.

On gray summer days, swelling with heat, we searched for red dragonflies among the cattails.

On blue days at the edge of winter, the sky the color of pigment squeezed from a tube, we watched for *vanessas* among the mamaki.

My mother put up nicely with mosquito fish in her laundry tub, an earthworm farm, white mice, parakeets, an orphan lamb, cats, a dog, an escaped blue crab that lived three days behind the refrigerator before it died and began to stink, but she would not have jars of dead insects lying about her house. The one room where they were permitted was my father's study.

I sat next to him at his big desk as he wrote out the labels for the new specimens we'd brought in. Slowly, meticulously, he printed the names: each letter a hieroglyph—a proboscis, a thorax, a pair of wings. When he was done he held up one of the labels he had written.

"*Vespidae*," he said.

I whispered it quickly for fear of getting stung.

"*Vespidae*," he repeated, laying down his pen. He taped the label he'd just written to the outside of the cigar box temporarily serving as a specimen case. Inside, rows of impaled wasps—black, iridescent blue, and gold—were suspended in flight, each anchored by a little tag naming genus and species, date and place of collection.

Carefully, my father tapped a couple more specimens out of

the collecting jar. He picked one up with a pair of tweezers and pierced it clean through with a mounting pin. His hands dwarfed the delicate instruments; his movements were patient and precise. "Here," he said, pointing to a dangerous-looking yellow hornet, "you try it now." He sat while I gingerly retrieved it by a wing—which promptly detached itself. The other wing and two legs fell off as I wrestled the insect onto the pin. "There," I said. Without wings the hornet resembled a very large and angry ant. My father pointed out that this resemblance was no coincidence. Ants, wasps, and bees all belonged to the order, *hymenoptera*, an irritable, industrious bunch.

When my mother came to call us for dinner, I showed her my work. She looked thoughtful. "Ah, poor bee; he has been killed twice," she said.

If you know the name of a thing, you know what it is, my father believed. When I was eight, he gave me a clothbound notebook with waterproof pages, like the one he carried everywhere. Here he kept a record of all the insects he'd observed with the details of their collection. If he did not know the name of an insect, he'd look it up later in one of his keys. On the outside of my notebook he had printed, A Book of Names.

As an entomologist for the Board of Health, it was my father's job to know the names of things. He supervised the inspectors who looked into the complaints of the public regarding infestations of various kinds. My father and his inspectors were responsible for finding where the trouble came from and getting rid of it. Though he's been retired nearly twenty years, this has been a habit that's proved hard to break. Now, when he comes to visit us in Michigan, he is the one to discover the termites in the woodpile, the ant trail in the mud room, the earwigs in the planter box next to the front door.

A few years ago, just after my husband and I started digging up the lawn and putting the perennial border in, I called my father, long distance, to complain about something skeletonizing the *crambe cordefolia*. I could sense that he was tracing a familiar men-

tal map, searching for a name. He had never seen a *crambe*;
"What family does it belong to?" he asked. I couldn't say. He
asked me to describe the physical characteristics of the plant, so I
waxed aesthetic about the clouds of tiny flowers floating above
the leaves on tall delicate stalks. There was a pause at his end, in
which he did not remark how I had forgotten everything he'd
ever taught me, but then he asked pointedly what the *leaves* were
like. I described the large, abundant foliage, and after we'd discussed more specifically how the damage looked, he said it
sounded as if the *crambe* were some kind of crucifer and that it was
probably infested with caterpillars. He told me to go out at dark
and check the undersides of the leaves. That evening, there they
were: *plutella maculipennis*, dozens and dozens of green cabbage
worms feeding.

*Popillia japonica, vanessa tameamea, megabombus pennsylvani-
cus.* These are the names my father taught me. I pictured the
names as fasteners, like specimen pins, holding what we could not
hold in our hands: red hibiscus afternoons, crickets ringing in the
grass, the rain smell rising from a forest floor. I loved to say the
names aloud, to hear the magic sound of them.

My father spoke of their precision. "They are like points
on a map," he said. Order, family, genus, species: they followed
a path. It was always the same path; the path was a story. You
are mine now, the story said. You are not strange to me anymore.

But there are the names older still than the ones in that
story. I remember reading somewhere that the Hawaiian language classifies insects under a different scheme—according to
whether they are big or small, creeping or flying, burrowing or
wood-boring, biting or not biting. Of much greater import are
the names attached to human beings. According to traditional
Hawaiian belief, a person's essence inheres in a name, which
might include conditions of birth, ancestral lineage, traditional
family occupations, and the particular form of mana—or spiritual power—possessed by a line. Above all, a name relates the

connection between a person and place; it is about a connection to the land.

My father does not imagine things in quite these terms, but for him, as well, the memory of place exerts a kind of somatic pull. Several years ago my husband and I took a trip with my father to Maui, where he grew up. Though he hadn't been back in many years, he never got lost. Progress had been almost everywhere we went, but he could see through what was there to what no longer was—the sites of disappeared sugar villages, the mountain routes he'd hiked as a boy, the best places along the shoreline for torching, throwing net, casting, and spearing. He showed us where he'd harvested honey from the wild beehives in the kiawe pasture and looked for hawk moths among the be-still trees. He pointed out where he'd gone fishing off Kipahulu the night before the tidal wave and caught nothing but sharks. Speeding down the narrow hilly road to Ulapalakoa, he searched for short cuts, no longer there, back down to the low country. It seems he has walked, climbed, fished, swam, driven almost every inch of the island—the memory of it like a map imprinted on skin.

"I remember," my father says, and the names open like windows. I have stepped into his nostalgia so many times, it almost seems mine, but I have never known a place in just that way. Since our early walks, I have come to see names in a different light—though I guess you could say I still collect them.

Often over the past ten years, I've wondered if maybe my grandmother's worst fears haven't come true and I haven't turned into somebody, or somebodies, else. At various times I have been Sylvia, or Cynthia, or Celia Wanatabe, WanTANabe, WANTanabe, Wabatabe, Whatabobby, Whatanade—my names choose me. They shift from day to day, moment to moment, depending on whether I'm talking to the mail order lady at L. L. Bean or the man behind the counter at the local post office. Lately, even my husband has begun receiving solicitations in the mail addressed to William P. Osbornabe.

I have gotten used to inquiries over the telephone as to whether my name is "Indian," or "African," or "Eskimo." Once, just after we moved to Grand Rapids, I went to a doctor I had never been to before. I could hear him rustling papers outside the examining room door. When he finally came in, he paused, a look of amazement on his face. "Why, you're not Polish," he exclaimed. "Not even close," I said. He had been trying to figure out my name from the medical file, and not being Polish himself, he said, that was the best he could come up with.

Another time, when I was trying to make a dental appointment by telephone, I gave my name to the receptionist, who was new. She asked—as I'd learned to expect—"What kind of name is that, where're you from?" When I told her Hawaii, she grew enthusiastic. "Well, Miss . . . Miss . . . Miss Wannabe, welcome to America!" she said.

I do not think anymore that a name is a kind of fastener that holds memory in place. Even now as I write, the signifiers are emptying out and refilling, changing shape, becoming something else. I find myself imagining the Polish African Indian Eskimo Sylvia Wampumabee and how she might tell this.

Nostalgia is memory looking off to one side. Any minute that thing you're not looking at might slide into view. Remember, my father says, or I say—but there is a place between now and before where we do not go. This is what we want to forget: Grandmother in the ambulance, Uncle empty of names.

When my mother became ill, the doctors could not name what was wrong. There was no map, no path to follow. She ached, she said, and they could say what the pain resembled—it resembled arthritis. Swimming therapy was prescribed, along with regular sessions on an Exercycle. We didn't learn till much later it was her liver that failed her. "It's funny when the thing that's killing you is called a liver," she said.

For months after she died, my father left everything as it was. Her footsteps whispering through the rooms, her breath in the air, her sleep still warming the unchanged sheets. He went about his day's routine as if she were the reason—waking when it was still dark in the windows, fixing six tiny meals of her favorite foods. He went for a walk some mornings, then cleaned house in the afternoons to her favorite soap operas; he couldn't say what was going on, but the sounds from the television belonged in the air. You get used to things, he said. And while he might, in time, become used to something else (he avoided the words *absence*, *death*), it was not yet that time.

Meanwhile, stacks of old newspapers collected in the hall. He collected beer bottles, cans, jars of all sizes (in case, as he said, he took up pickling), the cardboard tubes from rolls of toilet paper, two stray cats. He collected flotsam the way he once collected butterflies. All the items were organized by size and type—paper goods here, metal there—except the cats, who had a habit of wandering off.

A few months after the funeral, I was back visiting and we were sitting in the living room drinking beers. I said to my father, "What's all this, Pop, this is a firetrap, throw something out."

He gazed at the neatly sorted piles of this and that, then laughed. "These are the days of our lives," he said. "These are the days of our lives."

The signifiers are shifting.
The world is becoming unpinned.

My father and I have added forgetting walks to our repertoire. A forgetting walk happens when you walk into a room and do not remember why you are there. Or when you can't get past the fifth word of the sentence, "The other day I saw—now who was that— you know, what was her name, it was just there on the tip of my tongue. . . ." Or just before you are about to leave the house, perhaps to go on another kind of walk, when one of you remembers you have forgotten something. You wander from room to room, calling out, "Where are my glasses? Where are my keys?"

While she was in the senior care facility, my grandmother

went on her own naming walks. In the evening, after supper, she'd wheel down the hall, stopping at each doorway and putting her hands together in prayer. This annoyed some of the inhabitants who shouted rude things, but Grandmother continued, undeterred. Her last stop was the visitors' lounge, where she wheeled up to the refrigerator and pulled the doors open, just as she'd opened the doors of the tabletop shrine at home. Then she'd chant loudly into that cold white space, a single word, the Buddha's name over and over again.

Lately everyone in Hawaii is changing names; talk of Hawaiian sovereignty fills the air. There's Richard, the sansei poet, who now performs Hawaiian reggae liberation rap under the name of Red Flea. Then there's Diana, the novelist, who's become Kiana. And Carolyn Lau who has turned into Carolyn Lei-Lanilau. And Dennis, the college professor, who did not change his name but spent an afternoon getting his ankle tattooed in the traditional native manner.

I tell my father, who doesn't quite know what to make of all this, that he must also pick out a name for when the revolution arrives. He says that he already has one; he read it in the paper the other day. In an interview someone called local "orientals" *Neo-colonialists*.

"I guess that's your name too," my father says.

Forgetting is remembering.
I remember forgetting.

The scent of the night garden comes to me. The darkness brims with the sweetness of honeysuckle, pikake, nightblooming cereus—the creamy white blooms in the silver light. My father carries the net—it is long and deep, narrowing at the end like a magician's hat. I can see my mother through the kitchen window; she is washing dishes at the sink. She looks up and peers out, but cannot see us in the dark. She is beautiful in the yellow light.

My father passes the net once over the flower bed and a winged form appears in it. Army worm moth, drab little sister. He waves his net again and produces a flying cockroach. One more pass, and a grey sphinx materializes. This is it, my father says.

We take the moth into the light. My mother sees us now. "Don't you let that loose in here," she calls through the screen.

My father turns the net inside out, and the moth clings to the fine mesh, curiously still. I have never seen one like this before. It has a furry body, large red-jeweled eyes, and a coiled nose—like a pincurl. My father explains that this is not really a nose, but a proboscis, which is a kind of straw for sipping nectar. The moth's wings are slightly open, and they are light grey—almost silver— and covered with delicate patterns of grey, darker grey, black, and white. I brush my fingers against its wings and they flutter a little. They feel like air.

[SYLVIA WATANABE]

Because remembering, forgetting, identifying, and labeling experiences are all at the heart of "A Book of Names," I recently asked Sylvia Watanabe if there was one experience with her father she hoped she would never forget.

"Writing is a way of naming and naming is a way—not only of not forgetting—but of inventing memory," she said.

"My father, the man of science, would not agree with the latter, though my father, the artist, would understand perfectly what I mean. As a man of science and an artist, he taught me to look hard at things. This fall he visited us in Michigan. He had never before seen the colors and we went out on walks every day to see how they'd changed. It was my turn to tell him the names of things, though hardly with his precision.

"On the day he was leaving," Watanabe said, "the willow trees were just beginning to turn. 'Soon they'll be all gold,' I told him. 'It's too bad you couldn't stay.' 'Yes, but I can imagine them,' he said."

This winner of the Pushcart and O. Henry prizes for non-

fiction and fiction was born in Hawaii, on the island of Maui. For the last fifteen years, she has made her home in the Midwest, with commutes to Grand Rapids, Michigan, where her husband works; Honolulu, where her father lives; and Oberlin College in Ohio, where she teaches Creative Writing. Her first collection of stories, Talking to the Dead, was a finalist for the PEN Faulkner.

—C.O.

HEAVY WHEN IT'S EMPTY

Janet Ruth Falon

I'M WAITING FOR MY FATHER.

My mother and I are sitting in the Metropolitan Opera House, watching and listening to *Tosca*, and waiting for my father to make his entrance on stage. We're on the fourth ring, up about the fourth row, the second and third seats in from the aisle, and my mother smells of tea-rose perfume, which she's worn for nearly three decades. She's wearing clothes the colors of the Garden State Expressway in mid-October, her year-round palette, tones that match the gold leaf in the auditorium.

The empty seat on the aisle is on my right, and if he can change his clothes in time, my father will join us for the second and third acts.

My father is a supernumerary, a non-singing extra, a role commonly referred to as a "spear carrier." This is not his day job. He has no day job. The day job he had for more years than my mother has worn tea-rose perfume was as an elementary school principal in the New York City school system. He looked the part: He's six-foot-three, has a fringe of grey hair wrapped around his head like Julius Caesar's crown of laurels, and bushy gray eyebrows that reach toward each other when he's displeased. "Distinguished" is how people have always described him. When he was working he'd sometimes run into kids from his school in the supermarket; they always were startled to see him and surprised that he actually had to eat.

My father worked hard, and he had to; it was a demanding job, and the demands became weightier as the city grew more compli-cated. But underneath the severe exterior he wore to school like a superhero's insignia, my father entertained an ambition. He wanted to be on the stage: the opera, to be precise, with its grand themes and exaggerated emotional expression and elaborate stories that his own immigrant parents—if they ever went to the opera, which they didn't—might have called *bubbe-mysers*. Literally, "grandma stories." Preposterous plots and outlandish goings-on.

It's almost the end of the first act, and we're still waiting. On stage, below the spangly, starbursty chandeliers of the Met audito-rium, news of Napoleon's defeat has arrived. Preparations are made for a special service in the church of Saint'Andrea della Valle. The services begin. My mother elbows me to be on alert, that this is it, and I should watch out for my father. A great procession enters the church, row after row of solemn Christians shuffling in to the Te Deum. And there's my father, dressed as a priest, wearing a purple robe and matching skullcap, carrying a banner, looking as solemn and priestly as an aging Jewish man with a wonderfully Jewish nose can look, and I elbow back my mother, we look at each other—and we lose it. We laugh, and we try to muffle our laughter, but we go on for so long that we get shushed by the people around us. We can't look at each other because we'll trip each other off. It's one of those laughs you never forget, and always carry with you.

The act ends, and the people around us note who we are, then disperse for candy or a smoke. "Your father loves this," my mother tells me. "His feet don't touch the ground for hours after a show. He just floats."

My father the priest joins us about fifteen minutes into the first intermission. He's changed back to street clothes: gray wool slacks, a striped shirt, and a tweedy gray blazer. He looks distinguished. He doesn't look especially Christian. His hair is a little fuzzy, and he's flushed, partly from having scrubbed off his makeup. He kisses the two women in his life he knows best, and when he kisses me, I smell that comforting waxy smell that bald men often get after they've perspired under a hat.

"That was great," I tell him, and his face widens and glows. When we tell him about laughing, he laughs his "hm-hm-hm" almost-silent laugh. Each of his eyebrows is relaxed and keeps to its own side.

"Benjamin, your wife and daughter were hysterical," my mother says, proprietarily patting his hair into place, and we all keep giggling and playing off each other and stretching the moment into a memory.

"So tell me what's going to happen in act two," I ask, and we take our seats, and my father tells me.

My mother sewed a little purse for my father to wear around his neck, under his costumes, in which he keeps his keys and wallet. This, and a few other necessities—an extra pair of shoes, maybe, or a sandwich and can of V-8—my father carries to the Met in a canvas Channel 13 tote bag. It's on the floor now, underneath his seat, and my father, sitting next to me, waits for the curtain to rise on the next act.

I would wait for my father to come home from his school when I was a little girl. I'd look out the living-room window of our second-floor garden apartment in Queens, watching for the bus that might disgorge my father like Jonah from the whale. I was younger than eight, because that's how old I was when we moved.

The living-room window looked out onto Springfield Boulevard, a busy thoroughfare with enough hubbub to entertain me when I was sick with a cold, or home from school with chicken pox. I could see Shoe King Sam, the shoe-repair store that I loved to visit because of the little private stalls you'd get to sit in while waiting for your shoes, and the musky smell of leather. I could see the gas station where we'd take our big blue Ford to be fixed by Harold, the mechanic my father trusted (as much as anyone trusts a mechanic), which sat on a triangular plot that divided Spring-field Boulevard into two roadways like an island in a river. I could see White Tower, the fast-food restaurant where my mother would treat my brother and me for lunch before taking us to our father's school for a visit each spring; I'd have a hamburger, vanilla milkshake, and a Devil Dog every time. From the window I could see the bus stop, too. My father wouldn't look up to our window as he came closer, but I could see him, and he was always carrying his briefcase.

My father's briefcase was a rusty-brown briefcase made of a bumpy leather, and it had accordion pleats on the bottom and a flap that flipped over the top of the briefcase where it met the other half of a brass clasp. It could hold a heavy load. The bottom of the briefcase was wearing out—and, at the end of a day, so was he.

Education was my father's career choice for a variety of reasons. One was the security of the profession; having been scarred by want in the Depression, he wanted to be in a field with staying power. My father didn't need to—and wouldn't—make a lot of money, but schools, he figured, would always be in business. An-other big reason he chose education was that he—and my mother, who was a school librarian—would have their summers off. The trade-off was worth it: You give your heart, soul, guts, and various other components for ten months in exchange for two free months. For two months, you don't have to deal with the passions of par-ents and teachers and children. For two months, you're not the center of attention, and any burdens that you carry seem lighter.

I'd hear the key in the door. "Ben?" my mother would ask, stretching his name into a length that might merit several sylla-bles. "Honey?"

"Yes," he'd answer and walk up the stairs. Each step was dis-tinct and had its own tired sound. The stairs ended on a small landing that led into the living room or dining room. My father's desk—almost the same color as the briefcase—was in the far cor-ner of the living room, next to the big window, and that's where he'd drop his briefcase, right by the space into which he'd pull the desk chair.

"Hi, Daddy," I'd say, especially if I'd been sitting by the window, waiting, and he would come to me and kiss me. Not infrequently, his breath was sour, and his face was often drawn, the lines whittled deep. He'd kiss my mother, too, and for a few short moments we'd have the how-was-your-day kind of dialogue that's always funnied up for sitcoms.

"Dinner will be ready in ten minutes," my mother would say; even though my father's school closed at three, he rarely left right away, and then he had an hour-and-a-half commute on New York City subways and a bus. "Why don't you change your clothes and make yourself comfortable?"

And we would eat. And my brother and I would do our homework and watch whatever TV we were allowed. And my father emptied his briefcase, sorted through important papers, and did what he had to do. The apartment felt full, the way it was supposed to, and I could go to sleep. And then it was always the next day, and the same, and my father would return the papers to his briefcase and leave.

It was only in the summer, when my father left his briefcase at home and we went to a bungalow colony in the Adirondacks, that his face fully relaxed. He and I would go on early-morning walks to pick enormous blackberries, which would pop and burst as the pancake batter he'd put them in would fry on the griddle (the brand name of which was Happy Day). We'd go fishing out on Schroon River in a dumpy green rowboat with splintery oars, and we'd catch sunnies and throw them back in. My father would sing, too, songs like "Summertime" and "Go Down, Moses." He would put on his canvas rucksack with its drawstring closing—so much cruder than today's high-tech microfiber packs from L. L. Bean—and we'd hike in the morning, on the mountains, finding rocks with veins of shiny mica and pine cones sticky with their own juices, all of which we'd carry home in the rucksack to our bungalow and line up on a windowsill of the screened-in porch. As the day unfolded, the air smelled of the sweetness of warm spruce. The nights were illuminated by fireflies that never let themselves get caught and carried around in glass jars.

One autumn, nearly two decades after our last Adirondack summer—the year my father's eyebrows finally decided to declare themselves more gray than black—my mother bought him a gift: A new briefcase. It was one of those rectangular Samsonite attaché cases with hard sides and angles, and it was the color of a perfectly toasted marshmallow. It looked less lawyerly than the other one, and more modern. It looked like it would last for the rest of a fifty-seven-year-old man's career. The handle seemed like it would be easier to carry, too.

One night, when I was speaking to my father on the phone from my new home in a Philadelphia suburb, he told me about the gift. I immediately asked for his old briefcase. "You can have it if you want it," he said. "But it's in lousy shape. And it's heavy, even when it's empty."

"I know, and I don't care," I replied. "I just want it."

"What would you want it for?" my father asked, his voice one that I know goes along with mild irritation. "And it's all rubbed out, especially on the bottom."

"I'm not going to actually use it," I assured him.

"Fine," he said. "Done. If you want it, it's yours."

That was the year I was living alone for the first time. Not only had I moved to a new city, but I was gambling on a new job as a reporter, something I'd trained for in college but never actually done. I was living in an apartment complex, in a one-bedroom apartment on the second floor, with a living-room window that looked down onto the parking lot. I didn't have a lot of furniture yet, not even a real desk. I told myself I could keep stuff in my father's briefcase; I could hang on to things I didn't know what to do with but that I didn't want to throw away.

Tosca is nothing if not passionate, bloody, and thunderous. Although the final act begins peacefully, with the shepherd's morning song heard offstage, events build onstage and the music swells accordingly. There's the heartbreakingly sweet aria "E lucevan le stelle"—"the stars were shining brightly"—sung by Cavaradossi, the words those of the farewell letter he writes to his beloved

Tosca before his execution. The lovers sing a passionate duet. Cavaradossi is shot dead, and the grief-stricken Tosca climbs high on the parapet of the Castle of Sant'Angelo and flings herself to her death.

And everyone in the audience exhales, then stomps and whistles and cheers and claps as the lovers rise from the dead for their standing ovations. My mother and my father and I nudge each other and nod in approval to each other. "It was great," I say to my father, as the din continues.

"Wasn't it great?" he responds.

"Did you enjoy it, Jan?" my mother asks. And we all nod some more. It's one of those in-sync times when we're all on the same wavelength, like when my parents and I were in Paris together in 1973, and we all got a little tipsy at dinner and walked, arm in arm, over the Pont Alexandre III singing show tunes. Then, and now, we've temporarily left behind the irritations and disappointments between all parents and all children that can weigh them down like a suitcase full of stones. And not only is my father in on this Memorable Moment, but it's because of him that we're having it.

"It was really great," I tell my father, again, as we gather our coats and purses and his Channel 13 canvas tote bag and wait to join the lines of people leaving the auditorium. My father turns to look back at me, and his face is unlined and soft, fully fleshed out, like he used to look in midsummer in the Adirondacks, only older.

"Benjamin, you look like you're on cloud nine," my mother says, and we go home, to the small house they bought after leaving Springfield Boulevard.

The next day I come back to Philadelphia, to my latest home, a third-floor apartment where I live alone with my cat, and houseplants that are too stubborn to wither in spite of my lack of knowledge of their needs. When I look out my living-room window I can see a train station; fathers and mothers take this train to work, and so do I, my red nylon backpack filled with important papers so I can do what I have to do.

I find my father's briefcase in the closet. The bottom is rubbed out, like he said, but not so much that you can't trust it. I unburden it of its contents and tell myself that tomorrow I'll file or discard whatever papers I've stored in there. The familiar smell of old leather rises up to greet me, and I put the empty briefcase, ready to be employed, by the door.

[JANET RUTH FALON]

So often personal talismans, like the briefcase in Janet Ruth Falon's essay, are only cherished after a loved one is beyond our reach. How refreshing it is to read about a daughter who keeps one near, continually filling it with memories of a father who is heartily, wonderfully alive.

This type of old-fashioned affection clearly runs in Falon's family. Says the author, "My father still wears his ruby engagement ring every day, and my parents' wedding photo sits on his bureau. Both demonstrate to me his own brand of sentimentality and the important role of his fifty-three-years-and-counting marriage to my mother."

Falon, who is a freelance journalist, essayist, and poet, has appeared in The New York Times, Washington Post, Philadelphia Inquirer, *and* Boston Globe, *and is currently at work on a book of prose-poem Jewish liturgical readings. A documentary she wrote for public television was recognized with a local Emmy. She is also the author of* Kissed the Girls and Made Them Cry: Teaching Gender Respect to Children, *and* The Gender Respect Work Book. *She also teaches classes for adults and children at the University of Pennsylvania and Temple University.*

Born in Queens, New York, Falon now resides in Elkins Park, Pennsylvania, with her husband, two cats, a collection of 136 snowglobes, and, as she says, "more books than we will ever get to read."

—C.O.

MATTHEW 10, 34–39

AN EPISCOPAL HOMILY

Frederick G. Dillen

Do not think that I have come to bring peace on earth; I have not come to bring peace, but a sword. For I have come to set a man against his father, and a daughter against her mother, and a daughter-in-law against her mother-in-law; and a man's foes will be those of his own household. He who loves father or mother more than me is not worthy of me; and he who loves son or daughter more than me is not worthy of me; and he who does not take his cross and follow me is not worthy of me. He who finds his life will lose it, and he who loses his life for my sake will find it.

MATTHEW 10, 34–39

LORD, TAKE OUR MINDS AND THINK THROUGH THEM. TAKE our lips and speak through them. Take our hearts and set them on fire.

Four mornings a week I go to the gym at the YMCA in Gloucester and do thirty or forty minutes with the weights and machines and then work out for another thirty on the StairMaster, and the time on the StairMaster has become my time for prayer.

Actually I've exercised for years in gyms here and there around the country. It is only in the past year that I've begun to pray in one. With the prayer has come Jesus.

Not always, but not infrequently either, I have a sense while I'm on the StairMaster that Jesus is up ahead and to the right of me, sometimes almost within reach of my right hand and sometimes ten or twenty yards ahead. He leads me from forest into a thinning of trees and out toward light, toward the freedom and safety of open water. He doesn't lead me in any sort of noble parade, however. He is an athlete and I am not; he is resolute, and I am not. While I am on the StairMaster, he is, despite his odd clothing, the coolest camp counselor from my days as a twelve- to fifteen-year-old in a two-month summer camp of four-cot tents and deep-lake swimming. In those days the coolest counselor was in fact a version of God, and with that counselor, with Jesus, I become a child again who doesn't think he can make the hike, a child who wants to stop in the woods and might even, God help him, weep. So Jesus teases me as if I were one of the regular guys around the lake. He leads for a bit, and then looks back in mock amazement that I have fallen behind. He drops back to almost beside me and rolls his eyes and makes a disgusted effort to go as slowly as me. Sometimes he stops altogether and waits for me with his hands on his hips in exasperated impatience. He laughs.

That he laughs and teases means that I am in fact one of the regular guys and can make it to the light and the open water. It means he is with me, and we will make it together. It means that when we do make it, he will, without diminishing the effect by saying so out loud, accept me.

This is all silliness of course, a grown man's tapioca of adolescent theology.

It is also something else, however, because in today's gospel Christ says, "I have not come to bring peace but a sword." And in a world of swords, forests are real. The thickness of the woods and their darkness; those things are real. The promise of light and water matters. If it is true that I will make it out to the lake, it is also true that I must make it out. Jesus may tease me, but he does so because he knows it will keep me moving, which I have to do if I am to survive.

If in good seasons, survival has all to do with enduring thirty minutes short of breath on the StairMaster, in other seasons, those thirty minutes become all of time. The Lenten season of last year, when in fact I first began to pray at the gym, was one of the other seasons. It was, by no coincidence, the season that forest grew up around me. It was the season my father took hold of me.

In today's gospel, Christ says, "For I have come to set a man against his father."

Well, my father began for me as a kind, funny, educated man, but he drank himself to furious, solitary desolation and to death. He finished here in Boston, alone and on the street, possessing the clothes he wore and an extra necktie and a briefcase with cancelled insurance policies and papers from his naval service in World War Two.

I was twenty-seven when he died, and maybe he was alone because I was not with him, but I didn't think so when I came to claim his body and to persuade a plot for him in the veterans cemetery. I had been sent off to boarding school when I was twelve, and to summer camp the same year, because he was already on fire and setting our family on fire. In the way of catastrophic families, my mother died of cancer and my brother died of speed and smack, and my father outlived them both, and I survived because I was sent away and learned to stay away.

There was only one prolonged moment, in the year before my father died, that I thought to take care of him as all the clinics and institutes and tanks had not been able to do. I thought to bring him out to New Mexico where I was living. I had real as opposed to gymnasium muscles then, and I knew that I could physically manage him. I could punch him out if I had to, if I found him with a bottle. But I also had seen enough of alcohol by then to know that he would never be sober. And I had a wife and a new baby. And I had been sent away at twelve precisely to learn the common sense of separation.

Still, it stayed with me, that notion of saving him. I was a ranch foreman and a builder in the summers, to pay for writing fiction during the winters, and I could have fought with my father and with the booze on my own ground, on my own terms. I might have held my father's bald, blistering head in a headlock with one arm and never let go and still attended with my free hand to my own husbanding and fathering and building. But it was a nonsensical notion, and I knew it.

For the next twenty years I wrote unpublishable fiction and then at forty-eight sold a book and had a screenplay optioned and, as quick as I could, with the faith only writers of fiction possess, I mortgaged the farm so I could do nothing but write two new novels that didn't sell.

Would it sound more ridiculous if I said there was no farm to mortgage?

Yes. Suddenly my life was on fire, and I knew about lives on fire. Suddenly I was fifty-one years old, and I had been living on credit cards and I was so afraid I could not stand up straight. Overnight, it happened.

We were living in Los Angeles at the time. A friend called us with news of a cheap house in Gloucester, and we came back at the first of last year, and my father was everywhere. When I came to Boston to hunt up teaching work and hack business writing, he followed me. He waited for me down an alley behind Beacon Hill in a building that used to be an SRO hotel with a lobby where he could meet me as if he still had a club. He waited for me in Mass General, in Bullfinch Seven, where he had been brought when a Samaritan heard his good diction calling from a gutter. He called to me in the same diction from a boozers halfway house in East Boston.

I went, between interviews one day, to the Boston Public Library, to go to the bathroom down in the basement, and down there, in one of the doorless stalls, a bum in matted layers of winter rags and dirt and bare knees sat and wiped and wiped and wiped at himself, and he was not my father. He was no metaphor for my father. He was a man with his own horrific life, and he was also a future for me. I looked at him and knew that I could come to this bathroom when I had none of my own. Every fear I had ever possessed turned to the lure of despair.

I wanted to join my father. I wanted to be my father. I had found the truth of my life and wanted to abandon myself to no solace but the warmth and free paper of available doorless toilets. I wanted to be outside in the night on the street with nowhere else. I had never understood until then what had become of my father. Never truly understood. I had loved him, and he had loved me, and he had always understood. I wept for him and for myself.

And four days a week, I did the StairMaster, and the woods appeared and closed around me, and I said aloud on the second floor of the Gloucester Y, "Please, God, help me."

And Jesus appeared and teased me. He rolled his eyes and put his hands on his hips and spat. He led me through the darkest of the trees and then came back and walked beside me and looked at the bathos of my effort and shook his head and mimicked my sorry stride and glided out ahead again. He laughed back at me, and the trees thinned and there was light.

In the woods and darkness behind me, my father cried after me.

And I loved my father. He had sent me away to save me, but before he sent me, before the vacation nights that I had to look for him and drag him to bed, before all that, he played catch with me; he put his hand on my knee and loved me beyond words; he told me jokes that to this day make other jokes not good enough.

I ran behind Jesus who teased me on to strength and home, and my father cried to me from the loneliness of his last necktie and his useless briefcase and his terrifying nights. He called me back to be with him, not to let him die alone, and I chose to laugh at the Lord's teasing. I was glad of the teasing. I was that regular. I was the skinny kid at camp, and I ran to the light and the lake, and I did not look back.

I followed Jesus and would not hear my father.

For, "He who loves father or mother more than me, is not worthy of me, and he who does not take his cross and follow me is not worthy of me. He who finds life will lose it, and he who loses his life for my sake will find it."

Amen.

[FREDERICK G. DILLEN]

Frederick G. Dillen has lived in places that would be the envy of many writers, moving from location to location, almost as if his life has been an expanded travelogue of the United States. Born in New York City, he was raised in Connecticut, when at the age of twelve he was sent to St. Paul's boarding school in New Hampshire, sadly to escape his father's drunkenness. From there, however, his travels took a more pleasant route, starting with a degree earned at Stanford University.

After graduation, Dillen managed a small hotel on Maui and then ran a ranch in northern New Mexico. He had begun writing in Hawaii and continued it in New Mexico. A brief stay in Sacramento, California, was followed by a stint as a waiter in San Francisco and marriage to the actress and playwright Leslie Harrell.

Restaurants, writing, and the raising of two daughters continued to occupy his time, all of this intensifying with a return move to New York City. The more fiction Dillen wrote, the more plates he carried. As with many writers, he eventually sought a relief from the expense of city living, and after a brief detour to Los Angeles to try his hand at screenwriting, he relocated to Gloucester, Massachusetts, which he now finally calls "home."

Dillen's peripatetic lifestyle lasted long enough that one of his daughters has graduated from college and is married, while the other will soon finish law school at Berkeley.

Lest anyone think he has done more travelling than writing, Dillen's first novel, Hero, *was published by Steelforth Press in 1994; his second,* Fool, *by Algonquin in 1999. His short story, "Alice," was collected in the 1996 edition of the O. Henry*

Awards Prize Stories; his screenplay, Hero at Last, was optioned by the Samuel Goldwyn Company; and he was a screenwriter at the Eugene O'Neill Playwrights Conference.

One thing I found curious about Dillen's personal story was his desire to "join" his father in experiencing the man's worst states. It's an uncommon reaction. Normally adult children of alcoholics prefer to have nothing to do with that part of their parent's life.

"I don't have any sense of the norm in these things," he tells me, "but I can imagine, at least in part, why I feel as I do now.

"At twelve—and I was far from mature at twelve—I was sent away to boarding school and full summers of camp to avoid the blooming horror not only of my father's life but the life of my family in general. My brother was already wildly troubled, and before long my mother had begun a terminal illness. I was designated the normal one and provided with survival. The explicit message was that I was to live, emotionally as well as physically, somewhere else. I was a shy kid anyhow, and I took the message to heart and learned to close myself away from a fair range of emotional life.

"As a writer, not surprisingly, it has been a challenge for me to face emotional dangers in my work," Dillen says. "I have had to learn the symptoms of aversion and how, one way and another, to write my way through that aversion.

"Of course I want to be with my father. I missed him. I miss him now. I want to help him, as I did not do when I was a boy. I want to save him, as I never tried to do. And if I cannot manage those things, I want (a part of me wants) to suffer as penance exactly the horror I left him to suffer alone."

—C.O.

THE GEOGRAPHY OF LOVE

Mary Morris

"It's as if we even planned the weather," Rob said as his father adjusted his tie. Both men gazed out at the cloudless sky, the gentle surf, the stream of golden sunshine.

"It's true," his father said. "You couldn't ask for a nicer day." The night before neither man would have said that. There had been a deluge the likes of which no one on that part of the island could remember. It seemed as if the heavens had opened and drenched them. Some storm, a hurricane (Was it Dennis? When did they start naming them after men? Rob wondered.) had veered from the Carolinas, sending swirls of billowy water and steamy hot air.

But then, sometime in the night, the sky had cleared. The clouds had broken up, then drifted across the mainland. Stars had come out. Rob and Kimberly, his bride-to-be, had stood under that clear sky, and she'd whispered to him, "It will be a beautiful day."

"It will," he said, his arms looped around her. And it was. It was an exquisite day.

"There," his father said, as he straightened Rob's cummerbund one last time. "Let me have a look." His father put his hands on Rob's shoulders, turning him this way and that. "There. That

211

looks good." Rob fiddled with his tie once more, tugged on the cummerbund that was already rising up behind his back. "I'm proud of you, son." Rob and his father stared at his image in the mirror. They looked alike—same square faces, same blue-gray eyes. Once on the tennis court they'd been mistaken, briefly, for brothers.

Rob had to admit that he was proud of himself as well. He'd made it and he'd done it on his own. There were years when he thought he wouldn't, but somehow he had. It was one of the decisions he'd made years ago when he was still a boy. A lesson he'd learned early on. He would manage his own life. He would never blame anyone but himself for what had gone wrong. And he hadn't. He didn't blame anyone.

But nothing would go wrong today. Rob was struck by the feeling of perfection—a feeling that he wasn't entirely comfortable with. Normally he saw what was missing, what wasn't there. But today everything, even the weather, was perfect.

How had it all come out right? Because he and Kimberly had worked hard to make it so. This was their wedding, after all. They had planned everything down to the last detail. They had stayed up night after night, making lists, reams of things to do. Each moment of their wedding was a discussion, a decision, and then it found its place on the appropriate list. The buckets of roses the bridesmaids would carry; the pillows the ring bearer bore; the bridesmaids' dresses that blended into the sandy and green color of the dunes. Kimberly, a book designer, had thought of that. And she had wanted benches, not folding chairs. White benches. (Where are we going to get white benches? Rob had asked, but Kimberly had said, "We'll have them made.")

Kimberly was right about the benches, Rob thought as he looked down from the top floor at the deck that stretched along the ocean and the neat lines of white benches. As usual she's right about everything.

From the opposite window Rob watched the cars pull up, the guests file in. He saw valet parking take their cars. He saw the guests nodding, smiling, as they made their way up the gravelly path, admiring the tents of the palest pink, the gray-and-white clapboard house that loomed before them. He heard the "oohs and aahs" at the wrap-around water—the house, owned by a family friend, a friend who had taken Rob under his wing when no one else would, this house that sat on the edge between the sea and the bay, the sloping dunes, the wild dune grasses, the blunt lines of the fading light. Already the waitstaff was passing out sparkling glasses with Perrier and lime, the guests were taking their places on the deck. A sweet, gentle breeze blew from the south. Silk skirts rose and fell. Hair ruffled in the wind.

His father had left the room. He had given his son a pat on the back, wished him "good luck," and slipped out. Rob was glad. It gave him a moment to collect himself. Take a gulp. Catch his breath. He smiled, thinking of his mother. She would have been amused with all of this. It would have been an opportunity for her to toss her head back and laugh. The irony of the day would not have escaped her.

When he heard the first strains of the violin, the adagio for strings, Rob made his way down the wooden steps toward the deck. Their sixteen attendants (so many; like the Yale crew team) had lined up and Rob took his place beside them. He stood, hands pressed behind his back, as the bridesmaids made their way down the stairs, buckets of rose petals in their hands. As the adagio played, the first bridesmaid hesitated, lifted her skirt slightly, exposing her thin-heeled sandal.

They had not rehearsed this part—the girls coming down the stairs in their long skirts and shoes and now he cringed. What if one of them fell? What if Kimberly stumbled? But each of the girls made it down. It was all going so smoothly until the attendants sent the crash (that was what the red carpet was called; a crash. Over the past few months Rob had become familiar with the language of weddings) down the aisle too soon. He winced as the in-laws and grandparents walked on it. Only Kimberly was supposed to step on the crash. Kimberly alone.

The one thing, he thought, he hadn't planned was falling in love with Kimberly. It had taken him by surprise. For years now he had arranged his life down to the letter—planned what he'd study in prep school, the sports he'd go out for (football, crew, and soccer; he was too short for basketball, a game he'd longed to play) and where he'd go to college. It had to be Yale, his father's alma mater, and he'd even take an extra year of preparatory school to get into Yale. He'd planned his law degree (entertainment law) and he'd planned so many things, just as he had his wedding.

But he hadn't planned on Kimberly. He had liked her breezy, almost indifferent manner that seemed to match his. Her take-it-or-leave-it attitude. They had gone out perhaps four or five times when one night it was very late and they'd had too much to drink and there was a storm outside. He'd said to her, "Just sleep here." He'd made up the couch for her.

In the morning when he got up, she was gone. She'd left a note—a breezy note—on the dining-room table. *Rob, Sorry, had to leave early. Boy, do I have a headache. Where are your aspirin? Talk to you during the week, K.* He had been oddly crestfallen over this note, though he had no idea why. As he was going through the motions of changing the sheets on the fold-out couch (he had noticed the pillows smelled of her, a musky, healthy smell like hay, he thought, like the outdoors), he felt as if he'd wanted to cry. He hadn't wanted to cry since he was a boy and this surprised him. He sat on the couch to collect himself, the long weekend stretching before him.

It was then that he noticed the notes in the trash beside the sofa. The crumpled sheets of paper. There were at least six of them and he took them out, laid them on the dining-room table, beside the one he'd received. *Dearest Robby, I can't tell you what a good time I had. I'm so sorry I have to rush off . . . Robby, it was great to see you. Rob, sorry I had to leave.*

Months later, after they'd actually slept together, after they were talking about living together, she'd confessed to him. "You meant more to me than I let on."

"I know," he'd said.

"How do you know?"

He'd gotten up and gone to the drawer and produced them—

all the drafts she'd written, those crinkled slips of paper that told him how she'd had something to hide.

Like Rob, Kimberly wanted everything to go right. And so the day before the wedding they'd gone down their checklist—flowers, food, champagne, waiters, weather (well, they couldn't do anything about that, could they?), table seating, guests to pick up at airport, calligrapher to do place settings, toast (Rob), touch base with combos. Kimberly liked lists. She left them all over the apartment, on the refrigerator, taped to mirrors. All the things she had to do. And Rob prided himself on being able to look at those lists and memorize them. If Kimberly told him eight things she needed from the store, he never wrote them down, but he'd come home with just the items she'd asked for. He liked to amaze people with his ability to memorize a phone number (if he'd dialed it once, he never had to look it up again).

"You've written your toast, right?" Kimberly had asked the night before their wedding as they lay in bed.

"Wrong. I know what I'm going to say, I know who I'm going to thank. I feel entirely clear." She had rolled her eyes at him, that little sarcastic look he got from her sometimes that he found so sweet, so endearing. "I don't need six drafts to tell people I love thank you," he said, tweaking her nose.

"Well, I'm glad you don't, but I still think you should write something down, you know, like for the academy awards. They write down 'I want to thank my producer . . .' "

"It's okay. I'm good on my feet; I can take care of it all." But still she had made him write some notes. A list of names, the people he had to thank. And he had stayed up, just after she'd drifted to sleep, writing his toast, the people he would thank, the logical order he would thank them in, the way it would all fall into place as everything else had.

The music paused, then started again. Rob heard the vibrant strains of the wedding march. He gazed up and saw Kimberly at the top of the stairs, her body trim and bronzed, a broad smile just for him, and he knew. He knew they had planned it all just right.

Now she looked up, smiled at him, and took her first step

down the stairs to the red crash, to Rob who was waiting for her. Even this decision, Rob knew, as he watched Kimberly walk toward him, with no one escorting her on either side, had been right.

The minister seemed to drone on, talking of love and just what the vow meant. Rob could hear the guests, getting restless behind him. Overhead gulls called. He was swept up in the breeze, the sweetness in the air. And then it was over and the cocktail hour began. Rob made a brief announcement, telling his guests that they had an hour. They could roam around, enjoy the fading light. Champagne was served. Dozens of hors d'oeuvres were brought around—goat cheese and raddichio on toast, caviar puffs. Things Rob had never imagined.

People shook his hand. Kissed him on the cheek. "We are so happy for you," they all said. Rob was sorry that they had to spend most of the cocktail hour taking dozens of photos before the photographer lost the light. It had been awkward, but worth it, Rob thought, when the whole bridal party climbed on to the dunes. But after that the photographer promised that they could just enjoy the party. "The rest will be candid," he had assured him.

And then came the part Rob had been waiting for. Dinner was served and he escorted his bride under the pink tent, illumined with the globes of lemon yellow, orange, and lime green. He watched with pleasure as his guests had tittered slightly when they got their place setting. "Manhattan," he overheard. "What does that mean? I live in Queens."

Perhaps the most special touch of the wedding—the part they'd thought about the most—were the place settings. Each table named after a different city they had visited during the five years they had been together. In planning their wedding they had wanted to create a geography of love—each table representative of where they had been since they were together and who they had known and how that person had come to play a role in their lives.

They made their list of places. Chicago where they had met at a convention when he worked in the book business (he had since gone on to TV), Manhattan where they both lived, just blocks from one another it turned out, Fire Island where they'd fallen in love, Los Angeles where they'd gone on their first trip, Nantucket where his mother's family had a summer home, Montclair where Kimberly had grown up, Greenwich where his father and his new family lived, Rome where they'd gotten engaged, Honolulu where they were going for their honeymoon.

The division of friends and family, of colleagues and associates, even former lovers and exes and divorced spouses of family members (for they had often stayed in touch with both sides long after a divorce). There were steps and halfs and people who simply had not sat in the same room in decades. Now they were to be assembled once more and the place seatings were, of course, a major part of how the evening turned out. After much debate Rob had put his father and uncle, his two half brothers and stepmother at Greenwich; his mother's family, her siblings, his grandmother on the other side of the room at Nantucket (those tables were to be somewhat smaller, but it made the problem less obvious).

Rob wondered what his mother would have made of all of this. He thought she would have appreciated the floral arrangements—the creamy peach roses, the blue delphinium. His mother had loved flowers when he was a boy, but she'd never had the money to buy any. In fact she hadn't had money for much at all. So she'd kept imaginary vases around the apartment and often he'd pretend to arrange a vase, present it to her. "Oh, daisies. I love daisies," his mother would say. But these flowers were real. Everything here was real.

She had died, conveniently he thought sometimes, just after he'd graduated from college. In fact she had collapsed at his graduation dinner. He had been furious with her at the time, until he realized it wasn't one of her little games, but in fact she was sick. And perhaps she'd been sick for years. Perhaps she'd just been holding on for him until he had graduated and could make it on his own. He had planned her funeral as carefully as he'd planned his own wedding.

When his mother got sick, he'd tried to reassure her that she'd be fine. He had done the same thing the night before with Kimberly when the heavens opened and it had poured, a torrential storm. "Oh, there goes the wedding . . ."

"No," Rob said to Kimberly, even though he hadn't believed it at the time. "You'll see, it will be fine."

In fact it was a perfect night; as beautiful as anyone could have imagined. A sherbet sky, the light on the dunes. The pale pink tent with the floating globes. On each table the name of a place that mattered to them; at each table those they loved. There it was, Rob thought; everyone he had cared for in his life in his or her proper place.

Now it was time for his toast. The band stopped and Bradley, their wedding organizer, was calling him up, giving him that officious wave of his hand. Rob took a deep breath, then touched his breast pocket. He touched it again. Nothing was there. He touched it once more as if thinking it might suddenly, like magic, materialize, then he fumbled in the pocket, but it was empty. He didn't have his notes. He slipped his hand into his other pockets. When he closed his eyes, he could see exactly where he had left them. They were on the bedstand in their hotel room on the little white pad where he'd scribbled them the night before. He had never picked them up. But it did not matter. He hadn't wanted those notes in the first place. It was Kimberly who had insisted. Kimberly who liked lists after all. Besides, Rob had the photographic memory. If he closed his eyes, he saw the notes. There were five items. He could see them clearly. He knew just what he was going to say, how he would begin. He would begin by thanking his mother.

And he did. He took another deep breath, looked up at the room, overflowing with the people he knew and loved, and he thanked her. He eulogized her and said how she would have loved this party. How she would have loved the flowers and the tent and danced up a storm. Then he thanked his uncles and aunts, his godfather who had loaned them this house. He thanked his grandmother and his half brothers and then he thanked his bride.

That was five items, wasn't it? His beautiful bride and asked if she would be so kind as to have this dance with him.

As Kimberly rose, Rob was aware, but only dimly, of someone else rising, someone getting up and leaving the room. He couldn't tell if it was someone from Greenwich or Fire Island. It could have even been Honolulu. It wasn't quite someone in his central view, but he was just aware of a man in a tuxedo leaving the room. Perhaps it was his uncle, his father's brother, the one with the prostate problem. It was an older man who left so it made sense that someone had to go to the bathroom.

They had asked the band to play an old favorite of Rob's and his mother's when he was a boy. He heard them start to play "Imagine." It was a song he'd loved and now he and Kimberly would dance for just one minute. In fact a minute was all he'd bothered to learn at Arthur Murray dance studios where he'd gone, where Kimberly had insisted he go, because of his two left feet. "Okay," he said, "I dance, but for one minute."

"Aw, don't worry," his father had said, slapping him on the back at the rehearsal dinner. "One minute, then I get to dance with the bride."

Before them were their guests, almost two hundred of them, and the flickering lights on the tables, and all the places they had been and in his head he was counting, one two three four, one two three four. Counting and counting, until he knew it was more than a minute, and frantically his eyes roamed the room. Kimberly pulled him to her and practically shouted into his ear, "Where the hell is your father?" And then Rob knew that his father was gone. It was his father who had left the room.

The dance seemed to take forever. Kimberly whispered into his ear, "Just repeat what you were doing." He did, he tried, but he stepped on her foot. Later that night she would throw her shoes away. He lost count. Bradley, the wedding organizer, gazed around hopelessly. He checked his notes, shaking his head. The father of the groom was to cut in, but he was nowhere to be seen. The band leader hesitated a few more bars, watching the couple make a small square on the floor as they danced their lonely dance. Then he said, "All right, now, everyone dance." And everyone got up and danced.

When Rob saw that others were rising, he handed Kimberly to her father, squeezed her hand, then raced through the crowd, looking. Was his father sick? Had he gone to the bathroom? He asked a cousin, asked his half brother. No one had seen him. No one knew where he was. But Robby's uncle, Uncle Ted, knew. Uncle Ted, who had clearly had too much to drink, a good-looking man who'd had too many women, Uncle Ted went right up to Rob and spat into his face, "You forgot your father."

Rob paused, wondering what Uncle Ted meant and then he remembered. His toast. He had forgotten to include his father in his toast. "You're right," Rob said, mortified, "I did."

"You forgot to mention your goddamn father. You broke his heart, that's what you did. Ripped it right out of his chest and tore it in two. Let me tell you something in case you didn't know. Your mother was a goddamn psycho and her whole family is a bunch of psychos and you spend your whole speech thanking her, and you leave your father out . . ."

"You're right; I did," Rob said, "I did . . ."

"Your father was a saint, that's what he was. And your mother was a psycho and who did you thank, you thank that nutcase . . ."

Rob felt the room of two hundred people—people who had flown from around the world, from Tokyo and Anchorage, from Paris and West Palm—just to be there today—he felt them slip away. It was as if the only people in that room at that moment were he and his uncle and Rob was tightening the fist he intended to slug his uncle with. "So why did he let me stay with her? Why did he leave me with her?"

But already his uncle had walked away.

His mother had been a nutcase, everyone knew that. It was kind of the family joke, actually. "How's your psycho mother?" uncles on his father's side, long after the divorce, would say. She did lose it from time to time—sold houses they had just moved into, pounded pots and pans together to stop the neighbors from making noise. Sometimes she shouted out the window at people through a foghorn. And sometimes, there was no other way to say it, she had been cruel to Rob. Once, when he was no more than eight, she had locked him out of the house with all the gifts his father had given him that Christmas—a little train, a puppy, a sweatshirt. He'd spent the night curled in the sweatshirt, the puppy in his arms. A neighbor reported it to the police.

Though he'd only been eight, he'd begged his father even then, "Let me come and live with you, Dad," but his father said the same thing he always said—that he'd see, that he'd think about it. He'd ask Margot, his new wife, but then Margot had the first baby, which had come as a surprise, and so, he'd explained to Robby, it would be too difficult to bring yet another child into the house when Margot had just had a baby.

"I'll help with the baby," Rob had said, but his father had laughed. "No, Sport, you'd just be more work on Margot's hands." So then Rob had waited until he was ten to ask again, to beg his father to take him away and let him live with him in the house in Greenwich. Rob loved to go to that house. It smelled of pancakes and scrambled eggs, not dog piss and dirty laundry. The linoleum was clean and things didn't stick to your feet. He liked to run his fingers along the counter and see that it would come up clean. When Margot put a plate in front of him, sometimes he'd just sit and smell it or look at it. He didn't want to spoil the perfect beauty of that place or that table where people sat and ate food off plates and not on stools out of cans.

Often when he went to visit his father, they'd be planning a trip. Or they'd have just come back from a trip. Sometimes there would be skis in the vestibule, packed, ready to go to Aspen or Stowe. Or Margot would be putting pictures from France or Yellowstone into an album. "Oh, look at the boys with that moose staring at them." She'd laugh and point at the picture and Rob would laugh, too. He wondered what it would be like to go somewhere on a vacation. To go skiing or go to the beach. To sleep in a hotel room with clean sheets and have dinner brought to your room. Over dinner they'd talk about that. When he got home, he'd ask his mother if they couldn't go somewhere and she'd spit, "Ask your father. Ask him to take you next time."

But he never asked. Even as a boy, he knew better than to ask. Even as a boy Rob knew how to pick his fights. What he asked his father for was to let him come and live with him. He asked him strategically over the years and he always got the same answer. That his father had a new family, that it was too much for Margot. And then Rob was too old to keep asking. Instead he asked his father to send him to boarding school and his father did.

After that Rob had been more or less on his own. He had seen his father once or twice a month. His father had dutifully paid for whatever. They had always had animated talks on the phone and from time to time Rob even met his father in the city for lunch, during which time his father would give him advice about work opportunities or places to invest his money when he was older and had money.

Now Rob frantically scanned the room, the tables with the floral arrangements, the burning candles, their chattering friends and family and knew that his father was not under the tent and perhaps he was nowhere at all. Rushing out toward where the cars were parked, he began his search. He ran through the house out to the pool where the blue-green water shimmered, the tennis court, down the walk to the beach. He raced up and down but his father was nowhere to be seen.

He would find Kimberly. She would know what to do. But when he arrived back at the wedding where his guests were dancing to a medley of '60s dances (the pony, the twist), he saw his father at Manhattan, talking to the head of a publishing house. With his usual calm assurance, he was shaking a journalist's hand. Then he paused at Los Angeles on his way to Rome, careful to avoid Nantucket where his former mother-in-law and her surviving children sat. Rob tugged at the band leader's sleeve and whispered into his ear and the band leader nodded. Rob would ambush his father. It would be the way he'd make his amends. The music stopped and everyone on the dance floor paused, frozen it seemed for a moment in time, their arms waving as they did the funky chicken. "Excuse me," the band leader said, "we'd like to ask all of you to clear the dance floor so that the groom's father can dance with his mother."

Rob wondered how the band leader could be so stupid. How could he say such a thing when his mother was dead and even if she were alive, she would never have danced with Rob's father. Rob grabbed the microphone away. "Actually," Rob said, "my father is going to dance with my wife because these are the two people most special to me in the whole world. The two people who mean more to me than anything and I want us to give them all a big round of applause and let them have this special dance."

Rob's father stopped, stared up at his son. He could do nothing but comply. Had that sounded right? Rob wondered. He looked at his father, a smile on his face, his expression stony, made his way to the dance floor, as Kimberly came from another corner of the room, that slightly questioning smile on her face. This will make it right, Rob thought. This is what I needed to do. Still he wondered if he had said it right, if he shouldn't have said more, but what more was there to say? He had spoken from the heart before, but now, he didn't know what else there was to say. Rob hugged his father and handed Kimberly to him and watched as they danced, saw their heads tipped together as they spoke while dancing, smiles on their faces, and when the dance was over, he watched as his father walked off the dance floor, down the ramp, and out of the tent once more. This is what I know of my father, Rob thought. He is always walking out on me. This time Rob followed him. He raced after him until he saw that his father was heading for the bathroom. He saw his father go in and shut the door. He would let him go, then wait for him there.

When his father came out, Rob intercepted him. "Dad," he said, "can we talk? Can I speak to you?"

His father gave him an affable smile. "Sure," he said. "Why not."

Rob put his hand on his father's shoulder, led him off toward the shimmering light of the pool. The iridescent light reflecting off the pool. "So, what is it? What's up?"

"Dad, I'm so sorry. I left you out . . ."

"Yes, you did," his father said icily, though the smile had not left his face. "Why is that?"

"I don't know. I just didn't think of it . . ."

Even as he said it, Rob knew he had said the wrong thing. That was the problem, wasn't it? That he hadn't thought of it. He saw it in his father's blue-gray eyes, the same color as his own. In his father's thin red lips, also like his own. "Right," his father, the advertising executive, the man of few words, said. "That's the point."

"I'm sorry. It was an oversight. I tried to make it up to you, just now . . ."

"You thanked her. That crazy mother of yours and her insane family. You thanked her, that woman who made my life miserable."

Rob went back to that night when he was just a boy and his mother had locked him out of the house all night. He still remembered the long cold night he'd spent on the backstep. And he remembered when he'd phoned his father who lived two states away and his father had said it wasn't a good idea for him to come and live with him. He remembered when his mother got sick, even then, when he'd gone to visit his father, he had to sleep on the couch. There had never been a room for him. There had never been a place for him.

But he also remembered other things. That even though she did some crazy things, he knew she would have died for him. He had read about mothers who stood in front of oncoming trains. He had a mother like that. She had loved him completely. And she had never walked away. "She was all I had," Rob said.

"How dare you say that to me? How dare you?"

"Because it's true." Rob knew that this was not what he was supposed to say. That none of this was planned. "And you know it."

Now his father was shouting at him, berating him, calling him ungrateful, a looser. Telling him he was only what he was today because of him. "You went to Yale because of me. You got your first job because of me. Whatever you are, it's because of me." Rob watched a rage swell up in his father. For some reason he thought of the balloons in a parade and his red-faced father resembled one of them. He watched his father swell, get larger and redder as if he were being blown up with helium and was about to float away. "You came to us on weekends. I brought you home when I could. Margot welcomed you into our home."

"It was never my home; I never belonged there. You never wanted me," Rob said, sobbing now, the tears streaming down his face. "I never had a room to sleep in." In the distance he could hear the sound of his own wedding, glasses clinking, music rising. He could hear voices and the sounds of people having a good time. At any moment he knew Kimberly would come searching for him. Someone would come looking, but all he wanted to do was curl into a ball on a lounge chair and cry as he had when he was eight years old and locked out of his own house.

It was the photographer who found them. They were face to face, tears still running down Rob's face. "There you are," the photographer said. And that was the picture he took. It would be the only picture of father and son they would have from the wedding. The two of them, nose to nose. Then Kimberly came and rescued them both. She took them by the arm and said, "Where have you been? Everyone is looking for you."

It was time to cut the cake, to toss the bouquet and do whatever else had to be done to finish the wedding. Friends who'd travelled across the country came up to him, shook his hand. They had flights to get, rides leaving for the city. Where had he been? When could they get together again for some real time? He watched the night evaporate. The combo shutting down on schedule at eleven sharp. The waitstaff blowing out the candles. Guests scooping up the floral arrangements, toting them to their cars. Then dispersing into the directions from which they had come.

Their car was ready and waiting for them. It was not decorated. No one had thought to decorate it. Someone had written "Just Married" in the dew on the back windshield. Flower petals were tossed on their heads. The petals were squishy under his feet. They got into the car, waved at all their guests and friends, and drove the fifteen-minute drive in silence back to their hotel.

That night when they got into bed, Kimberly was in tears. "It was ruined," she told him. "Ruined." They would not make love that night. Instead Kimberly cried herself to sleep. When he heard her heavy breathing, the sound that she was asleep, he reached over to turn off the light and there they were. The little slips of paper he had written his speech on. He didn't need to look at them, at what he'd left out, but he glanced anyway.

There had been six items, not five. He had left out number four, the one just before he thanks his host and his bride. He had left out two words. Kimberly breathed heavily, almost snoring, beside him. He read those words "thank dad" as he crumpled the paper. Then he shaped it into a ball and took careful aim. Cupping his hands into a free throw, Rob shot—and a perfect shot, he would note later—the paper ball across the room in a smooth arc that made its way right into the trash.

[MARY MORRIS]

"For me a story is often a hopefully seamless blend of what I experience, what I witness, and what I make up," says Mary Morris, recipient of a Guggenheim Award and the Rome Prize in Literature from the American Academy of Arts and Letters.

" 'The Geography of Love,' " the author explains, "basically happened at a friend's wedding, but the shape it took and many elements, especially Rob's inner life, are invented. My friend did leave his father out of the toast, but not any toast he'd written. The incident inspired me to write it as a story. It came to me quickly and I had no doubt it was Rob's story, though it could easily have been the father's story.

"In the end, when Rob makes the basketball shot into the trash, I want it to be for Rob a statement of his own independence, but at the same time I can see Rob becoming his father at the end."

Morris is both a fiction and travel writer. Of her ten published books, four, including The Night Sky *and* House Arrest, *are novels. Among three travel memoirs to her name are*

Nothing to Declare *and* Maiden Voyages, *an anthology of travel writing she co-edited with her husband, Larry O'Connor. Her most recent book is* Lifeguard, *a collection of short stories. You will find her short stories and travel essays in such places as* The Paris Review, New York Times, Travel and Leisure, *and* Vogue.

Morris teaches writing at Sarah Lawrence College. She resides in Brooklyn, New York, with her husband and thirteen-year-old daughter.

—C.O.

"MICKEY LOU, I WAS JUST WONDERING…"

Mickey Pearlman

PART OF THE RESIDUE OF GROWING UP IN THE DEEP SOUTH during the 1940s and '50s is remembering that you had to endure what people in my adopted state of New Jersey—on their non-culturally advanced days—would call a lot of crap. First of all, every girl was automatically blessed at birth with two names, and every damn female you met was named something vile like Ida Mae, Ina Lee, Bettye Sue, Mary Jane, or in my case the doubly awful, doubly masculine, Mickey Lou. That moniker got me on the boys' gym list for twelve years, evoking hilarious laughter on a daily basis from pimply faced rednecks, and the guarantee that all my nonpersonal mail for the rest of my so-called natural life would be addressed to Mr. Mickey_____.

Then there were the ten (hundred) commandments without which no self-respecting Southern girl could mature into non-threatening adulthood and/or adorableness: *Sit with your legs together, Be sweet!*, (a big one below the Mason-Dixon line), *Elbows off table; Modulate your voice*, (this one never reached multiethnic New Jersey); *Ladies do not: Chew gum, Talk with their mouths full, Enjoy presents until thank-you notes are written*, etc. And of course,

"Sassy is not sweet," "It's as easy to marry a rich man as a poor one," *"Be nice to—* (fill in the blank here)," and, a particular favorite, *"Women who do not wear hose are doomed."* (Breathe deeply while I explain to you that there were NO pantyhose!) The aphorisms flowed faster than the molasses, one of the best being that hoary special, *"You have to kiss a lot of frogs before you find a prince."*

Now to get serious here, I *was* listening to all this malarkey, especially the one about the frogs, having grown up in the Land of Rock Pits and particularly detesting amphibians of all kinds (hence the D-minus in biology; "You expect me to cut up *this* thing?"), and I was even thinking about the philosophical implications of all this advice. That's when I wasn't thinking about how to get the hell away from the palm trees and into a world where leaves did not look like elongated sabers, and don't talk to me about phallic Freudian bullshit; I aced that course. But only now, late into middle age (epiphanies happening when they feel like it) have I realized that I had the prince to begin with and that I spent about twenty or thirty years kissing frogs.

Unfortunately I could not have married him—even if I had figured this all out—because *this* prince was my father, or as they're known in the South, my Daddy, since in *my* youth A Father was somebody that your Catholic girlfriend kept an eye out for when she was skipping Mass.

Actually, I should have known the prince was in the castle because in my childhood Floridian world of lime-colored trousers and flowered shirts, my daddy looked the part. He wore starched white, long-sleeved shirts (even *before* universal air-conditioning), silk bow ties, polished Florsheims, and double-breasted dark blue Hickey Freeman suits. He even dressed this way at the hometown college basketball games, at the Orange Bowl, and at Gulfstream Park Racetrack, where his law firm had box seats. There, the wipe-off-the-seat attendants—with whom he was hugely popular—addressed him as "Judge." *They* knew quality when they saw it.

The thing about my father (who by the way wanted to name me Michele Louise and is not responsible for my ruined psyche) was his emotional elegance, his soft Atlanta drawl, the way he said, "Mickey Lou, I was just wondering if you'd like to accompany me to the baseball game tonight?" I had my homework in my hands and was ensconced in the front seat of the gray Oldsmobile before my mother could find me in order to say No. Now mind you, we are not talking major league baseball here, we are not talking triple A, we are not even talking A ball. We are talking B league, a variety of baseball now exceeded by Macagna's Funeral Home, Vinny's Pizza, Bobkin's Fuel, and even, for God's sakes, by Vito's Pastry, and every other Little League team in my current hometown. We are talking about going three nights a week to see a team actually called the Miami Beach FLAMINGOS and managed by a then quite dilapidated Pepper Martin. Would it be redundant to add that although I've eaten in most of the best restaurants in New York, Rome, Prague, and Paris, nothing evokes culinary pleasure like the memory of my father's question as we entered the park: "Mickey Lou, I'm just wondering if you'd like a bag of peanuts?" And on the way home: "Mickey Lou, I'm just wondering if you'd like to stop at Howard Johnson's for a peppermint ice cream cone? I, however, would prefer pistachio." *Can we forget about cell phones, intergalactic travel, genetic cloning and please, please, learn how to stop time?*

Now don't get me wrong here. I've been an editor and/or a college professor for over twenty-five years and I've been forced to read and edit God knows how many papers on absentee, drunk, abusive, took-a-hike-on-the-day-I-was-born, sexually invasive, and even physically vicious fathers. Some days it seemed as if there were no other kind. So I've long understood how fortunate I was, even before that psych course where the professor explained in tedious detail about how a woman gets her sense of herself from how her father treats her. I know that, deep in my bones. And, as my daddy used to say in response to any gift, "I'm much obliged." What I don't understand is how he stayed so calm when I, his only daughter, whose grandmother had supported an entire family by making all the wedding cakes and bridal gowns in Savannah, flunked Home Ec? All he said was, "Mickey Lou, I'm just wondering how a smart girl like you could fail *Home Economics* when your mother is such a good cook and you both sew so wonderfully?" I guess my Southern belle mother didn't tell him it was because Mrs. Eulalia Blattner (doesn't God have a sense of humor with names?) made me make and remake white sauce and beaten biscuits ten times straight and I told her where she could put the next batch.

On reflection, his unspoken permission for me to be a full-fledged human probably started with my kindergarten graduation. I know that we wore white caps and gowns and I have the photograph to prove it. (This was the deep South, remember.) But the family myth goes something like this. Another rotten five-year-old, no doubt one of the blonde, blue-eyed ones named Mary Jane, wobbled across the stage and e-n-u-n-c-i-a-t-e-d my lines in the graduation play. And when I simply pushed her off the stage, (and, after all, she fell right into her mother's lap, for God's sake), all my father was reported to have said was, "Mickey Lou, I'm *surprised* that a nice girl like you would do such a thing." But "she said *my* lines, Daddy. She said MY lines."

Maybe it was because I looked exactly like him, the only two dark-haired, dark-eyed people in a family of redheads with green eyes. Maybe it was because in a room full of 300 kids you could have picked me out as his daughter. But I do understand the gift, that he let me be who I was, unabashedly, and without the usual lifetime price that females still pay for being assertive and/or different.

My father died, alone, sitting in his favorite white chair, while watching a baseball game on television. He was waiting for my mother's return from Hot Springs, Arkansas, and was planning to pick her up at the train station. I had flown in from Europe only the night before, with my ten-month-old son, after spending nine months in winter-logged Berlin, and was in the States mostly to see *him*. I was in Maryland at a friend's house, waiting for both of my parents to be reunited in Florida before I boarded the plane to Miami. I had been dialing their number all day, eager for the chance to talk again to my father without interruption or competition from another parent.

Instead I flew home at six A.M. for the funeral, never having had the chance to say either hello or good-bye. As I turned from the mourners' front-row seats to leave the funeral "parlor," I noticed a goodly number of Black people standing at the back of the room. Were these people here, among the 700 others, for the funeral in 1968 of a white, supremely Southern, Jewish community leader and synagogue president who probably had no practical working knowledge of, or emotional involvement with, concepts like "civil rights" and "integration." I noticed that Charlie Johnson was there, the gardener who had suffered over the mangled kumquat and frangipani trees with my mother after many a Florida hurricane. But who were the other mourners?

It took many years to find out that Charlie had once asked my father to secure and file the deeds on his church, in what was then known as Coloredtown. That was the beginning of a ten-year relationship that defies easy explanation but probably proves the existence of a Higher Power. Actually, what Charlie is reported to have said was, "Judge, I was just wondering if you could help us out a little here."

I am not wondering anymore. I even use Mickeylu as my E-mail address. I never miss a chance to watch baseball, and I always take a bag of peanuts with me to the game.

And thirty years and many frogs later, I am still lonesome, so lonesome, for the prince.

[MICKEY PEARLMAN]

Though she considers herself a devoted New Jerseyan, Mickey Pearlman was born in Miami Beach and is every inch a Southern gentleman's daughter. Having known her only a short time, I can still say that like her father, when something needs to be done, she gets it done, and with a quiet thoughtfulness that belongs to the old school.

Not that Pearlman is ever muted on subjects dear to her.

Hardly. She is a staunch promoter of writers and the written word, as is evidenced in her book Listen to Their Voices, and in a collection of interviews with writing women, A Voice of One's Own, that Publisher's Weekly called, "a treasure trove for readers of today's fiction." Three volumes of memoir: A Few Thousand Words About Love, A Place Called Home, and Between Friends have established her as an anthologist's anthologist.

In years past, she has taken life on the road to Vienna, Berlin, Tel Aviv, and Prague, but as all were "too far from Shea Stadium," now restricts her travel to lecturing and teaching at book events across the country. Closest to her heart is A Celebration of Readers and Their Favorite Books, an event she organized, which is held annually at Mohonk Mountain House in upstate New York.

"I think everyone in America should be signed up for a book club," she says. "Maybe when you get your driver's license or something."

Pearlman claims academic life is also far behind her but holds an impressive number of graduate degrees in philosophy, English, and American literature. She is also a member of the National Book Critics Circle and was named one of Mirabella magazine's 1,000 Women for the 1990s.

In "Mickey Lou, I Was Just Wondering . . ." she writes of the many wonderful gifts her father gave her, his time and love, her sense of self-esteem. Asking her if there was any one gift she wished she could give her father now, were it possible, I receive this response:

"My father had three heart attacks and, as noted, the fourth one killed him. If we are doing imaginary stuff, now that I know much more about heart disease than I did then, I would have liked to have given him more income and less stress and more years.

"My mother, always the wit, said (and usually disparagingly) that he was a man of 'the eighteenth century.' I don't think in reality that life was any easier then, but I know what she meant." Her father, she says, "should have lived in a different time when men of his background and education were taken care of in certain ways, did not have to worry about the minutiae of life, had the leisure to gracefully enjoy the years. Clearly my father did not have the resources to really compete in a materialistic world and was a man in love with the law instead of the dollar."

Pearlman is quick to add honestly, "Of course all this is classist as hell and is my take, not my father's."

—C.O.

THE WILD RUSSIAN

Rochelle Jewell Shapiro

"Block, Rosie," my father ordered. He threw a round-house at me in one of the mirrors he set up against the walls of our finished basement to watch himself box. My hands flew up to my face. I squealed and nearly toppled off the hassock.

His face got dark. "Don't scream," he hollered. Then his forehead got crinkled. His mouth turned down. He ruffled my hair. "Sorry I hollered, Rosie. Do like this," he said, softly. He raised up his arm, bent at the elbow.

I copied him. "Good," he said. My face felt like it would break from smiling.

Dad kept blocking as he threw punches. His eyes were narrowed and his mouth was tight. His muscles were like mountains that could move. He was wearing his boxing trunks and laced-up brown shoes with soft soles. He sprang this way and that, fists jabbing the air. He threw a left hook and Mirror-Dad came at him with a right. Sweat ran down my father's broad forehead. I liked watching him box more than I liked eating a Humorette. I even liked watching him box more than I liked playing chopsticks on the landlady's piano.

In the mirror straight ahead, I saw myself wearing the plaid dress I wore last week at my ninth birthday. I had a big green bow on top of my red curls. My father's hair was red too, but as he boxed, it got dark and his curls flattened. His eyes were blue like mine. I heard Mom upstairs smacking her Hoover into the furniture. I felt bad for her. I'd have stayed up there and kept her company or gone to the park with her, but Sundays were the only days Dad took the whole day off. I missed him and missed him. I noticed my fingers were bunching the ruffle on my hem, which made it wrinkle, but I couldn't stop. Mom was mad at me for watching Dad box. She said I was encouraging him.

Dad threw another punch. My hands flew to my face again.

His mouth twisted to one side, but he said, "At least this time you didn't make a peep. That's important, knowing how to be quiet. Me, I was only four when the Cossacks came. My mother hid me in the oven. 'Don't make a sound!' she warned me. I curled myself into a ball and listened to my father's dying screams. If I didn't keep my mouth shut, I wouldn't be here to tell you about it."

I wished Dad wouldn't tell me that story. It made me wake up in the night and call out for Mom. Mom held me and said, "That was a long time ago, Rosie. Nothing like that could happen now."

"If a punch is thrown to your chest or your stomach," Dad said, "you can cross your hands like this to block it." His elbows were down so his middle was covered. I copied him. Then he threw a punch and I blocked my face by mistake.

"You've got to concentrate," Dad said. "That's the secret." He punched the air faster, imitating the sounds his fists made when he was pounding the sandbag at Stillman's gym where his fighting name was "The Wild Russian," not Sol Polnikov. "Whomp, whomp, whomp." The gym smelled like onions left in the back of the fridge. Dad showed me off, introduced me to everybody. "Here's my best girl," he said. He let me try on his boxing gloves, the ones he wouldn't even let anyone else touch. I kissed his gloves, then raised them above my head and made them bump into each other as if I'd won a fight. Other kids weren't allowed there, but they let me stay because my dad was The Wild Russian. The other fighters watched him out of the corner of their eyes and

tried to copy his moves, and when it was time for sparring partners, my dad got the best. Abe, his manager, had gray and black
hair and crooked teeth. He would pat me on the head and say,
"Rocky (he called me that), do you know how good your dad is?"

"The best," I said, proudly.

Everybody was proud of Dad except Mom. Upstairs I heard a
big clunk. She bumped the Hoover into the radiator. She used to
brag about Dad coming here all by himself from Russia when he
was thirteen with only a change of underwear and two dollars,
landing a job hauling cases of blue bottles of seltzer from a ware-
house in Jackson Heights, training for prizefights. I loved to hear
her stories about him.

She had fallen in love with Dad's picture in a newspaper. "I
never in my life saw such cheekbones," Mom said. "And the way
he stood. Oh, my God." Even though she had never gone to a
fight before, she bought a ticket. Between rounds, Dad saw her in
the fifth row. He sent Abe to tell her Sol Polnikov wanted to meet
her. Their first date, Dad hugged her so hard, he cracked her ribs.
Now all she said was, "Those days are over."

Dad still loved those days. His eyes got bright when he told me
the stories. Mom used to stop at the gym to bring him a quart jar
of her lemonade. At his fights, she was at the edge of her seat,
chanting, "Sol, Sol, Sol." She'd dress up special in a hat with a
rolled-up brim and high-heeled shoes. If he got hit, she screamed.
The only thing that got the men's eyes off him was watching her.
He swore her Evening in Paris cologne cut through the sweat, the
thick air, working to make him fight harder, faster, better than he
ever had. After she had me, everything changed about her. Not
just her body, but how she felt. "Babies do something to you," she
had told me. "The world suddenly becomes a dangerous place—
and with me, it wasn't just for my little baby, but for my big baby
too." She was so scared Dad would get hurt that she couldn't
watch him fight anymore. He saw her there, but her eyes were
shut and he couldn't concentrate. It was the first time he got
knocked out cold. After that she stopped going. "But I need you
to cheer me on!" he said. "You're my good-luck charm. My Amer-

ican Beauty," he pleaded, but she shook her head. "Last time I was there, you got knocked out cold," she said. "But it was a fluke!" he insisted. "No, no," she said. "I can't take the risk of that happening again. I can't be responsible." She told me that even though she stayed away, she thought about him there. It still bothered her, just the same, the way you could think about a lemon and your mouth puckered up, even if there wasn't a lemon within miles. She'd pace the apartment waiting for him, and every time she heard an ambulance, she bolted to the door, flung it open, and stood there looking up and down the street, her hands on her heart. She began to beg him not to fight anymore.

"Sol, you're a father," she said. "You have to think about your future, our future."

"Fighting is in my blood," Dad said.

"Your blood is in the next room sleeping," she argued.

I never slept when they fought. I heard every word.

"Find something else to do," she had told him, but he kept right on boxing. She began to look for jobs for him. He could go to work for Max Stroller, the store that sold good suits. He could get an Arnold's bread route. And then she saw a deli for sale in the paper, cheap. She knew the business. Her uncle had had a deli. "If you buy it," Mom told Dad, "I'll help you run it. I could work right next to you. Rosie could help set the tables. We'd be a real family."

"We are a family," Dad said. "I train by running on the beach with Rosie on my back."

"If you keep boxing, I'm going to leave you and take Rosie with me."

I was Dad's best prize. I knew he would never want to lose me.

Now Dad said to me, "Block, Rosie." I knew what to do.

"Good, you're paying attention," he said.

When Dad finally bought the deli, I remember how excited Mom was. She hired three men to repaint the tin ceiling white. She bought frosted glass with clear vines trailing up the sides for the front windows and chose green leatherette for the booths. She painted roses on jelly jars and used them to serve mustard. It was called "Queens Deli" after our borough. But a lot of people called it "Dorothy's" because Mom made them feel so at home. People liked having me around too. They would give me nickels and stretch out one of my curls and let it go to watch it roll back like a party horn. "You're a real Shirley Temple," people told me. I watched Dad making sandwiches, his shoulders slumped as if all the fight was out of him. I felt as if it was all my fault. I puffed up my cheeks and crossed my eyes, but Dad's smile was like old ginger ale.

"I've got to get back in the game," he told Mom.

"No more prizefighting," Mom said.

One day Dad came home and went straight downstairs to the basement. He was down there a long time. Mom opened the basement door. "He's down there in the dark," Mom said. We went to find him. Dad was sitting at an old desk, his head in his hands.

"Sol?" Mom said.

He didn't even turn around. He just shook his head and said, "I have to get back to the gym. I'm not saying I'm going to fight. I just have to get in shape."

"Sol, you'll get hurt," Mom said.

"Dorothy, you're not letting me be a man. I'll just spar a little."

I squeezed Mom's hand. "All right," she said to Dad, quietly. "I'll get somebody to help out in the deli while you're at the gym. But training at the gym doesn't mean fighting real fights."

She hired a teenage boy and made him wear a hair net. But whenever Dad tried to go to the gym, Mom found some excuse. The refrigerator case was leaking; a big order had to be packed for delivery; it was too busy for him to go.

One day we heard sirens. Police were outside the door, but Mrs. Lipinsky still demanded her free refill of tea. Dukakis, the butcher, on the corner, had been held up.

"Thank God you're here with us," Mom said to Dad.

"What good will I be to you and Rosie if I look like Dukakis with his skinny arms and fat belly?"

After the robbery, Dad started going to the gym three afternoons a week. He came home with a new spring in his step. He bought me Snickers and Mars Bars and Nestlé's Crunch and let me find them in his pockets. He grabbed Mom and started whirling her around the living room in a dance that she didn't even try to follow. She kept checking his face and hands and if she found a bruise, she would wince. Then she'd start in about, "Sol, I know you. Once you start fighting, you can't stop."

"That's why we're a good match," he told her, laughing.

Mom couldn't be kidded out of her worry. "Promise me you'll never go back into the ring," she pleaded.

He got up, came to her, stroked her cheek.

But before long, Abe, Dad's old manager, began pressuring Dad. "Sol, you're not getting younger. It's now or never. Train full time and you could go the distance."

"I'm going for middleweight champ before it's too late," Dad announced.

I was glad for Daddy. I could imagine the crowd roaring for him. I could imagine me cutting out his picture from the sports page and bringing it to school for show and tell. But then there were terrible nights of fighting. I got out of bed and hid in the kitchen. When their voices died down, Dad came out for water. I'd watch him drinking. "Rosie," he said, tilting up my chin and then as softly as fly wings, bumped his fist on it. "It's going to be all right." He carried me to bed.

"Whomp," Dad said, landing a punch at me in the mirror. He looked scary. He looked like he was fighting for his life.

I forgot to duck. I forgot to block.

"Rosie, in this world, you've gotta have as many eyes as a potato." Dad undercut with his left, then jabbed with his right. "Ding," he called out. He grabbed a towel and wiped off his face. "Ten rounds and I only knocked myself out. I have a month more to get in shape. Come on, Rosie. We have to go up and face the music." Mom was the music.

She was on her knees in the living room trying to cover the nicks in the ball and claw legs of the coffee table with mahogany stain. It was five o'clock, but her hair was still in pin curls and she was wearing her flowered housecoat.

"Still not dressed?" Dad said.

"And what should I be dressed for? Did you take us to the
Loew's or to Horn and Hardhart? Did we go to the circus? Play-
land? No, you stayed in the basement with Rosie."

My name came out of her mouth like a spitball.

Dad went off to take a shower. He was in a good mood. I
heard him singing "Faigele, faigele, faigela, faigela, lox and
cream cheese mit the bagela." But what made him so happy—
boxing—was making Mom as bitter as the green tomatoes bobbing in the deli barrel. She slammed change down on the
counter and wiped the tables while the customers were still eating. I didn't know how to make Mom and Dad love me at the
same time.

The night of Dad's "Welcome Back Fight," as Abe called it, I
pleaded, "Daddy, I want to go."

"Rosela," he said, kneeling, rubbing his stubbled cheek against
mine, "there's no other children. You can't sit there alone."

"I can."

"No you can't," Mom said. "When you sit close to the ring,
blood sprays all over you. A boxer can get punched right out of
the ring and fall on you."

I imagined my father flying over the ropes into the crowd, his
body punched with little holes and spraying like our showerhead.
I imagined myself with blood all over me. I imagined myself
crushed like a sparrow in the road. Tears sprang to my eyes. I was
scared. Mom's fear had found an open seam in me.

"Dorothy, don't put bad thoughts in her head," Dad said.

After Dad slammed the door, Mom made popcorn. The little
kernels popping against the rising tinfoil reminded me of punches.
Mom kept it on the burner too long. The kitchen got smoky. The
popcorn was black. Mom started to cry as if it was the worst thing
in the world for the popcorn to burn.

"It's okay," I said. My throat was knotted. I couldn't have even
eaten one piece.

She took out a deck of cards. We played War. Her pile grew
and I had none left. Then she started walking back and forth in

the living room. I rocked on the couch and watched the clock. Mom didn't make me go to bed.

The big hand was past twelve when we heard the key in the lock. The door opened. Dad was in the doorway, leaning on Abe.

"On his way to middleweight champ," Abe called out as if he was using a megaphone.

Mom shrieked. Dad's cheek looked like mashed grapes and one of his eyes was blackened.

"Daddy!" I cried. I thought he was going to have to be taken to the hospital like the fish man down the block. The fish man never came home again. I thought of all Grandma's stories about people who were perfectly well one minute and keeled over dead the next.

"Don't cry, Rosie," Dad said. "I won." He tried to smile, but winced and drew in his breath.

He limped into the kitchen. As soon as he sat down, Mom flew at Abe, beating his chest with her fists. "Get out of here," she screamed.

Abe blocked and ducked. "Sol, you married a bruiser," he said. But he hurried down the stairs.

Mom dabbed at Dad's face with a cloth. "Oh, Jeeze. Take it easy," he said.

"I feel like hitting you myself," Mom said to Dad, but she wiped his face very gently, her eyes shiny with tears. Dad's lip was cut. Blood dripped onto his teeth. I couldn't look anymore. I ran to my room and threw myself on my bed, sobbing.

"Sol, look what you're doing to Rosie," I heard Mom say. "I love you, but I swear I'm going to take Rosie, pack up the Mercury, drive to my mother's, and never come back."

Grandma lived in Elmira. Mom and I went there three times a year. It took six hours to drive there and every time I couldn't wait to come home.

Dad came to my room. He turned on the lamp next to my bed. "Rosie," he said, "I only have a few fights to go before I get a chance at middleweight."

He looked at me sadly. I wanted to hear him singing silly songs. I wanted him to hear the ref shouting, "The winner and the next middleweight champ—The Wild Russian." Then I thought about how angry Mom was all the time now, like someone who should be boxing herself. I thought about Grandma in Elmira—the way she rolled her false teeth in her mouth to clean them with her tongue. I thought of all the ways I had heard of boxers getting hurt. Punch drunk. Bashed-in skull. Knock out. Dead. I couldn't get the picture of Dad all bloodied out of my mind. "Daddy, I want you to give it up."

He looked at me with his half-opened eyes and blew out his breath. "Okay, Rosie," he finally said. "If that's what you want." He stood up. The grace that always moved with him was gone.

Daddy was behind the counter at the deli again. Mom was joking with the customers like she used to. But Daddy couldn't even look them in the face, especially when one of them congratulated him on the fight. He went to Stillman's a few times to punch the bag and spar, but he left after an hour. "It's not the same if you're not training for a fight. I'm like a horse without a carrot in front of my nose."

Soon he stopped going. He ate, looked at the paper, except for the fight page, then fell asleep in his flowered armchair. He hardly talked at all.

One night he dozed off, his head dropping forward. "Papa!" he called. Suddenly, his head jerked up. His eyes snapped open. He stared at me as if he couldn't remember who I was.

"Daddy?"

He ground his fists into his eyes. His hands flopped back to his lap. Then he got up slowly. "It's like it all happened yesterday," he said.

"What?"

"Nothing. I'm just tired," he said and dozed off again.

I went into the kitchen. "Mommy, something's wrong with Daddy."

She sighed and went into the living room. "Sol, Sol, wake up."

"In a few more minutes," he told her.

"You've got to take an interest in something besides fighting," she said.

"Dorothy, will you please stop? Whatever I do, there's no peace."

Once Mom gave in to the fact that there was nothing she could do for Dad, she enrolled me in a Sunday morning dance class that I had never asked for. "It's not good for you to stay around the house all day," she said as if the way Dad was was an illness that I could catch.

A week later, she put on her red-and-white-checked topper and her hat with the pointy corners and took me on the A train. I thought of my father staring at the TV screen without bothering to turn it on. I pictured him nodding off. I was so used to the sound of his snoring that I imagined I heard it right in the train. Even if Dad didn't say a word to me, I wished I could be with him. It was too sad to think of him all alone on his day off. But Mom looked happy to be dressed up and out of the house and on her way to Manhattan.

At first I didn't like the class. The other girls had been going for a long time. They whispered to each other when I was right there and for them, tap dancing was no harder than taking a walk. I felt as if I'd never be able to do it, but after only a couple of weeks, I learned the time step and all the variations. I could even tap up and down my teacher's wooden platform and sing "East Side West Side," too. I began to love to hear my taps on the hardwood floor. It was like yelling into a tunnel and listening to your own voice yelling back at you. I tapped and tapped so long that I began to sweat like my father did when he was training.

By the third week, I began to sing and tap so well the teacher shouted, "Brava!" My face got flushed and I did a deep curtsy. All the way home, the whole world seemed to have stepped up its color. Through the smeary subway window, the hook-necked birds with the long skinny legs looked whiter against the marshes and the bay water looked as if someone sprinkled new pennies all over it. When I got home, the pink walls of my room were prisms and stayed like that even when it got dark outside.

But then I heard my mother yelling at my father and my room looked just regular to me again. I couldn't listen to them fighting any more. I went down to the basement and practiced the time step in front of Dad's mirrors. Even with the door closed, I heard Mom shouting, "This is no life."

"For just once can you shut your mouth?" my father yelled back at her.

I imagined my mother packing the Mercury. I imagined her driving to Elmira with our suitcases in the back. I imagined myself in Grandma's parlor, not being allowed to breathe on her chachkas, and Dad stuck in the deli with no dreams except bad ones. I got so upset, I began to shout-sing over their voices about the boys and girls together and me and Mamie O'Rourke.

My father came down to the basement. He sat on the bottom step with his elbows almost at his knees and his hands covering his ears. It looked like he was trying not to hear Mom even though she stopped hollering at him. He blew his breath out.

I started singing really loud about London Bridge falling down. He glanced at me. I kept tapping. Then he began to watch me. At first, him watching me made me feel as if I was going to trip over my own feet. Concentrate, I told myself, the way Dad used to tell me when he was showing me how to field a punch. Concentrate, the way I used to see him do at the gym. I kept dancing. I forgot all about him. I forgot about everything but the sound my taps made, the way my muscles sprang and stretched. I danced around the room so I could see myself in each mirror.

"Look at you, Rosie." Dad's voice was quiet. Amazed. "You've got technique."

He looked at me, straight-on, as if I had secrets he might need to know. He stood up and nodded. Even though it was just a nod, it made me feel as if a whole crowd was clapping for me. "So light on your feet," he said.

It was as if we'd been travelling in different countries and forgot how to speak the same language, and suddenly we were again. "Try it," I told him.

He hesitated. Then he got up.

"Hop," I told him. He hopped. "Now brush-brush." I swung my leg from the knee, making a double tap on the floor. He brush-

brushed, his leather slipper scuffing. "Step, step," I commanded and we stamped each foot. "Now faster." He broke right into the step and tapped along with me. He grinned a real grin. His eyes took on some spark. "Great, Daddy," I said. "Now let's take it from the beginning."

He took my hand and slowly, slowly, together we began to dance.

[ROCHELLE JEWELL SHAPIRO]

"You might say that I read and write for a living," says Rochelle Jewell Shapiro.

She is a working psychic who does readings from her bedroom office for "the famous and infamous." Her unique abilities lead her to appear routinely on radio, for programs such as "Talk Radio Network" in Colorado, "Morning with Murphy" in Kansas City, and "Conversations with Anne," of Radio One with Nancy Ross in Utah.

On the writing side of the equation, Shapiro's work has appeared in The New York Times Sunday Magazine, The Iowa Review, Astarte, *and* California Review, *as well as many anthologies. Recently she took up the challenge of writing her first novel. Quite naturally, it's about a psychic.*

Shapiro classifies "The Wild Russian" as a fictional memoir, with a few elements of truth behind it, the first being that "My father did survive a pogrom and come to America as a teenager. He did box in order to get the money for his business." A second truth, she says, lies in the fact that "I was a tap dancer and a Shirley Temple look-alike as a child."

Though her father's boxing days had ended before Shaprio was born, she put these two truths together because, she says, "Like the children of most survivors, I wished more than anything else that I could rescue my father. I wished I could bring him some relief, some distraction from his ghosts.

"*When I write about him, I get the opportunity to honor the man he could have been, the bond we could have had if he hadn't been too guilt ridden to enjoy me, if he hadn't been so tortured by violence as a child that he became violent himself.*"

—C.O.

SOMEWHERE NEAR SEA LEVEL

Dawn Raffel

HERE IS MY FATHER. HE IS TUCKING IN A TONGUE. COAXING. Lacing, doubling a knot. My ankles are weak. The rink is lit. My father's hands are darkly livered, veined. Use, he says, has done this.

"Can you stand?" my father says.

The ice, I see, is swept, wet, white. "Try standing," my father says. "Up." There is forcefully dampered music, piped. There is no sky. No rain, no threat. "See it?" my father says. "Look." No hint. It used to be something else, this forceful place. "Before your time," he says.

He looks like my father.

"Gone," he says.

"Dad?" I say. I am gaining my feet. There is something, I think, or nothing, hairline, cleft.

Deep. The voice. "Steady."

A person could be dizzy.

"You almost can see it."

"Dad?" I say.

It is dizzying.

"Things I could tell you," my father is telling me. He is inflection, timbre; unfamiliar and expected in the faraway, fatherly way he always has. "Gloves . . ." he says. "Folds . . ." I feel the after-rills of phrases, words between the words I am invariably failing to catch. "A curtain there . . . an arch . . ."

A ramp's slope.

What I want is to skate. I do. Want to. Want and want to want. Pulsing my toes, my fingers restless, ragged-nailed. "Now?" I say.

My father is talking marble and Saturday. "Nights," he says, whatever, I don't know. "Glass," he says, or "Hats," he says.

"Tails," he says.

"These skates," I say. "My toes."

My father is pressing for fit, says, "Gutted." I feel it. "Better?" he says.

I have had practice.

"Better," I say. "Better, please." My ankles flinch.

There is a woman in the middle of the middle of the ice, going backward. Curve and grace is what she is, and speed, and speed.

There is knowing in the body. My father is touching my elbow, glancingly, knowingly, fluidly moving beside me, before me, ushering me from behind.

"The center is lower," my father says, "in a girl."

The woman appears to me to be weightless.

"Why?" I say. "What center?"

"Didn't I tell you?" my father says.

She is all lift.

I am in a wobble.

"Never mind," my father says.

I am making my father fall, almost. I almost could.

"Easy, easy does it," my father says. "Use your head, for heaven's sake."

I am flailing for his arm. "Tell me," I say. "Now." My father is smartly just past reach. "Why?" I say.

"You know," he says, "a person cannot hear you."

Habit. Fearborne. Sleeves, snaps, cuffs. I am speaking to a bead, to a fearful pearlish glinting in myself. "This place," I say, "was what?"

"Careful," my father says.

There is a ceiling, of course. Always was. Flight's worth up. It burns, the ice, rebukes my back. Flat flung limbs. Nothing is broken, my father says. Birds, I say. It is terribly high, even given style, even given flights, even given tricks with scarves. A person could stand on a person's shoulders, given even balance, a bent for stunt, feint— a lady fluttering, swooning, waft and lilt and pale, light, sweet perfume, airily, deftly arcing off a balcony—taken down, removed.

My father is furrow and how many fingers.

"Who?" I say.

"Who do I look like? Please," I say.

"My name?" I say.

"What day?" I say.

"Wait," I say. "My ankle," I say, "hurts." It all comes back—oh, the power of the powerfully helpless. "Hurts," I say.

"Let me," my father says. "Will you?"

"Won't," I say. "Will not," I say, "help." This is only a portion of an answer in advance.

Now you see it: My father's skates are scarred, if from daring or storage, I do not know—in houses, cellars, wrecked and vaulted rooms, strewn, or bound, paired, dolled in attic rags, sleeves, yokes, the ruined drapes, the molded sheets—in plundered trunks, a chest; a lavish efflux: See under spawn and brackish fissure, over sunken seams, ridge, reef; see under floe; see under yaw, in another time zone, found.

By the way, I am married.

"Won't," I say, "help."

I am kneeling and fanning and lying.

I am not a child.

"Let me," my father says, "see it?"

I say, "Will you?"

I say, "Please," or I say, "Look," or "Hurts," I say. He is touching my elbow, hair, my arm. We are in an aisle; he is touching a veil, net, necklace—luminous, inherited; I am carrying lilies;

there is no breeze; I am carrying nothing, blood; we are in rooms, in years, in the rending of an instant, cleaving in the yawning dark, curled, here, gone. He is touching a shoulder—blade, wing—nobbed, insistent back. "What?" he says. "I can't," he says, "hear you, make sense of you, the way you turn away."

He is holding my foot, my father is. "Flex," he says.
The woman jumps.
"How does it feel?" my father says.
"Sore," I say. Impossible, the height. . . .
"Very sore."
. . . The woman lilts, floats, rises, impossibly rises.
"Sprained," I say. (I have had lessons.) "Horribly sprained."
"Not likely," my father says. "Couldn't. You hardly were moving."
"Was," I say.
"Can't be," he says.
"Could," I say.
"Could so," I say.
"You are so small," my father says. "You didn't have very far to—"
"Wait," I say. "There was a second in the air, I remember, when everything—"
"Slipped," my father says. We are all interruption.
"Spun," I say. "It—"
"—Most you did was slip," my father says. "Scratched, tops. More or less—"
"Please," I say.
"More or less nothing." My father is moving. "I am waiting," he says.
"Still waiting," he says.
"Can't hear you," my father says.
I am on bony, graceless knees.
The woman is glowing, effulgent.
I could be imploring.

* * *

"Tell me," he says. "What?"

There is a way that whatever you turn away from owns your heart. There is a way that it doesn't.

He is touching my neck, a clasp, mesh. We are under a shimmering sky.

He is still waiting.

I am in white. "Carry me," I say.

[DAWN RAFFEL]

"I used to go skating at an indoor rink that had once been a grand old movie palace," Dawn Raffel tells me, when I ask her about the inspiration for "Somewhere Near Sea Level."

"To me," she says, "it seemed an ideal setting for a father-daughter story because it evoked the layers of history in a father's life that a daughter can sense but never really see. I think we remain forever small in relation to our parents, our mythology of them. It is impossible, on one level, to ever apprehend our parents, yet we know them so intimately on a genetic level that it is difficult to accept the distance, the generational interruption."

Raffel's genius for seeking out glimpses of the unseen, fascinating twists and turns in the human character is evident in her short story collection, In the Year of Long Division, *in which "Sea Level" appears. After fourteen years at Redbook magazine, most spent as fiction editor, she has recently been named senior deputy editor for Oprah Winfrey's new magazine. Raised in Wisconsin, where all of her stories are set, she now lives in Hoboken, New Jersey, with her husband and two sons.*

Look for her first novel, Bedtime, *to be released soon.*

—C.O.

ON BEING DADDY'S SON AND DAUGHTER

Florence Cawthorne Ladd

OVER THE YEARS DREAMS OF MY FATHER, NOW DEAD A QUARTER of a century, have brought him back to me.

Appearing at first in his younger years, the years of my early child-hood, at the edge of a railway yard he stands next to his 1935 Ford, no longer new. I am perched on the hood of the car. Identifying the type of car, boxcar, freight car, Pullman, baggage car, caboose, engine, he points to passing trains.

Daddy often took me on Saturdays to watch the comings and goings of trains at a rail yard in northeast Washington, D.C., the city of his birth and mine. When I was five years old, Santa Claus delivered an electric train. There were other gifts that Christmas: a blue tricycle, a toy stove, and several dolls, but the major present was the train set. Dad built a train platform and installed a transformer that regulated the train's speed, whistles, and stops. It was too complex initially, he said, for me to operate. I knelt at his side and watched him turn the switches that maneuvered the train around the track. My mother whispered to relatives and neighbors, "Bill finally got himself an electric train." He also had in me a partner who shared his fascination with the movement of trains and the sound of wheels on rails, even the rattle of tin wheels of a toy train.

On Sunday mornings, Daddy drives me to Sunday School at Second Baptist Church. He remains in the car, drops me off, and drives away. When Sunday School ends, I come out of the church and find him waiting in the car, just washed and polished.

Although claiming membership in Second Baptist Church, my father rarely entered the church when I was a child. Only special events, such as baptisms, funerals, and pageants at Christmas or Easter, draw him within its granite walls. In his later years, only after the cancerous death of my sister, Ethel, and the passing of his parents did he become an active member of the church where he was a deacon with fiduciary responsibilities.

On a grassy field, he tosses a football beyond me. I run back and reach for it. Somehow I am there at just the right moment. "Good catch! Good girl!" he calls.

By the time I was seven years old, I somehow knew that my parents had hoped that I, their firstborn, would have been a boy. William Cawthorne III. Their second child, a girl, died in infancy. Then came my sister, Ethel. My mother seemed pleased to have two daughters. My father, however, had a "son" and a daughter.

Daddy and I engaged in a conspiracy of denial about my gender; I went along with his plan for the upbringing of a son. He took me to watch the local high-school teams play football. We rooted for Armstrong High, where he had played defense on the football team between 1915 and 1918. During halftime, he introduced me to his friends, the coaches. "Florence loves the game. She's a good athlete. She'd make a great scat back." In fact, I was a good runner; and I played touch football frequently with the boys in my neighborhood. Winter was the season for basketball.

Daddy and I were often in the stands at basketball games watching high-school boys run up and down the court. From time to time, he'd turn to me and say, "You're tall. You jump high. You should try basketball." A few years later, in physical education classes, I played basketball with other girls. I performed well in those mid-afternoon games played without spectators—games Daddy never saw.

A clerk-messenger for the Washington, D.C. public schools on weekdays, my father was a carpenter, amateur auto mechanic, and general handyman on weekends. Commissioned by neighbors, relatives, and friends, he made screen doors and built bookshelves. He also repaired radios. I was at his side in the basement workshop finding the radio tube he needed or giving him the appropriate screwdriver or pliers. "Hand me that Phillips screwdriver, Buddy." I liked his workshop name for me—Buddy. And I liked doing what apprentices do. It was an apprenticeship in becoming a son.

Daddy did his own auto maintenance work. I was invited to stand on the bumper and lean over the engine for lessons in changing oil, checking the water level in the radiator, and replacing a carburetor. When I sat in the front seat during an outing, it was an occasion for him to prepare me for driving with instructions about use of the gear shift, clutch, and brakes.

At Christmas there were gifts to reinforce the lessons of my apprenticeship: Lincoln logs, a tool kit, airplane models, and an erector set. At my request when I was ten, I was given a chemistry set. It was enormous—a small laboratory. My interest in chemistry had been inspired by a biography of Marie Curie; and Daddy encouraged my pursuit of chemistry, physics, and math. My scholastic performance was strong. Being a successful student mattered to him, too. Good grades were generously rewarded.

In my pre-adolescent years, my mother's interest in literature and music influenced my activities. I read books she suggested and took piano lessons. She also promoted tennis lessons and swimming. And during the five years I was a Girl Scout, Mom, in uniform, was the assistant troop leader.

My mother's passion about being well dressed began to influence my wardrobe. Toward adolescence, I found in my closet dresses not of my choice nor to my liking, a ruffled one that I never wore. She tried in vain to feminize me; however, my father's interests and influence prevailed into my early adolescence.

On a rainy day when tennis lessons were canceled, a boy in the tennis class taught me the rules of chess. Although he scarcely knew the game my father was delighted when he saw me at the chess board intensely engaged in a solitary game. At school, my chess partners were boys. We played during recess. I reported my wins and losses to my parents at the end of the day. Mom advised that I should "try to lose" when I played with boys, my only opponents. Ignoring her advice, I did what Daddy wanted me to do: I played to win.

When I was fifteen, one of my father's brothers (he had four brothers and two sisters), Uncle Warren, who wanted a nephew, introduced me to golf. A passionate golfer, he gave me lessons at the Langston golf course. In the same season, my father presented me with a .22-caliber rifle for hunting. He expected me to accompany him on autumn rabbit and deer hunting trips in Maryland and Virginia. On the rifle range, I was complimented for steadiness and accuracy. Daddy was proud that I was capable of handling a rifle well. Although I never took my rifle into the woods in search of prey, I had demonstrated to him that I was prepared to hunt.

We are driving on a country road. I am seated between Daddy and George, a boy my age—sixteen. George is the son of my father's best friend. I lean toward George, nestle against him. My father, looking straight ahead, is silent. George disappears. Daddy and I continue the ride in silence.

I don't know precisely when the moment of intervention occurred, when Dad (I no longer called him Daddy) and I sensed that we were no longer "buddies." Instead of calling me "Buddy," he began to address me as "girl" or "girlie" to underscore, I suppose, his recognition of my reorientation. I assumed my mother had "had a word" with him as she had with me. With the belated onset of my menstruation, she informed me that I was now at risk.

She told me to stop playing football and to start behaving like a lady. I assumed my mother had informed Dad of my biological womanhood and suggested that it was time for me to put aside my boyhood games, my tomboy talents, and the hobbies I had shared with him.

I didn't discuss my transition from boyhood to womanhood with my father. We both knew our relationship was irrevocably altered. Silence descended upon us. We no longer spoke of football and basketball and projects in his workshop; nor did we talk about cars, trains, and airplanes. In the company of others, Dad talked about me, expressing his abundant pride in my academic performance, scholarships, diplomas, and eventually degrees. When we were alone, we spoke briefly about the weather and other trivial matters, and then sat or walked in silence. Our bond broken, we were separated for several years by a wall of silence. Our conversations, punctuated by protracted silences, were terse, cheerful, and sincere, but inconsequential. I felt I had betrayed and abandoned him by electing to be a woman.

Later I redeemed myself by giving birth to a son. Widowed when Michael was thirteen months old, I made many trips from Cambridge, Massachusetts to Washington, D.C., where we visited my parents. In the five years that their lives overlapped, Dad and his only grandchild enjoyed a special relationship. In the role of proud grandfather, Dad crafted boy toys for Michael, gave him his first football, coached him at soccer, and crowned him with an orange hunting cap. I looked on with a sense of reliving episodes from my own childhood. Gradually aware that he was fatherless, Michael cherished his days in the company of a doting grandfather.

Recently I have had a recurrent dream about my father. *He appears as he was in his last year at age seventy-five: erect and sturdy, bravely concealing the cancer that ravaged him, smiling his death-daring smile. He comes and takes my hand. We stroll side by side along a tree-lined path in a park—probably Washington's Rock Creek Park, where we took walks long ago. We turn to each other as if to speak, to say some things that went unsaid. Moving apart with some distance be-*

tween us, we drift into a patch of fog and disappear. No words are spoken. There the dream ends.

I lie awake and wonder what we would have talked about, what more Dad and I might have said.

[FLORENCE CAWTHORNE LADD]

This is not the first time Florence Cawthorne Ladd has written about her father. The character of Henry Stewart, the father in her 1996 novel, Sarah's Psalm, *which received high marks from* The New York Times Book Review, *was shaped by her relationship with him.* Kirkus Reviews *pronounced the book, "An elegantly written first novel."*

"I continue to feel a profound attachment to him," says Ladd of her father, "and I know he always loved me. I also know that he was pleased with his contribution to my upbringing and satisfied with the outcome. The daughter he transformed into a son became a woman, scholar, wife, and mother he admired.

"Belatedly, I wish I had told him how much I valued my years as his son. I attribute many of my strengths to his disregard for traditional ways of rearing a daughter. I am brimming with unspoken gratitude.

"Thanks, Dad!" she says.

A psychologist and social critic, as well as author, Ladd lives in Cambridge, Massachusetts. She is a former director of the Bunting Institute at Radcliffe.

—C.O.

BUCKING TRADITION;
OR,
FATHER-SON RELATIONSHIPS
IN EASTERN NEVADA

Jesse Kellerman

To Dad—my partner in crime.

"No sound like it," sighed Mike "Big" Bucks as the explosion echoed dimly in the distance.

"Hm," agreed his son, Dave Bucks.

"Makes me wish I was twenty-two again, all fresh and in tip-top condition, straight outta the army."

Dave didn't answer.

"You wanna beer?"

"No, Pop."

"Sure?"

"Yeah."

Mike reached for the cooler, all the while not taking his eyes off the scene unfolding in the valley below. He grabbed a can, cracked it open, and took a slow, deliberate gulp, eyes watering with delight. Father and son, their legs crossed identically, sat in pensive silence, binoculars poised, rifles by their sides. After a moment, the sounds and images they had been waiting for—fire trucks, police trucks, helicopters from the east—emerged, staggering toward the city center like drunken actors in an avant-garde play.

"Look at that!" marveled the elder Buck.

"Uh-huh."

"This'll definitely get every front page in the nation."

"Probably."

Mike withdrew a small paper and pencil from one of the many pockets on his khaki vest and scribbled something. He scanned the paper's contents for a moment and muttered, "Jeez, I guess that makes twenty-one."

"Huh?" Dave asked distantly.

"Twenty-one states."

"States?"

Mike looked annoyed. "Twenty-one *states*. Before today it was twenty, and now Nevada. That makes us wanted in twenty-one states."

The statistic didn't seem to faze Dave in the slightest. It didn't even appear to register for a few seconds. His eyes indicated that he was elsewhere.

Mike tilted his head and narrowed his eyes. "There something wrong, Davey?"

The answer came slowly. "Nah."

"Come on, son. Tell your pop."

"It's nothing."

"Spill it, Dave," Mike said.

Dave's eyes flashed anger. "I'm twenty years old, Pop!" he said. "I don't need to tell you everything that's on my mind!"

His father was taken aback. "I just worry about you, you know, I want to make sure—"

"Yeah, well, never mind. I can handle this myself." Dave stood, turned away from his father, and walked to a nearby oak tree, dusting the seat of his pants absentmindedly.

Mike got to his feet with a tired shove, gawked at his son for a moment, and then looked down, running his hand over his stubble-covered cheeks. An eerie calm descended over the hilltop. The ruckus from the town spread out beneath their feet was a subtle hum over the shiver of the wind through untamed, grassy fields. Dave's voice sounded weary when it finally came. "Pop?"

Mike Bucks raised his gaze from his boot tips and cast a concerned glance toward his son, who was now looking at him steadily. "Yes?"

Dave paused and sniffled, stubbing his shoe in the dirt clods and wrinkling his upper lip. "I think I wanna start my own life."

Mike looked at his son like a tourist reading signs in a foreign language; there was effort and distress and confusion on his sun-browned face. His mind rolled and kneaded Dave's words for a moment. Then he said: "Davey, I'm not sure you know what the . . . the . . . im-pli-ca-tions of that statement are."

"I know what they are."

Mike shoved his hands into his pockets, spun around, paced, and spat, casually tossing back over his shoulder: "Fine, whatever you want, son."

"Don't talk down to me!" Dave commanded. Mike halted in midstep. Dave was breathing heavily.

"I'm not—"

"Pop! Listen, Pop, I gotta . . . I feel like . . ."

Mike felt anger creep up into his gullet. "You wanna go, go! I'm not standing here tugging at your pant leg! So go on and do whatever it is you think you have to do. I can make and plant bombs by myself just fine, thank you; I've been doing it for near twenty-five years, and I'm gonna keep doing it whether you're there to help me or not!"

Dave waited a second, trying to let his father reduce to a mild simmer, and then pushed it out. "Pop, I love you more than any-thing else, you know that, and I love to help you, and I think you're doing a great thing here. But I want . . . I'd like . . . I just need to leave the family business for a while—"

"Leave the family business!"

"—and do something I feel is, I dunno, my destiny or what-ever. You see? This—the blowing up buildings and running and never getting to know a girl any better than what color her panties are and maybe her first name, it's . . . *getting* to me, see? I want a family and a house and a dog and all of that stuff we've been working on blowing up for fifteen years."

Mike Bucks's eyes reached flood level and then spilled over.

He ran to his son and grabbed him in a mammoth bear hug. "Davey!" he wept, their long-unshaven faces scratching together. "Davey, you're so good at this, don't leave me, don't leave me—"

"Pop!" Dave pulled his father off gently. "Hey, Pop. I love you, right?"

"But, Davey," Mike said, "who's gonna set the blasting caps?"

"Pop," Dave said softly, "come on, remember what you said? You're the best, right? The original, right? The best serial bomber in the country! And I'm your son, your number-one guy! We're the Bucks family; don't you remember the TV and newspapers? FBI Most Wanted List for seven years running? Remain at large and uncatchable?" Mike nodded weakly. Dave continued with football-coach enthusiasm. "*Time* magazine, *People* magazine, tons of books, and a whole squad out there looking for us! All because of you, Pop. You're the best! You'll always be the best, and that's God's honest word. Right?"

Mike mumbled and began to sob again.

"Oh, now, look Pop, I'm not quitting *you*. I'm quitting this job. It's a great thing you do. I love it a lot, enough to have done it for this long. But, I'm a man now, and I want to . . . to . . . uh . . ."

"Take new steps?" Mike offered miserably.

"Exactly!" Dave's eyes were alive and bright. "Take new steps. And that's what I'm doing, right here."

Mike shifted his weight from foot to foot nervously. "Couldn't you just . . . just . . . become a slasher or something?"

"Pop, I wanna go *straight*. I don't want you to be disappointed in me."

"No." Mike frowned. "Of course I'm not." He smiled a small smile and said sheepishly, "I love you, son."

Dave Bucks let loose a wide, yellow grin. "I love you too, Pop. And I want you to know that if you ever need my help, I'll give it to you in a second."

"You're my number-one guy."

"I'm your number-one guy."

A brief silence settled in again. The Buckses, father and son, turned to consider the smoking debris they had created. Dave laughed and remarked, "It's still beautiful."

For a moment Mike thought Dave was going to relent. Then Dave said, "I'm sure gonna miss it."

Mike Bucks nodded wordlessly.

[JESSE KELLERMAN]

When I wrote to the Kellerman household, asking for biographical information, I ended up getting two bios on Jesse Kellerman, not one. First to arrive was an E-mail from his father, Jonathan, who told me Jesse was directing Sam Shepherd's Sympatico *at the American Repertory Theater.*

"It's a Harvard production," he said, "but getting the main stage at the A.R.T. is very tough for a student. What helped him is that he's directed several plays over the last couple of years and has acquired somewhat of a reputation for brilliance. The A.R.T. honchos are impressed."

As if this wasn't enough of an accomplishment for a twenty-one-year-old, "Jess has also written several excellent plays, is working on a novel, majoring in neuroscience, and doing research on the psychopathology of violence," the elder Kellerman wrote. "Some slacker, huh? Hell yeah, I'm obnoxiously proud. Don't get me started on my three daughters . . ."

In a second E-mail from Jesse, I got a slightly different spin on the same information. He confessed modestly that he didn't know what he should give me in the way of a biography.

"I have written many bad plays, several bad stories, and one bad novel. But I'm getting better. I love my mother and my sisters, and I hate the family dog. (My love for my father should be pretty evident from the story and its dedication.)"

Given "Bucking Tradition's" theme, I did ask Jesse the expected question about whether or not he felt pressured to follow in his father's and mother's creative footsteps. Both his parents are best-selling novelists.

Insisted the younger Kellerman, "I should say up-front that my parents are wonderfully unintrusive people. They've never pressured me to be anything but me. If I feel pressure to do as they have done, it's in the same way that any person feels compelled to live his life in accordance with principles set down by someone he admires. That is, I hold my parents in extremely high regard, and I think that they have led admirable lives, both creatively and morally. If I emulate them—if I only half succeed at emulating them—then I'll have done pretty well."

Then where did the idea for "Bucking Tradition" come from?

Not from Jesse's own personal experience, "but from listening to my father describe a musician friend of his whose son had left the music industry for a [more stable] life in finance."

"I fully intend to keep going in my parents' footsteps," Jesse wrote. "Heck, I'll be happy just to get their shoes on."

—C.O.

THIS IS AMERICA, MOM

A PERSONAL ESSAY

Zhu Xiao Di

As a child, I never dreamed of becoming a father. Today, over forty and a father twice over, I think I understand why. As a dad, you never stop worrying about your children and their future.

During a recent trip to China with my wife, Meirong, and our children, local protests broke out over the bombing at the Chinese Embassy in Belgrade. On our last night in China, we watched the news in our hotel room in Shanghai through a Hong Kong cable TV broadcast. As I translated the news for Alex from Chinese to English, our eight-year-old American-born son was as puzzled as my wife and I were shocked. Fortunately, no war broke out between China and the United States over this incident. My fear was that, had war broken out, our lives here in the United States wouldn't be easy, even if we were not to be put in camps like the Japanese-Americans were during World War II. My sons might be assaulted in school or on the streets by angry teenagers or even grown-ups as numbers of American casualties were to escalate. It was too painful to imagine.

I often wonder now how my late father functioned as a dad.

He joined the Communist movement in China in the 1930s during the Japanese occupation and became a student leader during high school and college. In the following half century, he was first a brave underground fighter, then an ideal comrade. He undertook his work with dignity and compassion and refused to follow the twists and turns in orthodoxy. As a result, he never received the promotions he deserved. In the late 1960s, both he and my mother were detained in labor camps. To some extent, he epitomized the Communist party's greatest promise and his victimization symbolized its greatest failures.

His love as a father shines through in an example involving my elder sister, nine years before my own birth. On the eve of the Communist victory in April 1949, as an underground fighter, he risked his life to deliver an important military map to the Communist army headquarters across the Yangtze River in the North. After the Communists took over Nanjing, the capital city on the southern bank, my mother saw my father again, in his new army uniform. Together holding their fifteen-month-old daughter, they both cried for relief and joy over her tiny body. My father's heroic action embodied his paternal love: to create a better society for the happiness of his own child and every other child, even if he himself might not live to see that happen.

If I had had the opportunity, I would certainly have wanted to learn from him how to be a good father. Yet, there was little chance, for as a boy I only saw him from a child's perspective, and when I grew up, he had become my niece's grandfather. What I discovered then was that fathers and grandfathers were really very different.

Once my father became a grandfather, every trace of him as a father melted into a benign smile. All house rules were broken. Now he permitted eating or drinking in bed, walking around while eating, leaving food on the plate unfinished, even having ice cream before dinner. Once my sister scolded her daughter at the dinner table and the little one began weeping and hiccuping. As a grandfather, my father said, "It's important to keep a child happy, and it is bad for the stomach, too, if someone is weeping and eating at the same time." It seemed to me that a grandfather often tried to undo things he had done as a father.

From my father I at least learned to be a responsible dad, particularly through one memorable incident. On a weekend evening in 1970, shortly after both my parents were released from detention at labor camps, my father told me and my mother that he had something to confess. It turned out that during his detention about a year before, he was once allowed to be escorted back to the city to visit a doctor. On his way across the Yangtze River, he recalled the trip he had made across this same river twenty years earlier as a young father. Life seemed to have betrayed him ruthlessly. During one short moment on the ferry, when the guard was out of sight, he suddenly felt depressed enough to jump into the river and end his life. Then he realized he did not have the right to do so—that would hurt his children both politically and culturally. Helpless as we were at the time, my sister and I still had the hope of seeing our parents come out of the camps alive. When my father finished this story, I felt I had suddenly grown up, although I was only twelve.

My father's rich life left an unexpected challenge for me as a father. How am I going to tell my sons that their grandfather was a lifelong Chinese Communist party member? I hope I won't hear them say someday: "What? Your daddy was a Commie?" The dilemma of being in the right but being thought to be wrong seemed to dog my father throughout his life. In China, he was often attacked for not following the Communist orthodoxy. Now that he is dead, he still might be misunderstood for his political affiliation. In life, one could be misunderstood or thought to be in the wrong for different reasons by different people or groups: the state authority, a majority of the people, or even an entire society. However, just as the Chinese proverb says, Real gold has no fear.

When and how can I explain all these things to my American-born boys, whose favorite restaurant—even in China—is still McDonald's? Before we left, I had hoped that this trip would help Alex connect with his Chinese roots. But just the opposite occurred! Sometimes he even openly scorns China. Why? Ordinary restaurants in China were often dirty enough to kill his appetite; and the luxury restaurants there all served fancy foods that were always too exotic for his stomach. Believe it or not, it was as simple as that.

The fundamental truth is that, born American, he is Americanized. This became evident at a young age. The first day we took him to day care, when he was only two and a half, just before he went in the door, he warned his mommy not to speak any Chinese, because "this is America, Mom."

It hurts me as a father to see Alex develop a snobbish attitude toward anyone who speaks Chinese but not English. As an immigrant, I constantly feel the pain of English not being my native language, even though I graduated from MIT and currently work at Harvard as a researcher. To make sure that Alex has excellent English skills I even postponed teaching him any Chinese, despite all the outcries from the Chinese community. My mother was very upset that Alex refused to talk to her at all in Chinese during our last trip to China. Although he understands us in Chinese fairly well, he often pretends that he doesn't and demands that my wife and I speak English.

Perhaps because of our ethnic, historical, and political background, we often talk about politics at home. We tell Alex that as immigrants we are not eligible to run for president of the United States, but, American born, he is. We tell him this is a democratic society where anyone who is native born and has lived long enough in this country is eligible to become the president. To our surprise, three months before his seventh birthday, Alex wrote a "campaign speech for the presidency," not as any homework assignment, but just for fun.

My wife and I were astonished and we insisted he read it aloud and let us videotape it. During the taping, he misread a few words, and I asked him why he didn't look at the speech as he spoke but stared at the camera all the time instead. "No, you don't get it, Daddy," he said. "You're not supposed to look at it. You have to look at your audience. Get it?" My wife and I laughed until tears rolled down our cheeks.

Here is the speech of my son Alex. The original spelling and grammar mistakes remain.

PRESIDENT SPEECH

I swear that our country should have freedom. We should be nice and responsible. I do not want anyone to use guns except the police and soldiers. And I want everyone to be safe.

I also would like everyone to be treated kindly. And I don't want any fighting. I want everyone to be caring for each-other.

I want everyone to be careful. We should share and take turns. Everyone should say kind words to each-other.

We should give people peace and quiet. We need to help each-other and lets be honest for each-other.

So if you want to have all that stuff vote for me!!!!!!

My first day of school at age seven was in 1965. The teacher announced that we were to elect a student monitor as a leader to assist the teacher in organizing and managing the class. As we did not know each other yet, she said, it would make no sense to hold an election that semester. Instead, for the moment she would appoint someone to the position on a trial basis. A real election would be held at the beginning of the next semester. Then she announced that I would be the monitor. I wasn't prepared for this and felt my throat tighten.

At home that evening at the dinner table, I excitedly talked a lot about voting, and my father patted me on my back proudly and explained that later in my life I would participate in more elections. "Our country is a socialist nation," he said. "When you become eighteen you will be eligible to vote for the president of China." I nodded my head vigorously to show I understood what he had said, although as it turned out, within a year his words no longer seemed true, and even he wouldn't understand what was happening. A political storm would sweep through China. Even the president of China would eventually die of hunger in a prison, and both of my parents would be sent to labor camps.

Just like all times right before other historical tragedies, life went on as usual without any particular sign or omen. Currently, we are living happily in a democratic society. But should we be concerned about its future?

If my son really wants to pursue a political career in this country, does he truly have a chance? As an ethnic Chinese, and born in a family with a Communist grandfather, does he?

A friend of mine (a native-born American, and not yet a father), who also knows Alex, tried to assure me that my late father won't be a political handicap or liability for Alex. As a father, or perhaps an overconcerned father, I have yet to be convinced. If my late father, who was a great father, truly became a political handicap for my own son born in this country, had I made the biggest mistake in my life to emigrate here? Or, maybe this kind of thinking just proves that, unlike my own father, I'm still a typical Chinese father, who cares more about his children's success than their happiness.

Today, my son already has a lot to complain about because he has me as his father. For one thing, I rarely play baseball with him, as other daddies do. Why? In his own words, "You stink at pitching!" To him, a daddy, or an American daddy, should know how to play this American game. Since I am not good at the game, I may not even be qualified to be a daddy.

Yet, I did one thing for which he is sincerely grateful. I left China a dozen years ago and came to the United States for freedom, among many other things. Will my children truly have that freedom? Will they be able to keep it?

[ZHU XIAO DI]

Because American readers do not have a great deal of familiarity with Chinese names, myself included, I inquired of Zhu Xiao Di if he might explain a little about his; for instance, which was his first name, which his last? After reading, "This Is

America, Mom," you may be tempted to pick up a copy of the author's engrossing book, Thirty Years in a Red House: A Memoir of Childhood and Youth in Communist China. If so, it might be a good idea to know how to pronounce his name.

"My name," writes the author, not the least perturbed by my question, "is pronounced as following (at least close): Zhu as in Jewish, Xiao as in shower, and Di as Dee. Zhu is my family name.

"There are a lot of confusions around Chinese names," Zhu explains. "The standard or official way by the Chinese government is to put the given names together and switch the family name to the end to adapt to the English way. But for famous people such as Deng Xiaoping, they would still keep Deng at the beginning and not change it to Xiaoping Deng, for that sounds weird to a Chinese ear. For the same reason, I don't want to switch the order either.

"Recently I found that in some cases, Korean names are spelled out in their traditional order in English, just as I spell Zhu Xiao Di, where the first word is the family name and the second and third are the given names." In some instances, the author notes, as in the example of Deng Xiaoping, the second and third given names are merged into one. "So, I guess it's really a power game. Whoever has the will and determination will eventually have his own way.

"Of course, there is a price to pay in the process," Zhu notes with a touch of humor. "A typical story is that the health insurance company has a hard time to recognize my family members as being in one family. I am Zhu Xiao Di, and my wife is Meirong Xu." Unlike Zhu, she followed all the rules to convert to the English name order from Xu Mei Rong, but she also adhered to the new rule, established after the Communist Revolution, which says Chinese women shouldn't change their family names. Adding to the insurance form nightmare, are the author's sons' names, Alex Zhu and Jeff Zhu.

"What a chaos!" he says.

Zhu emigrated to the United States in 1987, pursuing graduate studies, and received master's degrees from the University of Massachusetts, Boston, and Massachusetts Institute of Technology. He is currently a researcher for the Joint Center for Housing Studies at Harvard University. His writings are bicultural, including personal essays published in China and translations of short stories, and a novel from English. His academic works are published in both China and the United States.

—C.O.

CÉSAR BURGOS

EL PESCADOR (PESCADOR, N.M. FISHERMAN)

Sandra Benítez

CÉSAR BURGOS AWAKENED VERY EARLY. FOR A MOMENT HE lay in bed, catching the pitch of the wind and watching a slant of sorry light steal in under the door. "Beto," he whispered, drawing out his son's name, hoping to rouse the boy and trick him into a sleepy response. César was not above such tactics. He wanted his son to speak again. He wanted more from him than a grunt or a shrug. "Beto," César said again, but no answer came from across the room.

César swung himself up. He grabbed his trousers and tugged them on. He shook out his shoes for insect stowaways before slipping into them. The floor was cold, and in the room there was a chill that out at sea would send the fish deep. César pulled on a sweater. He stepped around his son's cot. The eight-year-old was tucked into a ball. The rebozo that had been his mother's, and that since her death he always took to bed with him, was pulled entirely over his head.

Going to the window, César lifted the curtain. The morning was gray. Little whirlwinds skipped along the road. César let the curtain drop and went across the room. At the stove, he lit its two burners. On one he placed the coffee pot he'd readied the night before. When the coffee grew hot, he poured a cup. Behind him his son stirred. César turned to him. Beto was propped up on an elbow. He had pulled the shawl down tight around his shoulders. He was dark, like his mother, with the same bow of a mouth that had been hers. "Did you sleep?" César asked.

Beto shrugged. He sank back onto the cot, drawing the rebozo over his head once more.

César stared at the boy enshrouded in the length of cloth that still contained his mother's scent. He thought about the way things had been before the day misfortune struck. Despite the shifting tides of a life dependent on the sea, he had been a man who lacked little: he had possessed a humble house, the companionship of a woman, good and true, and, above all, three sons, on whom he'd rested much of his hopes for the future.

César sipped his coffee. It was a Saturday, the start of norther season, and the sea was choppy. On days like this ocean fishing was not good, and César would take to estuaries where he knew the fish to be. Still, despite the weather, he would put out to sea today. Today, he needed the sea under him. Each time he stepped into his boat, he left his heartbreak on the shore. In his boat, he was shielded from the monstrous turn his life had taken.

"I want you out of bed," César said. He turned back to the stove, hearing the sternness in his voice that was his way of holding on. He removed the coffee from the burner and set a pot of beans on it. He lowered the flame on the second burner and laid three tortillas around it. This had been Concha's life. She fixed the meals and went to market. She kept the house swept and dusted. She cared for the children. Now it was he who had to tend the house and raise the one son he had left. In the two months since the accident he had done these things and gone to sea as well. He was doing a terrible job of it. The sea was so demanding that from June until November, when the weather was very good, it was fishing, fishing, morning through night, and who could raise a boy well with hours like that. Before he'd turned to fishing, he had done other kinds of work, but he did not want to contemplate leaving the fish when it was the sea that served him best.

When the tortillas were hot, César plucked them from the flame and stacked them on a plate. He scooped beans on, too, and set the food on the table. Beto had laid aside Concha's rebozo and now sat on the edge of the cot, pulling on the worn pair of Adidas he insisted on wearing without laces. He went over to the dresser and dunked a comb into a glass of water before running the comb through his hair. A tuft at the top of his head would not be tamed despite the effort, but César resisted the urge to point this out to the boy. Beto poured a cup of coffee and padded over to the table. "Coffee's not good for you," César said. "There's milk there."

Beto took a gulp of coffee. He screwed up his face against the taste of it.

César bit his lip. At school the boy was sullen and uncommunicative. When his mother and little brothers were alive, he was a different kind of boy. *Chinga*, César thought, who wasn't different then. They had been a family. Rodolfo and Reynaldo were curious, bubbly boys who loved their big brother and looked up to him. Beto was protective of them. When they got into mischief, he'd step between them and Concha if she picked up the broom and laughingly came after them. Frequently the three sat on Beto's cot, all propped against the wall, and Beto spilled out the seashells he collected. He told the boys stories. How this spotted shell had come from this place in the sea. How this small conch had left behind his brothers and how, if the boys placed the shell against their ears, they could hear the other shells calling. Now César glanced over at the window ledge on which Beto had kept the jars containing his collection. Sometime after the accident—César had not noticed exactly when—the jars had disappeared.

"Please eat your breakfast," he said to the boy.

Beto pushed his plate away.

"You must eat," César said, the edge of frustration building in his voice because right before his eyes the boy was languishing. To get a grip on himself, César turned his attention to the shrine that occupied the better part of the table. If the shrine was ever finished, he would place it on the side of the road at the spot where the bus speeding back from Oaxaca had not made the curve.

The shrine was a large square box built to resemble a chapel. It had a glass door in front, and on the top, over the door, a tall wooden cross. César Burgos had worked on the shrine for nearly a month, but every attempt he'd made to enhance it had failed somehow. He had painted the shrine pink, and then a blue like an early sky. Now it was white, and as he ran a hand over it, its plainness distressed him. He had asked his son for help, but the boy had refused.

César left the table and the dismal sight of the shrine and his son. He went to the window and looked out again. The wind had died down, but the sky was still gray. Between the shacks across the street, the sea was a dark smear, but still the sight of it was comforting. He loved the grandness of the sea, the formidable mystery it presented. He loved the creatures of the sea, those he saw and those he could only imagine. When he'd first arrived in Manzanillo—he had been born in the capital, but had left it for Veracruz and the sugar cane fields there—he had fished from the shore with harpoon and net, but later, when he had a skiff, he'd go out to sea. Each day he'd sit in his boat and chase the fish and savor his freedom, for there was freedom in fishing. Not so with the sugar cane. Fishing gave a man the time to think in silence. It brought the feel of water and its movement, the sight of the colors that played over it. It brought sky and clouds, sunlight and moonlight glimmering on the mountains or along the shore. Fishing brought perils, too. Peril from tides and winds and from the sea's creatures. But peril heightened vigilance. Peril provided the situation against which a man could test his mettle. Twelve years ago, when he was nineteen, he'd first come upon this sea. He had left Veracruz and crossed the width of Mexico to come to Manzanillo. Here he faced a new sea, and it took months to learn the peculiarities of tides and currents, to memorize the distances, the placement of rocks and, sometimes, of trees that served to mark certain depths or fishing spots. And the winds here were unlike the winds on the other coast of Mexico, and they affected these fish differently, and so there was that too he had to learn. But the stars above him had not changed, and it was a blessing to look up into the night and know the stars had followed him through all the journeys of his life.

When he was twenty-one, he had married Concha Ojeda. It was she who had allowed him to turn himself over to the sea. But now Concha was gone and in the months since the accident, the boy had gone mute and was clearly in decline. The boy needed a mother's love, he needed a father's strength, and there was none of one and little left of the other. César thought of Concha's sister, who lived in Oaxaca. She had asked for the boy. She would raise him with her own, she had said at the wake. Since that time, César Burgos had agonized over his sister-in-law's offer and there were moments when he thought he would have to let the boy go.

He turned to his son, who sat at the table, his chin dropped down onto his chest. "After a while, we'll go out on the sea," César said. Since the accident, the boy had rejected going out in the boat. But today César would insist. Perhaps the sea might turn the boy into himself again.

Beto said nothing.

"Did you hear what I said. I said we'll go out on the boat."

Still no response came from his son.

"Why don't you speak?" César cried, heat surging up his neck and into his cheeks. "In God's name, say something, say anything!"

Beto slumped into the chair.

César pressed the back of his neck, a sense of helplessness washing over him. He turned his gaze out the window again. There is nothing I can do for my son, he thought. *Nada. Absolutamente nada.*

Out on the boat, the sea was leaden. There were times when the sea was very blue and the water was silky to the touch and it gleamed and you could look down into it, seeing quite clearly the fishing nets ballooning down into the deep, seeing the schools of haddock or sea bass or dogfish heading in a silent rush for the nets. But today the north wind threatened, and the sea was dense, and you could not look past its surface. Overhead the sky was mottled, and soon fat raindrops fell, tiny craters forming where they struck the water. César Burgos ignored the rain. He sat in the stern of his boat, his eyes on his son's back. Beto's shirt collar poked out from his sweater and curved like a wide red petal around his neck. The boy's neck is like Concha's, César thought, and he looked away, toward the buildings that were staggered up the slope close to the shore. On some of these buildings' balconies tiny red and green lights twinkled. Christmas, he thought, Concha's best time and it was almost here again. César clutched the sides of the boat, remembering past Christmases, remembering the aroma of *pozole* and *empanadas*, the star piñata he hung from a tree branch in the yard, the fireworks lighting up the night sky of Manzanillo.

At the memories, the grief pent-up inside César spilled out and he began to weep. Since the accident, he had not allowed himself to weep, for a man must be strong. But now images of his lost sons and the pudgy flesh between their soft knuckles, images of Concha and the silent, hungry way she sometimes turned to him in the night broke his restraint. César cried out and he heard the sound he made. Though he felt the warmth of tears against his face, he could not hold his grief back.

César did not know how long it was before he felt the boat bobble. He opened his eyes and saw that Beto had turned around. Now his son planted his feet wide to steady them. In Beto's eyes his own despair shone out.

César wiped his tears with the heel of a hand. "I can't seem to make things right," he said. "I've tried to be a mother to you, a father too, but I have failed. I'm afraid for you, and I'm afraid for me. You are slipping away. First it was your voice and now it's the rest of you, and there is nothing I can do. Your tía Bersa, in Oaxaca, has offered to take you. I think of this sometimes and now I think it would be good if you went to live with them." César went silent, because the weight of his confession was like he'd dropped an anchor out.

Beto opened his mouth as if he would speak, but he did not. Instead, he shook his head. It was a slow, sad movement that tore open César's heart. César closed his arms around the boy and pressed him to his chest. "*M'hijo,*" he said finally, murmuring against the boy's head, using the words "my son" because it was what his mother always called him.

It was raining in earnest when the two reached home. They had rowed the boat in, dragged it up on shore, turning the boat over next to others secured in the sandy yard of the fishing cooperative. The two were soaked when they stepped into their house. César lighted a few candles, for the morning had gone dark. He turned on both stove burners to allow a little heat into the room. He and Beto changed into dry clothes and then César made fresh coffee. For the boy, he made chocolate, boiling up the water, dropping in a tablet of good Oaxacan chocolate, whipping up the mixture with the wooden beater just like Concha used to do. César brought the filled cups to the table, and the two sipped their drinks while the downpour beat an endless drumroll against the roof.

After a time, César dragged out a fishing net and the canvas bag that held his mending tools. The din the rain made was soothing, a perfect accompaniment to net mending. César selected a few lead weights and began to sew them into the rim of a turquoise net where some were missing. Soon after, Beto went to his cot and pulled three glass jars out from underneath. He carried the jars over and spilled his collection of seashells onto the table. César was amazed.

Beto went to the dresser and took out the balsa wood boat model and the tube of cement *el maestro* had given him after the funeral. The gift had gone untouched, but now Beto brought the glue to the table and lifted the cloth covering the shrine. He began to glue seashells to the outer surface of the box.

Concha! César thought, the word that meant "seashell." César laid down his own work and joined the boy who did not object.

A few hours later, when they were finished, the two stood and admired how it was they had elevated a mere box and cross into a proper shrine. Now the shrine was studded with turret shells and milky limpets. Glued on too were miniature horn shells in chestnut and violet, fig shells and auger shells in hazel and cream. Still, though the overall effect was splendid, there were gaps between the shells that needed filling in. "It needs something more," César said, pointing to the gaps.

Beto jumped up. He ran to his cot again and brought out another jar. He hurried back and turned the jar over. It was as if the boy had scattered jewels upon the table. What once had been bottle shards time and the sea had polished into gems. There were amber and aqua and rose colored nuggets. Nuggets as green as a wild parrot's wing. Nuggets as clear and as dazzling as diamonds. Until his mother's death, it had been the boy's greatest pleasure to stroll up and down the beach, his dark head bent in search of such miraculous transformations.

Beto selected a green nugget and fitted it between two seashells, holding it in place with his fingertips. He looked up to his father for approval.

"It is the crowning touch," César Burgos said, and for a few hours more he and his son picked over the gems, fixing each one to the spot where the shrine itself seemed to call for it. When their task was done they both stepped back, as if from a distance they could see more keenly. The shrine, faceted now with these polished colored jewels, brightened a room that for months had been drab.

It was almost two o'clock when they went out again. Though it had cleared, the daylight was still weak. César and Beto made their way carefully down the steep muddy road that led into Manzanillo. Once there, they caught the bus to Santiago. They were going to buy paper flowers from Chayo Marroquín, who made the best ones sold on the beach. The flowers would go on the inside of the shrine as the final touch.

When they got to Chayo's house, she was at the stove, making lunch. Because of the weather, Candelario was home too. He stood up from the table when César and Beto appeared at the door. "Hombre," he said to César. On many occasions the two had fished together, and they were as companionable as time spent on the sea permitted men to be. "*Entren, entren,*" Chayo said, wiping her hands on her apron and hurrying over to the door. She was young, in her twenties, yet there was a motherly air about her that made her seem older. The room was warm and brightly lit, filled with the odor of coffee, the sweet pungency of onions and tomatoes frying in a pan. Simply put, there was the aroma of home here, and César Burgos hungrily took it all in. The walls were bright blue. A wide yellow stripe formed a border along the ceiling. From the rafters, bouquets of paper flowers hung down like cornucopias.

"We built a road shrine for Concha and the little ones," César said. "We have come for flowers."

Chayo clapped her hands. "A road shrine. *Qué bueno,*" she said, deftly navigating around the room's happy clutter: the imposing double bed, the awkward dressers, the uneven table and odd matching chairs. Strung in a corner was a hammock within which a baby slept in spite of the noise. Chayo threw a plump arm around Beto, who hung back by the door. "You can have your pick of any of my flowers, but first a little something for the stomach."

César protested, but Chayo turned a deaf ear and soon they were sitting down to a table covered with a stack of hot tortillas and bowls of rice and beans and a platter of sauced green peppers dotted with bits of meat.

César was surprised at how greedily his son and he ate. When they had finished, Chayo removed the plates. "And now to the flowers," she said, pointing out the room with a sweep of her hand. César Burgos stood. He looked around. There was a garden of blossoms here—how could he settle on just the right ones? "Beto, you decide," he said. "I'll be outside." He left hastily because the room began suddenly to close in on him. He did not know why, perhaps he needed the spread of sky. Perhaps it was air he needed, though out in the yard the blessed smell of salt was hardly in it. He went to stand next to the arroyo. After a time, Candelario walked up. "So you finished the shrine."

"Yes. We'll put it up Christmas Eve. Concha always made so much of that day."

There was silence, because in silence there was more respect than in any words that they could say.

"How are you going?" Candelario asked at length.

"*¿Que?*"

"How will you get it there, you know, the shrine?"

César reeled at the question. The place of the accident was a good ten kilometers away. The shrine was awkward, heavy. He hadn't thought of how he would carry it. He felt like a fool. "The bus? The bus goes past there." He said this, but he couldn't bear to think about him and the boy and the shrine on the bus.

Candelario pointed next door. "Santos is my neighbor. He has a taxi. Santos can take you."

"*Ay, hombre, tomar un taxi es muy caro.*" César Burgos could not afford to take a taxi. Only once in his life had he done it, and that was on his wedding day.

Candelario laid a hand on César's sleeve. "No, hombre. Santos is a good man. He's reasonable. I'll arrange for it."

"*Gracias, hombre. La verdad, mi vida es una pura mierda.*"

César Burgos and his boy stood on what looked like the top of the world. They were on a wide shoulder that bordered the road to Oaxaca, a road of switchbacks and long curves. At the road's edge, the terrain tumbled, forming a ravine from which spindly pines and shrubs sprouted. As if to soften its severity, clumps of yellow flowers poked up here and there down the *barranca*.

It was early and the sky was a blue so brilliant that it looked like the sea.

Minutes before Santos had dropped them off. The man had helped to heft the shrine from the taxi's trunk and place it next to a thicket of young trees. When César dug into his pocket, Santos said, "No, hombre. Let a man do a man a favor." He had clasped César in an awkward embrace before driving off as it was planned that he would. César was thankful for Santos's kindness. He was thankful, too, to be here alone with his son.

Beto backed away from the ravine. He had not been here before. He had worn his dark cloth coat because there was a chill and because it was the most formal thing he had to wear. Over his shoulder lay the pack in which he usually carried his school books.

"It's very deep," César Burgos said, because he had twice

trudged the depth and breadth of the *barranca,* once just after the accident, and then again on the day he came to fix the spot where the shrine would sit. Now he looked out past the edge of the road to the place where officials said the bus had left the curve. In his mind he saw the bus. He saw it sail out into an emptiness he could not bear to think his loved ones had had the time to face. "We should get started," he said.

They hoisted the shrine up, carrying it to the base on which it would rest. The base was a simple concrete pedestal standing among sturdy cement shrines, crosses, and a few plaques. They lowered the shrine onto the pedestal, guiding the bottom of it carefully over the short rods that would anchor it.

"It looks very good," César said when at last the shrine was set. Behind the glass door, his wife's face looked out at him. She was somber in the photograph, her jet eyes steady, as if somehow back then she had understood what was to come. At each side of her was a photograph of a boy: three-year-old Rodolfo and four-year-old Reynaldo. A wreath of paper flowers trailed around the photographs, and the arch of the petals, the pinks and blues and violets, softened the graveness of the three faces.

Beto lowered the pack from his shoulder and took from it a parcel of folded cloth that César recognized as Concha's rebozo. It was black with crimson threads running through it. She had woven the shawl herself, had worn it for the first time on her wedding day. When the boys were babies, she had wrapped each one of them in it, cradled them in it against her heart.

Beto carried the rebozo over to the shrine as if it were an offering. Solemnly he draped it over one side of the shrine and up and around the cross and then down the other side.

César was perplexed by what his son had done, but before he could question him, Beto knelt before the shrine and began to speak. His voice was soft and slow. "Mamá," he said, "I brought you your rebozo because I don't deserve to have it. I should have gone with you, Mamá. You wanted me with you in Oaxaca. You wanted me to help you with the little ones, but I said no because *el maestro* does not like it when I don't come to school. But I was wrong to say no, Mamá. If I had gone, I would have saved my brothers. It was up to me to do it, but I was not there and so Naldo and Rody died. It was my fault, Mamá. *Yo tuve la culpa.*" Beto, the small penitent, lowered his head.

César was thunderstruck by what he had heard. He dropped down next to his son. "*No, hijo, no,*" César said. "*No tuviste la culpa.*"

"But I stayed home. It *was* my fault. If I had gone, I could have saved them."

"*No, hijo.* No one could have saved them. Everybody died in that crash. *Todos, hijo, todos.*"

As if pondering what César had said, Beto was silent for an instant, but then he spoke again. "Then I should have gone with them. If I had gone I would be dead too." He spoke haltingly, as if he had a measured number of words and they were soon to run out. "If I was dead now, I wouldn't be a bother to you, Papá."

César Burgos pulled Beto close and then drew away just enough to look into his eyes. "You are not a bother. You are my son. You are all I have in the world and I never want to lose you."

Beto buried his face against his father's chest.

"Come," César said after a moment. He stood and brushed at the bits of gravel clinging to the knees of his trousers. He went to the shrine and lifted his wife's rebozo, careful not to catch it on the seashells. He folded the cloth that was as soft as Concha's skin. "This is yours. Your mother would want you to have it now." He handed the rebozo back to his son.

Beto gave a little nod. He returned the shawl to his pack again and then stood beside his father.

"Concha would be proud," César Burgos said. He pictured the sea and his boat. And he pictured his son as a help to him in the future. César Burgos laid an arm across his boy's shoulders. They started off, toward the point down the road where the bus always stopped.

[SANDRA BENÍTEZ]

"I grew up in Mexico and El Salvador and had plenty of opportunities to be travelling down a highway to round a curve and come upon a roadside shrine," says Sandra Benítez. "From the car, I could not study these little altars that marked the spot of a fatal accident. Passing them, I was left with a blur of an image seared both in my head and in my heart. Who had died there? I asked myself. How did the end come? Who had they left behind to remember and reminisce?"

This was the kernel from which César Burgos's story sprouted and bloomed. In Latin America, Benítez says, she "learned that life is frail and most always capricious, that people find joy in the midst of insurmountable obstacles, that in the end, it is hope that saves us."

She was born in Washington, D.C., in 1941, a child of Puerto Rican and Anglo-American parents, and identical twin to a sister, Susana, who died only a month after birth. Until she was a teen, she lived in Latin America, and then was sent to live for three years on her paternal grandparents' farm in northeastern Missouri. There, she attended high school and was the first and only Latina in town.

Benítez came to the writing life at the late age of thirty-nine. Before that, this graduate with a masters in English from Truman State University taught English, Spanish, and literature at both high school and college levels. She also returned to her roots, travelling throughout Latin America as a corporate translator until 1980, when the fiction bug bit. Even with her clear and startling talent, it took her thirteen of her nineteen years as a writer to get published.

What shortsightedness on the part of the book world. Since the publication of her debut novel, A Place Where the Sea Remembers, *in which César Burgos appears, she has won or been nominated for a number of prestigious awards, including a 1993 Barnes and Noble Discover Award, a Los Angeles Times First Fiction Award in 1994, the 1998 American Book*

Award for fiction and, in 1999, a Bush Foundation Fellowship.

A new novel, The Weight of All Things, will soon join A Place Where the Sea Remembers and her second novel, Bitter Grounds, as favorites on readers' bookshelves.

Writing "César Burgos: El Pescador" will always be a seminal moment for Benítez, however. As she says, it "finally gave me the chance to pull up beside a roadside shrine, kneel before it, and take in the awesome fickleness of life."

—C.O.

THE FUNDAMENTAL THINGS APPLY

David Forsmark

THEY NEED A NEW CLICHÉ—THE WATCHED PREGNANCY TEST stick never turns blue.

At least that's my hope. As my wife watches in rapt anticipation, I put on a brave face.

Karen has been hearing her biological clock ticking for about three years of the three years and ten months we have been married. Now, we are the ripe old age of twenty-four. As a teenager I had doubted it, but here in my mid-twenties, I'm getting pretty sure that people actually have sex and give birth after age thirty. There is no big hurry.

My insistence that we are still young falls on deaf ears. Tick, tick, tick.

During the last year, it had gotten pretty bad. One time at a Sunday School class party, we were talking to a new couple, and within an hour it suddenly popped out.

"I really want to have a baby, but David doesn't," she confided to a complete stranger. Talk about your pregnant pauses in conversation. The woman glared at me. I just shut up and pretended to be fascinated by something else going on in the room. Of course it was all my fault. She didn't want to hear my rationalizations. What kind of jerk would keep this sweet, beautiful, petite woman from becoming a mother?

This happened more than once. Pretty much everyone in our church, family, circle of friends—people we nodded pleasantly to in the mall—knew about our difference of opinion. Anyone who meets us takes Karen's side automatically on any issue, much less this one.

At our dry, no rock and roll, Fundamentalist Baptist wedding reception, my mother even said in her typical brutally honest, but completely unmalicious way, "Some mothers think that no one is good enough for their darling boy. I worry about the opposite." She was trying hard not to be a cliché mother-in-law. At least, I chose to take it that way.

I freely admit that Karen is a nicer—and better—person than I am. Frankly, I wouldn't commit the rest of my life to someone who wasn't. I know me.

Sooner or later, I was bound to give in. I can't stand to see her genuinely unhappy. Once it got to the point where it was more than just this nagging gotta-do-it-pretty-soon thing, and a real source of distress, I was doomed.

I have to admit that sex was more exciting knowing that there was a chance you had just created a life. Of course, the guy playing Russian Roulette with three bullets in *The Deer Hunter* experienced a certain amount of excitement too. I didn't examine it too closely. Hey, I'm a guy. If men thought hard about the long-term consequences of sex, the world would be a lot emptier place.

We made a deal: If we were going to do this, we were at least going to do everything we could to have a boy. Nowadays, some people say you actually have some kind of choice in this. Soon, the nightstand, living-room end tables, and the floor next to the bed, were piled with books with titles like *Your Baby's Sex: Now You Can Choose*, or *You Can't Return to Sender, So Choose Your Baby's Gender*.

So we followed it to the letter. Face north, turn over, second day of the phase of the full moon, whatever. This, I also had to admit, was pretty fun.

Of course, I knew there were no guarantees. In fact, I had a sneaking suspicion it was all a scam. After all, about half the people would go away saying, "We followed that book and it really worked!" There were, after all, only two choices. The argument was basically over, but this way I could sort of fool myself that I had won some sort of point in negotiation, rather than having merely collapsed in the face of pressure. My male ego could pretend to be satisfied.

To my great relief, after all that, going off the pill didn't do the trick right away. "It will happen when God wants it to," I'd say piously.

Thank you, God.

Karen decided pretty quickly that God needed a little help. Her gynecologist wasn't too impressed by how long we'd been trying, but after a few months prescribed something.

If her pills don't work pretty soon, I am supposed to go masturbate into a bottle somewhere and see if I am contributing—or not contributing—to the situation. Maybe a successful test here wouldn't be so bad, after all.

Karen turns toward me, holding up the now blue stick. She's been staring at it so hard, I wonder if she's turned it blue through the force of her will. She is positively radiant; and looks so happy, that by some sort of strange alchemy, I sort of am myself.

Underneath her joy, however, there is an edge. She is looking into my eyes with the intensity of an industrial laser. I'd better look damn happy, and it had better be real, or the moment after the happiest moment of her life will never be forgiven.

Like the robot in *The Terminator*, my mind's eye quickly selects from the Options Menu. I click on Macho Ex-jock Expression of Triumph. That would be most in character and convincing. I clench my fist, put it up to my face, and as I bring it quickly down exclaim "Yes!"

It seems to work, or at least she isn't in the mood to press the issue. I have passed the test.

Or maybe not. Now, we get to talk about it. Time to explore our feelings.

"I'm so happy," she says through tears of joy. "Aren't you?"

"Of course," I say, still grinning like an idiot. "Come here," and I hold out my arms. When in doubt, hug.

But as she holds me tight, all I can think is, Yeah, you're happy now, but life as we enjoy it is over. No more picking up and heading to Mackinac Island or Toronto at a moment's notice because we feel like it. No heading out for a movie that starts in five minutes without making arrangements. That is, if we can afford that kind of thing after food, clothes, diapers, and then thirteen years of private school.

And no, no, no more just making love the second the urge hits us in midkiss and running off—or not quite making it—to the bedroom.

Sure, I'm worried about expenses. I've just gotten this selling insurance thing down pat, after some really lean years. Should a baby really have to depend on my inconsistent income?

Despite every financial bump in the road, every worry about whether next month's bills will be the ones that break us, living with Karen has been the best time of my life. I love our home together.

For the first time, home is not a place I stayed between fun things I did somewhere else. Not that I had some horrible, abusive upbringing, just that about half the things I enjoyed doing were verboten. Now, staying home is only one choice among several appealing options. That has only been true for about four of my twenty-four years. I'm not ready for it to change.

In bad jokes, people refer to the "old ball and chain." Not me. Marrying Karen was the most liberating experience of my life. Sure, there are guidelines. Dating, for instance, is out. But that was also a *really* small sacrifice. Face it, despite the so-called freedom of the single life, watching my single friends desperately seeking the approval of each attractive woman to come along is painful.

The bottom line is this. I don't want to share Karen. Everybody knows that mothers put their children above everything else. I love her the way I have never loved anyone before in my life. No contest, not even close.

Why introduce a little competitor?

I never really consider expressing those fears instead of making all of the usual shallow, clichéd arguments about money and lifestyle. Even though it might score some points with her on my behalf—not to mention keep my arguments from being the focus of conversations with strangers.

The problem with that is, once you express your real fears, they can be dealt with. They can be dismissed, allayed, and solved.

And then you lose the argument.

So, here we are, deliriously happy, on our way to becoming proud parents.

Lord, at least make it a boy. I can deal with boys.

People quit talking like normal people around life's Big Events. All of a sudden, the phrase "blessed event" becomes popular among our young friends. Even one of my best friends who is a vocal and avowed atheist used the term once. I look at him and grouch, "Have you ever even used that word before in your life?"

I'm beginning to think that the very thing that makes people lousy parents is the same thing that makes them become parents in the first place—they forget what it was like to be a kid.

Kids don't bring blessing to a house, they bring conflict, competition, and no small amount of angst.

And rebellion. Rebellion was a given.

"You'll never know the heartache we feel right now until you have kids of your own." The tearful admonition was a common one in our household, where there were no minor transgressions. "Just wait until you're a parent, then you'll understand," was the response to everything we found unreasonable.

Yeah, I couldn't wait for *that* to happen.

Fatherhood was also made to sound like a pretty grim burden by the way our pastor made constant references to "Crying out to God all night for the souls of his children," informing us that this was what all good fathers did. "Your father is as responsible for your soul as I am for those of the people in my church."

But aside from the heart-rending, crushing burden that being a father undoubtedly was, I also had no notion that parents and kids really could get along. After all, much of the pop culture of the 1970s highlighted the differences between young and old. It wasn't until later that I realized that teenage rebellion was natural, and that making it into some kind of ideology was a quirk of our times.

In my own family, parent-child tension predated my appearance on the scene and was a constant part of life, even into adulthood.

The way I understand it—and I've mostly heard my mother's side of the story—my parents dating life was sort of a Romeo and Juliet lite.

As unlikely as it seems, since my Grandpa Gustavson was a true-blue union loyalist skilled trades factory worker, and Grandpa Forsmark was also a GM tradesman, there was a class warfare edge, the Gustavsons' reaction to my father.

I barely remember Grandpa Forsmark, but he was an ambitious guy who bought and sold land, invested in the stock market—and was a GM factory worker. Grandpa Gustavson, on the other hand, really didn't have personal career ambitions outside of GM. When he retired, he retired. Now, at nearly ninety, he still does things like heavy remodeling, but only of his own house.

So this was hardly the class divisions of the Capulets and the Montagues.

My mother's parents, however, had bigger plans for their only child. Grandma Gustavson would throw birthday parties for my mom, and made sure that they made the society page of the Oakland Press. She had a good job in a hospital, and most likely figured her daughter would meet a young doctor someday, if she played her cards right.

In Grandma Gustavson's defense, some of their opposition could be accounted for by the fact that my dad *was* seventeen and my mother merely fourteen when they met on a ship to Sweden, as both families journeyed from Michigan back to the ancestral soil.

The Gustavsons didn't put roadblocks of denial in front of the young couple, but rather speedbumps of disapproval. So instead of quashing the romance—which they might have been able to do, since my father lived in Flint, about fifty miles away from my mother in Pontiac—this made it more romantic for them. At the same time, my dad deeply felt every dig, and every comment that implied the would-be construction engineer and his family didn't quite measure up.

When they married, the young couple settled in Flint, living not far from my dad's parents. Now, it was the Forsmarks' turn to get involved, give unwanted advice, and generally meddle. Of course, the Gustavsons didn't exactly step out of the picture, either, offering advice on everything from the color of the carpet to the number of kids my folks should have.

When my mother became pregnant with my sister—only her second child—my Grandma Gustavson, who'd only had one, muttered, "What're you going to do, have a litter?"

Non-Lutheran Swedes are about as rare as Jewish Catholics. One Sunday when the pastor of the trendy Lutheran church my dad grew up in made a statement that the Bible was a book with no greater authority than any other book, he thought, "Then why don't I just sleep in on Sunday mornings?" and never went back.

Instead, we began attending a large, fundamentalist Baptist church that the neighbors across the street invited us to. My parents soon converted to the traditional, orthodox Christian belief of a personal faith in Jesus Christ as Savior, and a literal interpretation of the Bible.

Soon, Dad, a man of intimidating intellect and withering rhetorical skills, was not only a deacon, but one of the arbiters of keeping North Baptist Church true to pure standards of Fundamentalism. The form he practiced went by the label of Separatism, which meant avoiding the vices of the world and the "compromises" of other less strict Christians.

Dad was a straightlaced guy who already had short hair, didn't drink or smoke, and even listened to classical music, *before* he became a Baptist. About the only things he had that he could give up in the name of piety were occasional movie theater attendance, his television, and, though he didn't gamble, the use of playing cards.

But the coolest thing about this proudly uncool form of Christianity was the way it could be used as a weapon.

Now the grandkids' contact with the Gustavsons could be

limited because of the bad influence of my grandfather's beer drinking, card playing, and his refusal to leave the Lutheran Church. We could be informed of *their* moral inferiority by the man who for a decade had been made to feel as though he didn't meet the standard.

At this point I should mention that the enforcement of strict standards and the imperative to proselytize has been misinterpreted by those who do not understand the Fundamentalist culture as spite or even hate. That is just plain wrong. If you think someone is going to Hell, it would be pretty hateful *not* to warn them.

Nearly all Fundamentalist Baptist families have their kids memorize Bible verses and say grace before meals. These are useful daily symbols of devotion to God that keep faith in the minds of developing young skulls.

These also became ways to dig back at the Gustavsons. Whatever message Dad decided his in-laws needed to hear on their upcoming visit could be thrown into the before meal prayer—which was four times as long when they came to visit and filled with words he didn't exactly use in every day conversation.

"Blessed Father, we come before thee thankful for this repast that is spread so bountifully before us. And we thank thee for the even greater gift of thy Son, Jesus Christ. Who died and rose again, so that we would not have to suffer the fires of Hell. And we thank thee that all we must do is accept his freely offered gift of salvation and that we do not have to work for it, nor can we . . ." and so on while the targets of the sermon—and his kids—squirmed and the food got cold.

The other indirect way for Dad to deliver the Message was through our memory verses for the week. Each time they came to our house, shortly after kisses were exchanged, and Grandma gave out whatever goodies she had brought for us kids, my sister and I would stand at attention, under Dad's stern perfectionist gaze, and stammer out our Bible verse of the week.

Though we were in our early grammar school years, we were well aware of our role in this little psychodrama. Grandma and

Grandpa were on their way to Hell, and how well we delivered our message could make the difference.

No pressure, there.

My grandparents never said a word about any of this. They endured, and at least pretended to respect, my dad's demands in these matters. They came to programs at the Christian school we attended and practically every church service that their grandchildren had a role in. They even came to a few special services my folks invited them to, which must have been sheer torture for them.

It wasn't until after I was married that Grandpa Gustavson even said a discouraging word about it. We were out bluegill fishing on one of the dozens of lakes that surround the Pontiac area, and out of the blue, he said in his Swedish accent that is still there after sixty years in this country, "You know, I'm not one to criticize a man's religion, and I think it has it's place. I sat through all those services and all those screaming hellfire preachers; but the one thing that really pissed me off was you poor kids having to stand up and recite those scriptures. You were so scared you would make a little mistake."

Unlike many rebellious teenage romances that fade after the excitement of getting under the skin of one's parents wears off, and the humdrum of real life sets in, my parents stayed wild about each other.

It's been said that the best thing a man can do for his children is love their mother. If that is true, then we were brought up extremely well. My parents loved each other madly, and we never saw them fight. Even now, as a grizzled veteran of years of marriage, it wouldn't surprise me to know that they never did. Mom and Dad were the united front. While other families in the neighborhood were breaking up with the newfound "freedom" for self expression, we were always secure in the knowledge that they wouldn't know how to live without each other.

On that united front, however, there was no outward doubt that Dad was the Boss. But despite all the father-is-in-charge and has-the-responsibility-before-God rhetoric in the home and at church, my mom got whatever she really wanted. We never had a clue that she'd had an idea vetoed, or that my father ever imposed his will on a situation. They just seemed to instantly and instinctively agree on every course of action.

While Gloria Steinem and the cultural elite were out condemning patriarchy and traditional marriage patterns, my mother did not chafe at her way of life. When she heard such things, she would give a scornful little snort and make a comment about "unmarried marriage experts."

My parents didn't always relate to us so well, but they sure related to each other. All over the darn house and all the time. I couldn't sit in the living-room recliner and read an Edgar Rice Burroughs book without having to try to hide my eyes behind it because they were necking on the couch. If I hadn't been too embarrassed to open my mouth, it would have been *my* turn to yell, "Go to your room!"

Thinking for himself as a young man and going his own way had certainly turned out well for my dad; but that didn't give him any confidence that we could be trusted to think for ourselves. His experience taught him how little parents could effect the ultimate direction of their children's lives; and it scared him. His bratty oldest son was far more likely to make serious, life-changing mistakes.

Of course all of this was heightened by the fact that I was growing up in a tumultuous time. For a Fundamentalist Baptist parent, the 1970s meant the certain knowledge that the world was going to Hell faster than ever before, and your kids were being actively recruited to help it along.

This line of reasoning had its strengths. While many who came of age in the 1950s and had become parents were shaking their heads and saying, "Kids today, whatcha gonna do?" and looking befuddled, Fundy parents were setting guidelines and not wasting any time worrying that their kids would think them uncool. As far as they were concerned, Dr. Spock was some pointy-eared alien who knew nothing about human children.

With Vietnam protests, race riots, and the sexual revolution, parents could find plenty to be worried about. But as things got more chaotic, a cottage industry of travelling speakers sprang up and added an edge of hysteria to the situation.

If you think about it, it's pretty hard to exaggerate about the tumult of the '60s, but these guys managed. And like Professor Henry Hill in the *Music Man*, they knew what buttons to push with their audience, how to exploit a sense of crisis, and what solution to sell them. Though in this case, you could call them the *anti*–Music Men.

Every so often, a few churches would get together for what they called a youth rally. The speaker would be somebody who said things like "dig" or "man" or "groovy" enough so that the adults would think, "Hey, he knows their lingo. Maybe they'll listen to him."

The guy might even have long sideburns—though no matter how long his hair was, it was likely to be improbably cut above his ear and chopped off at the collar—and would wear fairly wide bell-bottoms with his brightly colored sport coat and wide tie. If he was really pushing the envelope, he would wear shoes with two-inch heels. This cool cat would relate to us where we supposedly lived, but the real purpose of the meeting would be to scare the Hell out of us on one topic: rock and roll.

Even the antidrug and alcohol speech was subordinate to the rock and roll spiel. It would go something like this: Sally is now a drug-addled prostitute. Jimmy got drunk and wrapped his car around a station wagon full of toddlers. What did they have in common? They were good kids who got warped by listening to *rock music!*

The odds of finding a screwed up kid—or even a good one—who didn't listen to rock music by 1974 were never discussed. Nor was the fact that Sally and Jimmy both ate Cheerios while growing up.

One guy, Brother Bob, who made a living talking about the occult and rock music (as though they were one and the same) told the wildest story. "Some parents called me and they were frantic. There was nothing they could do with their daughter, and they said, 'Bob, help us, maybe you can reach her.' After talking to the young lady for a while, I said in a loud voice, 'Demon, I command you to tell me your name!'"

This brought gasps from the audience, and after letting this sink in, Bob continued. "Now the parents were about to kick me out of there, when a deep voice answered, 'My name is Legion.'

Now, they are really about to flip out, you dig? Like I can see most of you are. But in talking to this demon, he told me something that I will never forget."

As he paused dramatically, I elbowed my buddy Don and said, sotto voce, so a couple of rows could hear me, "Must have been good. Most people's conversations with demons are in one ear and out the other."

My youth pastor, as cool a guy as Baptist youth pastors were allowed to be in those days, hissed at me to shut up, then turned away; but I could see his shoulders shaking in laughter.

" 'I am the demon who invented rock and roll music,' " the speaker intoned. The audience gasped. My row cracked up. Some of the really square kids glared at me. If any of our group became demon possessed while listening to the radio, it was going to be my fault.

That kind of scare tactic, tacitly endorsed by the pastors they trusted, was what Fundamentalist parents had to live with in the '60s and '70s. Of course, it didn't help that there were a lot of radicals running around actually *saying,* "We're after your kids, you square repressive old Capitalist pigs."

Mining the statements of the radical fringe, the preachers succeeded in getting the rule-minding "good" kids to stream tearfully to the front, pledging never to foul their minds with the devil-worshiping jungle beat; while their parents thankfully filled the offering basket and lined up at the book, record, and tape table for ways to spread this word to their unenlightened friends.

In early 1975, my freshman year of high school, a world-famous evangelist came to town and filled the city's biggest arena. Billed as the Walking Bible, Jack Van Impe pulled from a broader spectrum of churches than most Fundy preachers and was making his pitch to be called up to the Billy Graham leagues.

His angle was prophecy, not so much the pop culture. Prying open the secrets of the book of Revelation has always been the surest way to fill the pews in a Fundamentalist church. Van Impe marginalized himself, however, after he started setting dates for Jesus' return to earth, and then had to modify them. His first blunder was in hinting that it would come in 1976. Just why God was so intent on helping us celebrate the Bicentennial was something he couldn't quite explain, but it added a patriotic flavor to a subject that can fill even the most listless of Baptist churches—the end of the world. It worked really well for Jack until about 1977.

Jack had yet another revelation for us. Sitting way back up near the rafters of the city auditorium with our feet on the backs of the empty chairs in front of us, my friends and I heard yet another amazing story about the origins of rock and roll.

Van Impe relayed word for word the conversation of Soviet Politburo members who were searching for a way to corrupt America's youth and make the United States fall from within. What did their mad scientists come up with? Rock music.

"That's why," Jack intoned, "they don't let young people listen to rock and roll in Russia."

Who could blame a good Fundy parent for being paranoid? They really *did* have enemies. Demons, Communists, and who knows, maybe even demonic Communists. It's a wonder we were ever allowed to leave the house.

For my dad, this revelation was a godsend. A chapter leader of the conspiracy-minded, anti-Communist John Birch Society, the "fact" that the Russkies had invented rock and roll made everything fall into place.

Actually, despite our protestations and logical arguments to the contrary, some of the preachers' rhetoric sank into us kids, as well. Perhaps there really were a bunch of rock and roll sluts running around trying to trap clean-cut young men like us. We only had one question. Where *were* they?

If you really want to discourage a behavior in teenagers, it seems a poor strategy to tell them everybody is doing it. Even worse, telling teenage boys that rock and roll is an aphrodisiac, is hardly the way to get them to avoid it.

As much fun as we made of the preachers' arguments, we all wanted to make sure the radio worked in the car, and we played music constantly on dates, just in case. I was rather surprised the first time I was told to turn the radio off because it was a distraction from the task at hand—or, rather lip.

Television was tolerated by rule makers—though we didn't have one in our house; but movie attendance was forbidden. Conduct codes for deacons, Sunday School teachers, and even choir members ruled out attending a movie house. You could watch them on TV, but even Disney movies were off limits if they played on a big screen.

The argument was twofold: One, supposedly by seeing wholesome movies, you were helping fund the theater that showed nasty films. In reality, what Fundies had done was remove a huge market for "family" films and give theater owners and studios less incentive to make and demand them.

Second was the even stranger argument that it was a "bad testimony." Supposedly, an unsaved person who saw you at the movies wouldn't know if you were there for the revival of *Dumbo* or *Last Tango in Paris*. Though why they would assume you used your television to watch *Monday Night Football* instead of the scandalous *Soap*, was not explained.

My dad, who loved Hitchcock movies, fell into line with the rhetoric, however. We went to see a double feature of *Winnie the Pooh*, and *The Ugly Dachshund* in 1966, around the time we began attending North Baptist, but then the movie houses became off limits soon after. My next big-screen feature was *The In-Laws* after I graduated from high school in 1979.

So for thirteen years—other than the television I could get in at friends' houses, or my grandmothers'—the closest I got to the popular culture was through the radio.

I could take a radio and an earplug down to the basement and listen while I made scale-model airplanes, go for bike rides with a transistor compact on my belt, or even hide it under the covers so I could listen to Peter C on Flint's pioneering radio station WTAC, after 10 P.M., when he played "underground" music like Hendrix and the Who.

But it was darn hard to hide a television under the covers; and the nearest movie theater was ten miles away—a long, long bike ride. *Star Wars* came out when I was a sophomore in high school.

Two of my buddies were suspended for a day from Christian school when they made the mistake of bragging about sneaking out to see it.

I spent enough time at Grandma Forsmark's house to become a bit of an old movie buff; but I didn't see *Star Wars* until a revival tour came through my freshman year of college. In the late '70s, this was the cultural equivalent of coming from a galaxy far, far away.

Fundy parents were worried about letting their kids out of the house, and we spent all our time trying to get out. But they found a way to keep us somewhat in line when we were out among the sex-crazed rock and roll fevered heathens.

They made us look like dorks.

I was able to vote before I had a haircut I would have chosen for myself. Hair was a big deal in the 1970s—a really big deal. Even the biggest musical of the era was named after it.

I didn't want to run around with a Tiny Tim hairdo down to my butt, I was a jock. I just wanted something that wouldn't pass muster at marine boot camp.

These days if someone digs out old high-school yearbooks at a party, the cooler you were in the 1970s, the more you get laughed at. Those of us who grew up Fundy have a lot less of a problem with our high-school graduation pictures. But compared to what we put up with at the time, that's small consolation.

I once had a fashion model–pretty blonde that I had an enormous crush on tell me rather wistfully, "You would be really cute if you had hair."

That echoed in my head for years and did wonders for my self-confidence with the opposite sex.

But hair was more than just the Baptist version of a male chastity belt, it was yet another ideological battle.

While out in the real world a guy had to have hair down his back to make some kind of radical statement, in the Baptist world, all he needed was hair that touched the ear or the collar.

Like the marijuana theory of drug use, we were told that hair on the ear was the next step to long flowing locks. And no one had hair that long without being a rock fan—and we all knew the road to Hell was paved with rock and roll records.

If there was a war over hair within Fundamentalism, our house was the Iwo Jima. I was determined to conquer the Mount Surabachi of normalcy, and my dad was as dug in at his position as any descendant of Samurais—or in our case, Vikings.

As soon as I started earning yard-work money, I tried to wrest some control of my scalp by buying my own haircuts. This would give me some control over length, I hoped—and get me away from my dad's home haircut kit.

His decreed Christian haircut was the "Princeton, short on top." Basically, a crew cut with short bangs, *not* exactly what the Princeton man was wearing in the 1970s.

It was, of course, pure coincidence that God's preferred haircut and music were the same as my dad's had been before his conversion.

When Mad Dad got ahold of those grooming instruments, every "Oops" meant an ever widening patch of razor stubble. By the time he was done, I looked even more like I was getting cancer treatments than I did a new marine recruit.

So, once I had the means and the "time to get a haircut" order was issued, I would hop on my bike the next Saturday morning and head down to the Barber College for a two-dollar haircut. Whatever trainee got assigned to me would step up behind the chair and invariably say something like, "Are *you* here for a haircut?"

"Yes," I would say grouchily. "Just make it a little shorter. I don't want whitewalls, leave enough so you can't see the skin through it."

"That doesn't leave me much room to work," came the doubtful reply. Here he was, trying to learn hairstyling—nobody got "haircuts" in the 1970s—and here comes some kid testing the steadiness of his inexperienced hand. It was a real challenge to trim hair that was maybe three quarters of an inch in length without leaving little gouges. Talk about splitting hairs.

When I returned to my grandmother's house, where we had Swedish pancakes for lunch every Saturday, my father would be waiting to commence inspection.

"I can't even tell you got a haircut," were always the first words out of his mouth. The argument went on from there.

"When you cut practically nothing in half, it's hard to tell the difference," I retorted. "If you like, I can ask Grandma for her magnifying glass; but since you didn't measure me on the way out the door, you won't have a basis for comparison, so what's the use?"

"When I was a kid, people would look at you and say, 'Time for a haircut,'" he pronounced.

"So?"

"So it's time for a haircut."

"When you were a kid, they had fins on cars, too."

"That's not the point."

"Yeah, it's the point. Styles change. Did God like fins on cars, did they serve some purpose back in the utopia of the fifties?"

"For one thing, car styles haven't changed for the better, they've gotten more boring—"

"Like your idea of a haircut?" I interrupted.

He went on like I hadn't said a word, "But they didn't change as a sign of rebellion. They didn't change because of the Beatles. You want to look like the Beatles?"

"Nope, the Beatles all have hair down on their shoulders, now, *and* they've broken up. There is no Beatles. Try to keep up."

"That, *that* is why you need a haircut!" Things had started out on a hostile, sarcastic note, but now the yelling was really getting going. "Just this little bit of freedom has made you rebellious and made you think you can talk to me like this!"

"Having a brain and being able to answer logically is a problem for you? I guess if you need to be able to make your argument, it would be," I said scornfully, not yet yelling. This made it worse.

"You are going back right now and getting a haircut!" he shouted.

"Why don't you come with me and explain," I challenged, finally yelling back, frustrated and tearful now that complete humiliation were the imminent stakes. "The guy complained that he couldn't find anything to cut in the first place!"

"It's not his place to comment on my standards!" he roared. "His job is to satisfy the customer."

"The customer is me, and he did his job the best he could under some stupid circumstances!" I was really losing my cool now. This was my head, and my back was against the wall.

"Don't you call me stupid! The Bible says, 'It is a shame for a man to have long hair!' You are not supposed to look like the feminized standards of the world. You will follow *my* standards!"

"This is not long. This is beyond short. I know the terminology may be a half inch '*long*,' but as an engineer, I would think you would understand the semantics, here."

"When I was a kid, that would have been long."

"When you were a kid, I was probably happier, because I didn't have some guy sending me out into the world looking like an idiot—because I wasn't born yet!"

"You need your spirit broken. *That's* why you need a haircut. You are going to get this haircut until you can learn to be satisfied with it. Until you learn to obey me and do it happily. Until you learn to be like Isaac, who voluntarily put himself on the altar as a sacrifice because his father told him that's what God wanted!"

"Come after me with a knife, and if you survive, you can tell the judge, 'God told me to do it,' " I yelled back, jumping to my feet.

My grandma entered the kitchen. She had pancakes to make and was tired of waiting for us to get out of her way. Haircuts were not a big deal to her, anyway. She cut her own because it was cheaper. As someone who vividly remembered the Depression, she wasn't parting with any of the hundreds of thousands my late grandfather had saved and earned over silly things like hairstyles.

Grandma Forsmark never quite understood her son's newfound religious fervor. She had brought her kids up in a very moderate Lutheran Church, but she now attended Riverdale Baptist with my folks because she didn't drive—and I think to her, church was church. She reached over and rubbed my head. "This is a nice, short haircut," she said. "This isn't long."

"Thanks, Mom," my dad said sarcastically. He was too tired to argue anymore. He sagged back into his chair, emotionally spent. "Why can't you just do what I say? Why can't you be more like Brian?"

Brian was the son of my dad's best friend, Jack. Jack's ideas made my dad's look mainstream. Brian enthusiastically jumped on board everything Jack proclaimed, and then tried to set himself up as the standard for behavior. He was also a wimpy, brown-nosing, emotional wreck, who would break into tears upon losing an argument, and who wet the bed well into late grammar school. (I know, because I had often been forced to sleep in his smelly bed years before, while our parents played board games at his house.)

"You really want me to be like Brian?" I gasped. "*That* would make you proud?"

Amazingly, my dad chuckled. He knew he had gone too far. "No," he laughed ruefully, "I don't want you to be like Brian."

I snickered, and he laughed. The argument was over, like a pressure boiler with a leaky valve, the steam had just escaped. "You're just going to have to go back sooner, and spend your money. That's your problem," he waved his hand dismissively; and I beat a hasty retreat while he was pretending he had won the battle.

As surreal as this conversation sounds, we weren't the only ones having this fight. While churches were fighting over dress codes and hair standards for what they would allow in their pulpits, Fundamentalist schools were hashing out hair codes for students; and having regular inspections to enforce them.

It was also gold to be mined on the evangelist circuit. Hal Webb and Theron Babock were a pair of travelling evangelists whose entire presentation was a primal scream against "worldliness." They didn't waste a lot of time on conspicuous behavior that the Bible condemns, like cheating, cutthroat grasping for power, or the elevation of self above God; no, they basically concentrated on anything that made one seem like they actually inhabited the decade in which they lived.

Unlike Brother Bob, they made no attempt to look cool. They used Brylcream like it was going out of style (which it had, the decade before), wore black-framed horn-rimmed glasses, and dark suits with narrow lapels and ties, which by 1976, they would have had to have custom-made. Either that, or they had stocked up at a J. Edgar Hoover fire sale.

They even set up haircutting stands where Hal would perform the ritual that to him was every bit as important as baptism for the new convert.

Hal was the preacher, and he seemed to have this default setting in his brain, that if the words "rock music" were mentioned— even if *he* was the one who brought it up—he would go into a squeaky falsetto and shriek, "Oh yeah baby, baby, get high and do it in the street!"

And don't even think about a fledgling new alternative called Christian rock. "Christian rock!" Hal would sneer. "You might as well say 'Christian sex!' "

Hal didn't clarify where Christian babies came from if sex was anti-Christian, but my friends and I decided that this attitude explained why, though married, he didn't mind spending most of his life on the road.

My parents figured that my grandpa, who didn't like hippies much, might enjoy hearing somebody else railing about the prevailing culture too. When Hal started curling his lips and screaming while jumping up and down on the platform, my poor grandparents got these stricken looks on their faces, like they had just walked into Jonestown. Getting them to stay for Kool-Aid and cookies afterward was definitely a nonstarter.

Even my mom, who was initially pretty enthusiastic about the duo, said to me afterward, "I don't think Mom and Dad were quite prepared for Hal and Theron."

Hal and Theron employed several gimmicks, including "Gospel Magic," and a pretty cool deal playing songs on something called a theremin, an antenna that put out an eerie science fiction–sounding wail, whose pitch was determined by how close the player held his hands. Appropriately, this was what was used as a sound effect in the movie *Village of the Damned,* when the eerie children used their power.

Another was the songwriting of "The Amazing Theron." People in the audience would call out a phrase, and Theron would have two minutes to write a song based on it. No one seemed to mind—or notice—that they all had the same melody.

They also put out record albums that featured Theron's longer form masterpieces. In terms of complexity, they made the tunes of a three-chord progression rock band, like local heroes Grand Funk Railroad, sound like Duke Ellington suites. This prompted a debate among my friends as to whether it was a contradiction in terms to call music a "One-chord progression."

Number one on the Hal and Theron Greatest Hits Chart was a ditty called "First Corinthians Eleven." It went like this:

First Corinthians eleven is still in the book
I know that it is 'cause I just took a look
For a man to have long hair it says is a shame
So why bring disgrace to our dear Savior's name?

The stanza that got the biggest laugh and applause was:

But mustn't the women take some of the blame
To resemble a man is as much of a shame.
If you must insist that his trousers you wear,
Then what can you say when he comes with long hair?

Now, I'm no archaeologist, but the way I understand it, the Corinthians had issues with cross-dressing homosexual temple prostitutes, not mop-headed pop singers. But hey, people using the Bible out of context to enforce their preferences is nothing new—and the people who loudly proclaim that the Bible is their only "rule in faith and practice" can be the best at it.

My dad liked to invite visiting missionaries and evangelists over to the house for dinner. Cool for him, but generally agonizing for us kids. We would be paraded out for show and required to act even more like Stepford children for the duration.

Hal and Theron came over, and after complimenting my dad

on the lack of a television in the house, Hal came over and rubbed my head. "Now *there's* a good Christian haircut," he commented.

"Yeah," I quipped sarcastically, "Jesus himself comes by every other week and buzzes my head for us."

I paid for that, but it was worth it. I got to brag to my friends, *and* hang out in my room for the afternoon and read Louis L'Amour, instead of performing like an organ grinder monkey for Hal and Theron.

Of course, this again brought up the pleas of "Why can't you just go along with what we want you to be?"

I didn't answer this way, but it was mainly because my suspicion was that following this life plan would have me leaving this world as a very old virgin.

Once in the course of a calmer discussion on this topic with my mom, she told me that she believed that God specifically picked the right type of parent for each kid. She also hinted that worked the other way around, too—that there was some sort of Baptist version of karma at work. If you were a pain to your parents, God would make sure your kids paid you back in kind.

My parents found out too late what kind of kid they were stuck with. I didn't want to make the same mistake.

My mom also gave me a bit of advice that I never forgot. I was a senior in high school and helping her make up the bunk beds that I still shared with my little brother in a ten-by-ten room. I was serious about Karen—so serious that I even let my parents in on it. Before that, I kept any interest I had in any girl strictly to myself, probably giving them something *else* to worry about during sleepless nights.

"Don't ever marry anyone you can see yourself being able to live without," she said.

That was advice I followed to the letter.

They say your life changes forever once you have children. But actually, your life changes a lot as soon as you find out the child is on the way. Our choose-the-baby's-sex books are suddenly replaced by stacks of prenatal-care manuals.

There are Lamaze classes for "birthing partners." Though in my class we are all fathers-to-be, the politically correct designation is still used. This is a series of ten one-hour classes into which they cram about two total hours of useful information.

We naively practice our breathing and coaching exercises, thinking, "Yes, this is how we will do it."

Both of us are pretty sure, however, that the slight pinch the birthing partner is supposed to apply to the mother's Achille's tendon during breathing exercises is not really an approximate simulation of labor cramps. Still, we faithfully chug through our "who, who, hee, hees" with all the rest.

Besides, they don't allow you in the delivery room without a certificate saying you've completed the course.

Doing the ultrasound, though, is an unbelievably cool experience. Karen, who had been born with an extra thumb on one hand that was removed shortly after she was born, anxiously has the technician doing her best to count fingers.

What I was looking for, however, only required counting to one.

I am breathless when we see the outline of the face and eyes, and the beating heart amidst the grainy, gray mess that looks like an Etch-A-Sketch that had been attacked by a hyper child with a magnet.

Looking into those hollow, alien-looking eye sockets is awe inspiring. "That's my son," I breathe. Nothing wrong with a little positive thinking.

About two weeks before the due date, we figure we'll get in one of our last shots at dinner and a movie. Mexican food, then Sigourney Weaver blasting the aliens. Right after my Michigan Wolverines take care of the hated Bobby Knight and his Indiana Hoosiers in the College Basketball Game of the Decade, we are headin' out.

I'm in the shower, when I get the news.

"Ba-abe," I hear the call.

"Yeah?"

"My water broke. We better get going."

I almost fall down and break my neck, but she's as composed

as can be. "Just take it easy," I yell, my voice an octave higher than usual. "I'll take care of everything."

But by the time I get out of the bathroom, she is packed, she's sopped up the puddle, thrown the rags in the laundry room, and is timing the contractions.

I sprint up the stairs, stumbling about halfway up, and she calls out, "Calm down, we have lots of time."

So, I calmly dress, my fingers shaking on the buttons, pick out a book for all the downtime—I can't stand staring at the walls; lines and waiting rooms are my earthly hells—and I mostly observe the speed limit on the way to the hospital.

When we get there, she is whisked away in a wheelchair, and I am sent to the maternity ward waiting room, which, amazingly, has no television, just the inevitable old magazines.

I settle in with Curtoon Stroud's *Sniper's Moon*, which is actually great enough to hold my attention in this situation. It's about 11 A.M. at this point, and a nurse tells me that from the timing and strength of the contractions, we're a few hours away from delivery.

Hmm. Maybe my new son and I can watch the late-afternoon Michigan game as our first bonding experience.

I flag down an orderly. "Can I get a television ordered in advance for my wife's room?"

She just looks at me. "Your wife won't be assigned a room until after we deliver the baby, sir. That's how we do it."

"Yeah, but you aren't sending her home. You know she's gonna need a room," I say reasonably.

"There's no need to be sarcastic, those are the rules."

"Look, our insurance is going to pay for the day, right? She's going to have a baby, today. You have this whole floor here, and only about four rooms seem occupied. You think someone is going to know the room was assigned a few hours early? I know we pay for the TV ourselves . . ."

"I can't help you, and I'm very busy," and she walks off stiffly down the dark hallway.

That is my first, and hardly most important, encounter with hospital bureaucracy.

Finally, they let me in to see her and inform me that from the strength of the heartbeat, "It looks like a boy."

For several hours, we faithfully do our breathing and watch the monitor during the contractions to make sure little Steven's heartbeat stays strong. Karen is doing great, keeping her composure and sticking to the method.

But as the contractions get closer together and stronger, she isn't dilating very much. My wife's small hips, which I considered pretty terrific around conception time, aren't so great for today's task. The baby's head just isn't coming through those bones; and isn't likely to.

Now we've had plenty of warning that this might be the case, so we take the news calmly. Our doctor had considered scheduling a C-section, but decided we would at least give "natural" birth a try.

So we are a little surprised to be informed that there is no anesthesiologist available for our "emergency" operation.

"How long is that going to take?" I demand.

"Not long," I'm assured.

"Not long" drags out into interminable hours in which Karen's labor pains increase, and her good temperament does not. Once she finds out that she is going through all this for nothing, her patience understandably gives out. They give her some limited painkillers to dull the pain, but they also serve to loosen her self-control. While I get to be the target of some of the cursing, the real venom is saved for the missing anesthesiologist.

About two hours into it, she snaps. "Don't give me that breathing crap! Why don't *you* try this for a while!" She then tells me to get out of her sight and go watch my damn basketball game.

The nurse tells me I should probably take a break, and I head down the hall. In every room, the Michigan/Indiana game is on and cheering from visiting fathers fills the halls of the maternity floor.

"How's it goin'?" I ask a guy who is leaning in the doorway. Over his shoulder, a Michigan player is soaring for a massive slam dunk. He's so far above the rim, it looks like the hoop is down around his knees.

"It's a slaughter." He grins. "Best I've ever seen U of M play!"

Yippee, yahoo.

I stop the nurse in charge of the ward. She's the daughter of our doctor and an old schoolmate. "Are we getting an anesthesiologist today?"

"Soon," she promises again.

"You know," I say crankily, "I'd better read about a train hitting a bus in the newspaper tomorrow, and that all the victims came here. This is insane."

The hours blur as I read my entire book, grab some food from the vending machines, and spend as much time in the prep room as Karen can stand to have me around.

When the anesthesiologist finally shows up, we are relieved enough that we don't mention his unapologetic attitude over the wait. Apparently, the waiting room Law of the Universe that states that only the doctor's schedule is important applies to this situation, also.

Karen is bustled out of the cubicle where she's been kept waiting in pain for about seven hours, and I am once again sent back to the waiting room.

Without a book, I am really at loose ends. I fidget, pace, and even look at some stupid magazines. It is probably only a few minutes later that they come and get me, but I would have sworn otherwise under oath. As we walk down the hall, the nurse explains to me, "Now they are going to make an incision in your wife's belly and bring the baby out that way."

Apparently, she thinks I'm still hanging around the hospital after being born last night, myself. "No kidding," I snap.

She's been doing this long enough not to pay attention to the moods of cranky fathers in waiting. "You can sit next to her on a stool and hold her hand and talk to her," she goes on, handing me a gown and mask. "Tell her she's doing great, everything is all right, keep it light. But you might want to concentrate on her, rather than the surgery. Some fathers have passed out from watching. If you feel faint, move away from the table."

For a second, I'm stunned. I have no reply, smart-assed or otherwise, to this. This is a new worry. I hadn't really considered the notion that I might pass out, fall on a scalpel, and cause the evisceration of my wife today. Until now, I'd actually felt pretty calm about the whole thing.

Now, I'm skittish as a cat at a rubber bone convention as they lead me into the delivery room. Everybody is standing around, seemingly awaiting my arrival. Karen is covered in a similar green gown as everyone else, except that her white, distended belly is uncovered. As I sit on a tall stool next to Karen, smile reassuringly, and tell her I love her, the rest of them go into action.

They draw a line across the top of her belly for the incision. Then I remember, Don't look, stupid! I turn back to my wife and smile. I focus on her. I am not going to pass out and be the topic of the nurses' lounge—not to mention family gatherings for years.

"I guess you won't be able to tell our son's dates horror stories about delivering *his* big head." I grin. Sometime during the first evening my mother met Karen, she trotted out the tale of delivering my big head. I think she figured since this girl was attracted to me despite my stupid haircut, it was time to add another layer of protection.

Karen smiles weakly at me. Jokes I can do. It's a heck of a lot easier than the breathing crap and yelling "Push!"

Then I hear the doctor say, "Here we are," and I can't help it. I have to look. Just as I do, I see him pulling the baby's head out. I forget all about the gruesomeness of the scene. I'm fascinated and in suspense. This is my first look at my son. Forgetting the rest of my instructions, I lean forward.

"What's happening?" Karen asks anxiously, as the doctor stops to clear the baby's nose with a turkey baster–looking thing. It starts to cry, loudly, opening its mouth wide, and letting her rip. It's the strangest thing I have ever seen. There's a screaming head sticking out a bloody gash in a woman's belly.

"Good strong lungs," the doctor laughs.

Still doing my darndest to keep things light, I say, "The head is out, babe. You look like you're in the movie, *Alien!*"

"Shut up and count the fingers and toes," she cries.

"I can't see them yet."

The doctor reaches down while a nurse holds the furious,

screaming head and pulls the rest of the body out of Karen. "Count the fingers," she insists again in her doped-up state.

Once again, there is only one thing I'm trying to count, and I can't.

It isn't there.

"It's a girl!" the doctor announces. "And she is beautiful like her mother."

It can't be a girl, I want to run back to the monitoring room and show them all the printouts from the heartbeat and contractions. There's been some kind of mistake.

"It's an Amanda," I tell Karen excitedly. That was the name we settled on for a girl. She has only ten fingers and ten toes.

After I cut the cord, and they give us a quick peek, the maternity crew takes charge of Amanda, cleaning her up and doing all their checks and tests. I sit with Karen while they put her back together. Forgetting my instructions now that I'm an old pro in here, I make the mistake of looking to see what they are doing.

Without the baby factor, this *is* pretty gross. Before, I was watching life come into the world. It was fascinating and wonderful. Now, I'm looking at my wife with her insides hanging out. I start to feel a little woozy, but hold it in check, taking a few deep breaths and looking quickly away.

When they are done, I am once again shooed down to the waiting room with my pocket full of dimes, where I make my phone calls. Both sets of parents promise they are on their way; other friends on the call list offer congratulations and say they will come up tomorrow.

The next couple of hours are a blur. The lack of food, the emotional exhaustion, and the tension finally catch up with me. I hold the baby, pose for pictures taken by both sets of grandparents, and get called things like "Proud poppa" a lot.

"Did you eat?" my mom asks, knowing that I tend to skip meals when I'm preoccupied. "You look as pale as she does."

"I'm fine. Just tired, been in this place too long. Too much waiting for that stupid anesthesiologist."

Karen's mostly out of it, and once our sets of parents leave, she conks out pretty quickly. I'm out of there as soon as she does.

The dog is pretty excited to see me—practically runs to me with her legs crossed, and I realize that I hadn't asked anyone to come over and let her out. "Well," I tell her, "the girls *way* outnumber the boys in this house now."

I'm exhausted and hungry, and now I'm worried. What the hell do I know about raising girls? All I know is they don't have any interests in common with me, and eventually, they become impossible to deal with—right about the time you have to worry about protecting them from teenagers like the younger me.

I start cursing and throwing things around. Unbreakable things, of course, I have another mouth to feed. I wolf down some leftovers, shower, and head up to bed to watch the basketball highlights.

For the first time in nearly four years, I'm sleeping alone in my own bed. This does not improve my surly mood any. I gradually drift off ignoring two of my usual rules: Don't go to bed mad; and don't just sit and channel surf until you fall asleep.

The next morning, I'm not a lot happier, but since I've always been an if-there's-no-solution-there's-no-problem kind of guy, I'm determined to make the most of things. I'm not going to be one of those idiots who wanted a son so badly he raises a confused, antisocial tomboy.

I decide I'm not going to get caught short again, so I take James Clavell's mammoth *Noble House, and* I take a backup book.

I get Karen's room number at the lobby information desk, pass the all-too-familiar maternity waiting area with a bit of a shudder, and bop into her room with a big smile and call out, "How are my girls today?"

The baby is on her belly in one of those bassinets on wheels with the clear plastic sides, and she immediately raises her head and turns and looks at me with sharp blue eyes. I stop in my tracks.

"Would you look at that?" the nurse exclaims. "What a strong baby! I've never seen one already lift her head the next day like that!"

Then the clincher: "She sure knows her daddy's voice!"

Okay, maybe that was sentimental baloney. Nevertheless, I fall hopelessly in love for the second time in my life. Of course she's a girl. Her name is Amanda. What else could she be?

It's my son Travis's second birthday party. The whole family is over, including my sister's three boys, so it is not a quiet gathering.

My youngest sister is pregnant for the first time, and now I'm the clichéd veteran father, dispensing bromides like "You find out what life is all about once you have kids. Before that you're just kind of a spectator in the world, blah blah blah . . ."

"You want a boy or a girl?" I ask my brother-in-law.

"A boy," he answers immediately and talks about getting a little race car driver or something.

I'm distracted from his answer by my macho, super-athletic son, who can already hit a pitched baseball and talk in complete sentences. "Look, Dad," he calls.

He's perched on about the fifth step leading to the upstairs of our hundred-year-old house. Before I can tell him not to, he launches himself into space. Every month or so, he adds another stair he can land from without falling down. It's like a regular training program with him.

He almost does it, but he's not wearing shoes and his feet fly out from underneath him as he lands on the slick wood floor, and he hits on his butt. This is not a big problem, thanks to the diaper.

In a moment, the smell lets everyone know that he had something else soft and squishy that helped to break his fall.

Batting? Yes. Speak in grammatically correct complete sentences? Sure. Potty trained? Uh-uh.

He grins. "Poo-poo, Dad."

Amanda protests, "Gross, Trav!" My perfect little blond girl with her shoulder-length curls has been busy organizing the older of my sister's two boys in some activity or another. She's not only a joy to have around, people ask to have her over to play with their kids so they can get things done. At six, she's already a semi-baby-sitter, and easily the smartest kid in her class at school.

I turn back to my brother-in-law, who is in stitches at the sight of my son sitting in his own filth with a smirk on his seemingly angelic face, and I let the naive man know he's all wrong about his preference.

"If you're lucky," I say, "you'll have a girl."

[DAVID FORSMARK]

Don't ever suggest to David Forsmark that he was scarred by growing up "Fundy" in the 1970s. It's given this talented Michiganian enough material to write a full-length memoir, of which the selection you've just read is part. Humorous and touching, Forsmark's experiences position him to be the Fundamentalist answer to Garrison Keillor; as well as demonstrating that a childhood in a restrictive household can still be filled with love.

While Forsmark's own children may have an easier time of it than he did, he is a strong believer in setting "a moral and spiritual tone" for his daughter and son.

"Spiritual activities should be given a top priority in the family's life," says Forsmark, "and you should lead by example. In fact, I think a father colors his kids' impressions of God, whether he means to—or even thinks about it—or not.

"If a dad is involved, fair, loving, and sets reasonable standards, his kids will have the impression, when they think of God, that He has similar traits and can be counted on. If a dad is distant, arbitrarily demanding, and judgmental, or selfish, their children will assume that God is off somewhere doing His own thing, and doesn't care much about them."

Adds the author, "It's important to have as few rules [as] you can get by with, but they should be strictly and fairly enforced. If you try to completely mold your children in your image, you are setting yourself up as kind of a tinpot god, and you can only fail—and alienate your kids in the process."

It must have worked, he claims, since he has kids he feels are nicer than he was at their age, and who like to go to church.

Although Forsmark makes his living primarily through the advertising agency he owns, he now spends a large share of his time writing about movies, television, and rock and roll for the Flint Journal. "All of the things I was not allowed to do while growing up!" he says.

—C.O.

ELECTRIC ARROWS

E. Annie Proulx

[1]

"YOU TELL ME," SAYS REBA, WRAPPED UP IN HER BLUE sweater
with the metal buttons. She's wearing the gray sweatpants again.
Her head is tipped back steeply on the long neck column as she
looks up at me, her narrow rouged mouth like a red wire. "Tell me
why anybody in his right mind would sit in The Chicken swilling
beer, watching fat men wrestle until midnight, why?"

I think, so they don't have to sit around in the kitchen and
look at moldy pictures.

Aunt pulls one out as thick as a box lid. I see milkweed blowing, the house set square on a knob of lawn, each nailhead hard,
the shadows of the clapboards like black rules.

There is a colorless, coiled hair on Reba's sweater sleeve.

"I couldn't believe it, open the door of that place and there
you are," she says.

Aunt's finger traces along the side of the picture, over the
steep maples, over a woman with two children standing in the
white road. Aunt smells of lemon lotion and clothes worn two
days to save on laundry detergent. The faces in the photograph
are round plates above dark shoulders, smiles like fern fronds. The

woman holds a blurred baby, she holds him forever. The other child is unsmiling, short and stocky, a slap of black hair across his forehead. He died of cholera a few weeks after they took the photograph.

Aunt points to the baby and says, "That's your father." He is unfocused, leached by the far sunlight. She clasps her thick, hard old palms together.

"I'm grateful I was there, Reba, when you come along needing your flat tire changed," I say.

"That part was good," she murmurs, as if giving me something I'd long coveted.

We are at the kitchen table inside the house of the photograph, waiting for the pie to cool. The camera belonged to Leonard Prittle, the hired man, who lived in this house once. We don't have a hired man now, we don't have a farm, we live in the house ourselves. Reba encourages Aunt with the photographs. And the Moon-Azures, hey, the damn Moon-Azures think the past belongs to them.

"Want me to whip the cream to go on the pie?" I ask Reba.

I do go down to The Chicken sometimes.

The maples in the photograph are all gone, cut when they widened the road. There is Aunt at the wheel of a Reo truck with her hair bobbed. The knuckles are smooth in the pliant hand. They widened the road, but they didn't straighten it.

Aunt takes another picture and another, she can't stop. She lifts them, the heavy-knuckled fingers precise and careful, her narrow Clew head bent and the pale Clew eyes roving over the images of black suits and ruched sleeves, dead children, horses with braided manes, a storm cloud over the barn. She says, "Leonard Prittle could of been something if he'd of had a chance."

Reba cuts the pie into seeping crimson triangles. Back when she worked she gave kitchen parties to show farm women how to get the most out of their freezers and mixers. Now it's all microwaves and the farm women live in apartments in Concord.

I pretend to look at the picture. The weather vanes point at an east wind. There are picket fences, elm trees, a rooster in the weeds. Hey, I've seen that rooster picture a hundred times.

Time has scraped away the picket fences, and you should hear the snowplow throw its dirty spoutings against the clapboards; it sounds like the plow is coming through the kitchen. The leftover Pugleys, Clews, and the Cuckhorns live in these worn-out houses. Reba was a Cuckhorn.

"Properties break apart," says Aunt, sighing and nipping off the pie point with her fork. We know how quarreling sons sell sections of the place to Boston schoolteachers, those believers that country life makes you good. When they find it does not, they spitefully sell the land again, to Venezuelan millionaires, Raytheon engineers, cocaine dealers, and cold-handed developers.

Reba mumbles, "The more you expect from something, the more you turn on it when it disappoints you."

I suppose she means me.

Aunt and I still own a few acres of the place—the hired man's house, where we live, and the barn. *Atlantic Ocean Farm* is painted on the barn door because my father, standing on the height of land as a young man full of hopeful imagination, thought he saw a shining furrow of sea far to the east between a crack in the mountains.

Reba puts plastic wrap over the uneaten pie, turns up the television sound. I go walk in the driveway before the light's gone. Through the barn window I can see empty cardboard appliance boxes stacked inside, soft and shapeless from years of damp.

You can see how nothing has changed in the barn. A knotted length of baling twine, furry with dust, still stretches from the top of the ladder to a beam. The kite's wooden skeleton, a fragile cross, is still up there.

I could take it down.

There is the thick snoring of a car turning in the driveway. It's not dark enough for the headlights, just the fog lights, set wide apart, yellow. The Moon-Azures. They don't see me by the barn. Mrs. Moon-Azure opens the car door and sticks out her legs as straight as celery stalks.

I go back in the house, let the cat in. Moon-Azure says, "Nice evening, Mason." His eyeglasses reflect like the fog lights. "Thought I'd see if you could give me a hand tomorrow. The old

willow went down, and it looks like we need a tug with the trac-
tor."

More like half a day's work.

When I look out the window I can see Yogetsky's trailer with
the crossed snowshoes mounted over the door, the black mesh
satellite dish in front of the picture window. Yogetsky is an old
bachelor. His cranky, shining kitchen is full of saved tin cans,
folded plastic bags, magazines piled in four-color pyramids. He sets
bread dough to rise on top of the television set.

Across the road from his trailer there's the Beaubiens' place.
The oldest son's log truck is parked in the driveway, bigger than
the house. A black truck with the word *Scorpion* in curly script.
The Beaubiens are invisible, maybe behind the truck, maybe in-
side the house, eating baked beans out of a can, sharing the fork.
They eat quick, afraid of losing time that could be put into work.
King Olaf sardines, jelly roll showing the crimson spiral inside the
plastic wrap, Habitant pea soup.

Yogetsky moved up from Massachusetts about ten years ago and
got two jobs, one to live on, the other to pay his property taxes, he
says. His thick nose sticks out of his face like a cork. He says, "This
trailer, this land," pointing at the shaved jowl of lawn, "is a invest-
ment. Way people are coming in, it'll be worth plenty, year or two."

He owns two acres of Pugley's old cow pasture.

Yogetsky is a reader. He takes *USA Today* and magazines of the
type with stories in them about dentists who become fur trappers.
His garden is fenced in with sheep wire. The tops of tin cans hang
on the fence and stutter in the wind. There's his flagpole.

[2]

We raised apples. Baldwins, Tolman Sweets, Duchess, Snow
Apple, Russet, and Sheep's Nose. The big growers were pushing
the McIntosh and the Delicious. I was nervy and sick, but I had
to help my father string barbwire around the orchard and down
through the woods. A quick, sloppy job. The deer would come in

late June, the young deer, and eat the new tender leaves, still crumpled and folded on the Baldwin seedlings. Nobody knew what was wrong with me. Nervy, Aunt said. Growing too fast. The Baldwins, torn and stripped, grew crooked.

The McIntosh apple ruined us. My father ruined us.

He said, "Children, it's a hard way to go to make money on sugar, but there's a good dollar in the Baldwin apple." And sold the maples for timber. And bought five hundred Baldwin seedlings. Your Baldwin apple is a dull, cloudy maroon color. It's got somewhat of a tender rootstock.

People wanted a shiny, red apple. Our fruit went to the juice mills. Now it's the other way around. All those old kinds we couldn't give away. Black Twig. Pinkham Pie. They pay plenty for them now.

Once your sugar bush is gone, it's gone for fifty years or forever.

My father sold pieces of the woodlot. Then pieces of pasture. Pieces of this, pieces of that. None of the Baldwins made it through a hard winter just before the war.

Aunt bites off the end of a raveling thread instead of using scissors.

Dad could make a nice stone wall, but he'd be off on something else before it got to any length. He preferred barbwire, get it over with. Still, he had a feel for stonework, for the chisel, without the dogged concentration you need for that work. He was silly. His excited ways, his easy enthusiasm made Aunt say he was a fool. I never heard anybody laugh like he did, a seesawing, gasping laugh like he was drowning for air. It was the brother that died young that had all the sense, says Aunt.

He let the farm drip through his fingers like water until only an anxious dampness was left in our palms. And his friend Diamond used to pick up first me, then Bootie, my sister, sliding his old dirty paws up between our legs, putting his tobacco-stained mouth at our narrow necks.

"He don't mean nothin' by it," Dad said, "quit your cryin'."

Dad told us, "The farmer's up against it."

You know where the golf course is, the Meadowlark condominiums, them sloping meadows along the river? He sold that

land for twenty an acre. Giving it away, even then. I told this to
Yogetsky and he moaned, hit his forehead with the heel of his
hand, said, "Jesus Christ."

We were up against it. There wasn't the money to find out
what was wrong with me, hey, just all kinds of homemade junk.
Bootie and I took boiled carrots to school in our lunch pails; the
cow's hooves made a thick sucking noise when we drove her
across the marshy place and that sound made me feel I didn't have
a chance. You get used to it.

The grand name for the farm, the hundreds of no-good trees
in the orchard, the heavy, tearing rolls of barbed wire strung
through the woods were all for nothing.

[3]

What can I tell you about the Moon-Azures?

They own the original old Clew homestead with its crooked
doorframes and worn stairs, Dr. and Mrs. Moon-Azure from Basil-
tower, Maryland. I was born in that house.

The Moon-Azures come up from Maryland every June and go
back in August. They scrape nine layers of paint off the paneling
in the parlor, point out to us the things they do to better the place.
They clear out the dump, get a backhoe in to cut a wide driveway. They get somebody to sand the floors. They buy a horse. Dr.
Moon-Azure's hands get roughed up when he works on the stone
wall. He holds them out and says admiringly, "Look at those
hands." A faint smell comes from his clothes, the familiar brown
odor of the old house. His wall buckles with the first frost heaves.

The Moon-Azures have weekend guests. We see the cars go
by, out-of-state license plates on Mercedes and Saabs. When the
wind is right we can hear their toneless voices knocking together
like sticks of wood, *tot, tot-tot, tot*. The horse gets out and is killed
on the road.

Nobody knows what kind of doctor he is. They go to him
when some woman from Massachusetts backs over the edge of the

gravel pit. Somebody drives to Moon-Azure's and asks him to come, but he won't. "I don't practice," he says. "Call the ambulance." He offers them the use of his phone.

They walk a good deal. You drive somewhere and here come the Moon-Azures, stumbling through the fireweed, their hands full of wilted branches.

Tolman at the garage says Moon-Azure's a semiretired psychiatrist, but Aunt thinks he's a heart surgeon who lost his nerve in the middle of an operation. He's got good teeth.

Moon-Azure says, "I'll never get used to the way you people let these fine old places run down." He's found the pile of broken slates that came off the old roof. It's been a tin roof since around 1925.

With Mrs. Moon-Azure it's information. What direction is west, when to pick blackberries, oh, kerosene lamps burn kerosene oil? She thought, gasoline. Like to see her try it. In the winter when they're in Florida, the porcupines get into the house, leave calling cards on the floor. "Look," she says, "bunny rabbits." She writes it all down. "My book on country living," she laughs.

She says "maple surple" for a joke.

"How's the hay coming along?" says Moon-Azure.

Once they come on a Saturday morning, smiling, ask Reba to clean house for them, but she says, "No." A teacup rings hard on the saucer.

They ask Marie Beaubien. They pay her more for wiping their tables and making their beds than any man gets running a chain saw.

"How's the hay coming, Lucien?" says Moon-Azure.

"Good," says Beaubien.

We could of used the money.

Marie Beaubien tells us, "White telephones, one in every room, and a bathroom all pale blue tiles painted with orchids. They got copper pans cost a hundred dollars for each one and more of them than you can count. Antique baskets hanging all over the walls, carpets everywhere."

It's not my taste.

My taste is simpler.

I like to see bare floorboards.

From the first the Moon-Azures are crazy for old deeds and maps of the farm, they trace Clew genealogy as though they bought our ancestors with the land. They like to think the Clews were farmers. He says, "Mason, looks like a good year for hay."

How the hell would I know?

They go down to the town clerk's office and dig up information on the ear-notch patterns Clews used 150 years ago to mark their sheep, try to find out if the early Clews did anything. One time they ask us to write down the kinds of apples. The orchards, black rows of heart-rotted trees, belong to them.

But all of their fascination is with the ancestor Clews; living Clews exist, like the Beaubiens, to be used. Dead Clews belong to the property and the property belongs to the Moon-Azures.

The Moon-Azures hire Lucien to clear out the brush and set up fallen stones. When I take Reba and Aunt for a ride up the road sometimes on the weekends you can see the Moon-Azures and their guests walking away from the cemetery, heads a little down as if they are thinking, not *sic transit gloria mundi*, but *this is mine*.

They post all of the land with big white signs stapled on plywood squares and nailed to posts every hundred feet. They set fence everywhere, along the road, up the drive, around the house, through the woods, all split-rail fence. Not an inch of barbed wire. But up in the woods the line of trees shows scars like twisted mouths from the wire we strung to keep the deer out of the orchards.

The Moon-Azures are after us, after the Beaubiens, even after Yogetsky for help with things, getting their car going, clearing out the clogged spring, finding their red-haired dog. They need to know how things happened, what things happened. Every year they go back to the city at the end of the summer. Then that changes.

Mrs. Beaubien polishes her spoon with the paper napkin and sifts sugar into her coffee. "The doctor is retired," she says. "They're goin' to stay up here until Christmas, then go off somewhere hot, then come back up here after mud season. Same thing every year from now on."

Aunt says, "Must be nice to have the jingle in your pockets to just run up and down between the nice weather."

"I never known one of them people to stick it out very long," says Mrs. Beaubien. "Wait till they have to scrape the ice off their own windshield. Lucien don't go up there for that, you bet."

I think, bet he will.

The Moon-Azures keep on walking. What else do they have to do after the first black frosts? In the shortening days their friends don't come to visit, and they have only each other to hear their startled exclamations that fallen leaves have a bitter odor, that the hardening earth throws up rods of cloudy ice. They come at us with their clumsy conversation, wasting our time. Beaubien and his son bring them wood and stack it. The autumn shrivels into November.

A week before Thanksgiving here comes Mrs. Moon-Azure again, walking down the field. She knocks on the window, peers in at Aunt. Cockleburs hang on her ankles. Her clothes are the color of oatmeal. Her eyes are gray. The refrigerator switches on as she starts to speak, and she has to repeat herself in a louder voice. "I said, I hear you have some remarkable photographs!"

"Well, they're interesting to us," says Aunt. She has flour on her hands, and dusts it off, slapping her palms against her thighs. She shows some of the pictures, standing them up on edge saying, "Mr. Galloon Heyscape doing the Irish clog, Denman Thompson's oxen, the radio of the two sweethearts, Kiley Druge and his crazy daughter."

"These are important photographs," says Mrs. Moon-Azure in the same way she said, "You ran over my horse," to Clyde Cuckhorn. We see how much she wants them.

Hey, too bad.

"I wonder they don't come right out and ask if we'll sell them," says Aunt after she's gone. "She'd give anything to get her mitts on these pictures. No, these are Clew family photographs, taken by a very gifted hired man, and here they stay."

Leonard Prittle, our hired man, took his pictures from under a large black cloak cast off by my great-grandmother, says Aunt.

How does she know?

What Aunt is afraid of is that the Moon-Azures will pass the pictures around among their weekend guests, that they will find their way into books and newspapers, and we will someday see our grandfather's corpse in his homemade coffin resting on two sawhorses, flattened out on the pages of some magazine and labeled with a cruel caption.

[4]

Maybe Dad never imagined himself doing anything but selling off the land and dreaming useless apple thoughts, but in the worst of it he got a job. And this was a time when there wasn't any jobs, and he wasn't looking for one. It wasn't even stonework.

Dad's friend, Diamond Ward, was one of those hard gray men who ate deer meat in every season and could fix whatever was broken again and again until nothing was left of the original machine but its function. Diamond was in the Grange, knew what was going on, and he was one of the first in the county to get a job through the Rural Electrification Act. He got my father in with him. The Ironworks County Electric Power Cooperative. Replaced now by Northern Nuclear. We got the alarm in the kitchen that's supposed to go off if there's an accident down there, everybody evacuate in a hurry.

Where to?

The two of them drove around all day in a dark green truck with a painted circle on the side enclosing the letters ICEPC and three bolts of electricity. Everybody called it "The Icepick." Diamond chewed tobacco, and the door on his side was stained brown. Bootie would get in the closet when she heard Diamond coming up the drive.

The kite's paper is gone, burned up in the seasons of August heat under the cracking barn roof.

There was something in my father that had to blow up whatever he did. He got a certain amount of pleasure seeing himself as The Lone Apple Grower up against a gang of McIntosh men. Now came a chance to be The One Bringing Light to the Farm. He could fool and laugh with people as much as he wanted.

He'd say, "A five-dollar deposit, the price of a pair of shoes, and we'll put the 'lectricity in. You'll hear the radio, hear Amos and Andy." He'd imitate Amos, laugh. "Get rid of them sad irons, use them for doorstops. Lights? Get twice the work done because you'll be able to see both ends of the cow. *Hawhaw.*"

He got up a mock funeral at the Grange, spent weeks laughing and talking it up. The men carried a coffin around the hall, then took it out and buried it. It was full of oil lamps and blackened chimneys.

Hey, I'm telling you, this is within our lifetime.

Television wasn't invented until 1938.

He'd list the things electricity was going to do away with. No more stinking privies. No more strained, watery eyes from reading by lamplight. No more lonely evenings for widowers who could turn on a radio and hear plays and music. No more families dead from food poisoning when Ma could keep the potato salad in a chilly white refrigerator. No more heating sad irons on a blazing stove in August. The kids would stay on the farm.

He'd look at somebody with his round, clear eyes, he'd say, "If you put a light on every farm, you put a light in every heart." He never missed a day in four years, until the afternoon Diamond got killed trying to get a kite out of the lines.

Dad always left the house at five in the morning, carrying his lunch in a humped black lunchbox. A thermos bottle of coffee fit inside the top, held in place by a metal clasp. He and Diamond set poles and strung line to canted, ancient barns and to houses settled down on their foundations like old dogs sleeping on porch steps.

He got the idea they ought to carry a radio around in the truck. A farmer did his own wiring in those days, then called up The Icepick and said he was ready. Sometimes they had a washing machine hid under some burlap bags all set up to go as a birthday present for the wife. But usually just a couple of ceiling fixtures, outlets.

Before they turned on the power, Dad got his radio out of the truck, rubbed it up a little if it was dusty. He'd plug it in. There stood the farmer and his wife and the children, all staring at it.

"This is goin' to change your life," Dad would say.

He'd go to the window and signal Diamond to turn on the juice. As the static-rich sound of a braying announcer or a foxtrot poured into the room, he watched the faces of the family, watched their mouths opening a little as if to swallow the sound. The farmer would shake his hand, the wife would dab at her watery, strained eyes and say, "It's a miracle." It was as if my father had personally given them this wonder. Yet you could tell they despised him, too, for making things easy.

I never saw how anybody could rejoice over the harsh light that came out of them clear nippled bulbs.

After Diamond was killed Dad decided to go into the appliance business. That's what I do out in the barn. I was never able to do anything heavy. We still sell a few washers and electric stoves. Reba helps me get them onto the truck. There's not much in appliances now. It's all sound systems and computers. You can buy your washing machines anywhere.

At noon in summer, if they weren't too far away, Dad and Diamond would come back to the farm, drive up into the field, and park the truck under the trees. They took the full hour. They had their favorite place. They'd spread out an old canvas tarp in the shade. There was a spring up there. There was a slab of flat rock. Sometimes Bootie or I would bring them up their dinner. We'd skirt wide around Diamond, he'd make mocking kissing sounds with his stained wet mouth.

Dad would laugh, "*Haw.*"

Sometimes Diamond was asleep with his shirt over his face so the flies wouldn't bother him, and Dad would be on his knees, tapping away at the rock with the chisel and the stone hammer for something to do. Bootie and I could hear the *tok, tok-tok* when we walked up the track. He was chiseling in the rock, chiseling out a big bas-relief of himself wearing his lineman's gear. We'd play a kind of hopscotch on his grand design.

"Look, Dad," said Bootie, "I'm standin' on the eyes."

In the winter Dad and Diamond sat in the truck with the engine running.

The old family plot, not used for eighty years or so, is up in back of the house. Diamond Ward is buried down in the Baptist cemetery in Ironworks. *A Lamb of God Call'd Home, His Soul No More Shall Roam.* Hey, we've seen that verse a hundred times.

His eyes reflected a knowledge of his terrible mistake, my father told us. "He looked straight at me, his mouth opened, and I seen what I thought was blood, this dark trickle, come out. But it was tobacco juice. He was dead there on the pole, lookin' at me. I was the last thing he saw."

After Diamond was killed, Bootie and I played at the best game we ever invented. We played it over and over for about two years. Bootie thought up the idea of the molasses.

It wasn't so much a game as a play, and not so much a play as acting out an event that gave us a sharp satisfaction. We'd get some molasses in a cup and go out to the barn where we had our things arranged. Pieced-out binder twine sagged between the ladder to the hayloft and a crossbeam. We argued about who would play Diamond first.

Bootie took her turn.

I'd say, "I'm Dad."

Bootie would say, "I'm Diamond." She would twist her face, hitch at her corduroy pants, kick at the floor.

"Hey, Diamond," I'd say, "there's a kite in the lines."

We'd look up into the dry twittering gloom. A kite hung there, as alert and expectant as a wounded bird.

"I'll get the goddamn thing out of our lines," said Diamond, taking up a long narrow stick. He climbed slowly, the stick hitting against the utility pole, *tok, tok-tok.* At the top Diamond turned and faced the kite.

"Be careful," I said.

The stick extended toward the kite, touched it.

[5]

A thin dust of snow falls. Visitors' cars rush along the road again, stirring up pale clouds.

"Must be havin' a party," says Aunt.

"Good-bye party, I hope," says Reba.

Mrs. Beaubien's little hungry face bobs into her window every time a car goes past.

Reba and Aunt and I get in the truck and go for a ride, careful to look straight ahead. There are eight coffee cans with dead marigolds on Yogetsky's porch. We can see the Moon-Azures up in the high field where the smooth, sloping granite lies exposed. We can see them among the poplars that have multiplied into a grove since I was a kid. Those trees all drop their leaves on the same day in autumn.

"That's the spring up there. Dad used to go up there at noon with old Diamond," I say. "Under the maple that went down."

"They can't be all that excited about a spring," says Aunt.

We see them bending over, one woman down on her knees with a pad of paper, drawing or writing. Dr. Moon-Azure leans forward from his hips with a camera screwed into his eye.

"They've got a body there," says Aunt. I can smell the faint lemony scent of lotion, the thick warmth of hair. The truck heater is on.

"More like a dead porcupine—probably the first one they ever see," says Reba. We turn around and go home and watch *The Secret World of Insects*. Our spoons clink and scrape at the cream and Jell-O in the bottom of the pressed glass bowls, the double-diamond pattern. It's just the field and the spring and the rock. Hey, I've been up there a hundred times.

The phone rings.

"What do you think," Marie Beaubien says.

"I think they've found a corpse in the bushes, one of those poor girls who'll take a ride from anybody in a red car," says Aunt.

"No, we would of seen that little skinny man, what's his name, over there in Rose of Sharon, the medical examiner."

"Winwell. Avery Winwell. His mother was a Richardson."

"That's right, Winwell. Yes, and the state police and all them. Whatever they've got there isn't no body."

"Well, I don't know what they could have found."

"Something."

The next day I walk down to Yogetsky's to get away from the sound of the vacuum cleaner. Reba knows it gets on my nerves.

Yogetsky is knocking the dead marigolds out of the coffee cans. Brown humps of dirt lie on the ground. He says, "See your neighbors found a Indian carving." I think at first he means the Beaubiens.

"What carving is that," I say.

"I got it inside in the paper," he says. I follow him into the kitchen. He washes his hands in the clean sink. The paper is folded over the arm of a chair. I look out the window and see our house, the grey clapboards stained with brown streaks from the iron nails, see the sign, CLEW'S APPLIANCES.

Yogetsky shakes out his paper until he finds the right place. He peers through his slipping glasses, his blunt finger traces across the text, and he reads aloud. "It says, 'Complex petroglyphs such as the recently discovered Thunder God pictured here are rare among the eastern woodland tribes.' It says, 'Discovered by the owners of a farm in Ironworks County.' " Yogetsky peers at me. "I didn't know there was no Indians around here."

He shows me the picture in the newspaper. I see my father's self-portrait cut deep into rock. In one stone hand he clenches three bolts of electricity. Around his waist is his lineman's belt. His hair flows back, his eyes fix you from the stone.

"Dad, I'm standin' on the eyes," said Bootie.

In our game the stick touched the kite, inexplicably fell away. Diamond swayed, his balance gone. Falling, his hand grasped the wire. His spine arched, his hand clenched living bolts of lightning. His eyes fixed mine, his mouth opened, and from the corner of his lips spilled the dark molasses, like blood, like uncontrollable tobacco juice.

I laugh, because isn't there something funny about this figure slowly cut into the fieldrock during the long summer noons half a century ago? And how can Yogetsky understand?

[E. ANNIE PROULX]

"My father," E. Annie Proulx told interviewer Alan Dumas for the Denver Rocky Mountain News, "was in textile and he moved a lot." From him, "I just got the habit of roaming. There's nothing I like better, absolutely nothing I like better than jumping in the truck and driving out. Just going."

This love of travel and exploration, instilled in her by her millworker father, is the wellspring from which Proulx's deft, detail-rich fiction flows. Her admittedly nonsentimental look at those who populate rural life have won her the Pulitzer Prize, National Book Award, Irish Times International Fiction Prize, and a nomination for the National Book Critics Circle Award, all for her debut novel, The Shipping News.

Proulx is an outdoorswoman through and through. Her greatest enjoyments are found in fishing, canoeing, camping, and skiing. When not outdoors, she prefers to settle down to write at the antique table in the wood stove–heated kitchen of her log house outside Laramie, Wyoming.

She came late to fiction at age fifty-two with the publication of her first collection of short stories, 1988's Heartsongs and Other Stories, of which "Electric Arrows" is a part. Prior to this, she spent decades collecting material as a journalist covering subjects such as apples, mice, mountain lions, weather, canoeing, African beadwork, and lettuces.

Born in Connecticut in 1935, she was the eldest of five daughters, and her father, a French-Canadian, left behind his ethnic identity to become a Yankee. For many years after graduating from the University of Vermont with an MA in history, Proulx lived in rural Canaan. As a divorced single mother, she struggled to support her three sons and one daughter, paying the bills with a meager journalist's income, and literally living in a shack.

Now the lonely Wyoming wilderness is her home, her "writing place," as she calls it, where she has worked on her novels Postcards and Accordion Crimes. In a new collection of short stories, Close Range, she observes life there in "Brokeback Mountain," about gay-bashing cowboys, a tale with a violent end that predates the Matthew Shepard killing by a year; as well as "Half-Skinned Deer," the story John Updike chose to end his anthology The Best American Short Stories of the Century.

Lastly, if you've ever wondered, as I did, what the "E" in her name stands for, it's "unwanted Edna."

—C.O.

THE GUN SHOP

John Updike

BEN'S SON MURRAY LOOKED FORWARD TO THEIR ANNUAL Thanksgiving trip to Pennsylvania mostly because of the gun. A Remington .22, it leaned unused in the old farmhouse all year, until little Murray came and swabbed it out and begged to shoot it. The gun had been Ben's. His parents had bought it for him the Christmas after they moved to the farm, when he was thirteen, his son's age now. No, Murray was all of fourteen, his birthday was in September. Ben should have remembered, for at the party, Ben had tapped the child on the back of the head to settle him down, and his son had pointed the cake knife at his father's chest and said, "Hit me again and I'll kill you."

Ben had been amazed. In bed that night, Sally told him, "It was his way of saying he's too big to be hit anymore. He's right. He is."

But the boy, as he and Ben walked with the gun across the brown field to the dump in the woods, didn't seem big; solemn and beardless, he carried the freshly cleaned rifle under his arm, in imitation of hunters in magazine illustrations, and the barrel tip kept snagging on loops of matted orchard grass. Then at the dump, with the targets of tin cans and bottles neatly aligned, the gun refused to fire, and Murray threw a childish tantrum. Tears filled his eyes as he tried to explain: "There was this little *pin*, Dad, that fell out when I cleaned it, but I put it back in, and now it's not *there!*"

Ben, looking down into this small freckled face so earnestly stricken, couldn't help smiling.

Murray, seeing his father's smile, said *"Shit."* He hurled the gun toward an underbrush of saplings and threw himself onto the cold leaf mold of the forest floor. He writhed there and repeated the word as each fresh slant of injustice and of embarrassment struck him; but Ben couldn't quite erase his own expression of kindly mockery. The boy's tantrums loomed impressively in the intimate scale of their Boston apartment, with his mother and two sisters and some fine-legged antiques as audience; but out here, among these mute oaks and hickories, his fury was rather comically dwarfed. Also, in retrieving and examining the .22, Ben had bent his face close into the dainty forgotten smell of gun oil and remembered the Christmas noon when his father had taken him out to the barn and shown him how to shoot the virgin gun; and this memory prolonged his smile.

That dainty scent. The dangerous slickness. The zigzag marks of burnishing on the bolt when it slid out, and the amazing whorl, a new kind of star, inside the barrel when it was pointed toward the sky. The snug, lethally smart clicks of re-assembly. He had not known his father could handle a gun. He was forty-five when Ben was thirteen, and a schoolteacher; once he had been, briefly, a soldier. He had thrown an empty Pennzoil can into the snow of the barnyard and propped the .22 on the chicken-house windowsill and taken the first shot. The oil can had jumped. Ben remembered the way his father's mouth, seen from the side, sucked back a bit of saliva that in his concentration had escaped. Ben remembered the less-than-deafening slap of the shot and the acrid whiff that floated from the bolt as the spent shell spun away. Now, pulling the dead trigger and sliding out the bolt to see why the old gun was broken, he remembered his father's arms around him, guiding his hands on the newly varnished stock and pressing his head gently down to line up his eyes with the sights. "Squeeze, don't get excited and jerk," his father had said.

"*Get* up," Ben said to his son. "Shape up. Don't be such a baby. If it doesn't work, it doesn't work; I don't know why. It worked the last time we used it."

"Yeah, that was last Thanksgiving," Murray said, surprisingly conversational, though still stretched on the cold ground. "I bet one of these idiot yokels around here messed it up."

"Idiot yokels," Ben repeated, hearing himself in that phrase. "My, aren't we a young snob?"

Murray stood and brushed the sarcasm aside. "Can you fix it or not?"

Ben slipped a cartridge into the chamber, closed the bolt, and pulled the trigger. A limp click. "Not. I don't understand guns. You're the one who wants to use it all the time. Why don't we just point our fingers and say *Bang?*"

"Dad, you're quite the riot."

They walked back to the house. Ben lugged the disgraced gun while Murray ran disdainfully ahead. Ben noticed in the dead grass the rusty serrate shapes of strawberry leaves, precise as fossils. When they had moved here, the land had been farmed out—"mined," in the local phrase—and the one undiscouraged crop consisted of the wild strawberries running from ditch to ridge on all the sunny slopes. At his son's age, Ben hated the strawberry leaves and the rural isolation they ornamented; it surprised him, gazing down, to have their silhouettes fitting so exactly a shape in his mind. The leaves were still here, and his parents were still in the square sandstone farmhouse. His mother looked up from the sink and said, "I didn't hear the shots."

"There weren't any, that's why."

Something pleased or amused in Ben's voice tripped Murray's temper again; he went into the living room and kicked a chair leg and swore. "Goddam thing *broke*."

"That's no reason to break a chair," Ben shouted after him. "That's not our furniture, you know."

Sally froze, plate in one hand and dish towel in the other, and called weakly, "Hey."

"Well, hell," he said to her, "why are we letting the kid terrorize everybody?"

He chased the boy into the living room. His murderous mood met there the torpor that follows a feast. The two girls, in company with their grandfather, were watching the Gimbels parade on television. Murray, hearing his father approach, had hid behind the chair he had kicked. A sister glanced in his direction and pronounced, "Spoiled." The other sniffed in agreement. One girl was older than Murray, one younger; all of his life he would be pinched between them. Their grandfather was sitting in a rocker, wearing the knit wool cap that made him feel less cold. Obligingly he had taken the chair with the worst angle on the television screen, watching in fuzzy foreshortening a flicker of bloated animals, drum majorettes, and giant cakes bearing candles that were really girls waving.

"He's not spoiled," Ben's father told the girls. "He's like his daddy, a perfectionist."

Ben's father since that Christmas of the gun had become an old man, but a wonderfully strange old man, with a long yellow-white face, a blue nose, and the erect carriage of a child who is straining to see. His circulation was poor, he had been hospitalized, he lived from pill to pill, he had uncharacteristic quiet spells that Ben guessed were seizures of pain; yet his hopefulness still dominated any room he was in. He looked up at Ben in the doorway. "Can you figure it out?"

Ben said, "Murray says some pin fell out while he was cleaning it."

"It *did*, Dad," the child insisted.

Ben's father stood, prim and pale and tall. He was wearing a threadbare overcoat, in readiness for adventure. "I know just the man," he said. He called into the kitchen, "Mother, I'll give Dutch a ring. The kid's being frustrated."

"Aw, that's okay, forget it," Murray mumbled. But his eyes shone, looking up at the promising apparition of his grandfather. Ben was hurt, remembering how his own knack, as father, was to tease and cloud those same eyes. There was something too finely tooled, too little yielding in the boy that Ben itched to correct.

The two women had crowded to the doorway to intervene. Sally said, "He doesn't *have* to shoot the gun. I hate guns. Ben, why do you always inflict the gun on this child?"

"I don't," he answered.

His mother called over Sally's shoulder, "Don't bother people on Thanksgiving, Murray. Let the man have a holiday."

Little Murray looked up, startled, at the sound of his name pronounced scoldingly. He had been named for his grandfather. Two Murrays: one small and young, one big and old. Yet alike, Ben saw, in a style of expectation, in a tireless craving for—he used to wonder for what, but people had a word for it now—"action."

"This man never takes a holiday," Ben's father called back. "He's out of this world. You'd love him. Everybody in this room would love him." And, irrepressibly, he was at the telephone, dialing with a touch of frenzy, the way he would scrub a friendly dog's belly with his knuckles.

After a supper of leftover turkey, the men went out into the night. Ben drove his father's car. The dark road carried them off their hill into a valley where sandstone farmhouses had been joined by ranch houses, aluminum trailers, a wanly lit Mobil station, a Pentecostal church built of cinder blocks, with a neon JESUS LIVES. JESUS SAVES must have become too much of a joke.

"The next driveway on the left," his father said. The cold outdoor air had shortened his breath. No sign advertised a gun shop; the house was a ranch, but not a new one—one of those built in the early fifties, when the commuters first began to come this far out from Alton. In order of age, oldest to youngest, tallest to shortest, they marched up the flagstones to the unlit front door; Ben could feel his son's embarrassment at his back, deepening his own. They had offered to let little Murray carry the gun, but he had shied from it. Ben held the .22 behind him, so as not to terrify whoever answered his father's ring at the door. It was a fat woman in a pink wrapper. Ben saw that there had been a mistake, this was no gun shop, his father had humiliated him once again.

But no, she said, "Hello, Mr. Trupp," giving it that affectionate long German *u*; in Boston people rhymed the name with "cup." "Come in this way I guess; he's down there expecting everybody. Is this your son now? And who's *this* big boy?" Her pleasantries eased their way across the front hall, with its braided rug and enamelled plaque of blessing, to the cellar stairs.

As they clattered down, Ben's father said, "I shouldn't have done that, that was a headache for his missus, letting us in, I wasn't thinking. We should have gone to the side, but then Dutch has to disconnect the burglar alarm. Everybody in this county's crazy to steal his guns. When you get to be my age, Ben, it hurts like Jesus just to *try* to think. Just to *try* not to annoy the hell out of people."

The cellar seemed bigger than the house. Cardboard cartons, old chairs and sofas from the Goodwill, a refrigerator, stacked newspapers, shoot posters, and rifle racks lined an immense cement room. At the far end was a counter and behind it a starkly lit workshop with a lathe. Little Murray's eyes widened; his boyhood had known no gun shops. Whereas in an alley of Ben's boyhood there had been a mysterious made-over garage called "Repair & Ammo." Sounds of pounding and grinding came out of it, the fury of metals, and on dark winter afternoons, racing home with his sled, Ben would see blue sparks shudder in the window. But he had never gone in. So this was an adventure for him as well. There was that about being his father's son: one had adventures, one blundered into places, one *went* places, met strangers, suffered rebuffs, experienced breakdowns, exposed oneself in a way that Ben, as soon as he was able, made impossible, hedging his life with such order and propriety that no misstep could occur. He had become a lawyer, taking profit from the losses of others, reducing disorderly lives to legal folders. Even in his clothes he had retained the caution of the fifties, while his partners blossomed into striped shirts and bell-bottomed slacks. Seeing his son's habitual tautness relax under the spell of this potent, acrid cellar, Ben felt that he had been much less a father than his own had been, a father's duty being to impart the taste of the world. Golf lessons in Brookline, sailing off Maine, skiing in New Hampshire—what was this but bought amusement compared to the improvised shifts and hazards of poverty? In this cave the metallic smell of murder lurked, and behind the counter two men bent low over something that gleamed like a jewel.

Ben's father went forward. "Dutch, this is my son Ben and my grandson Murray. The kid's just like you are, a perfectionist, and this cheap gun we got Ben a zillion years ago let him down this afternoon." To the other man in this lighted end of the cellar he said, "I know your face, mister, but I've forgotten your name."

The other man blinked and said, "Reiner." He wore a Day-Glo hunting cap and a dirty blue parka over a clean shirt and tie. He looked mild, perhaps because of his spectacles, which were rimless. He seemed to be a customer, and the piece of metal in the gunsmith's hand concerned him. It was a small slab with two holes bored in it; a shiny ring had been set into one of the holes, and Dutch's gray thumb moved back and forth across the infinitesimal edge where the ring was flush with the slab.

"About two-thousandths," the gunsmith slowly announced, growling the ou's. It was hard to know whom he was speaking to. His eyelids looked swollen—leaden hoods set slantwise over the eyes, eclipsing them but for a glitter. His entire body appeared to have slumped away from its frame, from the restless ruminating jowl to the undershirted beer belly and bent knees. His shuffle seemed deliberately droll. His hands alone had firm shape—hands battered and nicked and so long in touch with greased machinery that they had blackened flatnesses like worn parts. The right middle finger had been shorn off at the first knuckle. "Two- or three-thousandths at the most."

Ben's father's voice had regained its strength in the warmth of this basement. He acted as interlocutor, to make the drama clear. "You mean you can just tell with your thumb if it's a thousandth of an inch off?"

"Yahh. More or less."

"That's incredible. That to me is a miracle." He explained to his son and grandson, "Dutch was head machinist at Hager Steel for thirty years. He had hundreds of men under him. Hundreds."

"A thousand," Dutch growled. "Twelve hunnert during Korea." His qualification slipped into place as if with much practice; Ben guessed his father came here often.

"Boy, I can't imagine it. I don't see how the hell you did it. I don't see how any man could do what you did; my imagination boggles. This kid here"—Murray, not Ben—"has what you have. Drive. Both of you have what it takes."

Ben thought he should assert himself. In a few crisp phrases he explained to Dutch how the gun had failed to fire.

His father said to the man in spectacles, "It would have taken me all night to say what he just said. He lives in New England, they all talk sense up there. One thing I'm grateful the kid never inherited from me, and I bet he is too, is his old man's gift for baloney. I was always embarrassing the kid."

Dutch slipped out the bolt of the .22 and, holding the screwdriver so the shortened finger lay along a groove of the handle, turned a tiny screw that Ben in all his years of owning the gun had never noticed. The bolt fell into several bright pieces, tinged with rust, on the counter. The gunsmith picked a bit of metal from within a little spring and held it up. "Firing pin. Sheared," he said. His mouth when he talked showed the extra flexibility of the toothless.

"Do you have another? Can you replace it?" Ben disliked, as emphasized by this acoustical cellar, the high hungry pitch of his own voice. He was prosecuting.

Dutch declined to answer. He lowered his remarkable lids to gaze at the metal under his hands; one hand closed tight around the strange little slab, with its gleaming ring.

Ben's father interceded, saying, "He can make it, Ben. This man here can make an entire gun from scratch. Just give him a lump of slag is all he needs."

"Wonderful," Ben said, to fill the silence.

Reiner unexpectedly laughed. "How about," he said to the gunsmith, "that old Damascus double Jim Knauer loaded with triple FG and a smokeless powder? It's a wonder he has a face still."

Dutch unclenched his fist and, after a pause, chuckled.

Ben recognized in these pauses something of courtroom tactics; at his side he felt little Murray growing agitated at the delay. "Shall we come back tomorrow?" Ben asked.

He was ignored. Reiner was going on, "What was the make on that? A twelve-gauge Parker?"

"English gun," Dutch said. "A Westley Richards. He paid three hunnert for it, some dealer over in Royersford. Such foolishness, his first shot yet. Even split the stock." His eyelids lifted. "Who wants a beer?"

Ben's father said, "Jesus, I'm so full of turkey a beer might do me in."

Reiner looked amused. "They say liquor is good for bad circulation."

"I'd be happy to sip one but I can't take an oath to finish it. The first rule of hospitality is, Don't look a gift horse in the face." But an edge was going off his wit. After the effort of forming these sentences, the old man sat down, in an easy chair with exploded arms. Against the yellowish pallor of his face, his nose looked livid as a bruise.

"Sure," Ben said. "If they're being offered. Thank you."

"Son, how about you?" Dutch asked the boy. Murray's eyes widened, realizing nobody was going to answer for him.

"He's in training for his ski team," Ben said at last.

Dutch's eyes stayed on the boy. "Then you should have good legs. How about now going over and fetching four cans from that icebox over there?" He pointed with a loose fist.

"Refrigerator," Ben clarified.

Dutch turned his back and fished through a shelf of grimy cigar boxes for a cylinder of metal that, when he held it beside the fragment of firing pin, satisfied him. He shuffled into the little room behind the counter, which brimmed with light and machinery.

As the boy passed around the cold cans of Old Reading, his

grandfather explained to the man in the Day-Glo hunting cap, "This boy is what you'd have to call an ardent athlete. He sails, he golfs, last winter he won blue medals at, what do they call 'em, Murray?"

"Slaloms. I flubbed the downhill, though."

"Hear that? He knows the language. If he was fortunate enough to live down here with you fine gentlemen, he'd learn gun language too. He'd be a crack shot in no time."

"Where we live in this city," the boy volunteered, "my mother won't even let me get a BB gun. She hates guns."

"The kid means the city of Boston. His father's on a first-name basis with the mayor." Ben heard the strained intake of breath between his father's sentences and tried not to hear the words. He and his son were tumbled together in a long, pained monologue. "Anything competitive, this kid loves. He doesn't get that from me. He doesn't get it from his old man, either. Ben always had this tactful way of keeping his thoughts to himself. You never knew what was going on inside the kid. My biggest regret is I couldn't teach him the pleasure of working with your hands. He grew up watching me scrambling along by my wits and now he's doing the same damn thing. He should have had Dutch for a father. Dutch would have reached him."

To deafen himself Ben walked around the counter and into the workshop. Dutch was turning the little cylinder on a lathe. He wore no goggles, and seemed to be taking no measurements. Into the mirror-smooth blur of the spinning metal the man delicately pressed a tipped, hinged cone. Curls of steel fell steadily to the scarred lathe table. Tan sparks flew outward to the radius perhaps of a peony. The cylinder was becoming two cylinders, a narrow one emerging from the shoulders of another. Ben had once worked wood, in high-school shop, but this man could shape metal. He could descend into the hard heart of things. Dutch switched off the lathe, with a sad grunt pushed himself away, and comically shuffled toward some other of his tools. Ben, fearing that the love he felt for this man might burst his face and humiliate them all, turned back toward the larger room.

Reiner had undertaken a monologue of his own. ". . . you know your average bullet comes out of the barrel rotating; that's why a rifle is called that, for the rifling inside, that makes it spin. Now what the North Vietnamese discovered, if you put enough velocity into a bullet beyond a critical factor it tumbles, end over end like that. The Geneva Convention says you can't use a soft bullet that mushrooms inside the body like the dumdum, but hit a man with a bullet tumbling like that, it'll tear his arm right off."

The boy was listening warily, watching the bespectacled man's soft white hands demonstrate tumbling. Ben's father sat in the exploded armchair, staring dully ahead, sucking back spittle, struggling silently for breath.

"Of course now," the lecture went on, "what they found was best over there for the jungle was a plain shotgun. You take an ordinary twenty-gauge, maybe mounted with a short barrel, you don't have visibility more than fifty feet anyway, a man doesn't have a chance at that distance. The spread of shot is maybe three feet around." With his arms Reiner placed the circle on himself, centered on his heart. "It'll tear a man to pieces like that. If he's not that close yet, then the shot pattern is wider and even a miss is going to hurt him plenty."

"Death is part of life," Ben's father said, as if reciting a lesson learned long ago.

Ben asked Reiner, "Were you in Vietnam?"

The man took off his hunting cap and displayed a bald head. "You got me in the wrong rumpus. Navy gunner, World War Two. With those forty-millimeter Bofors you could put a two-pound shell thirty thousand feet straight up in the air."

Dutch emerged from his workshop holding a bit of metal in one hand and a crumpled beer can in the other. He put the cylindrical bit down amid the scattered parts of the bolt, fumbled at them, and they all came together.

"Does it fit?" Ben asked.

Dutch's clownish loose lips smiled. "You ask a lot of questions." He slipped the bolt back into the .22 and turned back to the workshop. The four others held silent, but for Ben's father's breathing. In time the flat spank of a rifle shot resounded, amplified by cement walls.

"That's miraculous to me," Ben's father said. "A mechanical skill like that."

"Thank you very much," Ben said, too quickly, when the gunsmith lay the mended and tested .22 on the counter. "How much do we owe you?"

Rather than answer, Dutch asked little Murray, "Didja ever see a machine like this before?" It was a device, operated by hand pressure, that assembled and crimped shotgun shells. He let the boy pull the handle. The shells marched in a circle, receiving each their allotment of powder and shot. "It can't explode," Dutch reassured Ben.

Reiner explained, "You see what this here is"—holding out the mysterious little slab with its bright ring—"is by putting in this bushing Dutch just made for me I can reduce the proportion of powder to shot, when I go into finer grains this deer season."

Murray backed off from the machine. "That's neat. Thanks a lot."

Dutch contemplated Ben. His verdict came: "I guess two dollars."

Ben protested, "That's not enough."

Ben's father rescued him from the silence. "Pay the man what he asks; all the moola in the world won't buy God-given expertise like that."

Ben paid, and was in such a hurry to lead his party home he touched the side door before Dutch could switch off the burglar alarm. Bells shrilled, Ben jumped. Everybody laughed, even—though he had hated, from his schoolteaching days, what he called "cruel humor"—Ben's father.

In the dark of the car, the old man sighed. "He's what you'd have to call a genius and a gentleman. Did you see the way your dad looked at him? Pure adoration, man to man."

Ben asked him, "How do you feel?"

"Better. I didn't like Murray having to listen to all that blood and guts from Reiner."

"Boy," Murray said, "he sure is crazy about guns."

"He's lonely. He just likes getting out of the house and hanging around the shop. Must give Dutch a real pain in the old bazoo." Perhaps this sounded harsh, or applicable to himself, for he amended it. "Actually, he's harmless. He says he was in Navy artillery, but you know where he spent most of the war? Cruising around the Caribbean having a sunbath. He's like me. I was in the first one and my big accomplishment was surviving the flu in boot camp. We were going to board in Hoboken the day of the Armistice."

"I never knew you were a soldier, Grandpa."

"Kill or be killed, that's my motto."

He sounded so faraway and fragile, saying this, Ben told him, "I hope we didn't wear you out."

"That's what I'm here for," Ben's father said. "We aim to serve."

In bed, Ben tried to describe to Sally their adventure, the gun shop. "The whole place smelled of death. I think the kid was a little frightened."

Sally said, "Of course. He's only fourteen. You're awfully hard on him, you know."

"I know. My father was nice to me, and what did it get him? Chest pains. A pain in the old bazoo." Asleep, he dreamed he was a boy with a gun. A small bird, smaller than a dot in a puzzle, sat in the peach tree by the meadow fence. Ben aligned his sights and with exquisite slowness squeezed. The dot fell like a stone. He went to it and found a wren's brown body, neatly deprived of a head. There was not much blood, just headless feathers. He awoke, and realized it was real. It had happened just that way, the first summer he had had the gun. He had never forgiven himself. After breakfast he and his son went out across the dead strawberry leaves to the dump again. There, the dream continued. Though Ben steadied his trembling, middle-aged hands against a hickory trunk and aimed so carefully his open eye burned, the cans and bottles ignored his shots. The bullets passed right through them. Whereas when little Murray took the gun, the boy's freckled face gathered the muteness of the trees into his murderous concentration. The cans jumped, the bottles burst. "You're killing me!" Ben cried. In his pride and relief, he had to laugh.

[JOHN UPDIKE]

Squeezing a biography, even a brief one, about John Updike into a few paragraphs is not just a serious problem; without the help of experimental physics, it's an impossibility. Living Legend, Icon of American Literature, these titles and others of similar notoriety have been ascribed to the author many times over. That Updike was chosen to edit the definitive volume, The Best American Short Stories of the Century *in 1999, pretty much puts the stamp of approval on him as the penultimate writer of the twentieth century.*

In reading a chronology of his accomplishments since he began writing for the Harvard Lampoon in 1950, it is a rare year that the author has not received some type of major award, prize, accolade, or fellowship. He is the winner of two Pulitzers, only the third American to be so honored; was awarded the National Medal of Honor by President Bush in 1989; has received three National Book Critics Circle Awards; two O. Henry Prizes; the Howels Medal; Ambassador Book Award; the French honorary rank of Commandeur de l'ordre des arts et des lettres; *and my favorite, in 1993, the Conch Republic Prize for Literature, presented to him in Key West, Florida.*

This is by no means a definitive list.

Readers of literary fiction probably know him best for his Rabbit novels, written about the character of Rabbit Angstrom, whose life is chronicled in four books, Rabbit, Run *(1960),* Rabbit Redux *(1971),* Rabbit Is Rich *(1981), and* Rabbit at Rest *(1990). Fans of popular movies are also likely to recognize his novel* The Witches of Eastwick *as the source for the 1987 movie starring Jack Nicholson, Cher, Susan Sarandon,* and Michelle Pfeiffer, which opens in a new incarnation, as a Cameron Mackintosh musical at the Theatre Royal, in London this year. His body of literary criticism spans five decades and numerous collections.

"Friends from Philadelphia," Updike's first short story sale, was to The New Yorker in 1954. Any struggling fiction writer reading this has probably just been struck by awe and envy, because that magazine is legendary as being the hardest market there is to crack.

Born in 1932 in Reading, Pennsylvania, Updike married Mary E. Pennington in 1953, the mother of his two sons and two daughters. He graduated from Harvard in 1954, and attended the Ruskin School for Drawing and Fine Art in Oxford, England, the academic year after. In 1955, he joined The New Yorker. Though he remained a staff writer for only three years, his name is synonymous with the publication to this day because of the prose it publishes from him on a continual basis.

His most recent works include the novels In the Beauty of the Lilies and Toward the End of Time, plus More Matter: Essays and Criticisms, which contains 900 pages of material.

Updike lives in Beverly Farms, Massachusetts with his second wife, Martha, where he has resided since 1982.

—C.O.